P9-DGR-107

BOOKS BY ELIE WIESEL

Night
Dawn
The Accident
The Town Beyond the Wall
The Gates of the Forest
The Jews of Silence
Legends of Our Time
A Beggar in Jerusalem
One Generation After
Souls on Fire
The Oath
Ani Maamin *(cantata)*
Zalmen, or the Madness of God *(play)*
Messengers of God
A Jew Today
Four Hasidic Masters
The Trial of God *(play)*
The Testament
Five Biblical Portraits
Somewhere a Master
The Golem *(Illustrated by Mark Podwal)*
The Fifth Son
Against Silence *(Edited by Irving Abrahamson)*
Twilight
The Six Days of Destruction *(With Albert Friedlander)*
From the Kingdom of Memory
Sages and Dreamers

THE FORGOTTEN

BY

ELIE WIESEL

TRANSLATED BY

STEPHEN BECKER

SUMMIT BOOKS

NEW YORK LONDON TORONTO SYDNEY TOKYO SINGAPORE

SUMMIT BOOKS
Simon & Schuster Building
Rockefeller Center
1230 Avenue of the Americas
New York, New York 10020

This book is a work of fiction. Names, characters, places and incidents are either products of the author's imagination or are used fictitiously. Any resemblance to actual events or locales or persons, living or dead, is entirely coincidental.

SUMMIT BOOKS and colophon are trademarks
of Simon & Schuster Inc.
Designed by Levavi & Levavi
Manufactured in the United States of America
1 3 5 7 9 10 8 6 4 2
Library of Congress Cataloging in Publication Data
Wiesel, Elie
[Oublié. English]
The forgotten/by Elie Wiesel: translated by Stephen Becker.
p. cm.
Translation of : L'oublié.
I. Title.
PQ2683.I3209213 1992
843'.914—dc20 91-46826
CIP
ISBN: 0-671-68970-3

For Marion, Always

Respect the old man who has forgotten what he learned. For broken Tablets have a place in the Ark beside the Tablets of the Law.

—The Talmud

ELHANAN'S PRAYER

God of Abraham, Isaac and Jacob, forget not their son who calls upon them now.

You well know, You, source of all memory, that to forget is to abandon, to forget is to repudiate. Do not abandon me, God of my fathers, for I have never repudiated You.

God of Israel, do not cast out a son of Israel who yearns with all his heart and all his soul to be linked to the history of Israel.

God and King of the universe, exile me not from that universe.

As a child I learned to revere You, to love You, to obey You; keep me from forgetting the child that I was.

As an adolescent I chanted the litanies of the martyrs of Mainz and York; erase them not from my memory, You who erase nothing from Your own.

As a man I learned to respect the will of our dead; keep me from forgetting what I learned.

God of my ancestors, let the bond between them and me remain whole, unbroken.

You who have chosen to dwell in Jerusalem, let me not forget Jerusalem. You who wander with Your people in exile, let me remember them.

God of Auschwitz, know that I must remember Auschwitz. And that I must remind You of it. God of Treblinka, let the sound of that name make me, and You, tremble now and always. God of Belzec, let me, and You, weep for the victims of Belzec.

You who share our suffering, You who share our wait, let me never be far from those who have invited You into their hearts.

You who foresee the future of man, let me not cut myself off from my past.

God of justice, be just to me. God of charity, be kind to me. God of mercy, plunge me not into the *kaf-ha-kallah,* the chasm where all life, hope and light are extinguished by oblivion. God of truth, remember that without memory truth becomes only the mask of truth. Remember that only memory leads man back to the source of his longing for You.

Remember, God of history, that You created man to remember. You put me into the world, You spared me in time of danger and death, that I might testify. What sort of witness would I be without my memory?

Know, God, that I do not wish to forget You. I do not wish to forget anything. Not the living and not the dead. Not the voices and not the silences. I do not wish to forget the moments of abundance that enriched my life, nor the hours of anguish that drove me to despair.

Even if you forget me, O Lord, I refuse to forget You.

MALKIEL'S WORDS

My name is Malkiel. Malkiel Rosenbaum, to be exact. I feel that I must set it down. Superstition? To ward off bad luck? Perhaps I merely want to prove to myself that I have not yet forgotten my own name. Could that happen to me, too? One morning I could pick up my pen and it would not obey me; it would refuse to follow my orders for the simple reason that I would no longer be capable of issuing them. Malkiel Rosenbaum would still exist, but he would no longer be master of his own identity.

I am forty years old. Malkiel Rosenbaum is forty years old. That, too, I must set down; it is important. I was born in 1948 in Jerusalem. I am as old as the State of Israel. Easy to remember. I am as old, and as young, as Israel. Forty. Plus three thousand.

What does it matter? Only memory matters. Mine sometimes overflows. Because it harbors my father's memories, too, since his mind has become a sieve. No, not a sieve: an autumn leaf, dried, torn. No, a phantom which I see only at midnight. I know: one cannot see a memory. But I can. I see it as the shadow of a shadow which constantly withdraws and turns inward. I hardly glimpse it, and it vanishes in the abyss. Then I hear it cry out, I hear it whimper softly. It is gone, but I see it as I see myself. It calls: Malkiel, Malkiel. I answer: Don't worry, I won't leave you.

One day it will call no more.

The shock was so violent that he lost his balance and almost fell to the damp soil; the name on the tombstone, tilted as if under the weight of its weariness, was his own. Malkiel ben Elhanan Rosenbaum.

A wild notion crossed his mind: could he already be dead? He could not remember living through his death. So what? That meant nothing. Who's to say that the dead carry their memories into the other world? Despite himself he leaned forward and deciphered the date: the month of Iyar 5704. May 1944. I'm a fool: I was not yet born. How can you die before you're born? But then, why am I here? Could I have forgotten? No, forgetting is not your problem, not yet, but your father's, right? I'm here to remember what my father has forgotten. But do I live only to remember? Suppose life were only your ancestors' imagination, or a dream of the dead?

Leaning on the tombstone of this grandfather who bore his name, he was suffused by an obscure and almost animal anguish, a black tide, menacing, portending disaster. Beyond the trees he saw the reddish-gray roofs of the town hall and the school. Beyond the tombs he saw the blood of the dying day and heard the moan of the yawning twilight. Living, he thought with dread. They call this living.

It's the same with love. They say, If I stop loving I'll die. And then one day they stop. And they're still alive. They call that loving. They call that choosing life. God has ordained that. As He ordains faith. So He always wins: the opposite of God is still God. To flee God is also to draw near Him. You cannot escape Him. Am I right, Grandfather Malkiel—you cannot escape Him?

Answer me. Help me. Come to our rescue. Your son needs you, and so do I. My father no longer understands anyone and no one understands him. As if he'd gone mad. But he hasn't. They say a madman, like an animal doomed to sacrifice, uses an intelligence different from ours, or at least a primitive form of ours. But my father's intelligence has been crippled. He's sick, Grandfather, and I'm fighting to help him.

His disease has a name, but he refuses to hear it. He will not let it be spoken in his presence. You'd say he was afraid of it. As if he were dragging a procession of soulless, faceless phantoms behind him. Strange, this apprehension. Is it because in his house, in the small town of his childhood, they avoided naming certain illnesses, certain disasters, for fear of being noticed by them? And now does he think he can fend off the disease by not naming it? Whatever his reason, I must respect it to the end.

He pressed harder on the cold stone, as if he wanted to embed himself into it, or at least leave a visible and lasting imprint.

From a distance a hoarse voice hailed him: "Hey, stranger! Where'd you disappear to?" It was Hershel, the caretaker-gravedigger, a clumsy giant with a head carved of granite and a face of blackened bark. He seemed out of breath. "I lost sight of you, stranger. You'll have to forgive me. I'm not so young anymore. My legs, oh my legs! If I were married I'd say they couldn't chase my wife anymore. Thcy don't carry me around the way they used to. It's not their fault. Here we say the years too can make us grow old. Ah, if I were your age . . ."

"I'm not so young either," Malkiel said.

"Cut it out. You're making fun of me. I could be your great-grandfather."

Well, thought Malkiel, my great-grandfather's grave is here, too; I must try to find it.

"But I'm talking, talking, and you have to leave. We're locking up. And be careful. A Jewish cemetery is a dangerous place even if it's abandoned."

"Dangerous for whom? For the dead?" Malkiel was a bit annoyed.

"For everybody. Except me. The gravedigger never has anything to fear. But other people . . . they don't realize. A cemetery is a special place, and an old one even more so. Look around you, how calm it is. And if I told you that was only appearances, a trick? You bet. The dead are like you and me: jokers slip in with the heroes, and between them they drive us crazy. They play all kinds of games. They will grab your coat and rip it, and grab your eyes and rip them, too. You're a happy man, stranger. You don't know about all that."

The gravedigger sat heavily on a low tombstone, across from

Malkiel. Mopping his brow with a huge patched handkerchief he'd pulled from an inside pocket, he went on. "Listen, stranger. A visitor from a nearby village showed up one day, a long time ago, before the war, and asked me to show him a relative's tomb. I showed it to him. All of a sudden he turned to me and said, 'Who's that open grave for?' Now, I'm the gravedigger, and I couldn't remember digging a grave, for the simple reason that no one had died that week. And maybe you know that tradition forbids us to dig a grave before the person has died, for fear of tempting the Angel of Death. So who dug that open grave? The dead themselves? So I said to this visitor, Listen, friend, if I were you I'd get out of here now and go far, far away, as far as you can. He refused. I don't believe in these superstitions, he said, disgusted. Well, you can guess the end. He left and went to the inn and a beam fell on him. They buried him the same day. In the grave waiting for him."

The gravedigger gestured as he spoke. He was enjoying himself. I'll give him a good tip, Malkiel decided; he's earned it. Any man who spends his life among the dead deserves a good tip. Do the dead enjoy his stories?

"All right, then, let's go," said Hershel the gravedigger. "In these parts night falls fast, because of the mountains."

Malkiel followed him out of the cemetery. At the gate a bucket of water stood ready for them. He washed his hands according to custom and gave Hershel two packs of American cigarettes. The gravedigger bowed low. "They're worth four bottles of *tzuika*," he said, patting his belly. "Listen, someday I'll tell you about the Great Reunion. I owe you that much. Tomorrow?"

"Tomorrow," Malkiel said.

Hands in his pockets, his throat dry, Malkiel walked along the river. Night was about to invade the town.

Arriving there two weeks earlier, on a beautiful morning in August —or Elul, by the Hebrew calendar—Malkiel had planned to stay only a few days: inspect the cemetery, stroll about, visit his family's old home, soak up the climate, the ambiance of the place, and find a trace of a certain woman whose name and address he did not know. Then he planned to go back, see his father and reconcile with Tamar. He could not have foreseen that his visit would extend for weeks.

The weather was fine that Thursday. The day promised to be mild, almost warm, with a clear sky and an invigorating breeze. In the distance pines bowed as if listening to a story. The dewy fields smelled sweet, fresh and rich. The familiar sights and sounds were those of a village waking: a bucket clattering up from a well, livestock being led to the trough. Outwardly, it was just another one of the villages that the traveler passes through between the Dnieper and the Carpathians. Cockcrow at morning, shepherd's flute at evening. Haughty horsemen, their hair flying; stooped and careworn laborers. Harsh-featured widows, old men with empty or suspicious glances.

Malkiel looked for someone to ask the village's new name. He chose a humpbacked, toothless peasant. Unfortunately, the man did not understand the question. Malkiel tried German; nothing. A word of Romanian? The peasant shrugged, muttered an unintelligible phrase and departed. Malkiel went on his way. He passed by the railway station and discovered, with some emotion, a sign: BOZHKOI. It was his great-grandfather's village.

To one side the valley with its earthen cottages, to the other the shadowy mountain, at once shielding and shattering. They slept when the mountain slept, they lay awake, huddled, when the mountain set its wild beasts howling in the storm. Then, young and old, men and women, believers and infidels, all took on the same face, hunted, resigned; they waited for the lull, to close their eyes and dream until the next day came with its pains and its pleasures; they showed their faith in nature's kindness.

Before leaving the village, Malkiel came upon a peasant woman talking to her cow. Which answered her. Farther along, a schoolboy, half asleep, emerged from his cottage and walked along close to the walls. Seeing Malkiel in his fancy rented car, the boy fled without looking back. There you are, Malkiel thought, you frighten children.

Finally he saw the town. From afar it seemed drowsy. Nearer he was surprised by all the activity.

Malkiel reached his hotel and filled out the obligatory form. Profession: journalist. Purpose of trip: to study the inscriptions on old tombstones.

Grandfather Malkiel, if you can hear me, heed my words. They are meant to be an offering, a prayer. They come from far off, a message of faith from your son, who needs your intercession above.

Let his health be restored, let his past not slip away. Grant him the power to break his solitude, and me the power to bear it.

Your son is devoted to you; he told me that so I would know, so I would remember.

If you can see, look at me: my father's memories are mingled with mine, his eyes are in my eyes. His silences, born of dread, frustration and despair, live in my words. My past has opened to his, and so to yours.

Your son is still alive, but can one call that living? He is walled into the instant, cut off from before and after. He no longer gazes at the heights, and his soul is a prisoner.

It would be indecent of me to feel pity for my father; but you, Grandfather Malkiel, take pity on your son.

That is what I have come to tell you. That is why I have come so far.

If I could gather a minyan *I would happily say a prayer for your soul; but there is no* minyan. *So all I can do is beg you to come to his rescue.*

"I waited for you," Lidia said. "Then got tired of it. In this country we spend half our lives waiting."

"How did you know where I was?"

"Ah, that's my secret," she said provocatively. "I have a right to secrets, too, haven't I?"

Malkiel's face clouded. She was trying to make herself interesting. Was she working for the secret police? Too bad if she was. That was a game they could play without him.

A languid breeze wafted spicy odors from the river. Malkiel caught a few and offered them, in spirit, to his distant lady friend. Tamar liked to say that she took in the world through her nostrils. Arriving in a new place, she sniffed the air before she even looked around.

"All right, I'll explain," Lidia said, taking his arm in a familiar gesture. "Obviously you're overcomplicated. The simple things go right by you. And yet everything *is* simple. I knew you'd go to the cemetery just like every day. And I decided that one of these days you'd be fed up with talking to the dead, or listening to them. To relax, you'd take a stroll along the river. Everybody does that here."

"I could have taken a stroll in the park."

"Too crowded this time of day."

"The garden behind the municipal auditorium?"

"Too near the police."

"In a nearby village?"

"Too far. Logical, no?"

"Absolutely. Logical."

They took a few steps in silence.

Behind them, in the little town with its gloomy streets and alleys, people were eating and drinking and laughing, stopping to scrutinize an unfamiliar doorway, to admire a woman, to make sense of their longings. A pair of lovers, close by. Secret police, perhaps? The boy was pointing to a sky streaked with violent color; the girl turned to look at the impassive river. Lidia was calm. Malkiel was not. A dozen times a day he felt an anguish that stopped his breath: he couldn't tell now if it was a weakness or an act of courage to call upon memory. Was it easy to let memory slip away? For his father it was not at all easy: he had watched it glide away inaudibly, smoothly, abandoning him to his emptiness, his heartbreak. Poor Father, wanting fiercely to pin time down, enclose it, tame it.

"You'll tell me when you're tired?" Lidia asked.

"I'll tell you." What an odd young woman, Malkiel thought. An odd interpreter, too: guardian angel or a shrewd policeman? Why does she follow me? What do I represent in her eyes? What does she want from me? A promotion at my expense? A pass? The chance of living some other way, dying somewhere else? I'm stupid; it can't be that. Then what is it? I am daydreaming.

He checked his watch. After eight. The trees were dense around him, and so was the silence.

"What are you thinking about?"

A flirtation? Is that what she wants? I'm not much good at that. My mind wanders. And I'm a bit too old for it. And then, I didn't come all this way to flirt, or even to dream, but to identify my father's dreams. Time now to separate them from my own, before I scramble them all together. Head in the clouds on a sunny day, that doesn't do the job.

But Malkiel could not help it. He was like that. A matter of character, of temperament. Of habit, too. There was a time when he fell in love quickly; he loved to love. A man in love, he thought, says "we" like a king. A man in love babbles of his childhood like an old man. But he spoke seldom about his early days. He had few memories of childhood; he had mostly dreams. Vibrant and intense, but nowhere sharply etched. Now he needed to transform those very dreams into memories. Not easy. In the mountains he dreamed of mountains. On the bank of the river he dreamed of the river. And in this town buried in the Carpathians, he saw himself in another town, buried in this one's heart. He hastened toward someone calling him, he ran, when he was actually groping for his way, he ran until he was out of breath, and onlookers cheered him along, and the dead inspired him: Faster, go on, they're waiting for you. And in truth just at the end, on a hill taller than the mountain, a young woman was waiting for him, beautiful and proud and anguished, not this one squeezing his arm, as if to remind him where they were, if not who they were.

"Lidia, who are you?"

"Oh, no! Don't you know that yet? I'm your professor of Romanian. Your interpreter. Your guide. The woman in your life, you might say."

Of course. Professor of Romanian to Malkiel Rosenbaum, reporter for *The New York Times,* on special assignment in Transylvania. The day after his arrival he had a visit from an official in the tourist bureau. The man welcomed him and put him through a courteous but searching interrogation. Did he speak Romanian? Hungarian? Not that either? But then how would he manage? "Well, don't you worry about it. I have someone for you. Recommended by the public affairs division in the foreign ministry. And by a rabbi in the capital. Believe me, you won't be able to do without her." Lidia came to see him that same day. With a grammar textbook. "Thanks, but I don't need it," Malkiel said. "It would take too long."

Was she disappointed? She gave no sign. "Whatever you like," she said, still polite. "We'll study without a textbook." He explained that he was not looking for a professor; he needed a guide, an interpreter. "I'm a professor of Romanian," she said, "but that doesn't stop me from working as a guide. And interpreter." Further proof that she was working for special services.

"Lidia," Malkiel said, "I didn't ask you what you do, but who you are."

She did not answer immediately. She thought it over. While she thought she ran her right hand through her hair. She seemed upset. Why this hesitation? What was she hiding?

"I don't believe," she said finally, in an artificially official tone, "that my private life can be of any interest to you."

Malkiel detected a trace of spite in her voice. Was she married? Unhappy at home? What was her game? He was about to quiz her but changed his mind. "Let's talk about something else, all right?"

Annoyed, she let go of his arm. The street stretched before them, empty and inhospitable. Low houses stood in rows like sand hills shot through with light and color.

"Why and how my life—"

He interrupted. "I'm a reporter, after all."

"Didn't you tell me you were in charge of obituaries?"

Malkiel bit his tongue. "You've got me there. I'm interested in the dead, that's true enough."

"Isn't it too late?"

"Too late for whom?"

"For the dead," Lidia said.

"Maybe. But when it's too late for the living, that's when things become serious."

She took his arm again and squeezed it, but said nothing.

For two weeks now they had met every day. In the morning before he went to the cemetery, and in the afternoon when he came back. Sometimes they dined together. Sometimes they strolled about in the evening. They chatted in English, or in German when Lidia couldn't find the proper word.

At first she tried to draw him out, make him talk about himself, his family, his work, his colleagues, his studies. With the real questions smuggled in: what was the true purpose of his stay in this insignificant village, shrouded more in legend than in history, with few tourists clamoring to discover its exotic charms? Why did he visit the cemetery every day? What was he looking for among graves the most recent of which was ten or fifteen years old? Malkiel knew how to avoid her questions; he wasn't a reporter for nothing.

A strange young woman, all the same. When she smiled, she was radiant. When she turned inward she was disturbing. Was she trying to seduce him? To gain intimacy? And yet he'd leave tomorrow and they'd never see each other again. So much the better. Father is ill; have I the right to amuse myself with an unknown woman? I'm betraying him, just as I'm betraying Tamar. Ah yes, Tamar: will you hold it against me if I sleep with her? Will you break off? Equally important question: Am I capable of making love to a stranger? She has beautiful eyes: when I looked into them that first day, I saw depths that dizzied me. True, it lasted only a second. Will you hold the dizziness against me, Tamar? And yet you know how I live for the moment. I am fascinated by it. I open my arms to embrace a woman, and at that moment she may believe herself happy, and I know myself open to happiness, to love. I also know the poison will take effect later, but I don't regret offering my hand. I smile at a child playing on the beach and he smiles back, not yet aware that he is doomed to grow up in a lunatic world; but I don't regret the smile. When I tell a beggar, Come on, I'll buy you a meal, I'm only emphasizing his solitude, his exile, but I don't regret speaking to him. Should I sacrifice the present on the pretext that it's fleeting? What do you say, Tamar? No, I mustn't think about you. You have no place here and now.

"Are you hungry?" Lidia asked.

"Not particularly. You?"

"Me neither."

All their conversations ended the same way: Are you sleepy? No? Me neither. Are you thirsty? Yes? Me too. In the center of town two or three cafés or inns were still open.

"Shall we?"

"We shall," Malkiel said. "But when we get there you're going to tell me who you are. Promise?"

"When I was a little girl, I promised my mother never to make promises."

When she was little, when I was little . . . What sort of boy was I? What was it like to be young? A gust of nostalgia drew him deeper into his shell. By turns timid and brash as a child, he had sought happiness where it was not to be found. So he invented it for himself. To play with it, destroy it and reinvent it.

Yet his childhood in New York was almost average. His father, careful not to lean on him, tried—sometimes without success—to stay in the background. Malkiel could ask his friends to the house for dinner. Loretta never complained at having to feed five unexpected guests. Elhanan respected his son's independence, even if it meant standing by while he committed foolishness. One day he said to the boy, "You should know, my son, that no one can suffer in another's place. All I can promise is that when you suffer, I'll be present." What an irony, Malkiel mused. Our roles are reversed. He's suffering and I can't suffer for him. I can remember for him, that's all.

"I'll tell you about me if you'll tell me about you," Lidia said.

"And then?"

"Then I'll know."

"What will you know?"

"Whatever you want me to know."

"Exactly. I don't want you to know."

She stopped, shot him a scornful glance and chuckled. "How complicated you are!"

Malkiel and Lidia came out onto a badly lit, still crowded square. The strollers seemed lugubrious, dragging their feet; they seemed to be slipping on the cobblestones. One moment they clung together, and the next moment, as if to flee an enemy, they dispersed. Malkiel looked inside an inn where singing drunkards were being scolded by waitresses. "Here?" Malkiel asked.

"No. Let's go somewhere else."

"You don't like the innkeeper?"

"He makes passes at me."

"Are you afraid he'll see us together?"

"He's too drunk to see anything but his bottle. And I'd prefer a quieter place."

"Do you know one?"

"Yes."

"Where the boss won't bother you?"

"No, he won't. I promise." And after a moment's reflection, "See? I'm betraying my principles: I just made you a promise. Shall we go, then?"

She led him toward a tree-lined alley. Once within, she began to hurry. A disconcerting interpreter, Malkiel thought. She intrigued him. Nothing unusual there. All women intrigued him. Because he never knew his mother, and sought her in each of them? Here in a Communist country he might do well to be wary, especially of women like this one. He'd read enough articles about it. Innocent tourists traveling alone, letting themselves be trapped by secret police who shoved a gorgeous creature into their beds. Then the crash of a door broken down, and flashbulbs, and an outraged husband lunging forward crying scandal, demanding an arrest: all burlesque. Reporter friends warned Malkiel as they said good-bye: "If it happens to you, enjoy it. You're not married and you're not risking a thing. They can't blackmail you."

"Seriously, where are we going?" Malkiel asked.

"To a serious place."

"Really."

"Trust me."

"When I was a little boy . . ."

"I wonder if you were ever a little boy."

Finally they stopped before a modest two-story house.

"Don't tell me there's a tavern in there."

She took both his hands. "You're a fool, Mr. Rosenbaum."

How many times in his life had he heard those words? You're a fool to stay in the house on a beautiful day like this, you're a fool not to go out with us tonight, not to go to the beach, you're a fool to spend so many hours with your old father, you're a fool to love too much or not enough. . . . You should, you could be happy, take advantage of life, sunbathe, give in to temptation. . . . You're a fool, such a fool, to seek and search when you don't have to, not to seek and search when you should. . . .

Lidia raised her head. "This is my house. I live here."

"I see. You live in a tavern."

"I can offer you a cup of bad coffee, but still better than the hotel's."

Yes, no? Malkiel wanted to say, Yes indeed, I like you, let's go to your place. But the image of his sick father rose within him. Drive it away? Of course not. Make love in its presence?

"Not tonight, Lidia. Don't hold it against me. Another time—I promise."

After a moment she smiled again. "I see you did *not* promise your mother not to—"

"No; I promised her nothing."

All right. Where now? The hotel? The café just off the main square? His father's house? Malkiel held his breath. He knew that house from doorway to roofline, although he'd never seen it. Every room and every piece of furniture: he knew the layout. Above the stove, in the dining room, the ceiling seemed low and blackened; two windows looked out on Barracks Road, and you could see the theater and the cinema, and the crowd rushing up to the ticket windows. To the left you could see the entrance to a garden where young people gathered on Saturday afternoons to wink at each other and gossip a little, just to get acquainted. Malkiel was gripped by a sudden desire to run over there, knock on the door, wake up the people asleep inside and live his dream to the end: invite his dead mother and his sick father to come and join him. Come on, I've fixed it all, restored everything; I've thrown out the intruders, the house is waiting for you, the nightmare is over; as if there had never been a war, as if there had never been deportations. The living are still alive, Death does not conquer all. Look, Father, you're home. I? For you, I am nothing but a suppressed desire, a muted voice.

"I'd better go home," Lidia said. "Don't you think?"

"Yes, Lidia. Tonight . . ."

"I understand."

A quick handshake. Lidia left him without looking back. In his mind Malkiel already saw himself running to his father's house.

Faster, faster. No more waiting. Give up this game and shout the truth to the whole world: "The *real* reason for my journey here? I lied to you; what I'm looking for is not engraved on headstones, but . . ." His train of thought halted. What am I saying? Where will I find what I'm looking for? And what am I looking for in the first place?

And yet the authorities had believed his story; it made sense. Editor of the *Times* obituary page, he was fascinated by ancient epitaphs. At the ministry an official had nodded and mumbled, "But of course, Domnul Rosenbaum, we understand; you were right to come visit our cemeteries. You'll stay awhile, won't you? At least we hope so."

And indeed he might linger. For long? How could he know? Only God knew all, always. Only God pierced the mystery of the future. Yesterday, tomorrow, never. These words don't have the same meaning in New York and Bombay. The beggar and the prince move toward death at different paces. What separates an individual from his fellowman? What keeps the past from biting into the future? All men need rain, prayer and silence; all forget, all will be forgotten. Me too? Me too. And my father, too? And God? He, too?

Oh, to recover faith! And the innocence of before. To live in the moment, to hold desire and fulfillment in one's grasp, to fuse with someone else, with oneself; to become infinity. For his father, unfortunately, infinity was merging with oblivion. The past like the future was only a vast black hole. Nothing more? Nothing more.

Malkiel felt a touch of nausea. He had eaten nothing all day. His body was taking revenge for being neglected, disdained and punished for no reason. What if he were to stop at the tavern for a bite, a slice of their bad cheese? Better still, he could retrace his steps, ring Lidia's doorbell and confess his uneasiness, his weakness: I'm stupid, Lidia; I'm hungry and I was ashamed to say so, I want you and I didn't dare admit it. . . . Well, Malkiel? Yes?

Seated on a bench in the main square, Malkiel attracted the attention of a few passersby, who watched him from the corners of their eyes. A sturdy fellow reeking of alcohol brushed past him. A woman whispered something he did not understand. Malkiel rose and walked back toward the river, which opened to the sky as if to rock it with melancholy. A bizarre urge seized him: to plunge in, float, let himself be swept as far as the sea and beyond, to be drawn up to the heavens and higher; to go away, to see nothing, to hear nothing, to feel nothing, to possess nothing, to sacrifice nothing. A death wish? A desire to forget death? To join his father in a common oblivion?

A loud, raspy voice saved him. "Come buy me a drink. It'll do you good."

It was Hershel the gravedigger. Where did he come from?

"How about it?" Hershel laughed. "God will pay you back."

"I thought gravediggers knew all about death, not God."

"But, my dear stranger, they work together, don't you know that? I have a lot to teach you! Come on, buy me a drink. We'll drink to God, Who created men in a drunken moment."

Malkiel did not reply. So between a beautiful woman and a gravedigger, I'll have chosen the gravedigger. What a life, he thought.

"My dear sir, you look depressed to me. What is it, now? Are the stars against you? Is the earth spinning backward under your feet? Will you feel better if I tell you about the Great Reunion?"

"Let's go have a drink," Malkiel said.

As they walked along, the gravedigger went on with his chatter. "People don't appreciate us, I swear. But what would they do without us? We're the only ones who know what death is all about. And the earth itself. Just let somebody try to muscle in on our work, and the earth will swallow him up like that, believe me. The earth is kind to us gravediggers. It doesn't complain, it lets itself be worked over. It accepts what we give it. It endures the assassin's arrogance and the victim's tears. It's open to everybody at any moment; the great conqueror is the earth, for it is the earth that tames the dead and feeds the living."

Was this gravedigger already drunk? Who taught him to speak with such eloquence? "Is the tavern far?"

"Nothing is far, for us," said the gravedigger, laughing.

That voice, Malkiel wondered, what gives it such force? Death? Is it the voice of doom and damnation?

"Will you listen to me?"

"Of course I'll listen to you, Father."

"You won't lose patience?"

"I'll listen carefully."

"And you'll try to remember everything?"

"I'll try."

"And take everything down?"

"I'll take everything down."

"Even the most insignificant details?"

"Details are rarely insignificant."

"You won't hold it against me if I sometimes tell you unpleasant things, sad things?"

"I won't hold it against you, Father."

"You won't be disappointed, later, when I express myself badly?"

"You've never disappointed me."

"But I have so many things to tell you, so many things!"

"I know."

"I worry and worry: will I have time to tell you everything?"

"Let's hope so."

"That's just it, my son. I feel hope deserting me, flowing out of me."

"You'll fight to hang on to it."

"Will you help me?"

"Naturally, I'll help you. Always."

"There's not much time."

"No, Father, there's not much time. You talk. I'll listen."

"All right. I'll tell you. The beginning, and what follows, everything, I'll tell you everything if God lets me. Are you listening? Try to remember what I tell you, because soon I won't be able to tell you anything."

Elhanan had to recall the village of his childhood for his own child. Malkiel must bear it within him as his father bore it, a landmark and a source of wonder.

Picturesque and colorful, it blended cultures and ethnic groups, diverse traditions and customs. Russians, Turks, Mongols, Germans, Hungarians and Romanians had left their imprint upon it. A modern Babel; its citizens spoke many languages. You might have said that men and women had thronged to this enchanted spot from all corners of history to build their temples, all too visible and not very reassuring.

You would find peddlers and merchants, acrobats and bandits, witches and healers. Just men who aspired to reach heaven, and primitive villagers coupling in the courtyard in broad daylight. Men who lived only for others and evildoers who lived only off others. Hard-hearted police informers and troubadours with smiling faces. Wise old men dreaming of God and upstarts who took themselves for gods.

"My grandfather lived far, far away," Elhanan told his son. "If you can, go and see the little hamlet where he had a farm just beyond a river, really a stream. . . . In summer I used to visit him."

With his mother Elhanan went there either by train, some twenty minutes' ride, or in a carriage, two hours or more. Elhanan preferred the carriage. When the coachman was in a good mood he let the boy hold the reins; and then, enjoying a new freedom and authority, the boy felt in tune with life.

The road wound its way through a forest. Elhanan gazed at the trees, which looked immense, all black with twisted roots, cracked and tangled branches: in them he saw the pleas of distorted and accursed creatures doomed to repentance. He closed his eyes, but still he saw them.

"I believed my grandfather stronger than a lion," said Elhanan to his son, "and wiser than a Wise Man. He spoke to me, and I listened; I spoke to him, and he listened. I listened even when he was meditating in silence; I meditated with him. It was he who taught me to love fields and valleys."

Elhanan did love the countryside. The shepherds' flutes calling their flocks at day's end, the stray lambs' tinkling bells, the wind rustling the leaves just before a storm. Every blade of grass possessed by its own song, said Rabbi Nahman. Elhanan loved hearing the song of the earth mingle with the song of the sky.

Elhanan's mother spoke often of her own mother, his grandfather's first wife. And the child loved her though he had never seen her. He was sure that she had been beautiful and sweet as his mother. On the other hand, he was wary of the morose woman his grandfather had taken for his second wife. He found her sullen and bitter; he resented her without knowing why.

Twice a year Grandfather came to town—without his wife—to spend the holidays with Rabbi Sender of Wohlnie, who lived opposite Elhanan. Grandfather admired this master naively and sincerely, and attributed to him virtues and powers that raised him to the ranks of the Just. Among his followers was a man who had damned his wife in an angry moment, crying out, "May fire take her!" Shortly afterward his wife died in a fire. Was it just bad luck? The rabbi reprimanded him: "You talk too much." After that the Hasid never uttered another word. A few years later, the rabbi told him, "Silence, too, has its limits." Whereupon the penitent immediately recovered the power of speech. But from then on, words tumbled together in his mouth; he became incoherent, and people thought he had lost his mind. The penitent asked, "Am I mad,

Rabbi?" And the rabbi answered him, "There are madmen of silence and madmen of speech; it is often difficult to choose between them." So the Hasid divided his life in two: he spoke in the morning and was silent in the evening.

Elhanan must have been five or six when his grandfather brought him before Rabbi Sender. "Bless him, Rabbi." The rabbi, with a majestic face, eyes sparkling with kindness and intelligence, took the boy on his knee and smiled down on him. "What blessing would you like from an old man like me?"

Elhanan answered, "May all the old men I meet be like you."

The rabbi laughed heartily. "I can guess what your grandfather wants. He wants me to promise him that you will grow up to be a good Jew who fears God and loves his Torah. But you're more original than he is, my boy. May you always be so." That exchange filled his grandfather with pride.

There was a Tempter in the village, a real one who wreaked havoc. He seduced young women and pushed them toward sin and suicide. Elhanan thought he had seen him once, near the well in the courtyard. He had heard him laugh, most often at night. A voluptuous, seductive laugh, a laugh that gave him goose pimples. His grandfather asked, "Are you afraid, Elhanan?" The boy confessed that yes, he was afraid, most of all on Saturday night, when the demons emerged from their prisons to come and perturb the living. His grandfather said, "Rabbi Sender will help you." Rabbi Sender did not make fun of the boy: "We should never mock someone who is in fear, especially a child. Here is what I suggest: Saturday night you and I will go together to listen to the Tempter. Would you like that?" Elhanan accepted. At midnight the rabbi and the little boy drew near the well. Rabbi Sender recited a brief prayer and said, "Tempter, if you go on frightening Elhanan, you will never free yourself from the punishment I have in store for you." A moment later, Elhanan heard whimpering rise from the depths of the well. "If you so wish," the rabbi said to Elhanan, "we have the power to chain him up for centuries to come. Do you want me to do that?" Elhanan had never felt so important. "I'd like to ask my grandfather's advice," he answered. And his grandfather counseled clemency. Elhanan adored him. Between the old man and the little boy there was a touching and comforting bond that no one could break. When Grandfather came to the house, they were inseparable. They slept in the same bed and talked on and off for hours.

One Rosh Hashanah night, his grandfather taught Elhanan a solemn and deeply moving song. Elhanan loved his voice: it summoned up secret universes. A holy flame flickered about his person: joy, warmth, light pervaded the whole house. In the early hours of the morning, his grandfather died, still singing. But for Elhanan his song was stronger than death. He was convinced that his grandfather would never stop singing.

"I loved my father," said Elhanan to Malkiel. "I admired him and I would have given my life for him. But I yearned to be like my mother because she was like my grandfather. My mother is present to me as you are present to me. If she could see me as I see you, if my grandfather could hear me as I hear you, everything would be so different. . . . Yes, Malkiel, so different."

Elhanan was speaking to his son, but he was alone. Or rather he felt at once alone and not alone. The room was lit and not lit. He trembled, seeing himself with his mother again in the snowy village. All these phantoms so near him, all these hysterical demons tangled together like conspirators, filled him with fear. Help me to cast out fear, Mother, and do not leave me. You're still there, I can feel it, my heart beats louder—why am I afraid? Ah, it's nothing. I'm just cold.

And because I'm talking to you, my son, and you are not here.

Do you hear me?

As a child Elhanan wondered where spoken words went, and glimmers of light and shared silences. Who gathered up the unheard prayers of the faithful? To whom did a dying man's regrets belong after his death?

Elhanan asked himself a good many questions. They bore on the mystery of life and of darkness. Why live, if it was only to cease to live? Why build, if it was only to wake up among the ruins? His father tried to explain to him that certain things remained inexplicable. His teachers took great pains to make him understand that sometimes it was better not to try to understand.

How sweet life was in those days! Stable, regular, incorporated into God's memory, it allowed the poor to go on their way singing, the prisoners to sleep, and the children to venture without fear on uncharted paths.

The Jews led a Jewish life, the Christians a Christian life, and the others—the emancipated—displayed equal scorn for both.

Naturally, an occasional crisis aroused distrust and rancor between the communities. When that happened Elhanan and all the Jewish children stayed home and worked alone or with their parents until calm was restored.

A memory: the fascists had seized power in Bucharest. Gangs of the anti-Semitic Iron Guard were planning a raid on synagogues and Jewish homes. Neutral, the police kept their distance. Protective measures were necessary, but which ones? A meeting was held in the house of Malkiel, father of Elhanan. All the elders were there. Solemn, grave, they talked and talked; and Elhanan's father advised and advised. Only Elhanan did nothing. He watched and he listened. He did not understand: why were they so worried? It was as if they expected the end of the world. At one point, his father had raised his head: "If all these rumors are true, it may be the end of the world."

In any event, the pogrom did not take place, thanks to Berl Brezinsky. You don't know Berl? That's odd; in the village everybody knew Berl. In short, Berl, who was rich and remarkably strong, went to find the head thug and said to him, "Listen, you, you have a choice. Either you hold back these bastards, and I give you ten thousand lei, or you refuse, and I beat you to a pulp."

Elhanan remembered Berl, as he remembered all the prominent men of the community, and also the less prominent. He felt close to Shammai, who told him, "It's hopeless, it's laughable," without ever explaining what drove him to despair. And to Yohanan, who confided to him, "I feel guilty and I don't know why; maybe you know?" And to one fool who spoke in a singsong: "People, people, are they annoying! Into the garbage with their fine words and their rantings and their pompous orations! The time for words is ended, and all that matters is the following fact: the world as it is does not deserve to survive." And to a beggar who told him of his grief one Sabbath afternoon in the synagogue, drowned in shadow: "I'm ugly, I realize that; it's poverty that makes me ugly. Tell me, you who are kind enough to listen, what becomes of my smile when I stop smiling?" And to a poet who said anything to anybody: "Ah, how I miss her, the woman I haven't met yet, the woman I'll never meet."

Dreaming of his childhood, Elhanan became a child again and rediscovered a naive language, sometimes prophetic and sometimes nostalgic.

There was an even more bizarre character. Something about him frightened people. Despite the warmth of the House of Study, the *beit ha-midrash,* where Elhanan had seen him the evening before, he sat bundled up near the hearth and seemed to be freezing; his lips moved, but he made no sound. Flushed and feverish, with a sickly gaze, he looked without seeing. Elhanan asked him, "Are you in pain, sir? Are you hungry? Thirsty?"

The stranger did not answer.

"Would you like us to call a doctor?" Elhanan could not seem to catch his eye; the man seemed to be moving through an unreal world, bewitched, beyond reach. "Who are you, sir? Where do you come from? From what hell have you escaped?"

Nothing.

"Who is tormenting you? Who wishes you harm?"

Still nothing.

At first he had gone unnoticed in the town. They were used to these wanderers, messengers bearing secrets, who appeared and vanished without a word of explanation. They gave them lodging in the vestibule of the *beit ha-midrash*. To feed them, the shammes sent them to well-off families, who gave them one meal a day. Some spent a night in the village, others seven years; the village accepted them all and respected their liberty.

Elhanan loved to talk with them, to draw them out; through them a distant, turbulent, altered world offered itself to him; thanks to them he roamed the earth from end to end without ever leaving his little village.

But this vagabond was not like the others. He seemed more a returning ghost. His beard and brows tufted, his arms scarred by burns, he might have survived a blazing fire.

At the evening meal Elhanan spoke of him to his father, who advised him to let the stranger be: "He may need silence and solitude; don't impose your curiosity on him."

Elhanan saw the man again the next day: seated on the same bench, in the same hunched position, with the same stare.

The boy watched him during the morning service; the stranger took no part whatever. He never even stood up for the *Kedushah*. After the service, Elhanan approached him again and offered to help.

"Stop nagging me, boy. You belong in school, not with me. You're too young to waste your time and too good to clutter up my fantasies. Scram. It's in your own interest to steer clear. If I start talking you are lost."

"I'm not afraid, sir."

"And you brag about it? Learn to be afraid. Like me. Like everybody."

"I'll learn." And in a burst of audacity, "Teach me."

The stranger grimaced suddenly. His gaze flared at Elhanan with painful force. "No, son. Find someone else."

"Please," Elhanan said. "Every visitor teaches me something. Don't be the first to send me away empty-handed."

The stranger appraised him at length and then broke into a smile. Elhanan thought, When I'm grown up I'll smile like him.

"So be it," the stranger said. "You won't go away empty-handed. You'll remember this meeting. You'll remember that once on the path of life you came across an old Jew, as old as the world itself, as stubborn as the world's memory. I'm not asking you to promise not to forget; he's the one who makes that promise."

The stranger smiled at him again, and Elhanan thought, No, I won't go away empty-handed; when I'm grown up I'll be generous like him.

Elhanan wanted to go on talking, but the stranger withdrew into himself, as if the boy were not there.

Elhanan wanted to cry, as if he guessed that the stranger would not be able to keep his promise.

Their first meeting. At the *Times*. At the end of the seventies. Tamar was a political reporter, and a star. Malkiel was a rewrite man. She brought in some copy and handed it to the editor, who scanned it quickly and dropped it on Malkiel's desk. "Cut it down a little, but not too much; be careful. Tamar doesn't like people tampering with her copy." It was a piece about some local political campaign. Charges and countercharges. Malkiel knew his stuff. Melt down the fat. Cut the cosmetics and coloratura. The classic rule of good journalism: honor the verb, sacrifice the adjective. And then the rhythm: be careful about pace and rhythm. An easy job, all technique, quickly accomplished. The piece ran on page one. His boss, nicknamed "the sage," was obviously pleased.

Not Tamar. She was famous, and she knew it; her successes, if not her pride, gave her the right to be temperamental. She stormed in next morning, furious, and planted herself in front of her surgeon: "You butchered my piece, you destroyed it, you turned it into a simplistic, id-i-o-tic caricature! Any reader with brains must have laughed at it!" She forced the words out between clenched teeth. "Who are you to massacre my story? Who told you to flatten my style? To make a fool of me in front of the whole world?" Standing there, she intimidated Malkiel, who wished he could crawl into a hole in the ground. If his esteemed colleague could have fired him on the spot she would have, and with pleasure. More, if she had had the power to cut off his fingers or even his head . . .

It was the sage, defender of the oppressed, who saved Malkiel from eternal damnation. He took her by the shoulders. "Calm down, Tamar," he said. "Do you want to drive him to despair? Just between us, he had nothing to do with it. In fact, he fought to keep it exactly as it was—and it was, by the way, one of the best pieces you ever wrote. I never saw him fight for any piece the way he did for this one."

The tigress calmed down immediately. "Is that bargain-basement flattery true?"

The sage, visibly sincere, flashed his special-occasion smile: "I swear it on the most beautiful head in the room. Yours."

She turned back to Malkiel, a bit confused and repentant. "You poor boy! I'm a monster. Why did you let me go on like that? You should have insulted me, put me in my place, told me to go to hell. . . . Don't be id-i-o-tic. Come on, I'll buy you a cup of coffee. By the way, what's your name?"

So they became pals. Accomplices. Everybody at the rewrite desk knew it: only Malkiel was authorized to edit Tamar. No trespassing. They were an elite team, blessed from on high. Inseparable. Tamar's style, Malkiel's editing, a real lesson for beginners. So much so that the sage, always ingenious, suggested they cover a story together. They took the shuttle to Washington, stayed at the Madison Hotel, and went to work. Tamar knew everybody in the Senate and the House. She had a contact in the White House. They called her by her first name, they teased her, they invited her to lunch, dinner, the "reception of the year." "Sorry." She shrugged. "I'm not alone." Malkiel blushed. Was he a burden to her, heavy baggage? "Are we doing the story together, or not?" Tamar asked. "Are we going to win the Pulitzer together or not?" Malkiel could only agree: "Of course, of course." She laughed ironically: "You *are* stupid. Look at these people—they're dying of jealousy. I love that."

Actually Malkiel was thrilled to be with her. He liked everything about her: the way she dressed, did her hair, gave orders—she knew how to make herself heard. Naturally, he was in love with her; naturally, he hoped she wouldn't notice; naturally, he was wrong. Too bright, Tamar. A penetrating intelligence. And beneath her professional cool she was rather romantic.

Why was she showing such an interest in her colleague? Because he wasn't competing with her? Or trying to impress her? Because he behaved like a lost boy with her? The others on the editorial staff were men and women of the world; they knew how to open doors. Not Malkiel. Shy and retiring, he listened in silence like a good boy, observed in silence, retreated into silence. Tamar suspected a secret within him. And Tamar loved secrets. She knew he had grown up without a mother. The poor boy. Tamar loved the sufferings of others. She came from a family where humor drove out sadness. Ah—she recalled that she had never heard Malkiel laugh. Never mind that; she'd teach him.

Their first night in Washington. After a long dinner with a local reporter, who boasted of keeping his ear to the ground, they went up to their rooms, but she paused at her door. "Are you sleepy?" Tamar asked. "Not really," Malkiel said, and averted his eyes. "We could work a little," she said. "Do you want to?" He did want to; he wanted whatever she wanted.

She opened the door; they went in. Sitting side by side on a couch, they went over their notes, elaborated on various strategies for the investigation, compared impressions, uncertainties, possibilities; it was midnight, and they couldn't seem to finish. It was two in the morning, and they lay in an embrace.

How did it happen? Who dared take the first step? Malkiel. He rose above his inhibitions and took the initiative. He had never in his life felt so whole or so real. Simply, without a word, he took her in his arms; and she submitted. Neither spoke. Yet he felt a powerful urge to talk, to dissipate silence and doubt. He had to make an enormous effort not to say what men always say in that situation: "I'm in love with you, Tamar, and always have been. You're the woman of my life. I've waited for you since I was born; only now am I starting to live." Other times, at the edge of abandon, at the heart of ecstasy, he knew a faintly bitter taste of farewell, of nothingness. At the eye of the storm, he sensed death guarding all the exits; as soon as one dipped beneath the surface of things, death was there, with open arms. Sadness heralded it; joy disguised it and staved it off.

Tamar asked, "What are you thinking about?"

Tell her? Tell her that he had a father who'd never recovered from the death of his wife, whose whole being was suffused with melancholy, who helped others triumph over theirs by listening, just by listening? "I'm thinking of my father," he said.

His father was not yet ill. He was passing through cycles of depression, that was all. Was his disease already working within him? If so, no one had yet noticed the first signs of it.

"I'd like to meet him."

"You will."

"Do you think he'll like me?"

"He'll like you."

Malkiel wondered, How can we come to terms with our own destinies? Two beings joined their desires, their movements, and became a crossroads where drives and dreams converge; and yet it is not this victory that floods my soul, but death—my mother's, my own. One day the last flash of intelligence and desire and light will drown in death. "What are you thinking about?" he asked.

"Your father."

He was suddenly frightened, and did not know why. Waves of fear swept over him, rising and swelling before they tore apart.

"Let's sleep," Tamar said.

"You're right."

She kissed him.

"I thought you wanted to sleep," he said.

"You think too much."

For Malkiel and Tamar, life became an unquenchable spring of gratitude. Their bodies were as finely attuned in yearning as in joy, in desire as in fulfillment; neither needed to protect his loneliness by silence.

Glorious days and festive nights. They were in love, and they exhilarated each other. The presence of the one never weighed on the other. At the very core of their union they had found a creative freedom that constantly renewed itself and enriched their every night. But all Malkiel had to do was think of his father, and time and space began to vibrate again.

"I'm afraid," Tamar said once, when they had become one as never before.

"You? Afraid? But of what?"

"Of happiness. Happiness changes people. It makes them better or worse. Pure or mean. Some people aren't made for happiness. Are you?"

Malkiel made no reply. His father was not; he knew that. His father's natural element was suffering and the memory of suffering.

"We'll have to do all we can to be happy, Malkiel. It won't be easy. Happiness is a jealous god. He possesses you but won't let himself be possessed. We'll have to fight. Will you fight?"

"I don't know," Malkiel said.

"I'll teach you."

Did they have the same notions of this battle? Of his chances for winning? Malkiel's heart grew heavy. Living for someone else is sometimes easier than living with someone else. What is a blessing for the one may be a curse for the other. "When will I meet your father?" she asked.

"Soon."

"And I want you to meet my parents." They lived in Chicago. "Suppose we went there for Thanksgiving?"

"All right," said Malkiel.

"But—your father?"

"He'll understand."

"He won't feel too lonely?"

"He has his patients."

A big family in a suburb of Chicago. Lots of commotion. Little ones stumbling, tumbling and grumbling, snacking, screaming for drinks. Tamar was the heroine, the princess. The small children clung to her skirts and wanted only her. For this festive dinner they all demanded to sit beside her. Malkiel occupied the place of honor, to the right of the lady of the house. She had roasted the traditional turkey. Unfortunately, Malkiel detested turkey. "Eat, eat, you'll enjoy it," Tamar's mother insisted, a true Jewish mother. "I'm a vegetarian," Malkiel said in apology. "Tamar!" her mother cried. "You never told me you were marrying a vegetarian. . . . What is that, a vegetarian? What religion is that?" Malkiel blushed in confusion; he was ashamed for Tamar and ashamed of himself. "Don't make a fuss, Mother," Tamar said. "You can be Jewish and vegetarian at the same time." Relieved, her mother explained, "But turkey is kosher, I swear it!" "Leave him alone," Tamar said. "He's not much of an eater." Thanks, Tamar. "Ay, ay," her mother said, "I feel for you. Men who don't eat well don't make good husbands." "Mother!" Tamar protested. Thanks, Tamar.

The following week Tamar accompanied Malkiel to his father's house. It was a Sunday in December, and the first snow was falling on the city. The Hudson's waves flowed slower. Tamar was quiet.

The moment Elhanan saw her he went rigid. His breath stopped. He muttered, "Not possible, not possible!"

Tamar went straight to him and kissed him on both cheeks. She'd hardly arrived but felt at home, in spite of his agitation. "Not possible, not possible," Elhanan repeated.

"What's not possible?" she asked.

"The resemblance," Elhanan murmured. "The quality of your beauty."

"Now, don't tell me you want to marry me." Tamar smiled. Lost to the world, Elhanan did not hear her. "What's the matter? Don't you like me?"

Malkiel spoke up immediately. "Father, this is Tamar. My colleague. You've read her articles."

Elhanan seemed to wake up. "Ah yes, of course. I remember. How happy I am to see you in my home!"

Elhanan had worn his blue suit. He wanted her to like him; she liked him. Tamar knew how to draw people out; soon she had him talking. About his students and his patients. She admired his erudition and his gift for analysis and introspection. A glowing Loretta served coffee. Tamar complimented her and meant it: "It's better than what they serve at the White House." "Tell the President," Loretta replied, "that I'll come give him a hand when he has important dinner guests." Malkiel excused himself to phone the newspaper. Elhanan took advantage of his absence to repeat, "Not possible, it's really not possible. You're beautiful, very beautiful . . . as my wife was once." Malkiel was back, and Elhanan spoke to him: "What are you waiting for, my son? Marry her! Hurry up!"

"I adore him, you know," Tamar told Malkiel when they were in the street again. "He's someone very special."

Thank you, Tamar.

"Do you see?" Tamar said, as they walked arm in arm down Broadway, looking for a cab. "Our parents consent. When shall we marry?"

"And your work?"

"I know myself: I'll be a good wife and a good reporter at the same time."

"I don't doubt it."

"I want children, lots of children."

"And your work?"

"Don't be a nuisance. I can be a good mother, a faithful wife and a great reporter."

"But—my father?"

"We'll take care of him. I can be a good daughter-in-law, a good wife—"

"I know, I know."

"Well, then? All right? All right with you? You'll give me babies? Five? Ten? If you knew how I love children . . . I love to watch them run along the sand, and dirty their hands, and make funny faces while they eat ice cream cones; I love them even when they're not really lovable. Promise me we'll make a lot of them."

"I don't promise anything." Children! By what right do we bring them into the world? And what a world! Can we be sure they won't curse us for having given them life? "I knew a man," Malkiel said, "who didn't want children. Not because he didn't care for them, but because he loved them; he felt sorry for them. He thought of their future and said, Better let it come without them."

Tamar blazed into anger. "Stop it! That's too stupid!"

In his apartment he tried to take her in his arms; she slipped away. "Listen," she told him. "Do you think I'm not afraid? I'm afraid of growing old, and ugly, and sick; I'm afraid of dying. But as long as I'm young I want my youth to make me happy; as long as I'm beautiful I want my beauty to intoxicate you. Of course everything's ephemeral in this life. But to say that because the future is threatening and death exists we have no right to love, and to life, is to resign yourself to defeat and shame, and I won't do that, ever."

"But—"

"Be quiet. I know: you think of your father and you despair. From now on I'll think of him, too, but I'll think of him so as *not* to despair. He's alone? But he's alive. He's melancholy? But he reacts, light gleams in his eyes. He's sinking into old age? We'll remember what he used to be."

Thank you, Tamar.

Malkiel had taken a studio downtown, halfway between the newspaper and his father. He spent the Sabbath and the holy days close to Elhanan, a custom that answered a deep need of his own: if the week's activities separated them, the special times reunited them. Every Friday night Elhanan lighted the candles and blessed them. Together father and son chanted *Shalom aleichem malakhei hashalom* in honor of the two angels that accompany every man and woman to the palace of the Sabbath Queen, to find joy and serenity there. Then Elhanan recited the kiddush, drank a sip of wine and held the cup to his son. Malkiel cut the challah and offered a slice to his father and another to Loretta, who went into raptures every time over its taste: "See that? My challah is better than any Jewish baker's. Admit it!"

It was during a Sabbath dinner that Malkiel caught the first indication of the disease that would ravage his father's mind. An apparently trivial incident marred the ceremony. Having begun the kiddush, Elhanan interrupted himself in midverse. Malkiel saw the veins swell in his temples, sweat bead on his forehead, his hands clutch the silver cup. He did not understand at first: "Do you feel sick, Father?" No, Elhanan did not feel sick. There was simply a gap in his memory. (Only later, much later, did Malkiel feel pain and pity in recalling the scene.) What should he do? Prompt him on the next line? Fortunately, Elhanan found a solution: "Do me a favor, Malkiel, and bring me the prayer book; it's in the living room."

Elhanan never again recited the kiddush from memory.

When he told Tamar about it, Malkiel could not erase the image of his father's crumpled face: "You can't imagine what he looked like. You would have thought he was a child who had misbehaved or a lost old man. He didn't understand what was happening to him. For him, forgetting the kiddush is like forgetting my mother's smile, or yours."

Another incident. Tamar was in California, and Malkiel took his father to Carnegie Hall. The soloist played divinely, people said; in his hands the violin sang. Eyes shut tight, the artist withdrew from everything but the piece he was playing. He seemed to be flowing through a universe of sound where fragmented melodies fled, sought one another, flowed together, tore themselves apart in order to say what the soul had been trying to tell us in its own language for an eternity: of its pain, its first and last yearning.

"Bravo! Encore!" shouted an enthusiastic, almost hysterical audience. "A triumph," wrote the *Post*'s critic. "He has surpassed himself," his colleague on the *Times* prudently agreed.

The young violinist let the audience plead, and finally reappeared for a short, light encore, demonstrating that his virtuosity was varied if not unlimited. Again the house gave him a standing ovation.

Malkiel was thinking he must mention this in his piece about the musician. He had a passion for music but had not come to this concert in the capacity of music critic. Personal curiosity or professional obligation toward the readers of his obituary page? He had to meet personalities of whom he would one day write. Sometimes while he was watching someone important, he would find himself thinking of his death. Not tonight. Tonight he was carried away by the artist's contained violence and dizzying perfection. "Did you like it?" he asked his father.

"Very much."

Outside Carnegie Hall, jostled by the crowd, they headed for Seventh Avenue, where the usual traffic jam blessed pedestrians with a pleasant feeling of revenge. How lucky I am not to own a car, Malkiel thought. "Are we walking?" Malkiel asked.

"Why not," said Elhanan. "It's a perfect, mild April evening."

Suddenly Elhanan stopped. Someone had called his name. He turned. A middle-aged gentleman approached him, hand outstretched. "Did you enjoy it, Professor Rosenbaum?" Elhanan said, "Yes, it was great." The man chattered on, and Malkiel noticed that his father was upset. Back in the apartment, Elhanan explained: "I know that man, but I can't remember his name."

"A colleague, maybe?"

"Maybe. I just don't know. All I know is that I know him, or rather I used to know him. While he was talking I identified him, but I couldn't dredge up his name. Brauer? Saftig? I had the strange feeling that it had simply vanished from my brain. Some ruthless criminal hand had snatched away my memory. I knew certain things without remembering them. Didn't you notice me trying to lead the conversation so he'd tell me his name? One single haunting question lashed my mind: Who is this man? My thoughts scattered, and roamed through my entire past. Nothing. I felt a sharp pain in my head. The phrase 'my head is bursting' became real to me. At that moment the man's identity seemed a more important question to me, more essential, than all the metaphysical problems of all the world's philosophers put together. I felt real panic. . . . Wait! I remember. His name is Rubinstein, Sender Rubinstein! He teaches mathematics at Hunter College. His people were Belgian."

"There! You see? You were wrong to be upset."

"You can't imagine what it was like, Malkiel. I was afraid of falling into a bottomless well, where the laughter of the Tempter was waiting for me. . . ."

And that, too, alas, was to happen. It was decreed on high that Elhanan ben Malkiel would be spared nothing.

In his moments of lucidity, which would later become increasingly rare and painful, he suggested an explanation of what was happening to him: "I am a guilty man. That is why I am being punished. Like Abuya's heretical sons, I gazed when I should not have gazed and turned my eyes away when I should not have. I saw a sin committed . . . a crime. . . . I could have, I should have, done something, called out, shouted, struck a blow. I forgot our precepts, our laws, that require an individual to struggle against evil wherever it appears. I forgot that we can never simply remain spectators, we have no right to stand aside, to keep silent, to let the victim fight the aggressor alone. I forgot so many things that day. . . . That is why I am forgetting other things now. Can there be anything worse than that?"

Yes, there was worse, there is worse: to forget that one has forgotten.

Malkiel was jumpy, out of breath, couldn't sit still.

Elhanan asked, "You won a Pulitzer Prize?"

Malkiel handed him an AP story. They were in the living room. Elhanan was in his armchair near the window, loosening his necktie. He was worn out, dissatisfied with the hour of therapy he had just administered. A couple of survivors, childless. They were very much in love, and that was why they wanted to separate. Each was suffering for himself and the other at the same time, and the load was too heavy.

"The OSI—the Office of Special Investigation—has turned up a former SS man who supervised the liquidation of the ghetto in Feherfalu. His trial starts next week. Tamar's going to cover the story, and I want to go there. It should be a big story. How about coming with me?"

Elhanan rubbed his brow with his hand, as if considering the matter closely.

"Why are you hesitating?" Malkiel pressed him. "Don't you care about learning how your own town—and mine—prepared for death?"

"I already know that," Elhanan said without looking up.

"But that SS man may tell us something you don't know!"

Elhanan was not persuaded. "I'll read about it in the *Times*."

Malkiel was surprised. His father was fascinated by Jewish history and insisted on keeping up with everything that touched on Jewish life, and therefore on Jewish death. Why was he now so recalcitrant? "I don't understand your reluctance," Malkiel said.

"It's complicated," Elhanan answered. "Reading stories about the catastrophe is one thing; meeting one of the criminals is another. Do you want to know the truth? I'm afraid. I'm afraid to see him. Afraid he'll see me."

Later Malkiel would realize that his father was afraid of something else too. . . .

With Tamar's help, Malkiel finally prevailed. Elhanan found a substitute for his classes and accompanied them to the federal courthouse. Rain mixed with snow caused gridlock that morning. Schoolboys laughed their way to school; their mothers called out, "Be careful! Button your coat!" People in the street slogged forward without looking left or right.

The courtroom was full. Television, radio, the print media: all the stars were there. Yet the defendant's life was not at stake, only his American citizenship. The prosecutor was trying to prove that the former SS man lied when he applied for a visa. If the defendant was worried, he didn't show it. His immediate problem was to dodge cameras and blinding flashbulbs.

An order rang out. The spectators rose. Judge Hoffberger warned the public to keep order and to refrain from emotional outbursts. Anyone disturbing the proceedings would be immediately ejected.

Sitting bolt upright and motionless, Elhanan listened intently. His eyes never left the defendant, a bald, puny specimen in an oversize gray suit. A twitch twisted his lips. His gaze was furtive, his hands nervous.

"He doesn't look like one," Malkiel whispered to his father.

"One what?"

"Murderer. Or rather monster."

There followed an exchange between prosecutor and defense attorney bearing on the identity of the defendant, who, upon arriving in the United States, had changed his name and falsified his age. The defense attorney claimed such alterations were common practice here. The prosecutor did not deny that, but . . .

The parade of witnesses began. The defendant watched them out of the corner of his eye. His lips tight and his eyelids drooping, he listened for flaws in their testimony. Often he pulled his attorney's sleeve and whispered into his ear.

PROSECUTOR: Your name, address and profession?

WITNESS: Jacob. Jacob Neimann. Butcher. Kosher butcher, of course. Sixteenth Avenue and Forty-seventh Street, Brooklyn.

PROSECUTOR: Place of birth?

WITNESS: Romania.

PROSECUTOR: Where in Romania?

WITNESS: In a small town that reverted to Hungary in 1941. Feherfalu. The white village.

PROSECUTOR: How long did you live there?

WITNESS: Until the end.

PROSECUTOR: Until the end of what?

WITNESS: Until the deportation.

PROSECUTOR: And when was that?

WITNESS: In May 1944.

PROSECUTOR: Do you remember the exact date?

WITNESS: May 17.

PROSECUTOR: And where were you on May 17?

WITNESS: In the ghetto.

PROSECUTOR: How long had you been in the ghetto?

WITNESS: Since Passover. They drove us into the ghetto a week after Passover.

PROSECUTOR: Who are "they"?

WITNESS: The Germans.

PROSECUTOR: How many Germans were there?

WITNESS: I don't know. . . . Not many. After all, they had the Hungarian police to help them.

PROSECUTOR: But who gave the order for the deportation? The Hungarian police or the Germans?

WITNESS: The Germans, of course. They were the masters. The Hungarians only followed their orders.

PROSECUTOR: Look at the defendant.

WITNESS: I'm looking at him.

PROSECUTOR: Do you recognize him?

WITNESS: I recognize him.

PROSECUTOR: Who is he?

WITNESS: Captain Hans Hochmeier of the SS.

PROSECUTOR: Are you sure of that?

WITNESS: Absolutely.

PROSECUTOR: You saw him in your town?

WITNESS: I saw him more than once.

PROSECUTOR: Under what circumstances?

WITNESS: The night before the first transport left, he came to inspect the ghetto.

PROSECUTOR: Was he alone?

WITNESS: He was accompanied by several officers, SS and Hungarian.

PROSECUTOR: And then?

WITNESS: After that he came back every day. He always had a riding crop in his hand. He inspected the deportees gathering in the courtyard of the synagogue. Then he went down to see them off at the station.

PROSECUTOR: He saw them off, and never spoke?

WITNESS: Oh yes, he spoke. He ordered the Hungarian police to be harder on us. To be crueler. They made us lighten or empty our knapsacks. Then they herded us into the freight cars and slugged us as we went.

PROSECUTOR: Are you sure it was because of him that the police were cruel?

WITNESS: He gave the orders.

PROSECUTOR: Was he himself cruel? I mean, did you yourself witness an act of brutality on his part?

WITNESS: Yes. At the station, a Jewish doctor approached him to report serious worries—there were three sick people in the boxcar; they needed room. . . . The captain listened and then struck him. The doctor fell to the ground. The SS captain kicked him until the doctor couldn't stand up and had to be carried onto the boxcar. The captain beat the men who were carrying him.

PROSECUTOR: You witnessed this yourself?
WITNESS: I was there. I was on the last transport. I saw it all.

Reporters were scribbling notes, the audience was holding its breath. The judge, somewhat remote, gazed upon prosecutor and witness in turn but seemed unaware of the audience. Elhanan had never felt more present, or more absent. His face hardened when the defense attorney cross-examined the witness; it betrayed pain and anger at the same time.

DEFENSE: Mr. Neimann, you seem to have a good memory. Am I right?
WITNESS: I believe I've always had a good memory.
DEFENSE: I congratulate you. If only all witnesses were as gifted as you . . . In this connection, May 17 remains vivid in your memory, does it not?
WITNESS: Yes.
DEFENSE: You rose early that day?
WITNESS: At dawn. To say my prayers. Dress. Get ready to leave.
DEFENSE: Your family also? Up early?
WITNESS: The whole ghetto—or what was left of it—rose at dawn.
DEFENSE: What day of the week was that?
WITNESS: A Sunday. Yes, Sunday.
DEFENSE: You're sure of that?
WITNESS: Yes . . . I think so.
DEFENSE: Then you're not positive.
WITNESS: Yes, I'm sure. . . . I think.

The lawyer broke off to consult his documents and, without raising his eyes, asked a deceptively casual question of the witness.

DEFENSE: What was the name of this SS captain in your village?
WITNESS: I told you before. Hans Hochmeier.
DEFENSE: You're sure?
WITNESS: Yes.
DEFENSE: Absolutely?
WITNESS: Yes . . . yes.
DEFENSE: Not Rauchmeier?
WITNESS: N-no. Hochmeier.
DEFENSE: How do you spell that?
WITNESS: Just like it's pronounced.
DEFENSE: With an *i* or a *y*?
WITNESS: With an *i*, I think.
DEFENSE: But you're not sure?
WITNESS: Yes . . . yes.

DEFENSE: I see that you hesitate. Perhaps you remember the defendant's rank more clearly?

WITNESS: I told you that before, too. A captain in the SS.

DEFENSE: But the SS was formal and exact about its rank: *Scharführer? Sturmbannführer? Hauptsturmführer?*

WITNESS: I don't know. . . . In the ghetto we called him captain.

DEFENSE: Ah, I see.

Another pause.

DEFENSE: So you saw the defendant in the courtyard of the synagogue and after at the station, is that right?

WITNESS: Yes.

DEFENSE: If you don't mind, Mr. Neimann, recall for us the color of his uniform that day. Was it light gray? Dark gray?

WITNESS: I think . . . dark gray.

DEFENSE: And was his holster on his left side or his right side?

WITNESS: The right side . . . I think. . . .

DEFENSE: Was the belt of his jacket tight or loose?

WITNESS: Tight. All the SS wore their belts—

The witness interrupted himself, embarrassed. He turned to the judge, then to the prosecutor, his eyes begging them for help. Then he shrugged, exhausted, beaten. He wept.

DEFENSE: That's all, as far as I'm concerned. I have no further questions for this witness.

A smirking defendant shook his head.

During the recess, Elhanan told his son he wanted to go home. Elhanan was sweating. He headed for the exit. Malkiel went out with him. Outside, whipped by an icy wind, Elhanan raged: "Did you see that? Did you see that bastard humiliate that survivor? Did you see the defendant snigger? That poor Neimann's memory is a graveyard, the biggest in the world, and the defense attorney wants him to remember the color of a uniform!"

"It's to be expected, Father."

"Details, details! How can we remember them all? Major events, and everyday incidents? What remains of the life of Moses and David is a few moments, a few words. And the rest? Has all the rest just disappeared?"

Next morning Elhanan called Tamar at the newspaper. "I wanted to thank you for your piece this morning."

She had written it in the first person and called it "The Tears of Memory."

. . .

Malkiel loved his work. He threw all his talent and energy into it. Every day he felt like thanking God for his job on the *Times*. He liked his colleagues, the secretaries, the errand boys; the moment he stepped into the editorial offices he perked up. The irregular hum of the teletype machines, the constant shrill of telephones, the word processors lined up on desks like an army awaiting the signal to move out: Malkiel would not change places with the most exalted prince on earth.

He had never followed any other calling. As a student at Columbia, he had applied for a job at the *Times,* which took him on as campus stringer. Luck smiled upon him: it was the year of the student demonstrations. Malkiel phoned in his stories three or four times a week, then every day. They won him his boss's friendship, his fellow students' admiration, and the anger of the administration. And what was bound to happen happened: he devoted more time to his reporting than to his literary studies. His father seemed unhappy about that, but Malkiel reassured him. "Why do we study? To prepare ourselves for a good job, right? Well, I already have one." Just the same, he promised to complete his degree before going to work full time. "Is that better?" Yes, that was better. Not best, but better. "What's still bothering you?" Malkiel's father seemed worried. Malkiel was used to his father's anxieties. He knew how to deal with them. But when he seemed sad, Malkiel felt helpless. And he was sad now, Malkiel's father was. He was no doubt thinking about the woman he had loved: If she had lived, she would have been proud of her son.

Malkiel lowered his voice: "Are you thinking of Mother?"

"I'm always thinking of your mother."

"Is that why you're so sad?"

"You're why I am sad, too."

"What have I done?"

"Nothing; nothing bad. On the contrary, you've justified all the hopes we had for you. It's just that . . . I wonder if a good journalist can in the end be a good Jew." For Malkiel's father, being a good Jew was at least as important as getting a good job.

Malkiel was aware of that. "Don't worry," he said. "In the old days all reporters were cynics; but no more. Trust me. I won't let you down."

The day came when he was awarded a diploma. Father and son sat on a bench on the banks of the Hudson. It was a beautiful evening in June. All around them students were popping corks out of champagne bottles. "Long live life!" they shouted. The students hugged and kissed. "Live it up!" "Aren't you going to join them?" Elhanan asked. Malkiel replied that he had no desire to. Elhanan tilted his head back and stared up at the starry sky: "I'm proud of you, Malkiel." He could not conceal his emotion.

Next day Malkiel started work at the newspaper. The atmosphere was invigorating. A newspaper was society's nerve center; its problems, upheavals and aspirations were refracted through it as through great theater. A play two hours long could cover thirty years of existence; so thirty pages of a newspaper contained thousands of events, which could fill a hundred volumes. And then a newspaper was a brotherhood, too. Despite intrigues and feuds, camaraderie on a newspaper was unlike anything else. Anyone's success was a credit to all. Any victory over injustice, won by reportage or an editorial, justified pride in the whole team. A newspaper was a living organism, pulsating with affection, determined to accept only truth. Of course there was often a gap between the ideal and reality. There were compromises, deals, someone was always passing the buck; all that was normal. But your eyes—at least at the beginning—were on the heights, even if they were unattainable. Even if you had to begin the climb again every day.

It wasn't going so well this evening.

Malkiel was working on a story from the Buenos Aires correspondent but couldn't seem to concentrate. His boss had praised him often for his powers of concentration: Malkiel listened well, read quickly and understood even more quickly. When an editor was in a hurry, he called on Malkiel.

But this evening it wasn't the same Malkiel. He was trying to recall: what time did he see Dr. Pasternak? At eleven in the morning? Not earlier? He had known for only nine hours? Borne the weight of this curse for only nine hours?

Dr. Pasternak was treating Elhanan. Casually dressed, with a loosely knotted tie and horn-rimmed glasses. In his sixties. A hard, clipped voice: "Thank you for taking the time, Mr. Rosenbaum."

"Tell me what's going on."

A routine question, but deep down Malkiel knew it was bad news about his father. He could not admit it to himself, but he was afraid the doctor would say, "Your father is sick. He has cancer."

"Your father is sick," said Dr. Pasternak, his hands clasped demurely before him on the desk.

"Is it serious?"

"Very."

"Cancer?"

"No," said Dr. Pasternak.

Thank God, Malkiel thought. If it isn't cancer it can't be too serious.

"It's actually worse than cancer," the doctor went on.

Impossible, Malkiel thought; I must have misunderstood. What could be worse than cancer? "I don't understand," he said in a changed voice.

"Cancer is not always incurable. Your father's sickness is."

"I don't understand," Malkiel repeated. His heart was pounding, bursting. A migraine had struck again. Nausea rose in his throat.

"What we have here is an extreme case of amnesia," said Dr. Pasternak. "Elhanan Rosenbaum has a sick memory; it is dying. Nothing can save it."

Malkiel was drenched in sweat. He groped vainly for a handkerchief.

"Doctor, may I use your washroom?"

"The door to the left, behind you."

He washed his face, took a few gulps of water, breathed deeply to overcome the nausea. In the mirror, a face pale and gloomy announced an approaching misfortune.

"Forgive me, Doctor."

"Not at all, Mr. Rosenbaum. Perhaps I should apologize. I should have given you the news less brutally."

"Go on, please."

Dr. Pasternak explained that the nervous system was annihilating itself. Symptoms of senility, and even dementia. A loss of orientation. Of identity. An inexorable process that might take months or years: it was impossible to predict. And even more impossible to slow down. The doctor inspected his hands, his nails. Perhaps he was embarrassed; had he not just confessed his impotence? As for Malkiel, he was living through a scene outside reality. It is not true, it cannot be true, he decided. It can happen to anyone? Yes, but my father is not just anyone. "What are we going to do? What can we do?"

"Do?"

"I mean, about my father. Are we going to tell him?"

"I don't think it's necessary."

Malkiel did not understand. Did his father already know? And had he said nothing? Once more he remained alone with his secret.

"Your father is a very intelligent man," Dr. Pasternak said. "For some weeks now he's suspected what was happening. He came to see me, which was natural. I spoke frankly to him. I respect him too much to deceive him."

"When was this?"

"Yesterday afternoon."

Yesterday afternoon? Malkiel reproached himself: Why didn't I go to see him then?

Tamar was standing at his desk, feverish, impatient. "What's the matter with you, Malkiel? Are you sick? Good God, you look shattered."

"It's nothing."

"I've been standing here—you haven't even noticed me."

"I'm sorry," Malkiel said. "I'm hot." He found his handkerchief, wiped his forehead and the back of his neck. "I'm almost finished. Do you want me to read your piece?"

"No; there's no hurry. Come on. I need some coffee."

Unsteadily he followed her to the cafeteria. Their friends were swapping newspaper jokes and political gossip.

"I'm worried about you. You look like it's the end of the world. What's wrong?"

Lie to her? "It's my father. He's a sick man. Very sick."

She wanted to say "Cancer?" but asked, "His heart?"

"Worse," Malkiel said. He repeated his conversation with Dr. Pasternak. Tamar listened in silence, her eyes filling with dread. Malkiel tried to compose himself. "Let's go upstairs. We have work to do," he said.

They rose, and Tamar took his hand. "Don't let this change anything between us." And after a pause, "Do you hear me? Don't. Your father isn't my father, but I, too, am struck by his misfortune; I, too, am pained by it. I need you more now than before. Promise me you'll try?"

"I promise," Malkiel said, wondering how he could think about her article. A few words from the mouth of a doctor, and the whole world is upside down.

He finished rewriting the Buenos Aires story, read Tamar's piece and sent it on to the political desk.

"Page twenty," said the layout editor.

Ordinarily Malkiel argued with him, always after more prominence for Tamar's pieces. But not this time. Too many words and pictures bouncing around inside his head. He could not even figure out whether he wanted to stay or go home.

"Shall I come with you?" Tamar asked him in the elevator.

Malkiel did not answer.

"I'd like to," she insisted.

Malkiel remained silent. They walked up Eighth Avenue, with its shops full of exotic fruit and its sleazy bars and clubs. At the Coliseum they stopped for a red light.

"I think I need to be alone with him for a while," Malkiel said. "But please, come and join us later."

When the light turned green he walked on, leaving Tamar behind. A few taxis passed, but he preferred to make his way on foot. Loretta rushed to give him a hug. "He's in the living room," she said. "By the window. All he's done since yesterday is look outside. He won't sleep or eat or drink, and he won't talk to me."

For a long moment Malkiel stared at his father's back. "Good evening, Father," he said quietly.

Elhanan seemed not to hear him.

"Father, I should have come yesterday. Can you forgive me?"

Elhanan sighed and said, "Come over here."

Together they looked out at the night, and the lights of the great city. How many fathers and sons confront their destiny at the same moment?

"Speak to me, Malkiel."

What could he say, and how could he say it without breaking down?

"Speak to me. I need to hear your voice."

"I saw the—"

"I know. I don't want to hear his words, but yours."

With his throat tight and his eyelids heavy, Malkiel had to lean on the table behind him to keep his balance. Overwhelmed, blinded by emotion, he saw himself walking a tightrope over an abyss: one false step, one awkward word, and he would fall, dragging his father with him. "Listen to me, Father. You've always been at the center of my existence; and you always will be, to the end of my days."

A sob shook Elhanan. "God of my fathers," he said, "let me remember those words when I have forgotten everything else."

He extended a hand to his son, who took it in his own. An hour later, Tamar found them the same way.

. . .

Her name was Blanca, but she preferred, God knows why, to be called Bianca. Tamar had introduced her to Malkiel, as she had introduced Richard and his snooty friend Rhoda; and Max and Serge, two distinguished art dealers who thought no one was aware of their deeper relationship; and their rich clients Jean and Angelica Landman, who argued even when they said nothing. . . . Tamar knew a few people.

Dining with Tamar's friends, Malkiel was really sitting in for her. She was in Washington. More investigative reporting on the Pentagon. That was what she did best: ferreted out secrets, turned them up and classified them, processed them and revealed them to the public—she loved all that as much as she loved love. I miss you, Tamar.

"Hey, Malkiel, you off in the desert?" Bianca asked.

"Pardon?"

"Come on, you naughty boy. We're here, and you're here, but your head's somewhere else. Don't deny it."

"I'm sorry." Malkiel blushed.

"At least tell us where I brought you back from."

"Nowhere, really."

"You're a rotten liar. I've never understood what Tamar sees in you."

A forgotten memory resurfaced, upsetting him. A summer Sunday on Fire Island. Tamar in a bad mood because she was scooped on a story. Malkiel, who had nothing to do with it, was annoyed that she wouldn't snap out of her sulk. So he, too, sulked. As usual, Blanca—pardon: Bianca—took matters in hand. Sweet Tamar, she said, I know a sure cure when things go wrong: grab hold of your man and kiss him till he passes out. Doctor's orders, you hear? Tamar wouldn't dignify that with an answer. Bianca flared. Listen to me: you give your imbecile lover a big kiss right now or you'll be sorry; I'll take care of him myself, you understand? And as Tamar still did not react, Bianca proved how she kept her word. There she was in front of Malkiel, sitting on the sand, facing him. Languorously she kissed him on the mouth. Hey, she cried, that's good! She did it again. Tamar was disgusted and never even looked their way. Playing the game—was it a game?—Malkiel let himself be swept along. He closed his eyes, thought of something else, and received the kisses. Opening his eyes again, he saw Bianca's smiling face close to his own, he noted her tanned breasts. The blazing sun beat down, and Malkiel turned away. Beside them, Paul, Bianca's husband, laughed as if at a good joke. Tamar was not laughing.

That evening she would tell him, "You let me down, Malkiel. I know it was a game; but love isn't a game you can play with just anyone."

"No," Bianca said again, "I really don't know what Tamar sees in you. You kiss well enough, but—"

"Stop it," Malkiel said.

"Why?"

"I can't hear what you're saying. Too much of a crowd. Too much noise. Hard to hear. Hard to think."

"Now you're boring me. No one's asking you to think. As far as I know, you're a reporter. It's your job to listen. And to amuse people."

"That's not on the menu," said Pietro, the maître d', who took personal care of this table.

But apparently it was; yes, it was. Paul was brilliant, Bianca charming, Susie drinking and Angelica flirting. Max and Serge were describing their last auction.

They all seemed happy. "Business good?" Damn good. "And the new gallery in San Francisco?" Almost ready to open. "And you, Malkiel? Still working?" Still working. "Who stars in tomorrow's obits?" An eighty-eight-year-old Indonesian general. A dancer. A model. AIDS. Malkiel felt better: They had something else to talk about. The twentieth-century plague. Punishment from heaven? "Poor heaven," Bianca said. God should find another way to pass the time.

At the newspaper, a special team was assigned to cover that disease, or that evil, depending on how you saw it. Two reporters were following several victims, three others were interviewing specialists, a reporter with a medical background was setting up a round table with six researchers from Sloan-Kettering and the Pasteur Institute. They were even thinking of inviting a scientist from Moscow. Also joining the discussions: the theologian James Wienfield, and Malkiel. "God and death are linked to this problem," the sage had told them; the editor was famous in newsrooms everywhere for his humanism. The theologian could only approve; for him, God was linked to everything, and therefore to death. One day he said, "If I had to choose between the God of death and the death of God, I'd take the God of death." As usual Malkiel teased him: "In my tradition we talk about the Angel of Death. Our God is the God of life." James retorted, "We should never talk theology with Jews; they take God too seriously."

"When's this round table on AIDS?" Serge asked.

"In a month or so."

"And how many will die between now and then?"

The dinner guests ventured guesses. Paul quoted Professor Leventhal's statistics. Bianca mentioned an article in the *Times*. Malkiel said nothing. For him, figures obscured the tragedy instead of clarifying it. Every death deserved to be thought of as the first, unique. Every time the disease struck, it meant one more human face obliterated, one more family in mourning. Every time, they should give the death all the prominence and attention and compassion that it deserved. "You'd like to fill the paper with your obits," one of his assistant editors told him. "But reality is something else again." Malkiel answered, "Reality can wait. Death doesn't."

"Any news from Tamar?" Paul asked.

"No news is good news," Bianca commented.

"You two ought to get married," Paul said.

"Are you crazy?" Bianca said. "Get married? What for?"

"For children," her husband explained.

"Children? You can make them without a marriage license."

Malkiel let them argue. It was their favorite pastime. In his mind, he joined Tamar. His loving friend Tamar. His accomplice, his ally. Tamar's smile. Tamar's gestures. Tamar's caresses. "When you're in love," she said, "you have no right to hold back. When you're in love you let your body choose its own ways of loving." Sparkling eyes and impertinent lips; her view of love was definite.

"Just the same, you ought to get married," Paul insisted.

"Oh, leave him alone," Bianca snapped.

A light gust of yearning made Malkiel blush. He had known a few women. Passing fancies who left no traces. Tamar was different. With her he could not drop his guard. Demanding and critical, she kept him alert. She wanted him perfect even in his imperfections: "For a man to interest me, the woman or the reporter, he has to be noble or a son of a bitch; if he prefers the middle ground, he can go to hell." Did he love her? Yes, he loved her. And his father loved her, too. Elhanan could not look at her without smiling. He would be happy to see her come into the family, if only to assure the survival of the line. Poor Father. To give him pleasure, Malkiel and Tamar should marry as soon as possible. While he could still take part in the ceremony. How much time did he have before vanishing in darkness and emptiness? Poor Father. How could they save him? How could they help him? Often in bed Tamar would sigh, "Poor Malkiel."

He rose abruptly. "Forgive me. I have to leave."

"Heading back to the newspaper?"

"Are you kidding? He has a hot date. Poor Tamar."

Full of anguish, as he was each time he thought of his father, Malkiel urgently needed to see him again.

One evening early in his illness, Elhanan asked his son to sit down opposite him. "I have grave matters to discuss with you, my son."

Malkiel's heart stopped. Elhanan hastened to reassure him. "Don't be afraid. We'll fight back. We'll hold out. We'll learn how."

Father, I admire your courage. Your confidence. Your way of fighting resignation. But how long will it last? More and more you move awkwardly, more and more your memory slips. . . . But we will fight to the end. Even if it's hopeless. After hours of talk that evening, you even managed to sum up, a philosophical conclusion for both of us: "The important thing is to be aware of the present. The moment possesses its own power, its own eternity, just as love creates its own absolute. Hoping to conquer time is wanting to be someone else: you cannot live in the past and present at once. Whoever tries to runs the risk of locking himself into abstractions that separate a man from his own self. To slip out of the present can be dangerous—suddenly man finds himself in an ambiguous universe. In our world, strength resides in the act of creating and recreating one's own truth and one's own divinity."

Oh yes, Father. You tried to persuade me that even for you nothing was truly lost. To live in the moment is better than not to live at all.

"It takes no more than a moment," you told me that night, "to tell your fellowman that you love him; and in so doing you have already won a victory over destiny."

I remember: despite your weariness, despite your fear, you were in a kind of ecstasy. You were talking to persuade yourself as much as to reassure me; you were celebrating the present so as not to retreat from it.

"The future?" you said to me. "The future is an illusion, old age a humiliation and death a defeat. Certainly, man can rebel. But his only true revolt is to shout 'No' in the present against the future. As long as he can move his lips he'll be telling fate, 'You challenge my right to live a full life—well, I'll do it anyway; you challenge my happiness under the pretext that it is futureless, that because it's severed from its roots it can never be perfect—well, I shall taste it anyway.' "

Your eyes were shining, Father. You were breathing hard. I was, too.

"I have the feeling," you told me, "that fate is making fun of me. Because I cultivate memory, fate has decreed that I be deprived of it. Well, I say 'No.' When fate laughs at me, I'll laugh at it. And I'll be happy even if in my situation it's absurd to do so."

At dawn you broke off our conversation. You were suddenly exhausted. So was I.

"You're young," you said to me. "At your age you can be desperate and proud at the same time. It's not so easy at my age. But I refuse to go under."

Me too, Father; me too.

What to do?

Elhanan was reading. Despite the late hour, he was waiting for Malkiel to return. A matter of habit. Even before the disease struck, he'd had a hard time falling asleep without chatting with his son, if only on the phone. Now it had become an irrepressible need.

"Have a good day?"

"Good enough," Malkiel said.

Stretched out on an old sofa beneath the yellow light of an old lamp, Elhanan was leafing through newspapers from the 1930s and '40s. "Who died?"

"An Indonesian general. A Belgian painter. A clothes designer, still young. A university president somewhere in Virginia."

"Page one?"

"Twenty-eight."

Elhanan Rosenbaum took an interest in his son's work, as if he knew something about it, which was by no means true. But he did know that the front page was better than the twenty-eighth. He knew that for his son's career the position of a piece was important. "It's unfair," he sighed. "Only unimportant people are dying nowadays." The disease had not weakened his sense of humor. "And Tamar?"

"She sends a kiss."

"I'm very fond of her."

"And she of you."

"Why not—"

"Because."

"Really, my son. You ought to—"

"I know, I ought to marry her."

"What are you waiting for?"

"A sign, maybe."

"What would you need?"

Malkiel bowed his head. His father was right, wanting to see his son stand beneath the *huppah* before . . . before . . . "I understand. But it's not so simple." He took off his jacket, poured himself a glass of mineral water and sat down again on the hassock across from his father. Loretta brought in a platter of fruit. She seemed sad. "Father," Malkiel asked, "why have you never thought of marrying again?"

Elhanan Rosenbaum stiffened. His brow wrinkled. "Why do you ask? Why now?"

"Just a thought. Perhaps to get back at you. What about you? You could have found someone."

Elhanan propped himself on one elbow. Loretta came back in with two glasses of hot tea: she thought hot tea could cure anything. Elhanan waited for her to leave before he answered. "I no longer know, Malkiel. I'm sure I once had a good reason."

"Is it because you loved Mother too much?"

"Too much? When you love someone it's never too much."

"Do you still love her?"

A pause. "Yes, I still love her."

He stretched again. A remote dream made him happy and sad. Malkiel, too, felt sad. He loved his father with total, all-encompassing love. No one had ever been so close to him. This was the man who raised him, who sang him lullabies, who took him to nursery school in the morning and brought him home in the afternoon, who stayed at his bedside when he had the flu, who took him in his arms when nightmares came. Of course there was Loretta, too, the marvelous black maid from Virginia, who was always there and in complete charge of the household; and Malkiel was attached to her. But it was not the same. He loved his father. Just looking at him, or making him a pot of tea when Loretta was on vacation, he was overwhelmed, sometimes to the point of tears. In grammar school and high school he had friends, pals. But his closest friend was always his father. Then why had he made him suffer? "Tell me about Mother," Malkiel said. "Tell me something I've never heard."

"I thought I'd told you everything. Have you forgotten?"

Forgotten. The word struck Malkiel. So it's true, he thought. There are words that hurt more than sticks and stones. "No, I haven't forgotten a thing." He rose and touched his father's shoulder. "And I promise I never will."

"I believe you," said Elhanan. He closed his eyes.

Once upon a time, my father was another man. Upright, proud and open to the sounds of life. Everything interested him; doubt fascinated him; evil repelled him. His patients swore by him. His students adored him. He knew how to bring an ancient text to life; he made it speak. It was as if Isaiah were to address each of us individually; as if all were present to watch Titus enter the holy of holies.

I liked watching him at home. At his worktable, beneath his dusty lamp, which Loretta never dared to clean, he conversed with invisible companions. I used to hear him murmur, "But no, that's impossible!" He would set one volume aside and pick up another, and I would hear him admit, "Okay, you're right." And at my childish astonishment, he would explain: "You see, Malkiel? When I speak to Abraham ibn Ezra, it seems perfectly normal, and when he answers me through his text, that seems normal, too."

His greatest pleasure: reconciling texts and authors. He managed to find common ground between the school of Shammai and the school of Hillel, between an interpretation by Maimonides and one by his implacable adversary the Raavid; then he radiated happiness. "To you, to life, to the survival of your teachings!" he would say, as if addressing them, a glass of wine held high. For him, this was a celebration.

At school his colleagues found him a bit odd. "He ought to get married again," they said. "His son needs a mother, and he needs a wife." They were wrong. We needed each other, and that was all.

A woman called Galia Braun, a native of Ramat Gan, was in love with him. Madly in love with him. She taught biblical geography and blushed every time she looked at me in class. She was quite beautiful and somewhat strict but never with me. She loved my father through me.

It was my father who taught me to read and write. I remember a story he told me during our first lesson. "In my village there was a man, a porter, who refused to learn the alphabet. One day I asked him, 'What have you got against the alphabet?' And he answered, 'Words say the same thing to everybody; I want them for myself.' 'But prayers,' I asked him, 'how then do you pray?' And he answered, 'That's easy. I don't like to repeat other people's prayers. I prefer to make them up.' "

Later he would hold me spellbound with his stories of other times. He often described his childhood to me, and his adolescence. The wise men, thugs, madmen, beggars—he remembered all in such detail that I was constantly amazed. "In those days," he used to say, "the whole village meant a few people—a few relatives, a few friends, a few rivals. I knew the others existed, but only in a vague way. Now I love them all. The poor, I wish I could enrich them; the rich, I would like to save them."

I admired my father not only for his kindness and intelligence, but also for his memory. He could quote long passages of the Talmud and Plato, the Zohar and the Upanishads. He could recall in rich detail his visit to the ghetto in Stanislav, his first skirmish as a partisan, his arrival in Palestine. He envied the character of Rabbi Nahman of Bratslav, who remembered what he had done in his mother's womb and even in his father's desire.

Immersed in his own past and the world's, my father was nevertheless a man of his times, reacting to all its convulsions. Politics stimulated him, and so did the international situation. Famine in Africa, racial persecution in Indonesia, religious conflict in Ireland and India: what men did to other men they did to him. When someone said that as a Jew he was wrong to care about anything but Israel, he answered angrily, "God did not create other people so we could turn our backs on them." And yet he loved Israel with all his heart and soul. Why didn't he go back there to end his days? He did not know, and admitted that to me. "Maybe it's cowardice on my part. Maybe in Jerusalem every stone and every cloud would remind me of your mother; I'd be too unhappy." Another time he told me, "I know it's convenient to love Israel from a distance. It's even a contradiction, but I'm not afraid of contradictions. In creating man in his own image, didn't God contradict Himself? Except that God is alone and free while man, still alone, is never free."

When he was already sick and felt himself going under, he said something that made me want to cry out, or die, every time I thought of it: "Soon I will envy the prisoner: Though his body is imprisoned, his memory is free. Whereas my body will always be free, but . . ." He never finished the sentence, but his face betrayed such anguish and sorrow that a lump came to my throat and I wanted to console him. "Soon," he said, "I will be absent from myself. I'll laugh and cry without knowing why."

Now nothing excites him. Nothing interests him. Everything happens outside him. And I, his son, take his hand in mine and no longer know what to do.

Her name was Talia, and she trailed happiness in her wake. All she had to do was toss her thick head of hair, and her gloomy friends perked up. She rejected their gloom: "I refuse to see you like that. Cheer up or I go." As if by a miracle, they felt better, uplifted. They promised the young tyrant any gift from any shop, any color from any rainbow, if only she'd stay. "All right, then, I'll stay," she said, "but make me *want* to stay. I want to see smiling faces. Understand?" Yes, they all understood. No more long faces when she was around.

Elhanan Rosenbaum had also understood, but his sadness was stronger than he, stronger than the young girl. Elhanan was chronically depressed. The others sang; he withdrew. Boys his age found ways to amuse themselves, but not he. To please Talia he made an effort to appear happy, but he never succeeded.

Germany, 1946, a camp for "displaced persons." An orphan, alone in the world, Elhanan was waiting for his "certificate" to Palestine. Thousands of survivors were in the same position. Representatives of the Jewish Agency preached patience. Some refugees, at the end of their rope, applied for visas to the United States or Canada. Displeased at that, Zionist activists organized political meetings. Passionate oratory, popular songs and dances: the young people's blood ran hot; they were seduced by the fascinating history embodied in the Zionist ideal. Of course there were quarrels between Weizmann's followers and Jabotinsky's. As they did everywhere, left wing and right wing waged interminable combat. Elhanan took no part in it all. A loner by temperament, shy by nature, he fled crowds and hated noise: he had endured enough during the war. He liked to read, to study. Books in Hebrew, Yiddish newspapers.

One day when he was in line for his cigarette ration, he had the shock of his life: Talia, the princess with countless suitors, accosted him. "They tell me you speak Hebrew. Is that right?"

"They're exaggerating."

"We'll find out. My name is Talia. Yours?"

"Elhanan."

A smile came to the young woman's lips. "Are you kidding me?"

"No, not at all. That's my name."

"Elhanan?"

"Don't you like it? It's a very old name, and some very wise men have had it."

"I know, I know, but—it's too old for you." Her face became solemn. "If I've offended you, I'm sorry."

Elhanan nodded; he was forgiving her.

"Are you a practicing Jew? I bet you are."

"My father was."

"And you?"

"I used to be."

"And now?"

"I still am. A little."

"Me too," she whispered into his ear. "A little."

They had reached the counter. Elhanan picked up his ration, broke open a pack, tapped a cigarette free and offered it to Talia.

"I don't smoke."

They walked back toward the barracks in silence.

"Do you know what I'm doing here?"

"Yes," Elhanan said. "The Zionists sent you."

"That's right. They sent me here to shape the young people, to teach them Zionist ideals. And organize their departure to Palestine."

"You're doing good work. I congratulate you."

"I never see you at the meetings."

"Not my kind of thing."

"Aren't you interested in meeting other young people? Preparing for your future in Palestine, or at least dreaming about it?"

"I dream better when I'm alone."

She stopped; so did he. "Would I be intruding on your solitude if I shared it now and then?"

"No, not at all."

"Thank you," she said. "Thank you for trusting me."

They saw each other the next day, a Friday. At nightfall, after the service and before the Shabbat meal, everybody was dancing in front of the mess hall: in singing and in joy, Jews welcome the

Queen of the Sabbath. As usual, Elhanan was watching the dancers from a distance. "Come," said a familiar voice, in Hebrew. He had no time to resist. Talia was already whirling him into the dance.

"I'm mad at you for this," Elhanan said.

"I love it," she answered, laughing.

"What do you love?"

"Hearing you speak Hebrew." And after a moment, "Even if it's only to tell me that you are mad."

Elhanan realized that she had called him by the intimate "thou." That is the rule in Hebrew: I and thou. I detest you, he thought, so as not to admit that he loved her.

Talia Oren: twenty years of sun, laughter, a free and savage joy, were inscribed on her fine and angular Oriental face. Born of a Yemenite mother and a Russian father, she joined the mystery of the Orient to the intellectual pragmatism of the West. Her smile ironic but gentle, her eyes dark and glowing, she seemed forever alert, hearing music meant for her alone, forever meant to rouse men to happiness and love.

"Your mother," Elhanan said. "How I loved her! I may have had a premonition. I may have known from the start that I'd have to love her for you, too.

"Did she suspect, during our first few meetings? We saw each other often. She was a year older than I but seemed younger. I'm sure she wanted to protect me, educate me, focus my life. But she wasn't right for the role of big sister. And she was too clear-eyed not to know that I was in love with her.

"Thanks to her, I adapted to the communal life of the camp—I, who since my time in the battalion and then with the partisans longed only to sleep alone, eat alone, keep my distance from the groups that inevitably multiplied in the camp. I adjusted to life. I spent less time thinking about the dead. I never talked to her about them. She would only have scolded me. She loved to do that—show men how immature they were. Make them understand that the past must bury the past. That suffering can and should be eradicated from Jewish existence. That redemption was not by divine work but by human hope. . . . We listened to her, we never dared contradict her. We feared her anger but even more her sadness. Because she became melancholy, your mother did, when anyone contradicted her. To bring back her good humor, we were ready to do anything.

"And so was I, even more than the others. Ready for anything? Your mother insisted that I take part in celebrations, discussions, all their group activities. It was not my sort of thing. Even the beasts of the field don't live alone, she told me. Have you forgotten the Bible? It's in Genesis; read it again. It is not good for man to live alone. . . . I loved to see her that way—passionate, fervent; anger made her even more beautiful. Then when she calmed down I reminded her that the verse she'd quoted was about Adam before Eve's creation. God wanted Adam to marry. I asked her, Do you want me to marry, too? Yes, she said. I asked, Who? dreading her answer. Me, she said. I was so stunned that she burst into laughter. So did I.

"After the noon meal on the next Sabbath your mother suggested I come to a Zionist meeting with her. I tried to resist. She took me by the hand and said, It's no use, Elhanan Rosenbaum; I want to be with you, and I have to go to that meeting.

"The auditorium was jammed. The main speaker talked about the underground war that the three resistance groups were fighting against the British occupation.

"He was an impressive man: in his forties, muscular, square jaw, abrupt gestures. He personified the fighting man's implacable authority. He spoke in Yiddish. Talia's Yiddish was not good, so I interpreted for her. It was a fiery speech, slightly demagogic. Short, explosive sentences, simplistic arguments. The Jewish people were persecuted because they had no state of their own. Scorned everywhere, the Jew was of interest only to his enemies. If we'd had a Jewish state in 1939, millions of men and women—'your parents, your brothers, your sisters'—would have been saved.

"It was like an oven in the hall; we were drenched in sweat. Unperturbed, the crowd applauded. The speaker—I think his name was Aharon—carried us away. Like him, we had just observed Sabbath in Jerusalem, whose light and silence are like nowhere else in the world; we breathed the perfume that gardens in the hills of Galilee gave off; we sang the beauty of the valley of Ezreel and prepared for the struggle that would join the Jewish people to the Jewish state. I remember a few of his phrases and expressions. For the first time in history, he said, a people would put an end to two thousand years of exile and wandering, and found a sovereign state on the land of their ancestors. . . .

"Was it the magic of his speech or the strength of our longing? We swayed to a rhythm at once exotic and captivating, we moved through an ancient and revolutionary dream, we took part in imaginary operations beside the heroic characters who had nourished our people's legends. If at the end of his speech Aharon had challenged us to move out *now*, hundreds of us would have done so.

"All the more because no other country cared about us at all. Understand this, my son: the survivors' tragedy did not end at their liberation. The world made them feel their inferiority. In a pinch, some would have treated us as invalids, but not as equals. In Palestine, Aharon said, you will be welcomed not as immigrants but as brothers returning home after a long absence. Any refugee was susceptible to that kind of argument.

"And yet I hesitated. First of all, to leave for Palestine meant choosing illegal immigration and parting from Talia. And then there was something else: I wasn't mature. I mean intellectually mature. No, I mean morally mature; that's more exact. Was I worth redeeming? One afternoon I talked about that with your mother. She flew into one of her rages. 'What is all this idiocy? A Jew's place is in his history, in his own land, and that's all there is to it! It's *there* that you'll find Jewish dignity! Or *there* you'll create it! Don't tell me you'd rather rot here and wallow in the memory of your humiliations. . . . Listen. They're putting together a secret convoy, and you're going to be part of it, all right? If not . . . ' 'If not?' I asked. She broke into sudden laughter: 'If not, I'll give you a kiss.' Which she did. She kissed me full on the lips. It was the first time. 'You're leaving,' she said. 'And you'll see: you'll be happy in Palestine.' I wasn't so sure, so she quickly added, 'I'll see to it myself.'

"Next morning I registered for the convoy."

The police officer seemed courteous and amiable. He rose to greet his visitor and the interpreter. He shook the stranger's hand and begged him to have a chair. He went so far as to offer refreshment. A cup of coffee? A glass of *tzuika*?

"Water," said Malkiel.

"Bravo. It pays to be careful, especially in the morning."

An orderly brought a bottle of mineral water with three glasses. The official, a perfect host, poured. Malkiel sipped at his; Lidia was not thirsty.

"And how has your visit here gone along, Domnul Rosenbaum?"

"Very well."

"No problems?"

"None at all."

"Have you seen what you came to see?"

Shrewd, this fellow. "Not everything," Malkiel said.

"I don't understand."

"They must have told you—my specialty is funerary inscriptions, epitaphs. You have an abundance of them here."

"They did tell me. But . . . why choose our cemeteries? Why not the ones at Cluj or Satu Mare?"

"These are older."

The official consulted a file before going on. "You won't tell me that the cemetery is the only part of our little town that interests you."

"Indeed I won't. My charming interpreter was kind enough to show me other places."

The official turned to Lidia and said a few words that made her blush.

"What did he say to you, Lidia?"

"He suggested I persuade you that the living are more fun to be with than the dead."

"And that's all?"

"That's all."

"Tell him I get the impression he doesn't believe me."

The official's face darkened. "Am I wrong?"

"To suspect me? Frankly, yes. And anyway, what do you suspect me of?"

"I don't know yet. But rummaging through cemeteries strikes me as suspicious."

"Don't tell me you're afraid of my contacts with the dead."

"I'll tell you whatever I like."

"Did I offend you? I was only joking."

The official inspected him for a moment and then brightened. "Well, so was I. Your health, sir." He raised his glass of water.

"And yours, sir," Malkiel said.

"How long do you plan to stay with us?"

"That will depend."

"On whom?"

"On my boss."

The official jotted a note in the file. "Do you plan to publish articles about your stay here?"

"Of course."

"All on the cemetery?"

"All for the obituary page."

The rest of the interview was devoted to the weather in New

York and Bucharest, to the pleasures of world travel on an expense account, and to friendship among the peoples of the world.

"Thank you for coming," the officer said, extending his hand to Malkiel. "I hope your visit here continues to be pleasant and peaceful. See to it, miss."

Lidia refrained from translating her reply.

Driven by his overwhelming need to tell all, to omit nothing, Elhanan spoke in breathless tones. "Are you listening to me, Malkiel my son? Do you remember our lessons in Talmud? And Rav Nahman? Before his final breath he begged his friend Rava to tell the Angel of Death to spare him pain. He feared suffering more than death. . . . You must tell him yourself, said Rava; isn't your voice heard on high? I know nothing about that, Rav Nahman confessed, but I know that there is no defense against the Angel of Death. And the two masters went on talking, and then Rava said, I have a favor to ask: could you return from above to tell me if you did suffer in leaving this world below? Rav Nahman promised to do that. And after his death, he appeared to Rava in a dream. Rava asked, Well? What is it like to die? Is it painful? And Rav Nahman said, Not at all. It's like when you pluck a hair out of a bowl of milk; that's how the soul leaves the body. And yet, he added, if God, blessed be His name, asked me to come back to earth, I would answer, No, Lord; I am not strong enough for that; I would be too afraid of death."

Malkiel did remember that Talmudic legend but had forgotten its profound beauty. On first hearing, it had sounded more like an anecdote. Now it resonated within him.

That occurred before the accident. His father was sick. But it was nothing serious, a chill, the flu. But running a high temperature, Elhanan feared death. "Do you understand me, my son?"

"I understand you," Malkiel said.

"Right now, when everything hurts, what bothers me most is that I can't see you clearly."

"I'm here, Father."

"And yesterday? Where were you yesterday? And the day before? And last week? I closed my eyes, opened them, looked for you. You were somewhere far away."

"I didn't know you'd caught cold."

"I'm burning up, aren't I? Aren't I burning?"

"You have a fever. The doctor said it was a touch of pneumonia. It will run its course."

"Is the whole city burning, too?"

"It's snowing out."

"And in Berlin?"

"I don't know, Father."

"Isn't Berlin burning?"

"It's wintertime, Father."

"What were you doing in Berlin?"

"Covering a story," Malkiel lied.

A lie, a shameless lie. Malkiel had spent a few weeks in Berlin because—because a young German reporter, a woman, was there. Love at first sight? More like a fleeting madness over a stupid quarrel with Tamar. In a rage she'd shouted, "It's all over between us!" All he did was nod stupidly. Tamar rushed out, slamming the door, and Malkiel did nothing to hold her back. Days of depression, nights of gloom. "Couldn't you send me on assignment somewhere?" he asked his boss. "I need to clear my head." "How about a trip to Germany?" the sage answered. "Germany! Never! Anywhere but Germany." He preferred not to think about Germany. For him, Germany was pained Jewish memory. And he had had enough of that. Enough of living in the shadow of Silesian smokestacks. Enough of remembering those Jews beaten and destroyed, those children incinerated, those women shamed, those starving old men whose huge eyes stared out at a cold and cynical universe. Enough of moving about under the gaze of the dead. Let them vanish, let them leave the living alone. . . .

By a bizarre coincidence he met Inge on the ninth day of the month of Av, on Tisha-b'Av, a day of mourning and commemoration, of fasting and affliction: on that day we remember the destruction of the Temple in Jerusalem. Inge and Malkiel met in the elevator at the newspaper. They walked along together in Times Square, made small talk and introduced themselves. "Inge Edelstein, German."

"Malkiel Rosenbaum, Jewish."

She threw him a startled glance. "It doesn't bother you to be walking with a German girl?" No, it didn't upset him; a reporter can't always choose his companions. "Shall we stop for a cup of coffee?" Why not? He was about to take a sip when he remembered his father: Elhanan was fasting until sundown. "You won't drink it?" No, he wouldn't drink it. "It's not good coffee?" No, it wasn't that. "Then what is it?"

He explained to her.

"No," she cried. "You can't be serious. Your temple was destroyed two thousand years ago and you're grieving *today*?" Yes, as if it had happened only yesterday. "A lot of people have told me the Jews were crazy," she said. "They were right." Yes, we're crazy. "It's human nature to forget what hurts you, isn't it? Wasn't forgetfulness a gift of the gods to the ancient world? Without it, life would be intolerable, wouldn't it?" Yes, but the Jews live by other rules. For a Jew, nothing is more important than memory. He is bound to his origins by memory. It is memory that connects him to Abraham, Moses and Rabbi Akiba. If he denies memory he will have denied his own honor. "So you insist on keeping all your wounds open?" Those wounds exist; it is therefore forbidden and unhealthy to pretend that they don't.

They met again the following Sunday. And Monday. And Thursday. They loved each other. . . .

"Fever, my son. I feel the mists rising again. Exhausted, the body can do no more. Defeated, the spirit listens in vain for even a bitter music. How can I put the world together again? Those hands holding me down are not my own; how can I cast them off?"

Tamar, Malkiel thought; Tamar would have known how to cast them off. Reconstruct a whole world? Tamar would have known how to do that, too. Why did I follow Inge to Berlin? Didn't I know it would bring unhappiness to my father?

Like an idiot, he had gone knocking on the boss's door. "I'll do it. I'll go to Berlin if you want me to."

"A good idea," said the sage, scrutinizing him. "Isn't the Jewish cemetery in Berlin one of the largest in the world? Readers will go for that."

The sage was no fool. He knew it wasn't the cemetery that drew me to Berlin. And my father in all this? Left alone, and sick. Nothing serious? Nothing that antibiotics wouldn't cure? Nothing linked to the disease that would destroy him later? Such excuses were too convenient. I was wrong to go.

"The mists are rising," Elhanan said. "I see Jerusalem. Would you like to know what I see?"

"Yes, Father. What do you see?"

"Near our home in Jerusalem, in the Mea Shearim neighborhood, was a garden where old men came to live out their last days. They spent hours sitting there motionless, like statues. Sometimes I went up to them and asked questions. 'What did you do before you came here?' They looked at me in a daze. The word 'before' stunned them. But among them was a woman of incomparable sweetness. She invited me to sit down beside her, and said to me, 'We have a whole life to live, just as you have, even if it only lasts one hour, the last hour—and no flowers to pick.' The next morning I went back to the garden with a bouquet I'd promised myself I would give her. Only . . . she was no longer there."

Did he come down with that stupid fever because of me? Loretta, Loretta, why didn't you pay more attention, keep a closer eye on him? And Tamar, why did you send me away?

I should never have gone. I was wrong to follow Inge, wrong to leave my father alone, wrong to lie to him, wrong to begin an affair with that German girl.

And yet Malkiel had fallen in love with her. And she with him. In Berlin their love seemed even more miraculous than in New York. Each embrace brought them new discovery of their bodies, new potential, a flight of each beyond the other, within the other. Together they bridged the gap between Jew and German, promise and threat, happiness and suffering. Together they defied fate, lending it an innocent face, the smiling face of reconciliation if not forgiveness. Hand in hand they strolled the lively streets of the Third Reich's former capital, lingered at elegant shopwindows, visited museums, public gardens, libraries, admired rebuilt neighborhoods, applauded at the theater and at concerts, laughed with the schoolchildren they passed in early morning or late afternoon. It was so simple to attract happiness; all they had to do was set aside the past, turn the page. All Malkiel needed to be happy was not to think of his father. But . . . he thought of him. Even more than before. The man who changed his money at the bank—where was he during the war? And this bureaucrat explaining Berlin's municipal politics—how old was he in 1943? Was he old enough to have served in the SS special units? And Inge—did she have parents? Who were they? Slowly, bit by bit, Malkiel felt his happiness drain away. In the end Inge noticed the change. She wanted to be clear in her own mind about it. It's my father, Malkiel confessed. My father keeps me from forgetting. And, the height of paradox, she said that Elhanan was right. I know, she told Malkiel; none of it must be forgotten. I love you because I don't want to forget; you can't love me because you have to remember. Intelligent, Inge. Honest and demanding. It's because I think of your father, she told Malkiel, and of his father, and of all the Jewish fathers that our fathers murdered, that I love you with a love that is doomed. Muddled, torn apart by urges and loyalties, Malkiel sank into despair.

On the eve of Yom Kippur, Inge went to synagogue with him. Old men were chanting the Kol Nidre, that overwhelming poem by which the Marranos had reaffirmed their loyalty to the covenant. Seated among the women, Inge could not watch Malkiel. He was weeping like a child. Like the child within him that had not wept at his mother's death. As he did every year, he fasted until Yom Kippur was over, and attended all the services. Inge, too. "Do you still love me?" he asked her when they met in the evening. "More than ever," she answered. "Do you know," he asked, "that the most common word in our Yom Kippur prayers doesn't relate to forgiveness, or expiation, but remembrance?" She did not know that. They spent the night rediscovering each other.

That was long ago and far away.

"You're doing better," Malkiel said. "You'll be fine now."

A fresh wave of fever racked his father's body. Elhanan had to make an effort to speak. "One day in Kolomey . . . did I ever tell you what I saw in Kolomey?"

"No. But don't talk anymore now. Tomorrow, all right?"

"In Kolomey I saw what I see now: a woman slipping into shadow, another writhing in pain under a blazing sun. I want to know them, tear off their veils, but I'm afraid to see them close up; I'm afraid I'll discover death's claw marks. Still, isn't it worth trying? Even if it hurts? Even if it scares me?"

"The will to live is always worth it."

"That's what your mother always told me. Did I tell you about your mother, Malkiel?"

"Not enough, Father."

"You must never forget her. I must never forget her."

Did he already sense that an illness of another kind would transform his mind to heartbreak?

Outside, on the Hudson, a thousand shadows huddled beneath the rain.

"So, Malkiel my son, you've finally made up your mind?"

"Yes, Father, I'm leaving."

"When?"

"Tomorrow night."

"Nonstop?"

"One stop in Paris."

"You'll be careful?"

"I promise."

"You won't forget?"

"Forget what?"

"Keep your eyes and ears open, look and listen: you must represent me. I want to see everything with your eyes, and hear everything with your ears."

"I'll do my best."

"And then . . ."

"Yes?"

"There is one point which is essential."

"What is it?"

"It's at the core of my blurring memories; thanks to it, the memories are still mine."

"What are you talking about?"

"You'll know at the right time."

"When? Where? Over there?"

"Yes. Over there. Or when you come back. But to know it, you must first go there."

"You can't tell me now?"

"I must not, Malkiel."

"And if I come home empty-handed?"

"You will not come home empty-handed."

Why had Elhanan Rosenbaum insisted that his son, Malkiel, visit his hometown? To dig up what secret? To meet what phantom? To do what ritual penance?

It was only to oblige his already sick father that Malkiel had agreed to leave him for a few weeks. He could not refuse him this favor, perhaps the last he could do for him.

"You must go," Elhanan repeated, more and more obsessed. "Believe me, you must."

"Are you hoping I'll find you there, as a child or a young man? Think again, Father. You're not over there but here. Entirely."

Entirely? Not really. Day by day Elhanan Rosenbaum deteriorated. Each morning new regions of his past seemed to have been detached from him, to have vanished. "What are you waiting for, Malkiel? For the last spark to die? For the last door to close?"

Malkiel had no choice.

. . .

He had made another journey, several years earlier, far from the excitement of New York, far from his father, who was flourishing as a teacher and psychotherapist.

In Asia, the earth—or rather history—was trembling. Gigantic mass graves had been discovered in Cambodia. The phrase "boat people" had entered the language. "I want to go over there," Malkiel told his boss. "I *have* to."

"Why?"

"I don't know. But I *have* to."

The sage, chin resting on one hand, studied him for a moment. "Because of Tamar? To put some distance between you?"

"No."

"Because of your father?"

"Not that either."

"We have Henry over there. He's doing a good job. He doesn't need help, as far as I know."

"He's willing to have me come over," Malkiel said.

The sage sounded annoyed. "You spoke to him before speaking to me?"

"We're friends."

There followed a lecture on journalistic protocol and ethics, which ended in a handshake. "If I understand correctly, you already have your visa?"

Malkiel nodded.

He rushed to tell Tamar; to telephone his father. That very night he left for Bangkok. Henry was waiting for him at the airport. "What's a nice Jewish boy like you doing here?"

"Just looking," Malkiel answered. Of course Henry knew why Malkiel was there.

"I didn't book you into a hotel. You'll stay with me."

"What I'd like to do—"

"I know. You'd like to leave for the border right away. Let me take care of things. Tomorrow morning we'll go up together. First you're going to take a shower. And change. I have tropical clothes for you."

Good old Henry. The perfect friend. A great reporter, with a Pulitzer Prize, at home everywhere. And ready for anything.

Next morning they entered the camp at Aranyaprathet, not far from the Cambodian border. Thousands of eyes followed their every move. Eyes burning from sunlight, exhaustion, suffering. Malkiel would never forget those eyes, or the devastating smiles of starving children.

"I look at them and I want the whole world to look at them," Henry said.

"I look at them," Malkiel said, "and they look back at me. And I think of other children in other places, after the war in Europe."

They trudged through the camp's streets and alleys.

"Your pieces are the best you've ever written," Malkiel said. "Nobody can read them without a sharp pang of guilt."

Day after day, Henry's dispatches appeared on the front page of *The New York Times,* describing men and women whom the Khmer Rouge, in their murderous insanity, had deprived of all hope and joy. One piece ended, "How can this outrage be happening? Can a whole people die?"

"How did this madman Pol Pot persuade so many people to kill so many others?" Malkiel asked.

"You know the pattern," Henry said. "Pol Pot calls himself a revolutionary. You can justify anything in the name of revolution. He was hoping to bring history back to zero."

"To begin again? Like God?"

"Great killers want to be gods."

"And they just let him do it?"

"Apparently, yes."

"I don't understand."

"You don't understand? And your father doesn't understand either?"

Malkiel gulped. "Yes. My father understands."

A sun at once leaden and coppery beat down like a curse on the tents and barracks. Women passed out in the heat; nurses brought water.

"Come along," Henry said. He led Malkiel into a special barracks apart from the others, where two hundred young men lived. They seemed to be infantrymen and noncoms. They were disciplined, doing calisthenics, training rigorously—for what purpose? They refused to talk to strangers.

"Take a good look at them," Henry said. "They're Khmer Rouge."

These killers were fourteen or fifteen. The word was that they'd tortured their own parents and executed their own brothers and sisters, always in the name of their revolutionary ideal. Hangings, drownings, shootings: Malkiel searched for traces of violence in their impassive faces.

In nearby tents, Cambodians talked about their agonies. Henry translated. Terror, flight through the forest, life and death in the swamps. Could anyone imagine a whole country transformed into a hermetically sealed ghetto? I can now, Henry said. Could anyone even conceive of a regime, in 1980, for which remaining human is a crime punishable by death? I can now, Malkiel thought.

In his mind he saw his father and talked with him: "You see? The Jews aren't the only ones to suffer."

"I never said they were."

"But to hear them you'd think only their suffering mattered."

"You weren't listening closely, Malkiel. When a Jew talks about suffering, he's talking about other people's suffering, too."

"In that case they don't talk about it enough."

"Possibly. They are timid; they refuse self-pity. Try to understand them. If they talk too much, people resent it. If they don't, people resent them for *that*."

When I come back to New York we'll continue this discussion, Malkiel promised himself.

He would spend several weeks in Aranyaprathet. Khao I Dang: one hundred ten thousand people jammed into a compound that might house a quarter of that number. Sa Keo: thirty thousand refugees . . . Malkiel wanted to know everything, to take it all in. He spent his evenings with French, Israeli and American volunteers; he visited the infirmaries, the schools, the kitchens. Henry spared him none of this education: he too remembered. In 1938 his father fled Hitler's Germany. Fifty thousand visas could have saved all the Jews in Germany.

Malkiel interrupted his investigations and turned volunteer, working for a rescue committee. He helped some refugees fill out emigration forms, others to find vanished relatives. He played with children, taught them a few words of English; he slept little and hardly ate. Henry warned him: "You want to help them, of course you do. But you'd help them a lot more with a good piece on all this."

"Logically you're right," Malkiel said, "but I checked my logic at the door."

Was he thinking of his grandfather, the benefactor whom he resembled so? Elhanan spoke of it one day: "You know, my father—whose name you bear—did much for the Jewish people."

A Thai doctor, young still and refined, watched discreetly over Malkiel's health. One night he collapsed, fell to the ground; she was there to have him carried to the infirmary. "Overwork and exhaustion," she said. Malkiel was given an injection and woke up forty-eight hours later.

"Well, my friend," Henry said, "I have a telex from the sage, may God grant him long life. He demands that you take the first flight out. They're waiting for your copy." He winked. "Not to mention Tamar; she's impatient, too."

The Thai doctor also urged him to leave. "If you stay with us you'll work yourself into the ground; will the refugees be any better off? Go home and tell them what you saw here; find the right words, and we'll all be grateful."

Gaunt and weak, Malkiel left Bangkok. On the flight to New York he wrote the first article.

"You did well to go there," Elhanan told his son. "Do you want to know why? Because no one bothered to help us when *we* needed it."

That night he read his piece to Tamar, who said nothing for a long moment, and then thanked him in her own way.

A child swept away by a tempest. A young waif jolted by tragic, inexorable events. A disoriented youth, lost and bewildered, singled out by fate.

When hostilities began in 1939, Elhanan was thirteen years old. An only son, he divided his time between his yeshiva studies and his father's office at a lumber company. At home, his mother, still young and elegant, represented Western culture: she kept up with the artistic life of the capital, while her husband read only religious works. It was a close and happy family. The two servants followed instructions: they were never to turn away a beggar without offering him shelter and a meal, and they were to show him warmth and understanding. "Even if he doesn't deserve it?" asked Piroshka, the cook.

"I don't know of any human being who doesn't deserve a crust of bread and some change," was the blunt reply of Elhanan's father, Malkiel. "We never know. The nameless beggar may be the prophet Elijah himself, a vagabond Lamed-vovnik, one of the Just, a rabbi in exile."

Elhanan once broke into the conversation. "And if the beggar in question is someone we know?"

His father smiled proudly. "A good question, my son. But remember that in every beggar there is an element of the unknown."

It was a turbulent and tormented year. Czechoslovakia was torn apart. Poland was attacked, bombarded, dismembered. Then came Romania's turn. Soon the small town of Biserica Alba reverted to its Hungarian name, Feherfalu. Overnight they would have to change the names of streets, schools, shops, cinemas. At school the students were forced to learn songs to the greater glory of Horthy Miklós. And yesterday's idol, King Karol II? Banished and repudiated.

The situation was almost stable for the Jews. Previously threatened by the Romanian anti-Semites of the Iron Guard, they were now threatened by Hungarian anti-Semites of the Nyilas movement. So? You can learn to live with anything, especially the worst.

After the fall of Poland, Jewish refugees appeared in the little town. Not surprising: the town was perfectly situated for people who wanted to cross the border illegally. A crossroads of four or five countries, it absorbed foreigners because everybody here spoke all their languages. Austrians, Slovaks, Czechs, Poles—Elhanan's father took care of them all with a devotion that preachers everywhere mentioned in their sermons. "Look at Malkiel Rosenbaum. He is the embodiment of the rare virtue *Ahavat Israel,* which signifies Jewish solidarity and compassion." He found lodgings for them, documents, work; he helped them flee to other towns and other havens. Many refugees headed for Romania, Turkey, Palestine came through Biserica Alba, now Feherfalu.

In memory: 1941, Sukkoth, the Feast of Tabernacles. Malkiel brought home a guest for the evening meal. Elhanan was struck by the stranger's pallor and gauntness. A threadbare raincoat shrouded his hunched shoulders. Through thick lenses his myopic eyes gazed at the middle distance, as if to capture an evil omen. The night was pleasant, yet he had his collar turned up and he shivered. Elhanan's father asked him about the situation in Poland. "Bad, sir, very bad," replied the visitor, and his lips tightened. But how? Tell us more. The visitor refused to go into detail. "We haven't enough time," he said. "If I start I'll never stop. But I must say good-bye soon, as you know; my train leaves at eleven." His Yiddish was Germanic, his tone fearful. After the meal and the customary chants, he said, "You've been a great help to me. How can I thank you? Yes, I know how. I will give you a piece of advice; follow it. Do not linger in this country; the enemy will rise up here, too; don't wait; take your family and go; as soon as possible and as far as possible. Take pity on your son and his mother; take pity on yourself." He shook Malkiel's hand, wished Elhanan and his mother a courteous good night, and walked out into the sleeping town.

For a long moment the three Rosenbaums were speechless. Father took hold of himself. "It is fear speaking through his mouth. He has surely been through a terrible time, and he sees the enemy everywhere."

Mother was not so sure. "I don't know. . . . And if it was the truth? If he was right when he said we should go?"

Father raised his voice, a sure sign that he was upset. "Go? Go where?" Sitting in the *succa,* they thought it over. A gentle breeze whispered along the roof. In the neighboring *succa* people were singing, celebrating the holiday with exuberance. "And you, Elhanan, what do you think?" asked Father.

"He frightened me."

"Me too," said Malkiel.

Elhanan cried out: "Look! The stranger forgot his briefcase!"

To lighten the mood Malkiel said, "Maybe he's an absentminded professor. Go on, son. Run to the station and give it back to him."

Elhanan snatched up the briefcase, which he found rather heavy, and rushed to the station. Their guest was seated on a bench in the waiting room. "Sir, sir, look, you forgot this!"

Expressionless, the stranger raised his head, took the briefcase, set it down beside him and murmured a vague thank you.

Obviously, thought Elhanan, he has other things on his mind. The boy said good night and turned to go home, when the stranger called him back: "Sit down." Elhanan sat. "Can you guess what's in this briefcase?" No, Elhanan had no idea. "Look, then." The stranger opened the case, and Elhanan almost fainted: it was full of gold coins. "That is my whole fortune," said the stranger tonelessly. "That is all I have left."

Elhanan could not understand. "Then how could you have forgotten it?"

The stranger shrugged. "You'll understand someday. You'll understand that a fortune doesn't mean much in times like these."

Elhanan glanced at his watch. It was still early; the train would not be in for half an hour. Go back home? He preferred to keep this refugee company, this man who suddenly broke into a smile and said, "It's funny. When you handed me my briefcase I was foolish enough to wonder just how happy I was, and I had to admit that the taste in my mouth was not the taste of joy." Aside from the ticket agent dozing behind his counter, they were alone in the waiting room. "Nevertheless," said this stranger in thick glasses, "I owe you a little present. I'm going to tell you some stories. Real-life stories. You can go home and tell them to your parents."

That night the train was late.

Rumor raged through the town like a pack of wild dogs and roused the local Jews from their lethargy: it was said that all those who had disappeared were already dead.

This was in 1941. The Hungarian government had ordered the

expulsion to Galicia of all "foreigners," meaning all Jews, who could not prove their Hungarian citizenship.

All massacred, rumor said. Buried in mass graves dug by the victims themselves. Children, too? Yes, children, too. And their parents. And their grandparents, and each in the presence of the other.

In Feherfalu they said, Impossible. Things like this don't happen in the twentieth century.

But in 1941 the impossible was possible. Some people believed it. All the more because the rumor had started with a Hungarian officer just returned from Galicia. His outfit was bivouacked near Kolomey. Some of the soldiers had seen the massacre from a distance, and with their own eyes had seen the killers lining up the victims at the edge of the ditches; they had heard the crackle of machine-gun fire. Similar scenes near Stanislav. Are you sure? I'm sure, said rumor, adding hair-raising details: none of the victims wept, and some went to their death in silence, impelled by a strange feeling of dignity and defiance.

"You will remember those massacres," said Elhanan to his son. "Will you promise me to remember them especially?"

"Why do you insist on especially*?"*

"Because . . . I'll explain it to you. History itself is often unfair to its victims. Some were luckier than others. Consider those at Kolomey and Stanislav. Nobody's erected a monument to their *memory. Few scholars devoted their research to them, while there is a literature about all the others. The Jews killed at Stanislav and Kolomey were second-class victims, and they deserve better. You agree?"*

"I'll remember, Father. I promise you that."

"You'll say aloud that they were among the first that the enemy engulfed in night?"

"I will say it."

"You will repeat it as often as possible?"

"I will repeat it."

"You will not let oblivion humiliate them day after day?"

"I will not permit it, Father."

"Remember, my son. Without even knowing it, I must have walked across their graves."

. . .

An urgent meeting took place at the home of the community's president. Another at the chief rabbi's house. The first was devoted to practical problems: financial and political steps to be taken, should the rumors prove true. The second was of a strictly religious nature: if those who vanished had been put to death, how could it be verified, so that those who survived could properly mourn them? The two groups arrived at the same conclusion: send someone to Galicia to investigate.

A Hungarian officer, Major Bartoldy, agreed—in return for a whopping bribe—to escort an emissary as far as Stanislav and bring him back. Elhanan was chosen, first because his uncle lived there, and then because he spoke perfect Hungarian. And also because he seemed older than he was: in uniform he would easily pass for the *szazados*'s orderly.

Of course Elhanan's mother objected. "If he leaves I'll never see him again, may God not punish me for those words!"

Her husband reassured her. "Under the protection of a major in the Royal Hungarian Army, Elhanan is not in much danger."

Their departure was set for a Sunday between Easter and Shavuoth, the Holiday of Weeks. Before donning his uniform, Elhanan had to see his sidelocks clipped off, and it was a mournful loss: he was proud of those *peyot,* which he curled around his fingers while he plumbed a difficult passage of the Talmud. "Consider it a sacrifice," his father said. "On the day of judgment," said the chief rabbi, "your *peyot* will be weighed in the balance along with your good deeds."

At ten in the morning Major Bartoldy and his orderly took their places in a staff car, a convertible. Elhanan's mother wiped her eyes while his father ran through his instructions once more: questions to ask his uncle, messages for the local rabbi, the code to set up for an eventual correspondence, with the major as go-between. "I don't believe I've left anything out, my son. May the God of our fathers watch over you." Brusquely he embraced the boy. His heart heavy with foreboding, Elhanan closed his eyes so as not to see his parents grow small in the distance and then vanish.

The car passed Christians on their way to church. A cloudless sky. Trees in leaf and blossoms. Farewell, Biserica Alba—pardon: Feherfalu. See you soon, Father and Mother. Good-bye, my childhood. I am no longer a boy; I must be strong and not give way to emotion. I am a major's orderly. A soldier. A soldier does not give way to emotion, even when saying good-bye.

With a stolid driver at the wheel, the car traversed fields and mountains, towns and hamlets. Children in their Sunday best were playing hide-and-seek. Girls with flowers in their hair acted haughty to attract their beaux' attention. Old men in straw hats dozed before their huts. To the strains of a fiddle, a blind man sang a heartrending *doina.* Here and there a Jew on foot or in a ramshackle cart glanced up, curious about the car raising a cloud of fine dust. Greet him? Elhanan wondered. Too risky. A Hungarian soldier, and an orderly at that, does not greet Jews. It is up to the Jews to salute. A crazy notion made him smile: I ought to salute myself.

About one in the afternoon they reached the border. The duty noncom, at strict attention, saluted this officer, who quizzed him condescendingly: "Everything all right?" Yes, sir, everything was all right. If the noncom had any questions about the orderly, he kept them to himself. They raised the barrier. The car started up again and roared through Galicia's disquieting countryside. At dusk they stopped before a two-story building on the main square in Stanislav. The major's rooms were on the second floor. "You'll sleep in the hallway," he told Elhanan. "Tomorrow you'll go see your uncle. You have his address?" Elhanan knew it by heart. "You're crazy, boy. Your uncle does not live there anymore. I know this town. You'll find him in the ghetto with the rest of the Jews. Didn't you know that?" No, Elhanan did not know that. No one in Feherfalu knew it. At any rate, no one had said anything about it. Was it a forbidden topic? Taboo? From time to time, in the synagogue, one would speak of the fate of the Warsaw ghetto, that was all. A ghetto so close to Feherfalu? Unthinkable. "All right," said the major. "We'll wait for tomorrow and find a way to slip you into the ghetto."

Elhanan slept badly on the floor; his uniform bothered him. And the word "ghetto" ran through his head like pain through a wound. Just what was a ghetto? He remembered tales of the medieval ghettos. Tomorrow he would enter the Middle Ages. And then?

He woke early in the morning and washed at a tap; he saw that the driver was still asleep and took advantage of that to run up to the attic, wear his phylacteries and say his prayers. Fact is, he thought, I'm taking unnecessary risks. I'll be in the ghetto in a little while and can find a synagogue there. The ghetto: he was impatient to be there.

The major had to report to his unit, camped outside town. Elhanan went along with him. Adjacent to the main encampment was another, smaller and dingier, where the uniformed Jewish laborers, the *munkaszolgálat,* lived. They were not permitted to bear arms and were made to dig ditches, build roads, chop down trees and cook. A yellow band on the left arm distinguished them from the Hungarian soldiers. Hearing Yiddish spoken, Elhanan greeted a tall fellow with a frank and jovial face. "Who are you?" the man asked. "What are you doing here? Why aren't you wearing an armband?" Elhanan told of his odyssey and his problem: how was he going to find a way into the ghetto? He had to make his way inside; that was of the first importance. He was on a mission. "I know I seem young, but in wartime young people are old." "Go on," said the big fellow, whose nickname was Itzik the Long. Elhanan didn't understand: go on about what? "I like the way you talk. Go on." Embarrassed, Elhanan got mixed up, repeated himself, pulled himself together. "Yes indeed, you're still young," said Itzik. Their eyes met, and a friendship sprang up: a hard and free friendship of which only lucid men and desperately courageous children are capable. "Don't worry about it," Itzik the Long said, clapping him on the shoulder. "You're on a mission? Then I'll help you accomplish it." "But how can you—how can I—" Itzik laughed. "It's easy. You'll see. I'll take you in tonight." They would meet just off the main square, at six in the evening, sharp.

Informed, the major congratulated his orderly's resourcefulness. "I'm giving you two days' leave," he said. "Be back Wednesday morning at the very latest. That's an order. If you're not here on time, I'll go back to Hungary without you." Elhanan understood.

Itzik the Long knew a secret passage connecting the ghetto and the town. They were in no danger as they used it. No one saw them slipping into the shadows.

The ghetto: a caldron of humanity. Hard to push your way through, hard to see anything in this mob. Hard to talk, with the stench of sweat in your throat. Hard to make out faces, suffering had distorted them so. All the aimless strollers walked with the same jerky gait, and all the mothers were lamenting their children's fate, and all the orphans were chanting the same complaint. How to find an address, an apartment, a person? Luckily Elhanan's guide knew a member of the Jewish Council. The council member knew someone who often saw the young emissary's uncle. The uncle was dressed in rags and living in an overcrowded room. He greeted his nephew as a savior: "Is it you, is it really you, son of my brother? Let me touch you; come here and let me look at you; it's really you. How's my brother? What's he living on? How are the Hungarian

Jews getting along?" Amid a crowd of "tenants," uncle and nephew conversed as if alone together. Late in the evening someone cried, "Go do your talking somewhere else; we want to sleep!" They slipped out to the yard and went on with their desperate talk. "Tell me the truth, Uncle," Elhanan said. "Are the Germans really murdering the Jews? Is there really no hope? Are all the exits closed?" His uncle could only sob, "Yes, yes." And Elhanan could not console him.

He spent all the next day in the ghetto, his uncle acting as guide. Elhanan wanted to see everything. Remember it all. The system carefully laid out by their oppressor. The function of the Jewish Council, the activities of the Jewish police, the needs of the Jewish aid committee. What must they do to survive for another week, another night? What were the limits of solidarity and the frontiers of death? At fifteen Elhanan knew more about life and fate than most men of seventy-six. I will have to tell it all, he thought. Yes; all of it. My memory must store it all away. Yes; all of it. It's vital, it's essential. If I tell the story well, if I report it faithfully, the Jews of my town will be saved. And my father will be proud of me. I will have accomplished my mission.

His second night in the ghetto was as dramatic as the first. His uncle took him to visit a clandestine yeshiva, where students were teaching scripture to young children who had escaped the roundups. And an attic where mystics were calling upon divine names and numbers to hasten their deliverance. And a basement apartment where boys and girls were debating armed resistance. This, too, I must remember, thought Elhanan, begging heaven to stimulate his memory and its powers: every word is important, every sign may be a matter of life and death. Father will ask questions, and I must not let him down, I must not bring shame upon him. "Uncle," he asked, "will you do me a favor?" Of course. "Ask me about what I've seen and heard. Ask me in detail." They spent all Tuesday night reviewing the report that Elhanan, this young emissary in the uniform of a Hungarian soldier, was going to make to the anguished community of Biserica Alba now Feherfalu by the grace and order of the Führer.

Only Elhanan would not be going back so soon.

At dawn on Wednesday the Germans sealed the ghetto. Mute houses, defiant glances. Hoarse shouts: "Outside, all Jews outside!" Rifle fire and pistol shots. Dogs barking. Doors broken down, bodies smashed. The operation lasted until nightfall: a thousand Jews were led off to the forest. Elhanan's uncle was among them.

Sheltered by strangers, Elhanan managed to escape the roundup. They waited in terror until dusk. A happy accident or a miracle: the shelter proved truly safe. At six in the evening, the Germans withdrew. The ghetto, revived in the wink of an eye, heaved a sigh of relief. The few lucky survivors embraced.

Itzik the Long reappeared when the situation was back to normal. Elhanan had no strength, and no desire, to talk to him; the boy collapsed, drained. All he could say was, "My uncle! My poor uncle!"

Itzik the Long tried to bring him back to reality: "You better get out of here fast. Hurry up!"

But Elhanan could not stop moaning, "And my uncle, my poor uncle?"

Itzik explained. "There's nothing you can do for him now. Not you or anybody." They left the ghetto the same way they came in. Itzik asked, "Are you going back to your major?" Yes; Elhanan must explain the special circumstances that accounted for his delay. "All right, we'll go together. If there's any trouble, stick close to me." There was trouble, all right, big trouble: the major had gone back to Hungary without his orderly.

A dark panic gripped the Jewish boy. "What's going to happen to me now? What's going to happen to my report?"

Itzik the Long made up his mind without even thinking about it. "Come with me. If you stay here, they'll arrest you. You can join us and put on a yellow armband. You'll be one of us, at least for now."

Elhanan joined the Jewish labor battalion. When he returned to his village later, centuries later, it had changed.

So had he.

Malkiel son of Elhanan son of Malkiel. Here I am, Grandfather. Malki-El: God is my king. But your king did not protect you, Grandfather. Ask Him why, as a favor to me. You're there, on high, so near the celestial throne; speak to Him. Tell Him that even in their distress His people go on glorifying Him. Now, what does He make of such praise?

Standing at his grandfather's grave, Malkiel was speaking to him but also to himself: How do we stay Jewish in a world that rejects Jews?

You were lucky, Grandfather. There were people who envied you here in your grave, do you know that? You were the last to be buried in consecrated ground. The others? Better not to talk about the others. Grandmother: Ah yes, much better not to mention her death.

Malkiel knew how his grandfather had died. Thanks to his father, who had sought out the story among the rare survivors of the ghetto. Grandfather Malkiel had been the invaders' first victim, but they envied him all the same. What luck, people said. He had a proper funeral. He died an individual death.

The ghetto was established in April of 1944, when the Red Army was already closing in, just beyond the mountains.

The Germans summoned old man Rosenbaum and appointed him elder of the Jews. He declined the position. "I mistrust power," he explained. "I don't know how to give orders." He was about to go on, but a blow to the head stopped him. Another knocked him down. They beat him senseless. They revived him with cold water. "Now will you accept the job?" He still declined. The torturers went back to work. Same result. In the morning the Germans summoned the chief rabbi and other notables: "You make him listen to reason." Before the prisoner's eyes they shed bitter tears: " 'Woe unto me, to see you like this,' " the chief rabbi moaned, quoting a Talmudic verse from the time of the martyrs. "Take the job," said the president of the community. "Be our spokesman to the Germans; if you refuse, they may appoint an opportunist." Grandfather Malkiel let himself be persuaded.

The ghetto lasted a month. No more. The Russian front was going to explode any day, and Adolf Eichmann was resolved to do his job quickly. There were still six hundred thousand Jews in the Hungarian provinces, and the killers had only a few weeks to deport them.

Despite the decrees raining on the ghetto, its inhabitants clung to hope. "It can't last long," they said in the streets. Anxious about fairness and justice within the confines of the ghetto, the Jewish elder and his associates worked day and night organizing aid to the poor, the sick, refugees from nearby villages. Not everything went smoothly, far from it, but at least they got used to waiting. Even with hunger and isolation, the situation seemed tenable, livable. Medical services, an employment office, housing offices, all operated more or less efficiently. True, local anti-Semites took advantage of the occasion to let off steam: they stopped religious Jews to cut off their beards, spat on women, insulted parents in the presence of children, forced respected old men to lick sidewalks clean; but these ordeals were, as people said, in the natural order of things.

"May no worse thing happen," they prayed. A certain Zoltan, fanatical leader of the Nyilas, popped up often in the ghetto, and then the streets emptied. He sowed terror among the residents. He bludgeoned, mutilated, killed whoever crossed his path. The committee suggested, "Let's keep our eyes open and set up an alarm system. With warnings we can take shelter before Zoltan strikes." In short, things could have been worse.

Soon they were.

One Sabbath morning the Jewish elder was summoned to the Kommandantur. An SS officer from Eichmann's team broke the news to him: the Jews were going to evacuate the ghetto. "Where are they sending us?" Somewhere in Hungary, was the reply. "When do we leave?" Tomorrow, was the reply.

The officer, unusually amiable, went on: "Don't worry. This measure is due to the military situation. The Russian front is getting closer. If we remove you from the front, it's for your own security." Then he ordered him to keep the matter secret. "No one must know about this. Not before tonight." The elder was about to withdraw, but the officer called him back: "One more thing. You will supply me with a list of ten names. Ten Jewish names."

"For what purpose?"

"So they can serve as hostages. If one Jew escapes from the ghetto, one of the ten will be shot."

The elder had been on his feet throughout this exchange, and now he felt dizzy. His head whirled and his knees gave way. His vision blurred and his heart pounded. What can I do, God in heaven, to keep this danger from others? "Officer, sir," he replied, "I understand your request, and my answer is affirmative. You shall have ten names. But not this minute. Tonight. It is the Sabbath, you see, and I am not permitted to profane the holy day by writing."

The SS officer stared at him, dumbfounded: was this Jew making fun of him? He must have decided that no Jew would dare laugh at an SS officer, because he dismissed the elder with an order to return that night with a complete list.

The elder went home and asked his wife to go to see a certain number of Jewish dignitaries and invite them to join together in a *Minhah* service at the chief rabbi's home. There he told them of his conversation with the SS officer.

"So this is the end," murmured the chief rabbi.

The president of the community asked, "And the list? Are you going to hand him his list?"

The elder's answer was yes. Barely masking his anguish, the president of the community asked, "Which names will you give him?" The elder replied, "Not yours."

That night he handed the officer a sheet of paper folded in half. The officer opened it and saw the elder's name written down ten times. He froze for a moment, deliberating. Then he slammed the elder against the wall and began punching his face, methodically: right cheek, left cheek, right cheek. Without a word, with no sign of anger, he slugged his victim until the old man fell to the floor. "Pig!" the officer shouted, crushing his jaw under the heel of his boot. "Try to trick me, eh? You'll get the punishment you deserve: you will die ten times." Ten times the elder passed out under torture, and ten times he was revived. Unrecognizable, he had become a lump of flesh without will, a bloody body without life. When the officer fired a bullet into the elder's head, he was assassinating a dead man. To terrorize the ghetto, he had the body delivered to them. They buried him that evening. Later the Jews of Feherfalu nodded as they said, "Yes, yes, he was lucky; he is lying in his own grave."

A crazy idea flashed through Malkiel's mind: if he were to die now, he would like to be buried here.

"You again?" It was Hershel the gravedigger, with his monstrous dark head. "Well, then," he brayed, "you finally going to buy me that drink?"

The afternoon was drawing to an end. A gentle breeze murmured secrets from one gravestone to another. A branch creaked. The trees bowed, as if to show respect for this ground, where so many of the dead had found eternal rest.

"Didn't I promise to tell you about the Great Reunion? Buy me a jug and you'll see. I know what a promise is. What do you say?" Hershel relaxed on the dewy grass. Sitting, he seemed even more misshapen. He crossed and recrossed his legs; his herculean torso stayed motionless. "You're rich, and I'm only a poor bastard," he said. "Pity a poor bastard who's also the last remaining Jewish gravedigger in this town! Can you imagine what it's like living here? My only friends are dead people. But dead people are stingy; they never buy me a drink. But you, Mr. Stranger, you are alive and well; and you offer me nothing?"

Malkiel inspected him more closely. He had never in his life seen a more grotesque creature. Everything about the man was wrong. His ears were too big, his eyelids too heavy, his mouth was gaping and half toothless; and his hair was all dark, dark as jet, and shockingly thick, as if covered with bark. "Your promises don't interest me," Malkiel said.

"Listen, you trying to insult me, or what? You too good to drink with me?"

"Forgive me. But I prefer stories, certain stories."

"You do?" Hershel beamed. "I know stories. I know as many stories as God Himself. And mine are cheaper."

"All right, here's a deal: for each glass, you tell me a story."

"Ah no, what do you take me for? A street peddler? I'm a wholesaler! I deal in bottles, not glasses!"

"All right."

"You want me to tell you the story of the Great Reunion?"

"No."

"Hey, it's a fantastic story, believe me! You're not interested?"

"Yes, but some other time."

"Too bad. That's your loss. What story do you want me to tell you now?"

"The story of Malkiel Rosenbaum." Pronouncing his own name, Malkiel felt, irrationally, that he was lying to the gravedigger. He felt guilty. And if he were to confess that it was his own name too?

Hershel said, "Malkiel Rosenbaum? The last dead man from the ghetto?"

"Did you know him?"

"Did I know him? You're asking me did I know Malkiel Rosenbaum? I knew him better than his own son, better than his own wife. After all, my poor sir, I was the last one to see him. Come with me now, my boy, and you'll hear stories, real horror stories that will make you tremble; I swear it to you. . . ."

They left the cemetery. The customary basin of water was ready; Malkiel washed his hands, and the gravedigger wet his own. Near the park, at the corner of an alleyway occupied by a grocer and two butchers, the tavern was open but half empty. Malkiel knew the place, thanks to Lidia; sullen husbands dropped in to cheer up, and hard-featured widows, and empty-eyed old men.

"Shall we take a seat in the corner?" Hershel asked, seething with thirst and impatience.

Behind the bar a waiter was reading the newspaper. He was obviously bored. Malkiel called to him, with no luck. He called louder, and did no better. "What's his problem? Is he on strike?"

"That's my fault," the gravedigger said. "He can't stand me. He's a dummy; he claims I drive his customers away. Why? Because they think I'm ugly and stink of death. I scare them, he says. That's not true, believe me. I don't scare anybody. They scare themselves."

But the waiter was probably right. Suddenly the few customers still in the tavern were on their feet, paying their bills.

"One of these days," Hershel said, "I'm going to grab my cane, the one I used the night of the Great Reunion, and I'm going to come show that son of a bitch what I really think of him."

"Forget it," Malkiel said. "Tell me instead—"

"Malkiel." The gravedigger grimaced. "Malkiel Rosenbaum. I remember him as if he were here, right in front of me, as if he'd asked me to have a drink, like you did."

"Tell me about him."

"Hey, you're in a hurry! Something to drink first!"

Malkiel rose and went over to the waiter, who ignored him. "Hershel, tell him in Romanian or Hungarian that if he's friendly he may land himself a nice tip."

The gravedigger called out from his corner. The waiter answered. "He says he wants his tip in advance!"

Disgusted, Malkiel pulled out a sheaf of Romanian bank notes and set it on the bar, right under the waiter's nose. It was not enough. "The son of a bitch says you have to pay him back for all the customers I drove away just now," said the gravedigger.

A second sheaf brought a smile to the waiter's face. He was suddenly efficient. Three large glasses and a bottle of *tzuika* appeared on the table. They all three hoisted a glass.

"I'm listening," Malkiel said.

"When he goes away. He annoys me."

"He doesn't speak Yiddish."

"I don't like his face! If he doesn't leave, I leave! With the bottle!"

All right, all right; the waiter went back to his newspaper.

"Malkiel Rosenbaum," the gravedigger said, and wiped his mouth with a corner of his jacket. "I knew him, you bet I knew him! But when I took him in that Saturday night, in the funeral parlor, his own mother wouldn't have recognized him. His head was a bloody bundle of rags. His body was a housepainter's body —blue and red and green and black, a real rainbow, you know? I dug his grave, and it's crazy but I was laughing—and no, you may not ask me why—I was laughing with rage and pride all at once, because Reb Malkiel was stronger than his murderers. I was laughing, but the whole world was crying. His funeral was something to see. By candlelight the chief rabbi, the widow and about twenty leaders came for the burial service. The chief rabbi recited the special Kaddish that you only recite then. 'He was a great Jew,' said the head of the community. A saint, the vice president corrected him. One of the Just. He sacrificed himself for the honor of the Jewish people; may his soul rest in peace in heaven among the shepherds and sages of Israel. . . . It was almost dawn when they went back to the ghetto. Nobody was asleep. They were all preparing for the deportation. The leaders told them what Reb Malkiel had done and how he had done it, and Jews blessed him as they said their good-byes. He was somebody, Malkiel Rosenbaum."

Hershel emptied his glass, filled it and emptied it again. I must tell all that to my father, Malkiel was thinking. He deserves to know everything. But—will he still be able to understand?

"And I didn't go back to the ghetto," the gravedigger went on. "You want to know where I went?"

"Where?"

"Nowhere, at first. I stayed at the cemetery. Then I went to join the partisans. Surprised?"

"Nothing about you surprises me."

"You must be wondering how I stayed alive, isn't that what you were wondering? If I guessed right, you order another bottle."

Malkiel ordered another bottle.

"The dead protected me," said the gravedigger, rubbing his left knee with his right hand. "The cattle cars carried off all the Jews, but they left me behind. The Germans forgot about me. Maybe they thought I was dead; I thought I was a dead man myself. It's no fun to be the only living man among all the dead."

"No fun for whom? For the dead?"

Outside, night had fallen. A lone car sounded its horn for no reason; there was no other vehicle to quarrel with. A boy opened the tavern door, spotted the gravedigger and flung a stone at him. He ran off without closing the door. A moment later an old witch appeared; she spat insults, lifted her skirts, and then she too disappeared.

"You know what the night of the Great Reunion was?"

"No. I don't know."

"Do you want to know?"

"What'll it cost me?"

The gravedigger closed his eyes, as if to relive a scene of long ago. "It was during the week of all the transports, the ghetto's last week. I spent the days in the woods with the partisans; at night I slipped back to the cemetery. Most of the Jews were gone. The ghetto had shrunk. A few streets, a small square. At night I sat on a grave and talked out loud to myself: You disgust me, Hershel; you ought to be with the living on their way to death, not with the dead; the dead are in no danger. You're a Jew, aren't you? So many Jews die, and you want to live? Not nice, Hershel, not nice at all . . . One evening I was ready to give it all up and run to the Jews who were dying all day and all night, but some unknown voice held me back: Hershel, it said, don't abandon us; we need you, too. . . . It wasn't the first time the dead had talked to me. Nothing unusual about that. They have nothing to do, the poor creatures, so they talk to me just to pass the time. . . . But usually they told me what was going on in heaven—interesting things happen, even exciting things. You wouldn't think so, would you, Mr. Stranger? Jealous angels: who wins first prize this week? And the Just, who care so little for pleasure except in study, even up there. And the demons playing with fire, hey? Oh, if you only knew! But this was the first time a dead man asked me to do anything but listen. Not only that, but I couldn't identify the voice talking to me. Whose was it? Well, it was short on courtesy and never bothered to introduce itself properly, so I snapped: Hey, Mr. Dead Man, who are you to talk to me like that, and ask me for a favor to boot? What you tell me is all very nice, and very flattering, but all the same, you could tell me who I'm talking to, couldn't you?

"So the voice realized it had lacked manners, and introduced itself: 'I am Rabbi Zadok, the first rabbi to have the honor of serving this holy community; for three and a half centuries now I have watched over it from this grave.' Well, I wanted to tell him what I thought of that: You have a funny way of watching over your community, my good rabbi; go take a stroll around town. But I didn't say it. You understand, by the nature of my job I have to show respect for rabbis. So I just said, 'I'm happy to meet you, and what can I do for you?' Well, believe it or not, he had work for me. 'Do you know the last rabbi's house?' he asked me. Well, sure I knew it. I told him, I've been there a thousand times in connection with my job. 'Good,' said Rabbi Zadok. 'Go into the room he used for an office. In the closet, on the left, you'll find an old cane that used to be mine. Bring it to me.' Tell you the truth, I was scared silly. As long as I was at the cemetery, in the dark, I felt safe. But outside? Outside, there were Germans. And Hungarian police. And wild Nyilas. And the worst of them all, Zoltan, may his name be blotted out. Why run dangerous risks? But the first rabbi of our holy community calmed me down: 'Don't be afraid, Hershel. You'll be safe, I promise. And you must know that I always keep my promises. Go and do what I ask of you.' How could I get out of it, a poor little gravedigger like me?

"So I stood up, pulled down the cap I inherited from the last gravedigger, sent a quick prayer up to God and headed for the gate. I opened it carefully and took a look in the street. Deserted. Good for you, Hershel. Let's keep going, Hershel. I moved out even more carefully, hugging the walls. It was pitch black, but I can see in the dark. It's the third house after the great synagogue. There's the synagogue, there's the house. Nobody around? Nobody. Some police in the yard, maybe? The yard is also deserted. And the stairway? I'm all alone. Hey, watch it, I tell myself, you may bump into a burglar in the rabbi's apartment. No. Not tonight. All's quiet. I go into the living room. It's empty. I mean, really empty—looted, cleaned out. The bedroom: the same. So the looters must have taken the cane! No. It's there. It waited for me. That amazing first rabbi, four centuries ago, he's somebody. He knows what he's doing. The cane's right where he said it would be. I take it in both hands and carry it like a dead baby, like that, out in front of me, to the rabbi's grave. I set it gently and respectfully on the tombstone. 'Thank you, Hershel,' says the now familiar voice. You're welcome, I say, ready to flee. 'No, no,' says the voice, 'your job has just begun. Take that stick and go knock on Rabbi Mordecai's tomb, and Rabbi Yehuda's, Rabbi Israel's, and the tombs of all this community's rabbinical judges. Tell them that Rabbi Zadok son of Chaim summons them to his presence tomorrow at three in the morning. Tell them in my name that it is a matter of our people's survival.'

"I don't much like this, it's not my line of work, but do I have a choice? I do what the voice told me to do. I take the cane and make my way through the cemetery. Of course I know every lane, and where each tomb is, and how each stone tilts. I can predict the exact moment when a leaf will fall, and how long it will take to reach the ground. So there I am walking around waking the dead. I come to Rabbi Mordecai's tomb and I knock on it with the cane and I say, 'Rabbi Mordecai son of Shalom, forgive me for troubling your sleep, but this congregation's first rabbi, Zadok son of Chaim, sent me. He summons you to a special meeting at three in the morning. It's about saving our brothers and sisters.' I wait around for a while to see if the message has been received. A murmur rises from the depths of the earth. I could hardly hear it, but oh, did it scare me: Yes, the message has been received.

"I move along to Rabbi Yehuda's resting place and knock three times with the cane and say, 'Rabbi Yehuda son of Joshua, I've been sent by Rabbi Zadok son of Chaim.' I do the same thing and say the same words for all those summoned by the congregation's first rabbi. And then I go back to report on my mission: they were all invited, they'll all come. Rabbi Zadok son of Chaim says he's pleased, and adds, 'Don't run off, Hershel; I still need you. A rabbinical court cannot sit without a shammes, a beadle: you'll be our beadle.' Well, that was all I needed. Me, a beadle? Not on your life. Not for anything. But how can I turn down the first rabbi of a congregation I've seen live and grow and die? At your service, good rabbi, I tell him. 'Thank you, Hershel,' says the voice. 'And now rest. It is after midnight. You have less than three hours to restore your soul. To enjoy repose.' Easy for him to say, enjoy repose. On one hand, I have all these Jews disappearing and on the other, all these illustrious rabbis gathering, and he wants me to enjoy repose. Well, all right, I think, I'll try anyway. If my friend the first rabbi wants to help me out, I'll fall asleep. It can't do any harm. So where are you, angel of sleep?

"I woke up just before three o'clock. No: something woke me, and I don't know what it was. A strange sound, or the feel of a hand tugging at my arm. Maybe a drop of rain, or dew? Whatever, I was at my post on time. Suddenly Rabbi Zadok's voice rose over the cemetery: 'Beadle,' it intoned, 'are all the participants present?' I answered timidly that I don't know. How would I know? I can't see the dead. 'Call the roll!' Well, all right, I could do that. I knew the names well enough. I can recite by heart every name on every tombstone. Rabbi Yehuda. Rabbi Shalom-Shakhna, head of the rabbinical court from 1880 to 1914. Rabbi Israel and Rabbi Mordecai. So I called them all, one after another, in the same order as Rabbi Zadok son of Chaim, and one after another they answered, 'Present.' Our village's first rabbi said, 'I took the liberty of calling you together to ask your help: our community is dying, and it is our duty to save it.' Someone answered, 'God of Abraham, I didn't know. I was asleep.' Another echoed him: 'God of Isaac, I was lost in my studies.' And a third lamented, 'Why is this punishment visited upon our sons and theirs?'

"Then came a learned discussion, too learned for me. They all chimed in, each one with a different thought. Everybody knew how to revoke the decree. And there I was, listening but not understanding. How much time passed while they debated? I don't know. I only know that the color of night faded and dawn was about to break. The council realized this, too, because Rabbi Zadok called to me, 'Hershel, listen carefully. It is too late now for us to go into town, but we'll go tomorrow night. You will guide us. We want to enter every house of study or prayer, in all the synagogues, and find out firsthand what the enemy is planning for the people of Israel. We also want to visit the homes of its children. You will show us the way, and you will point out the most deserving among them, so we can bring help and consolation to our descendants. Do you understand what I have told you?' Well, like the fool I am, instead of saying, Yes, yes, good rabbi, I heard it all and understood it all —I had the gall to give him advice. 'Why don't you ask one of your companions to be your guide? Go and ask Reb Malkiel Rosenbaum. He'll explain the situation. What he suffered, very few of our martyrs suffered; what he did, no one else will ever do; he knows what's going on. Let Reb Malkiel guide you along the pathways of Jewish torment.'

"I was sure the whole council would blast me in all its authority and all its wrath; who was I to tell them what to do? But to my great surprise, the illustrious Rabbi Zadok son of Chaim spared me the thunder of his displeasure. For an endless moment he said nothing, so I wondered if he'd even heard me, if I'd actually spoken the words I shaped in my head. And then, with a sweetness unheard of, infinite sweetness, a sweetness that moved me to tears, he said to me, 'You're right, Hershel. I did not think of Reb Malkiel; I should have, but I forgot him. May he forgive me. I'll ask him to join us tomorrow night. You're right, Hershel; he is the perfect guide.' And then, after such kindness from an illustrious *tzaddik* that I'd never met before, I couldn't hold back the tears. And I who never cry, I sobbed like an orphan on his father's tomb.

"Instead of disappearing into the woods with the partisans, I slept all the next day. I was exhausted. Too many emotions and too many happenings; my poor head couldn't take it all in. I wasn't hungry and I wasn't thirsty. I was sunk in the deepest sleep, and I dreamed, but I can't remember my dreams. I only remember that before midnight I was back at Rabbi Zadok's tomb. They were all there, Reb Malkiel included. First he led us to the great synagogue; it was full of excrement, and it reeked. And Rabbi Mordecai, the one they call the *tzaddik* with the broken heart, cried out *avinu malkenu,* our father and our king, Your enemy profaned the sanctuary, what is left to us to do? Then Reb Malkiel led us to the hasidic *shtibl* of Wizhnitz; the sacred scrolls lay in the dust. And Rabbi Israel, the one they call his people's ardent soul, uttered a cry that must have pierced the heavens: 'God of our fathers, are we guilty? Could we have prevented this scandal, this shame?' Then Reb Malkiel led them to every other synagogue in the town: the tailors', the dreamers', the traveling salesmen's. All pillaged. Broken windows, smashed pulpits. And Rabbi Yehuda, the one that the poor particularly adored, began to sob: 'Is there then no place for You, O Lord? In this city of sin, who will console You?' And Reb Malkiel opened the doors of all the empty homes in the ghetto, to find a moldy crust of bread, a child's slipper, a prayer book with torn pages. But where are our children? cried the rabbinical council. Where are their parents and their teachers? And all the council wept, and cried out in pain—all but Reb Malkiel, whom the enemy had already rendered mute. Then I went up to him and said, 'You can't speak, Reb Malkiel, so I'll speak for you; in your name I say that one day the children of these children will come back here and take their revenge; they will punish this city that did not resist evil.'

"I wonder if the people sleeping in that city heard us. The dead made a noise not of this world, believe me. It wasn't noise but something else, something beyond. A quake: not an earthquake but a time quake. Thunder so powerful that the living, suddenly deafened, confused it with silence. My head was splitting. You don't know me, but you can believe me when I say that nothing impresses me. That night I wasn't myself. Our procession marched through the shadows with more zeal than any since the world is world. Have you ever seen dead people walking and talking at the same time? Dead people imploring the living to stay alive, dead people who want to become avengers? That night I saw dead people —I who have seen many—who filled me not with pity but with admiration.

"Shortly before dawn Rabbi Zadok, surrounded by his companions, stopped and asked if he could speak in their name; they answered yes. 'God of our ancestors,' he cried, 'in the name of all who have guided this holy Jewish community, I say again what our teacher Moses said to You one day in the desert: Yet now, if Thou wilt forgive their sin—and if not, blot me, I pray thee, out of Thy book which Thou hast written.' Well, believe it or not, he'd hardly finished talking when a bolt of lightning split the sky over the cemetery. 'Too late,' murmured Rabbi Yehuda. 'Too late,' acquiesced Rabbi Mordecai. And suddenly I heard myself, bolder then I ever dreamed I was, saying, 'No, it isn't too late. The Jews in the last convoy aren't dead yet. They're in the train on their way to death, but they aren't dead yet. They can still be saved.' You won't believe this, but all those rabbis who sit there near the throne, they congratulated me for showing them the way. 'And if we go to the train?' asked Rabbi Mordecai. Rabbi Zadok said, 'A good idea, but impossible; you know we cannot leave this city until the Messiah comes.' A discussion broke out: from the Halakic point of view, could they or could they not soar from here to the train? Rabbi Zadok gave his opinion: 'The law is the law.' 'No,' said Rabbi Yehuda, 'the law applies only to the living. But we may ask God to blot our names from His book if the Jews on the train aren't saved.' 'Too late,' said several indistinct voices. On the horizon, night was already withdrawing behind the mountains. 'Woe unto us,' said Rabbi Zadok in a low voice. 'We are the dead rabbis of an extinct congregation.'

"At dawn, after visiting every empty home, after weeping over every vanished soul, they returned to the cemetery. Like a good beadle, I followed them at a distance. At the tomb of Rabbi Zadok son of Chaim they gathered in silence for a minute or an hour or more. Then Rabbi Zadok turned to Reb Malkiel and said, 'Now then, Malkiel: is it really too late?' And Reb Malkiel nodded his head, which was as it had been before the beating: Yes, it is too late. And all cried out, Woe unto us, it is too late! And Rabbi Zadok son of Chaim said in a clear strong voice, 'God of our fathers, there will be no more prayers to You from this city! The voices of children reading Torah will never again be heard within these walls! The hearts of these people will never again yearn for their Redeemer! Is that what You wished?' I'm sure God heard him; I'm even sure God answered him, though I never heard God's voice. I heard Rabbi Mordecai's voice, murmuring, 'Since the enemy has taken our children and their parents into captivity, since he has delivered them unto death, how can I find sleep again?'

"Now dawn was breaking in the east. 'We must go back now,' said Rabbi Zadok son of Chaim. 'Stay where you are, Hershel, and as you are. You must deliver the sentence. Every night except the Sabbath and Jewish holidays, you must come here with my cane. You will knock at the tomb of Reb Malkiel the Martyr. And the sleep of this city's burghers will be broken.'

"You may take me for a fool, but that's just what I do, every night. Except once, when I decided to go and knock somewhere else: on the door of a real son of a bitch, the worst . . . I really wanted to put him to sleep for good."

He swallowed another glass of *tzuika* and began laughing and sobbing at once. Malkiel thought, There we go, he's drunk. I'm spending my day with a drunkard. Malkiel was sure he had made a mistake, as if someone at a crossroads had given him bad advice and sent him down the wrong road.

The gravedigger leaned toward Malkiel and breathed, "And you, Mr. Stranger—what are you doing in the cemetery at midnight?"

"But I'm not in the cemetery at midnight," Malkiel protested.

"That's what you think," said the gravedigger, laughing louder. "You can cheat the others, but not me, and not the dead. We're keeping a close eye on you. Tell me, what are you looking for, at the grave of Malkiel the Martyr? What's your mission? And who sent you on it?"

Tell him the truth? Admit everything? Tell him about Elhanan's illness? Explain his true mission, his need to rescue Elhanan's memory? Tell him the story he could not know, the story of Elhanan and his shrinking universe, a universe expiring from moment to moment, from memory to memory? "I don't sleep well," he said at last. "I have insomnia. So I take walks. I wander around."

The gravedigger pounded the table with both hands, upsetting the glasses. "That's a good one! You don't sleep well! But in this damn town everybody sleeps badly. That was the wish of Rabbi Zadok son of Chaim. As long as this cane is in my hands, the people of this town will not sleep at night!"

Malkiel shuddered. "And later on? When you're gone?"

"Don't worry about it. Somebody else will take my place."

"Who?"

"Well, aren't you nosy! I have faith, I do. Rabbi Zadok will find someone, believe me. He can even do without someone if he has to. The cane will do the job all by itself."

"And it will come and tap on your grave, too?"

"And on yours," said the gravedigger. His face was visibly swollen, a clown's face, the face of a monstrous, gleeful giant. And his eyes: red, wild, fierce. They were glaring at the tavern, the street, the whole town, from every tree, every roof. His eyes were the stars. If he closed his eyelids the whole town would sink into shadow. And not just the town. I am beginning to understand, Malkiel thought. And if forgetfulness was linked to fear?

An image: hunched over an ancient book, my father called to me. He was upset, and his breath was labored. I sensed that he was more distressed than usual. "Did I ever tell you the story about the Rabbi of Apt?"

"Which one?"

"The one about his promise."

"No, Father."

"Before he died, the famous Rabbi Abraham-Joshua of Apt made a strange promise to his weeping disciples: to do all he could, up there in heaven, to hasten the coming of the Messiah. 'I know,' he added, 'that other masters have made the same promise. The first, transported directly to paradise, naturally forgot his promise. The second, drunk on divine light, forgot it on the threshold of paradise. The third, knowing what had happened to his predecessors, swore to his followers, "I shall resist: I shall make my plea heard the instant I leave you here below, before I have even glimpsed the gates of paradise." And indeed he held fast against the angels who wished to take him before the celestial court. "I will not move a step," he said. "My people have suffered too much and too long, and they deserve deliverance. If the Messiah will not descend to earth, then too bad, I refuse to budge." At that, the angels had an idea. They half opened the gates of paradise; that way the Rabbi could hear the other sages studying Torah in fervor and with love; what he heard seemed to him so beautiful, so original, so true, that he ceased thinking about anything else, and he forgot his promise.

" 'I shall not forget,' promised the Rabbi of Apt.

"Apparently, he too forgot," said my father. "But he had a good excuse: he was already dead. I have no excuse; I'm not dead and yet I'm forgetting. True, I made no promises. But you, my son, you made a promise to me. I'm counting on you."

. . .

Have I been a good son? Malkiel stood before the house of his father. Most of the time surely yes, but not always. There were his affairs, his journeys, his mistresses. Inge. He shouldn't have. Leila. He shouldn't have. A wave of remorse broke within him. Was that why his father had sent him here? To repent?

Like all teenagers, Malkiel had had misunderstandings and disagreements with his father. He wanted to go out more often, and Elhanan tried to dissuade him: "Have you done your schoolwork? Did you revise that composition?" Malkiel would happily have gone to every baseball game of the season. Elhanan claimed it was too much. "You're not of my generation," Malkiel said. "You can't understand." How many times had Malkiel said those words? He remembered them now, and they seemed childish and wicked. I made my father suffer, he thought. I made him doubt his own authority. Not for long; but it was still too long.

A memory: father and son at dinner. Both silent. Loretta tried to start a conversation. No luck. Malkiel said something; he stared at his plate.

"What's on your mind?"

"Nothing."

"Then why are you so moody?"

"I'm not moody."

"Don't you trust me?"

"Of course I do."

"Why don't you talk to me?"

"I don't feel like talking."

At that Elhanan's eyes filled with night.

Another time: Malkiel put on his overcoat, ready to go out.

"Where are you going?"

"I have a date."

"With whom?"

"A friend."

"Who is he?"

"A friend." A trace of hostility in his voice, Malkiel added, "Haven't I told you that I don't like questions about my personal life?"

Elhanan bowed his head. "And here I thought I was part of your personal life."

Another scene: Elhanan was dressing, putting on his best suit.

"Tomorrow is Rosh Hashanah. Are you coming to synagogue with me, Malkiel?"

"Maybe."

"You're not sure?"

"I'll think about it."

"Were you expecting to pray somewhere else?"

"Maybe."

"But you know how I like praying beside you."

"I know."

"Malkiel."

"Yes?"

"Why do you go out of your way to hurt me?"

Now, in Feherfalu, Malkiel thought, That's true. Why did I sometimes feel that perverse need—even if it was unconscious—to wound him? To be like the other kids? To punish him for bringing me into a world that is ugly, unjust, stupid, doomed? To break free of his hold on me? To put a distance between his nightmares and me? Still, before he got sick he rarely talked about the past. I knew when he was thinking about it, though. He would grow peaceful, serene. He would rejoin my mother, and his eyes would become veiled. Then he would meditate on all things with a kind of primordial clarity. And me, did he see me at all?

Well, I know: all adolescents stumble over the same difficulties with their parents; but my situation was different. First, I had no mother. And my father? Didn't he belong to my dead mother?

One day during a stormy argument Elhanan tried to explain the complexity of our relationship. "You're the center of my life, Malkiel. It's you who make me invincible. But it's you who also make me vulnerable: if anything happened to you I couldn't stand it—I'd die."

"You have no right! You have no right to saddle me with a burden like that! Let me live my adolescent life. Don't force me to grow up so fast!"

"Now it's my turn to say you don't understand me. You don't understand that only you can make me happy—or make me give up all hope of happiness."

"I refuse!"

"To understand?"

"No. I understand, all right. I refuse the role you want me to play!"

"You refuse to be my son?"

"I refuse to be anything *but* a son to you!"

"And you don't see that your refusal is a repudiation?"

"Repudiation of what?"

"Of my whole life." And gently, sadly, he went on: "How many times have I described my concept of a Jew, Malkiel? We are all cloaked in the memory of God."

He went on talking, and I had a date with a charming young girl, the prettiest in my class. I stood up. So did he. He walked to the door with me, and for some unknown reason he dragged his chair after him, as if it were a corpse on a deserted battlefield.

Malkiel scrutinized a window in his father's house as if he might find there an answer to his question. Why did I make him suffer? Of course that phase didn't last. But the question does.

"Sleep well, Lidia?"

"Very well, thank you," said the young interpreter. "Is my sleep so interesting?" Lidia was in a bad mood. Natural enough. No woman likes to be rejected. Even, or especially, if she's working for *them*.

It was early in the day, and the main square was bustling. Surly peasants, civil servants in a hurry, schoolteachers and housewives, still half asleep: the day's whirl brought these men and women together before dispersing them.

Seated on the hotel terrace, Malkiel and Lidia discussed the day's plans as they did every morning. Of course. To inform others she must inform herself. Like Satan, Malkiel thought. He, too, needs to be everywhere at once, to shatter alibis and excuses. Satan: the creature of a thousand traps. And Malkiel thought of Satan, which reminded him of Rosh Hashanah. When would it be? Soon, in a few weeks. And where would he be? Where would he go to pray? Was there a synagogue in this town? His father had told him of several, but Malkiel could not locate them. The Communist authorities had either closed them or changed the street names. Ask Lidia? She would then tell her superiors, who . . . what for? There was no Jewish community left in Feherfalu.

"What's on the agenda?" Lidia asked. "The cemetery again?"

"Why not?" Malkiel said. "There are still plenty of inscriptions to translate."

"And of course you don't need my help."

"Not unless you read Hebrew."

Scowling, Lidia sipped her coffee, her mind far away.

"Are you mad at me?"

"No," she lied. And then, "Yes, I am. Do you behave like that with all women? Attract them just to reject them?"

"That's not it."

"Then what is it?"

An answer came to his lips, but he held it back.

"Are you afraid of me?" she went on. "Suspicious of me? Do you think I belong to *them*? Is that why?"

He experienced a sudden, curious pity for her, as if for a defenseless child. As if it were she that the police were watching. "Give me your hand, Lidia," he said softly.

Still pouting, her eyes hard, the young woman seemed defensive. Then she held out her hand, and Malkiel covered it with his own.

"I'll explain everything someday," he said.

"When?"

"Someday."

"Someday is a long way off. And it's vague, and I don't like vagueness."

Malkiel kept her hand in his. She made no effort to pull away.

"Last night," she said.

"Yes?"

"Last night I wanted to love."

She did not say "to love you" but "to love."

"Why me?"

"That I don't know. I felt as if you were in another realm. Walled off from love. A man who spends his life in cemeteries doesn't love life. I thought I could help you. Cure you."

Malkiel felt himself falter, ready to drop his guard. Lidia was no beauty, but there was something else. She was real. Mouth open or shut, brows arched or furrowed, whether speaking or listening, she did not lie. When she loves, she loves with her whole body; and when she is on the lookout, all her senses are on alert.

"And after love?"

"I don't know what you mean."

"What comes after love?"

She withdrew her hand. "I feel sorry for you," she said harshly. "I pity everyone for whom love isn't an end in itself. What is it to you? A game? Then what are the rules?"

Malkiel felt an unpleasant sensation. "Let's talk about something else."

"As you like."

Love, love. Sooner or later you collided with it. Did his father endure the same trials? There was Vitka, and Lianka. . . . But after Talia died? In any case, he had never talked about it; and he never would. The truth was that Malkiel's father had never known any woman but his own wife. A matter of fidelity? Not even that: only love. Which writer said that you could love two women but you could only be faithful to one? Malkiel's father might have known an occasional surge of love, but he had loved only one woman. She was always present to him. Sometimes he spoke to her, asked her opinions. He missed her and told her so.

Malkiel thought back to the women who had counted in his own life. His cousin Rita. One year younger than he, she fascinated him with her fiery temper, her mischievous, sparkling wit, and the power of her sensuality. She wanted to be a liberated woman. She said it over and over. Free in act and commitment. "God's equal; free as He." So she defined herself. Proud and stubborn, Rita was. . . .

They saw each other often from the earliest years. They attended the same grade school and the same religious high school (where she provoked one scandal after another by trying to seduce her professors). Sometimes they had dinner together and took in a movie. Malkiel felt a sort of tenderness for her, mingled with dread: she intimidated him and encouraged him at the same time. He had never dreamed that there could be anything serious between them. But in time they went on trips to the Catskills together. Or swam in her parents' pool. They were playmates, that was all. Cousins are meant to tease one another, to plot together, to make fun of the grown-up world, but they seek adventure on their own. One evening Rita suggested that they spend the weekend at Tanglewood. It was the beginning or middle of August; New York was crushed by a heat wave. Why not go off where it was cool and enjoy beautiful music at the same time? Rita drove a convertible and cursed the drivers who passed her. Her hair streaming in the wind, she steered with her left hand and drew Malkiel to her with her right. At first it was innocent: to show him a billboard, an old tree, a cloud formation. Malkiel sensed her warmth, but their closeness seemed of little consequence. Malkiel thought of nothing special, nothing new, and neither, no doubt, did Rita. They reached Lenox early in the afternoon and proceeded to the motel where they had reserved two rooms. Unfortunately, there was only one left, the clerk informed them, apologizing for the confusion. To make up for it, he would give them the room at half price. "Okay?" she said. "Okay," he said. It was the beginning of a beautiful and stormy affair.

The concert beneath the stars was majestic. The magic of Schubert and Bernstein: total strangers, spellbound, exchanged greetings. "Beauty makes us all dreamers," said a girl with shoulder-length black hair, a music student. "It makes me shiver," Rita said. Yet the night was warm. Their summer clothes clung to their bodies. "Let's go for a swim," Rita said. "The pool at the motel looked inviting." It was late, but Malkiel agreed. The swim did them good. So did dinner. The truth was, Malkiel would have lingered; he was strangely uneasy about being alone with his cousin. The room had one bed, a small sofa, two chairs and a table. Well, he'd sleep on the floor. But Rita had other ideas. "Are you crazy?" she asked. "The bed is plenty big enough for two." He was stammering a timid "All right," when she interrupted: "You know, we're really not living in the fifteenth century. And we're all grown up, aren't we? And cousins, after all." That settled it. Deep down he was even pleased at the way things had developed. Rita took a shower and emerged from the bathroom wrapped in a towel that barely covered her suntanned breasts. "It's yours," she said. He took the longest shower of his life and reappeared in blue pajamas. Stretched out on the bed, impassive, Rita was reading a newspaper. Malkiel tried to busy himself. He hung up his shirt and pants, inspected his socks, went back for a glass of water. "You're making me nervous," Rita said. "Come to bed." He wondered what he was feeling. Desire, apprehension, curiosity—all that and more. Shyly, cautiously, he stretched out along the edge of the bed. "Do you want the paper?" she asked. "Thanks; I have my book." She wanted to know what he was reading. His answer was muddled, unfocused. "Hard to say what it's about," he told her. For a long moment they read in silence. In the hall, young people were calling noisy hellos and good-byes and making dates for the next day. Tense, Malkiel tried to picture himself among them, so that he would not picture the half-naked young woman beside him. And then, neither knowing how or why, their two bodies touched. And Malkiel soared to seventh heaven before plunging to seventh hell. In torture, in ecstasy, he wanted to sing and to weep; he had never felt so torn or so whole. "Was that the first time?" Rita asked. He was ashamed to admit the truth but admitted it anyway, not going so far as to tell her what he felt now: a mixture of guilt and remorse, a sense of defeat. His whole religious memory was suddenly judging him. Had he not violated one of the Ten Commandments? How would he answer at the Last Judgment? What would his uncle think? "Got the blues?"

Rita teased him. "You poor virgin. Come here and let me cheer you up. . . ."

And Leila. The beautiful Muslim, fierce and exasperating. His fellow student at Columbia. She was a Tunisian, a diplomat's daughter, extremely intelligent and dynamic. One of the activists at the forefront of the student protest, she stood up to her professors, whom she called every name. And to the administration, which she repeatedly sent to hell. Malkiel had come to interview her for the *Times*.

It was the end of 1968, a turbulent, even volcanic period. The students were front-page news. Inflammatory speeches; financial demands, and sociopolitical, educational and philosophical ones. The professors could only hold their tongues and mind their manners, because their students, being younger, knew more than they. Down with the rich and culturally privileged! Down with the powers that be! Make way for idealistic youth, whose future is at stake, make way for the purity of their motives and the generosity of their aspirations! A wave of fervor and words swept through the campus. Down with everything old, and up with everything new; time to start again! Every speechmaker saw himself as Danton, every agitator was Robespierre. Smash the idols, unmask the priests, demystify all those received ideas and beliefs: that was the goal. To accomplish it they invoked the individual's fundamental right to immediate happiness and knowledge, to friendship without taboos, to the magic of LSD, and also and most of all to love without limits or inhibitions. Opposing them, in what they disdainfully called "the establishment," adults saw things differently and denounced the promiscuity of mindless young people, their depravity and simplistic slogans. The students ridiculed their critics scornfully: "They're all impotent. Their ideas aren't even worth examining."

To "cover" the rebellion, Malkiel interviewed its most prominent leaders, among them Leila, the movement's Passionaria.

"So, Mr. Reporter, you've already sold out to money and power, at your age?" That was how she greeted him. Their first interview took place outside, in front of the library. At the top of the stairs a spokesman was reading out the latest resolutions adopted by the executive committee after a night of stormy debate. The crowd cheered for each paragraph as if the fate of the world depended on it.

"Could we talk seriously?" asked the reporter.

"You mean that the needs and demands of your own generation aren't serious? Just what do you want anyway?"

"I need answers."

"Then let's have the questions. What do you want to know?"

"Why a beautiful girl like you raises hell."

Leila glared at him. "What are you? A boy scout? J. Edgar Hoover? Do I owe you any explanations? Who are you to talk to me that way?"

Against the tirade Malkiel could only stammer, "Sorry, sorry." In an instant, the young reporter lost all his assurance and became what he was, the son of a refugee.

"Enough of all that," Leila said. "Let's talk. You can be useful to us. The capitalist press has exploited us long enough; now it's our turn." She plied him with propaganda, overwhelmed him with news "from an unimpeachable source," "top secret" analyses, "confidential" rumors. Happily, a rewrite man restored perspective. Under Malkiel Rosenbaum's byline, the article was a reasonably accurate account of the situation at Columbia. Next day Leila promptly insulted him. No jeer or insult was omitted. Too timid to defend himself, Malkiel let her wear herself out. Finally she asked him, "Don't you have anything to say for yourself?"

"Yes. I still want to know why a beautiful girl like you goes around raising so much hell."

She shot him another scornful glance and left. They saw each other several times after the protests had quieted down. She ran into him at one of the campus gates and asked, "Is a capitalist reporter rich enough to buy me a cup of coffee?"

"I think my newspaper can afford it," he said. That same night they became lovers.

Malkiel often considered telling his father about her. But Elhanan would have taken it badly. He would have cried, "What? You, a Jew, with a Muslim woman? I'm sure she hates Israel. . . ."

And indeed she did. Leila, a future follower of the PLO, was already anti-Israel. Between her and Malkiel, argument followed endless and sometimes violent argument. Yes, yes, Israel has suffered, she would say; but does that give them the right to make Palestinians suffer?

Malkiel: You know very well it isn't Israel making them suffer! You can blame the Arab governments for their tragedy; why did they exhort them to flee their homes in 1948? And then let them live in refugee camps?

Leila: You Jews did all you could to uproot those people and drive them from their land, and now you blame the Arabs? If you hadn't come along, there would have been no tragedy!

He: We didn't come *along*, we came *back*. Easy enough for you to forget!

She: I'm not forgetting anything, but you forget that the Palestinians have been living on that land for centuries, and you abandoned it two thousand years ago!

Malkiel lost his temper: *Abandoned?* You dare to say we abandoned the land promised to Abraham, Isaac and Jacob? And shown to Moses? And conquered by Joshua? Aren't you ashamed to falsify history? They expelled us from that land, but we never repudiated it, or forgot it, or abandoned it! Since King David there have always been Jews in Jerusalem, and Galilee, and Gaza.

She: Oh yes? And the big cities?

He: The big cities? Do you mean Haifa, Netanya and Tel Aviv? Do you want to tell me who built them? You, maybe? You were a smattering of people in the desert—do you dare deny that?

She: That's the Afrikaner argument in South Africa.

He: I forbid you to compare us to those racists and their apartheid! Racism and Judaism are incompatible! We suffered too much from racism to use it against others.

She: There you go again with your suffering! As if you were the only people who ever knew hardship!

Their relationship lasted only a few months. Malkiel matured in the course of it. Of all the women he had known before Tamar, it was Leila who intrigued him most. Shrewd, determined, politically committed, she sought extremes and rejected compromise and equivocation alike. "Do you think I love you?" she asked him during one of their quarrels. "You're a dreamer, poor boy. I like you well enough to sleep with you, and you interest me enough to make me make you want to sleep with me." Malkiel thought she was saying that to antagonize him, to affirm her power over him, to wound him; he was wrong. Leila loved him because he was a Jew. And after she left him she detested him for the same reason.

Did he feel guilty for living with a pro-Palestinian Muslim, an enemy of Israel? Sometimes after a sleepless night he dreamed up all sorts of scenarios. Suppose Leila was a spy. Suppose she'd seduced him solely to make him an Arab agent. Would he have been capable of following her that far? Of betraying his own people? Of mocking and desecrating everything his father believed?

Later he would wonder if his father's illness was not a punishment for the love he himself had borne for an Arab woman.

AN EXCERPT FROM ELHANAN ROSENBAUM'S DIARY

Dr. Pasternak broke the news with extreme delicacy. He is a nice man, Dr. Pasternak. A bit awkward, rather prudent. When he talks to me he inspects his fingernails, which, between you and me, could use a little care. He is "my" doctor and he wants to spare me. What is he afraid of? Seeing me distraught, wiped out? I'm strong. I've always been. The proof is that Talia is dead and I am still alive. I am holding on.

"It's something of a rare disease," he said.

"Tell me all, my friend."

"We don't know much about it. What causes it? What might keep it from worsening? We'll know someday. For now it's incurable, as they say. But only for now."

He went on. The brain is deteriorating and the memory eroding; researchers are optimistic. Encouraging. In Stockholm and Rehovot, New York and London, eminent specialists are working relentlessly. They will surely corner the enemy and render him harmless. Everywhere medicine is winning stunning victories.

"Keep fighting. In this kind of battle, it's essential. You're your own best ally. Keep telling yourself that memory possesses its own mysterious powers, which are even stronger than imagination."

He went on at some length, Dr. Pasternak did. He wasn't inspecting his fingernails now; he was studying me. I stopped listening. I only heard a word here and there. His whole speech could be summed up in a single fact: slowly, and then not so slowly, but at an unforeseeable pace, I was going to forget my whole existence, forget all that I had been.

"The main thing is not to give up," the doctor repeated, walking me to the front door. "Miracles do happen."

In the waiting room his receptionist, Susan, offered me a smile and a candy: "Don't tell the doctor. Chocolate's not good for you."

I did not go straight home. I took a walk. Was it warm or cold that day? I have no idea. It was spring, but I couldn't care less. What did I think about? I have no idea. My legs carried me along. My legs did the thinking for me.

Wandering along Broadway, I stopped at a bookstore window. Classics and popular works beckoned me to leaf through them. Not interested. Farther along, a clothing store. Not interested. Near the subway station a beggar accosted me: "I was rich once and I lost everything." I looked at his open hand and his closed face. I took out my wallet and pulled out a five-dollar bill. "It is for you." He seemed perplexed, frightened. "It's too much," he said. And then, hardly knowing what I did, I gave him all the money I had on me. "I was rich too," I said, "and I'm going to lose everything."

With that, I felt liberated. I glanced at my watch: I would be late for my class. If I hurried, I could just make it.

My students noticed nothing. In fact, it was probably the best class of the year, if not of my whole career. We were discussing biblical poetry and its effect on prophecy. I remember my conclusion: "Jeremiah was an activist, but what remains of him? The politician? No. The poet." Dina, my best student, was waiting at my office door. "Thank you," she said, "for making us love Jeremiah."

I reached home at dusk. Loretta announced that dinner was ready. "I'm not hungry," I told her. She looked closely at me, and her hand went to her mouth. She retreated to the kitchen. I could not erase Dr. Pasternak from my mind. I had to make an effort not to call him and ask, "How much time does 'for the moment' mean? How deep will the erosion go? And just what do you mean by the word 'miracle'?"

As a Jew, I believed in miracles. Our survival is just that. But according to the Talmud, miracles ceased with the destruction of the Temple. Since then, miracles of another sort, daily and ordinary, occur before our very eyes. I speak to someone who understands what I say—isn't that a miracle? I love someone who loves me—isn't that a miracle? Any encounter involves the miraculous. We find it also in the connection between the event and the story of that event. And in the hidden meaning of that story.

The hidden meaning of the written word. There again, I am too much a Jew not to cling to the word. At first it calms me; then it disturbs me.

That's how it is. I've done all I can. There comes a time when words are like stars or prayers, and then all turn to dust.

I am thinking of Zarathustra. We read him in class, I can't remember when. Nietzsche had him return to the mountains and the solitude of his cave, where he "withdrew from men, waiting like a sower who has scattered his seed. But his soul grew full of impatience and desire for those whom he loved, because he still had much to give them. For this is what is hardest: to close the open hand because one loves, and to keep a sense of shame while giving."

Why Zarathustra? Why Nietzsche? Why recall my lectures? To persuade myself that I still have things to give? Is that why I am writing? To remain modest by forgetting what I can no longer give?

Malkiel, one day you asked me why I did not write down my own story.

"I must not," I answered.

"Try," you told me.

"I must not even try."

Fact is, I did try. Several times. I tore up the pages as fast as I filled them. The gaps between my memory and words seemed unbridgeable. Despite the perils of syntax, paradox, and faded images, I'd have hoped for coherence, not perfect but enough to convey the essence of memory. Unfortunately, I never managed to connect all the fragments to a center; too often the words surfaced as obstacles. I fought them instead of making friends with them. And after the battle, exhausted, I contemplated them as if they were corpses. Sometimes, thinking of the dead whose memory I have sworn to preserve, I told myself, To write this story you'd already have to be dead; only the dead can properly write their story. Would forgetting be worse than dying?

I hope that when I sense my end I shall have enough strength to write this: I write these words to say that I can no longer write.

"Malkiel."

"I'm here, Father."

"Give your mother something to drink. Can't you see she's thirsty?"

"She's not here, Father. You know she can't be here."

"I say she's here. Talia, tell him you're here. Your mother is here, I tell you. And she's thirsty. What kind of son are you? How can you show your own mother so little respect?"

"Father, look at me. I'm here beside you. In this room there are

only the two of us. Even Tamar isn't here. There's only you and me, me and you."

"I don't believe you, and you don't believe me. Talia, tell him it is a son's duty to believe what his father tells him. Tell him it is not good to contradict one's father. Tell him, Talia."

"I could make you feel good, Father. I could go along with your fantasy and win your praise. But it would be unhealthy, false, harmful. If I let you go on like that, I'd fall alongside you. And then we'd both be lost."

"But I see her!"

"You want to see her, so you see her. But remember—" Malkiel bit back the words: his father could not remember, and there was the tragedy.

"I see her as well as I see you, Malkiel. I don't see anyone else. Talia, my magnificent Talia. Come close to me. Sit, sit. Our son is not wicked. You'll see; he'll bring you something to drink."

"You're thirsty, Father. Here's a glass of seltzer."

"Didn't I tell you, Talia? What a fine obedient son we have! Aren't you proud of him?"

"You mustn't, Father. You mustn't give in to fantasy. You remember my mother, and that's good. Every time you remember her is important. But remember, too, that my mother is no longer of this world; I never saw her; I never kissed her cheek. Make an effort—your mind and your life depend on it, and maybe mine, too!"

Slumped, Elhanan seemed old, truly old. "If you're right, son, help me, help me not to see your mother right here before my eyes just as I see you. Help me—I need your help badly."

Malkiel got his father to bed. Then he went into the other room. He opened the window and let his thoughts wander through the hostile night.

At first Elhanan wanted to keep his sickness a secret. Rumor had it that he'd had a heart attack. And that he needed total rest: no visits, no aggravation. His sickness was surely not shameful, but he allowed no discussion of it.

One day a colleague came to see him. Without phoning ahead, he rang the doorbell. Loretta, brave Loretta, still hoping for a miracle, decided not to turn him away.

"Elhanan! How happy I am to see you! You look fine. Not in bed? You cannot imagine my joy on hearing that your heart is growing stronger. We worry about you at the university, you know."

Elhanan listened, but could not quite focus. What did these pleasant banalities have to do with him? He scarcely reacted, so his visitor concluded that he was tired, perhaps depressed. To distract the patient, he retailed rumors and gossip about mutual friends. Elhanan feigned interest and answered, "Is that right? Imagine that. . . ."

Later on, Malkiel and Tamar encouraged visitors. They helped to fill his days. And who could tell—a word, a tone of voice, might help him recall something of the past.

An Israeli diplomat passing through New York insisted on spending an afternoon with him. Lean, almost ascetic, tense, this former Haganah officer had fought beside Elhanan in the Old City of Jerusalem. Together they had been shipped to the Jordanian desert as prisoners of war. "So you're on sick leave, are you?"

Elhanan was in an armchair, a woolen blanket over his knees.

"Sick of extra duty, is that it?"

"It will pass," Elhanan said.

"Do you remember that boy who brought us water? He had a limp, poor kid. And the Jordanian sergeant who made us search the tents twice a day, remember him? We used to make fun of him."

"The boy," Elhanan said. "The Old City."

"Yes. He slipped through the cellars and rubble like a mouse. You were fond of him."

Suddenly the veil parted: Elhanan saw it all clearly. Jerusalem, 1948. "It's coming back to me," he said. "That was Israel's time of glory."

"Glory? And sorrow."

They stayed up past midnight swapping old memories. Tamar and Malkiel, in the background, listened without making a sound. They were moved by an absurd hope: All was not lost. With the right key, you could unlock the doors of memory. And keys were easy enough to come by.

A few weeks later, when summer had arrived, Elhanan was visited by a woman he had treated for a nervous breakdown. She was young and frail, her expression warm and generous: she liked to give, to give of herself. "I heard you were sick, Professor," she said at once. "Is there anything I can do?"

Elhanan recognized her but could not place her.

"Do you remember me, Professor?"

"Of course, of course."

"A mutual friend, one of your colleagues, referred me to you. I came to see you. Anyway . . . one disaster after another: divorce, sickness, disappointment—I was suicidal. Without you, who knows . . . ?"

Elhanan nodded.

"How many times did I come to burden you with my personal problems? You listened patiently and—how shall I say it?—seriously. And once you told me something I'll never forget: Sometimes you let yourself be taken prisoner so you can help other prisoners escape, and it's the same for certain diseases—make use of your own to cure someone else's."

Elhanan was startled. A moment of his past came back to him in gusts. He should have devoted more time to therapy. But what about the teaching? Was he wrong to combine the two callings?

The woman took his hands. "Now it's my turn to help you," she said. "Just tell me how."

"Another time," Elhanan said.

She left in haste. At the door, out of his sight, she burst into tears.

Other visitors came to the house, former students and patients. Malkiel had never realized it, but his father enjoyed a solid reputation in the academic community. Because he was likable? and good? and wise? Because he greeted every man and woman without condescension? No one had ever heard him raise his voice.

"Do you see?" Malkiel asked him. "When you talk, your brain works better. Why not try to tell us more about your life?"

Very late one evening, Elhanan asked for a glass of hot tea, cleared his throat and invited Malkiel and Tamar to sit on the edge of the bed. "Usually," he said between sips, "a man talks and cannot make himself heard. Just imagine if a man could make himself heard without talking! I would have liked to be that man."

Without consulting each other, Tamar and Malkiel kissed him on his forehead.

Old Haskel, shivering Haskel, Elhanan remembered him. He was always cold, Haskel, hence the nickname. Beard, mustache, bushy sidelocks—he rubbed his hands for warmth while he talked, while he prayed, even while he ate. Elhanan was fond of him. He saw him in the morning, at the *mikvah*. Haskel was in charge of the ritual baths, and he never spoke. He greeted his guests with nods and indicated by gestures where they could go to undress.

Was he mute from birth? They said he had been a preacher in a Ukrainian village. They said he drew great crowds, and made them weep, and incited them to repentance. They said so many things about him. Did he know that? He never showed it.

Yet there was some truth to the rumors, as Elhanan learned from his father. Haskel was not a simple bath attendant. His muteness was not a whim. It was imposed upon him by his talent and his preacher's calling.

Some years before, on a Thursday afternoon, he had appeared—hungry, haggard, a bundle on his shoulder—before the rabbi of Feherfalu, to pay his respects and ask permission to preach that Saturday afternoon in the great synagogue. The rabbi questioned him, and admired his learning as much as his piety, and granted permission. Better yet: the rabbi promised to come himself and listen.

The synagogue was full, as if it were the eve of Yom Kippur. Men old and young, learned Talmudic scholars and simple artisans, students and merchants—they were all there. They all wanted to hear this preacher, whose reputation had preceded him. Was he really so eloquent? Yes indeed, he was. Draped in his tallith, he ascended the bimah, kissed the purple velvet cloth that covered the holy ark, leaned on the pulpit and commenced his discussion of the week's *Sidrah* in melodious and incantatory tones. His text was Joseph's reunion with his brothers in Egypt. The text says, "*Vayi-*

tapek Joseph, Joseph controlled himself and refrained from bursting into tears." From which we draw the lesson: It is better not to display our emotions; secret sobs are more real than the others. The orator developed this theme for an hour, dazzling his audience with Talmudic quotations, legends from the Midrash and references to Mussar literature. In the front rows wise men nodded and agreed with his every conclusion. The Hasidim loved these stories. The rabbi, eyes closed, listened with an air of admiring concentration.

And suddenly the preacher stopped. He looked at his audience and seemed to hesitate. Would he go on, or would he not? He shook himself and, in a quieter voice, more intense and intimate, began to speak not of the remote or immediate past but of the present. "But there comes a time when one cannot, one must not, contain one's sorrow. To weep, Joseph had to leave his brothers. I am only a simple Jew." Abruptly he pulled the tallith down over his forehead. They could not see his eyes. They could see only his mouth, twisted in pain. "Joseph wept," the orator went on. "Why did he weep? Because he had just found his brothers again? I shall never find mine. Joseph's brothers were still alive, and mine are not. The enemy has killed my brothers." The narrative followed, a chain of bitter tragedies. In the balcony, women sobbed. Down below, the young students could not understand why the old men had lowered their gaze. At some point the rabbi, who had been seated on the bimah, approached the speaker and whispered a few words in his ear. The orator looked at him from beneath the tallith and answered in a loud, clear voice, "I know, I know that today is the Sabbath, and that one has no right to be sad during the Sabbath, but my pain is too great."

The rabbi asked him most gently, "Is it *piku'ah-nefesh*? Is it a matter of life and death? If so, you may continue; if not . . ." The rabbi went back to his seat. After a long silence the speaker stepped backward down the steps of the bimah and went to sit at the rear of the room.

When the Sabbath was over, Reb Haskel was called to the rabbi's house. The two men remained sequestered until dawn. They went to the ritual bath together, and to the morning service, and took a glass of tea together and plunged into their studies until evening. Next morning the itinerant preacher left town.

He reappeared three or four years later. He was unrecognizable, like a beggar or penitent. He no longer wished to preach in the synagogue; in fact, he no longer wished to speak at all. What had changed him? They said that in distant communities he had spent his time trying to tell all that he had seen and lived through, to people who refused to listen. He called out to them in the synagogue, in the marketplace, in their homes. "Do not turn away from me," he cried. "Your lives and the lives of your children depend upon it." They were all happy to hear him discourse on the Bible and the commentaries, but as soon as he touched upon the present, they turned a deaf ear. They pitied him, they avoided him, they took him for a madman. Did he choose silence, or was it imposed upon him?

Elhanan had loved this man.

Today he loved him even more.

In August the labor battalion of Hungarian Jews left Stanislav for the Russian front, where Major Bartoldy's division was committed to battle as part of the German formation.

How many times did Elhanan try to return to his hometown? His companion Itzik the Long moved heaven and earth to dig up a smuggler somewhere to cross the border illegally, but it was no use. They were too close to the frontier, and the whole region was under tight German surveillance. To be stopped meant arrest and death.

"Be patient," Itzik said. "Stay with us. The battalion moves around a lot. Sooner or later we'll wind up in your town."

When word of their departure for the front came through, they greeted it with a sort of skeptical confidence. "Who knows? Maybe God has heard our prayers."

No. The battalion did not return to Hungary. It crossed Poland as far as the Ukraine, and went on toward White Russia. Berdichev, Zhitomir, Rovno, Kiev, Minsk: rubble and ruins everywhere. Terror and hatred sown by the invader. Why did Elhanan whimper so often at night? Because he was ever farther from his parents? Or because the names of these places roused warm and melancholy yearnings? Berdichev he knew. In his memory Berdichev was the famous Rabbi Levi-Yitzhak of Berdichev, celebrated for the exalted love he bore his people. The Defender of Israel is what they called him, and the title suited him. He never hesitated to lodge a complaint with the Creator of the Universe, to force Him to come to the aid of his unfortunate children. Where are you now, Rabbi? Elhanan asked. Since you are up there in heaven, do something! Look at your city: where are the Jews hiding? Elhanan looked for them. They had disappeared. In Oman, too, he sought them. Disappeared. Swallowed up.

"So stop praying," said Itzik. "What good does all this lamentation do you?"

"Oman," Elhanan answered. "You don't know Oman. For me Oman is Rabbi Nahman, Hasidism's incomparable storyteller. His grave is here. I'd give anything to visit it." His wish was granted. The battalion spent a night in Oman, and Elhanan persuaded Itzik to come to the cemetery with him. They were not alone. The whole battalion gathered there to chant psalms and Kaddish. *"You, Rabbi, who love stories, hear our own, the story we are living."*

The battalion celebrated Rosh Hashanah in Kiev. Miracle of miracles: the major allowed the Jewish laborers to observe their holidays. Yes indeed, while the Germans were systematically massacring the Russian Jews, a few hundred Jews in Hungarian uniforms were living, working and praying as Jews. During services they were surprised to see three men join them. "We live in hiding in the forest," they said. "They told us that Jews were celebrating the holiday, so we took a chance and came to mingle our prayers with yours." After the service, they described the death of Kiev's Jews. Between Rosh Hashanah and Yom Kippur the year before, the Germans assassinated ten thousand Jews a day in the ravine at Babi Yar. "It's the same everywhere," they said. "Borisov, Smolensk, Vinnitsa, Poltava, Dnepropetrovsk—the German angel of death swooped down on all these communities. And others. If it keeps up this way, there won't be a Jew left under the sun." Huddled and incredulous, the Jewish laborers listened, frozen in disbelief. This is only a nightmare, they told themselves. The world has not gone mad. Elhanan said to Itzik, "It's crazy. All the Jews dead, and we're still alive. It's crazy." The three visitors from Kiev left them at nightfall. "If you come back this way, we'll see you again." "God keep you, Jewish brothers." "You too."

Few of the laborers slept that night. Lying on cots or straw pallets, they whispered their fears to one another. Should they believe this or not? No one doubted that the Germans were killing Jews. There had been massacres; that was certain. But Elhanan and Itzik could not believe that this criminal enterprise had attained such a degree of perfection. "You don't kill hundreds of thousands of men, women and children just like that," Itzik said, "without the earth itself trembling."

"But those three Jews—"

"On one side you have three Jews. On the other side you have common sense. Which are you going to believe?"

All the laborers joined the debate. "Itzik," Elhanan said, "when I reach home they'll ask me about all this. What shall I tell them?"

Itzik thought it over for a while before answering. "Tell them we chanted psalms in Oman."

"And?"

"We celebrated Rosh Hashanah in Kiev."

"And?"

"Tell them that . . . that if we had to weep for all the dead, the world would drown in our tears."

Should he speak of the sadness that never left him? The anger that welled up inside him, at once clear and dark, ready to pour over a powerful and evil people which had placed itself at the service of Death? How could he find the words for it? And who would listen to him? Who would believe him?

Behind the front lines the Jewish labor battalion was never in real danger. Elhanan and Itzik, inseparable, were attached to the Quartermaster Corps, chopping wood and repairing the officers' uniforms and vehicles. Elhanan escaped the hardest work because he was so young. In winter he worked in the kitchens. That did not protect him from a severe case of flu. Bedridden for ten days, he had a visit from Major Bartoldy. "I'm going back to your hometown," the major said. "I'd like to take you with me, but it's a long way and too risky. Is there a message for your parents?"

Despite his fever Elhanan filled a sheet of paper: he was doing well, there was no need to worry, he hoped to be home soon and would never leave again. The major returned two weeks later and delivered a package of food, some warm clothes and a letter. "We pray to God to bring you home quickly. The house is empty without you. Life goes on here. . . . I hope," his father wrote, "that you are not forgetting to wear your tefillin every morning."

After Stalingrad the front contracted inexorably. Now the Jewish battalion was ahead of the Hungarian army. The latter, hounded by the Russians, suffered serious losses. "You see?" Itzik said. "We're going home." They retraced their route, passing through the same towns, the same villages. But now these places were in ruins. They found families in mourning and orphans with numb expressions. In Oman the Jewish laborers again visited Rabbi Nahman's tomb. A peasant told them that men came there every night and had been heard praying. In Kiev they stopped for two days, hoping to find the three escaped Jews. Itzik and Elhanan combed the desolate city from end to end; not a Jewish face in sight. Not a Jewish voice in the whole area. Killed, the last Jew in Kiev. In their bivouac at night the Jewish laborers were reunited with their three local friends. "The Germans are on the run," they said, laughing strangely. "How sweet it is to see them go! Their days of pride are over." And their days of cruelty? "No, no, they're just as vicious as before, maybe more so." Elhanan wondered why these three survivors laughed so oddly. There was no joy in their laughter, no triumph, no satisfaction or pride. "It's a laugh that comes from beyond happiness and sadness," Itzik said. "From beyond faith and anger. It's a laugh that only the dead could appreciate." And their three visitors confirmed it: "That's the truth, we're not alive anymore; we saw too much and heard too much. That's why we could take such risks. We're partisans. We'll have our revenge; not enough, but we'll do our best." The one who did the talking was called Volodia; the others laughed like him and with him but contributed only isolated words, half-sentences. Volodia was a strapping man with broad shoulders and strong hands. The second was called David, an avowed Communist and atheist; he was short and younger. Lev was the eldest of the three; he was secretive and sad. "How do you become a partisan?" Elhanan asked. "How do you become an avenger?" asked Itzik. "Come with us and we'll show you," Volodia said.

The partisans left at dawn and promised to be back the next night. "We'll take whoever wants to join us," Volodia said.

"What shall we do?" Elhanan asked Itzik. He could not hide his confusion, and Itzik was no less confused. In their battalion they were at least under the protection of the Hungarian army, but if they fled . . . The next night David appeared alone at the bivouac. "Where are your friends?" they asked him. "We had a little firefight with the Germans," David told them. "Volodia's dead. Lev's badly wounded." Elhanan was stunned and cried out, "Volodia dead? He was so strong, so . . . so . . ." He had admired Volodia, was drawn to him, and could not imagine him dead. "Don't weep for Volodia," David said. "He died a hero's death. He took a bunch of those killers with him." A heavy silence set in. What were they to do now? Move out? "It's not that easy," David said. "The Germans have sealed off the whole area. We'll have to wait for our moment." Sure of his route, knowing every corner of the region, David left the bivouac alone to rendezvous with his fellow partisans. "We'll meet again soon," he said to Elhanan. "And when we do," Itzik put in, "we'll show the Germans what we're made of."

The retreat continued. Germans, Italians, Hungarians, Romanians all evacuated forest after forest, region after region, harassed by intrepid partisans and pursued by implacable Russians. Despite cold and hunger, fatigue and anguish, Elhanan rejoiced to see the lords of bloody conquest in flight. They had invaded Russia singing, and now they were howling in anger, insulting the Italians and their mandolins, calling the Hungarians cowards and despising the Romanians for their poverty. The warriors were no longer so happy to be waging war.

One day when the battalion was resting in a Ukrainian village, a German officer came out of nowhere and ordered ten men to follow him. Itzik the Long hurried to find the Hungarian officer who in the major's absence assumed command. "I have two vehicles stuck in the mud," said the German. "I need ten men to pull them out."

"My men are exhausted," said the Hungarian officer.

"This is an order."

"We're the same rank. I don't take orders from you."

Impassively the German pulled his revolver. "If you don't follow orders from an officer of the Wehrmacht, I'll shoot you down."

They glared, full of hate, awaiting some sign to start fighting. In the end the Hungarian yielded. "They're only Jews. Take as many as you need."

The German put away his revolver and shook hands, all elegance, with his comrade in arms. "Were you ready to die for a bunch of Jews? I don't understand you."

"Not at all," said the Hungarian. "I was ready to die for a principle."

"But you see," said the German, smiling, "I am ready to kill for a principle."

Of the ten laborers, only seven returned. The German officer had shot the others in cold blood. "You surely know," he told the survivors, "that an officer of the Third Reich follows his Führer's lead: he keeps his promises."

These gratuitous murders made up Itzik's mind. "The first chance we get, you hear me? The first chance we get, we take off. They'll see how a Jew takes revenge."

A few weeks later, Major Bartoldy was blown to bits by a shell. The officer who replaced him, a young Nyilas, insolent and hateful, announced to the Jewish laborers that their "loafing" was over; he would personally see to it that not one of them left these snowy fields alive.

It was a frigid November night. Ghosts drifted through the petrified forest. Better dressed than ordinary soldiers, who had only their patched uniforms, the Jewish laborers were ordered by their new major to take off their sweaters and warm underclothes: "There's no justice," he shouted. "Brave Hungarian soldiers defending their fatherland against a Bolshevik plague are freezing to death, and you good-for-nothing kikes think you're at the winter Olympics."

Zelig, Maurice, Peter and a jovial weaver—Wolfe Neuman—came down with pneumonia and died quickly.

"All right," said Itzik. "Understood? Let's be ready."

In early December the cold clamped down even harder. You couldn't stick your nose outside. The battalion was paralyzed. The machinery froze. The living dug in like the dead. The front stabilized, but for how long? The Polish border was close but seemed as inaccessible as the Holy Land. Where would they find partisans? If God willed it, anything was possible. God willed it.

And it was David who served as messenger—David, the survivor of the three friends. The Communist, the atheist. In the dead of night he showed up at the bivouac. Parka, fur jacket, fur-lined boots: he looked like a wild animal, though friendly and mischievous. He pulled out a bottle of vodka, which he passed around. "Tell us everything, David!"

"It's been a while since—"

"Where have you been? Tell us."

He was glad to tell them. The partisans had followed the battalion. Their tactics were to stay mobile and keep ahead of the front, mounting sabotage operations in the enemy's rear so as to hold up reinforcements. "We're not far from here, men," he said. "So don't be foolish. Come fight alongside us. Tomorrow will be too late. Jump aboard before the train pulls out."

It was four in the morning. With no warning the anti-Semitic major barged into the tent. "What the hell is this?" he roared. "A midnight meeting? A plot? An insurrection? I'll teach you how to live. I'm going—"

He wasn't going anywhere; or rather he went a long way, as far as death itself. David smashed the major's skull with one blow of the bottle. Terror spread across the Jewish faces. A mutiny meant the firing squad.

"Good riddance," the young partisan said. "Now there's no turning back. Strip him. Take his boots. I'll take his pistol."

Someone felt that the dead man was entitled to a moment's pity.

David feigned agreement: "You're right. The poor son of a bitch may freeze to death."

Some fifty of them escaped. Two partisans were waiting about ten minutes outside of camp. David questioned them briefly. "No problems?"

"None."

An hour or two later, they reached the partisan camp, where Elhanan discovered whole Jewish families, children too.

"Surprised?" David laughed. "You think only grown men make partisans? Everybody's welcome here. Even children. If you only knew how daring Jewish children can be."

A new life began for Elhanan Rosenbaum. Instantly adopted by the *otriad,* the Hungarian-Jewish laborers were quickly integrated. Still inseparable, Itzik and Elhanan were assigned to a unit that attacked German convoys. A week after they arrived, they had already liberated one machine gun and one pistol from the enemy. David offered public congratulations: "Well done, you two. Elhanan, now we know what a Talmudic scholar can do."

A young woman from Kharkov, her hair hidden by a fur hat, kissed him on the mouth. Her face glowed with beauty and warmth. To Elhanan she was the woman he had never encountered. "Listen, young man," she said. "You look shy and brave to me. If you want, I'll take care of you."

"What do you mean?" Elhanan stammered.

"Don't you feel lonely here?"

"No. I have Itzik. He's my best friend."

"It's not the same thing."

Partisans started to needle him gently. "She doesn't bite. What are you scared of?"

"Leave him alone," she said.

When the others had gone off, he asked, "What's your name?"

"Vitka. My name is Vitka." She was a widow. Her husband and two children had been killed.

"You were married young," Elhanan said, to show that he was not as shy as she thought.

"Go on," she said. "I love flattery."

Elhanan coughed, and hesitated, and then decided. "I would like to be with you," he said, not looking at her. "On one condition: don't try to separate me from my friend."

"I promise."

So they formed a team with Itzik the Avenger, as people called him from then on. He wasn't interested in demolishing tanks with Molotov cocktails. What he liked to do was kill Germans. "If they're so fond of Death, let them marry it."

Of course Elhanan was in love with Vitka. Of course he didn't dare show it. Of course everybody knew it.

"Go love her," Itzik said. "She loves you, too, believe me. I know all about love. If you let her slip away, watch out, some other man won't be so slow!"

"Who?"

"Me." Itzik laughed.

"I don't believe you," Elhanan said.

After all, wasn't friendship stronger than love?

In a little Ukrainian hamlet the *otriad* was assaulted by a band of urchins. Emaciated, ravenous, they had no strength left to beg; they only stared. But such suffering shadowed their eyes that Itzik and Elhanan gave out all the bread they had. "Who are you?"

The children were afraid to answer.

"Jews?"

Panic-stricken, they looked for ways to flee.

"Don't be afraid," Itzik said. "We're all Jews."

The children exchanged incredulous glances.

"You speak Yiddish? We do. Listen." Itzik and Elhanan conversed briefly in Yiddish.

Relieved, the children grimaced. "Yes. We're Jews."

"What did the Germans do to you?"

The Germans had locked them into a barn. Without food. Several days, a week. Some had gone mad, others had died of thirst.

"Who liberated you?"

"A peasant."

"No, it was a logger."

"No, it was a robber."

"It was the prophet Elijah."

As they devoured their bread they went on squabbling. Poor kids, Itzik murmured. He stared at them for a few moments and then seemed to reach a decision. "Come on, kids. Follow me."

He led them to a cabin at the edge of the village where six German prisoners were being held. He turned to one of the boys, handed over his submachine gun and said gently, almost tenderly, "Fire, boy. Fire at the whole lot!"

The boy trembled. He looked at the weapon, examined his own hand, seemed to hold a debate with an invisible presence and finally said, "I don't know how."

"Don't worry," Itzik said. "I'll show you."

The boy lowered his eyes and said, "No."

Itzik turned to another. The same answer. A third. Still the same answer.

Itzik clapped them all on the shoulder and said, "All right, all right, I understand. Later on you'll know how."

God of Israel, Elhanan thought, watch these Your children and be proud.

Somewhere in Polish Galicia one night the *otriad* sheltered a Soviet paratrooper. He was carrying a radio and passed along an order from headquarters to David: stop a convoy of German armored cars. Moscow considered this operation of the highest priority. The partisans prepared feverishly. David brought his lieutenants together to organize the attack. The convoy was to pass through the village of Turek early in the afternoon three days later.

Elhanan and Vitka, disguised as peasants, bundled up from head to toe, trudged to the village to reconnoiter. How many Germans were on hand? How many police collaborators? It went well. Vitka and Elhanan brought back accurate and useful intelligence: so many soldiers, so many police. All in all, the village was thinly populated, almost a ghost town. There were many cottages without smoke.

"You're sure of that?" David was insistent.

"As sure as anyone can be," Elhanan said.

"Are you ready to go in again tomorrow?"

"Why not?"

"We have to know where to set up our machine guns. Find two or three empty huts along the roadside, near a bend if possible."

Vitka and Elhanan went back to Turek. They inspected several huts, prowled outside three or four wooden houses, and broke into the wrong one. Elhanan was taken prisoner. Vitka got away.

"Come here," said a shrewd and surly Polish policeman. Elhanan obeyed.

The policeman punched him in the face. "That's just to get acquainted," he explained politely. Another blow, and a third. "Now, while I rest, you're going to tell us who you are, what you're looking for and who sent you."

Elhanan understood Polish but spoke it badly. In any case he would have held his tongue; once you started answering, you ended up telling all.

"Hey, men," said the Polish policeman, "we got us a tough guy. Come look at this."

Three smiling torturers set about beating Elhanan. His head, his chest, his stomach. He felt as if he were floating on air and falling down a well. Blood gushed from his nose. He was suffocating. He passed out.

He woke with a heavy, aching body, on a farm the Polish police had requisitioned to interrogate chicken thieves, black marketeers and drunks, far from German surveillance. From time to time they brought in Jews with false documents who were trying to pass for Aryans. "Now, my little kike, no more aggravation, all right?" The same policeman was kicking him, not to hurt him, only in fun. "What's your name? Avrom? You're a kike, we know that, we took down your pants. So we know what you are but not who you are. Who's been sheltering you?"

Elhanan wondered, How long have I been here? Through the slit of his swollen eyelid he saw an oil lamp on a large kitchen table. What time is it? Nighttime yet? He pictured Vitka: let her be free and safe, O Lord.

There, too, if God willed, anything could happen. And God was good enough to will it. Vitka was free. She had rejoined her comrades and was trying to talk them into following her to the village, attacking the farm and liberating Elhanan. A few of the men objected. "Is it worth it, to kill us all for the sake of one?"

The Soviet paratrooper made a weighty argument. "This raid may be the right thing to do, but won't it compromise the mission general headquarters has ordered?"

Vitka lost her temper. "I don't see why. I take four men with me, volunteers, of course, and before you can blink we're back with our—"

"In saving your friend, you'll reveal our whereabouts to the Germans."

Vitka was no amateur. "The Germans know very well that we're around."

David made a decision. "We'll do it. Solidarity is not an empty word." And to the paratrooper, "Also, Elhanan knows our plans. Let's save him before he cracks."

Vitka protested, "He won't crack."

David threw her a stern look; she swallowed the rest of her speech.

Elhanan was half conscious when he heard, as if in a fever, the sounds of a fight. They had broken down the door and invaded the farmhouse. The three policemen were on their feet, hands up, and they stank of fear.

"All right, little one. It's all over," Vitka said. Kneeling above him, she was wiping his face. "Did they make a mess of you?" When Elhanan gave no answer, she turned to the policemen. "Which one beat him?" Silence. "Which one is the interrogator?" Silence. Staring straight ahead, the police shook their heads, no.

"Let me do this," Itzik said. They left him alone with the policemen. Half an hour later, he came out. "They won't be beating any more Jews," he growled.

They made it back to camp without incident.

That night Elhanan and Vitka did not separate. She bandaged his wounds and comforted him, stayed at his bedside and watched over his sleep. In the morning he woke before the rest. Vitka smiled at him. "Better?"

"Much better."

She held him to her. "Sleep. It will do you good."

"One question, Vitka. What did Itzik do to the policemen?"

"I don't know."

"He didn't say?"

"Not a word."

"What do you think he did?"

"I don't know, but—"

"But what?"

"I'm sure they got what they deserved."

Elhanan fell back asleep.

Next day they attacked. It went off as planned. Four machine guns in huts at the entrance and exit to the village. Mines, Molotov cocktails and grenades. Organized to be the *otriad*'s most ambitious operation, this would remain its biggest success. Two tanks on fire, eight vehicles destroyed, thirty-odd Germans killed. For the partisans, two dead and five wounded. Among the dead, Vitka.

Elhanan wept in secret; the whole *otriad* wept openly. All but Itzik, who clenched his teeth and vowed revenge.

Vitka and her comrade were to be buried in the forest, as was customary. Elhanan had a better idea: "I saw a Jewish cemetery nearby."

"Let's go there," David decided.

A nighttime burial. Solemn and sorrowful. Shadows digging two graves for shadows. Murmurs instead of words, mute tears as the funeral oration. Who will say Kaddish? They all said it, in a low voice. Lianka, who was younger than Elhanan, took his arm during the prayer. "I know how you feel," she whispered on the way back. She had lost her boyfriend the year before.

The *otriad* moved on. Other goals and other targets awaited them. Soon Elhanan and Lianka were a couple. Had he forgotten Vitka? Of course not. It was something else altogether: because he had loved Vitka, he was capable of loving Lianka. He had loved Vitka so much that the love overflowed; there was still enough in him for Lianka and the whole *otriad*.

In spring the partisans pitched camp about seventy miles from Feherfalu. Purim in the Carpathians. Passover in a remote mountain village. Being youngest, Lianka asked the four ritual questions. "Why is this night different from all other nights?" David improvised a response: "Because the Jews are fighting their enemy and we have sworn not to lay down our arms until he is defeated." And Itzik added, "Because we know that revenge is near." And Elhanan thought, Because I'm close to home, almost under my parents' roof. The Seder ended with the traditional promise: "Next year in Jerusalem."

"I wonder how many of us will live long enough to keep that promise," Elhanan said to Itzik.

"You and I will be there. But between now and then, a flood of German blood will flow. That, too, I promise."

"All you can think of is revenge."

"And what do you think about?"

"My parents. Where are they? How are they doing? Who are they celebrating this Seder with?"

He had not noticed Lianka coming closer. She took his hand as if to say, I know and I understand.

Over the following days Elhanan tried to persuade David to send him into Feherfalu.

"Are you crazy? There's the whole front between us and the town."

"I know every inch of it."

David would not be persuaded. "Patience, Elhanan. You'll show me your town before too long. You'll introduce me to your parents. Be patient."

Nervous, worrying, Elhanan hardly slept nights. He pictured his homecoming. His mother and father. Had they changed, had they aged? He'd introduce Lianka to them. He was sure they'd like her.

Unfortunately, the front stabilized. The Russian offensive pausing for rest? Stiffer resistance from the German army? Battles raged, but if they advanced a few miles one day, it was only to withdraw the next. April passed, and then May. In June the offensive picked up speed again. Now the Red Army was operating in full liaison with the partisans. David's group was attached to the divisional staff, just as divisional officers were assigned to the partisans.

Elhanan struck up a friendship with a one-armed captain. He had a mustache and was called Podriatchik. He was from Borisov and had been in the lines since the German invasion. Elhanan loved hearing his stories. The Russian's voice was a solemn, melodious bass, and he chanted as he spoke. He sensed Elhanan's curiosity. "You want to know how I lost my arm? I got careless because I was impatient. I wanted to take out a tank with grenades. But I pulled the pin too soon. The grenade went off and my arm with it. A partisan should have known better."

Elhanan's impatience increased when he heard that the unit was to infiltrate Stanislav and blow up a military restaurant. Of course he volunteered. David hesitated. "You're not up to it. You're running a risk—emotion may take over. One precipitous move, one careless gesture, and the operation fails."

More stubborn than ever, Elhanan argued that, on the contrary, his presence would be an asset. "Two men know this territory," he said. "Itzik and I. We've been in Stanislav. All right, I've never lived there, but I know my way around. I bet the military restaurant is on the main square. It may even be in the house where I spent my first night away from my family." He argued with logic and passion, took care not to let himself get carried away, be overcome by the enthusiasm, the exaltation that flooded his heart. "Listen, David, you need somebody like me. Why are you holding me back?"

"You're not yourself these days. I'm worried about you."

"I'll be careful. I promise."

He won Itzik's support, and David gave way to their combined pressure. He was still worried, but he gave his consent.

The plan: Lianka and Elhanan would go down to Stanislav as scouts, reconnoitering and evaluating. Itzik and his group of ten—including two peasant girls, Lisa and Dora—would infiltrate alone or in pairs from different directions and converge on the square at six in the evening. With grenades, pistols and Molotov cocktails, they'd wait for Itzik's signal to launch the attack. Problems: how to approach the target without attracting attention; how to make sure the restaurant wasn't empty; how to coordinate the attack for maximum efficiency. Elhanan had an idea. "I remember a movie on the square—am I right, Itzik?"

"Right. I remember it too."

"If we all stood in line for tickets?"

"A good idea—if the movie's open."

"If it's closed we can stand in line at one of the stores."

"How will we know?"

"Lianka and I are going in first. We'll find a way to tell you."

David approved the plan. Itzik and Elhanan shook hands, in perfect complicity.

Very early the next morning, two young villagers joined the hundreds of peasants and workmen trooping into Stanislav. Their anxiety looked normal. What would this day bring? Lianka hardly spoke. She was like that, reticent, shy. Elhanan tried to cheer her up, but it was no use. Anyway, they had to stay alert. They spoke Polish badly. More precisely, they spoke a mixture of Russian and Ukrainian that might, in a noisy room, pass for Polish. Better to keep quiet and go unnoticed. Fortune smiled on them. There was no checkpoint at the entrance to town. The streets were crowded. There were lines forming at the municipal offices for ration cards and travel permits. Elhanan noticed the movie house. A large sign announced that it was reserved for German soldiers. Too bad; they'd have to find something else. The building next door: a hotel. Reserved for German officers. Across the street, a restaurant. *The* military restaurant for staff officers. On the ground floor. No guards. The Germans felt safe. From the partisans' point of view, the unprotected target was ideal: they would only have to open a door or break a window, throw an incendiary bottle—thirty to sixty seconds and it would be all over. While the grenades blew, it would be easy to withdraw. To race out of town and head for the forest. But how to relay all this to Itzik? Lianka stopped in front of a shop and couldn't suppress her excitement. "Look," she said.

A notice like so many others. Distribution of sugar and flour for A-1 and D-3 coupons, from five to seven that evening.

"Bravo," Elhanan said. "We'll stand in line."

And how would they keep busy until then? If they loitered, they'd be spotted.

"Shall we go to the ghetto?" Elhanan said.

"You're crazy. You think you can go in and out just like that?"

"I know a secret passage."

They found it. Was Elhanan excited? Overexcited. He wasn't walking, he was flying. He dragged Lianka behind him, and she had to quicken her step. They might have been rushing to meet a vanished relative. Elhanan struck a match. Another. A third. He pushed at a manhole cover: they were outside again, free and clear.

Lianka asked, "Are you sure we're in the ghetto?"

"What a question . . ." But he was suddenly struck by doubt: was this the ghetto? Then where were its inhabitants? Why this silence, why no living soul in sight? Where were the children, hollow-eyed with hunger, the mute, blind old people, the mad-eyed mothers—what night had engulfed them?

"I don't understand," he said. And then, "I'll never understand."

"I do," Lianka said, her hand on her lips.

Immersed in his bitter, dark memories, Elhanan seemed so remote that Lianka shook him. "You look desperate, Elhanan. Let's get out of here. If they see you they'll know you're a Jew; they'll know by your face. Think about Itzik, about all the others and their fight, our fight."

She dragged him into a dilapidated house. It smelled musty and seemed abandoned. Broken dishes, torn books, dirty clothes, were all that remained of one Jewish family's treasures. Elhanan sank to the floor, and Lianka joined him. She grew older, Lianka did. Riper. Tender, infinitely tender.

"You have to forget, Elhanan," she said, taking his hand.

"I can't forget. I don't want to forget. In my mind this ghetto was alive; now it's dead. It's as if I'd killed it myself."

"Don't talk nonsense. You know very well you had nothing to do with it. Make an effort. For now anyway you must forget. Otherwise you'll be like Itzik: possessed. All he thinks about is revenge."

"Are you judging him?"

"No. What right have I to judge him? But I'm not sure revenge is the answer."

"Why wouldn't it be? Why not punish murderers? Why not make their accomplices tremble?"

"I don't know, Elhanan. Those are good questions. Ones that matter. But can I answer them? I may be young, but I've learned enough to be suspicious of avengers."

"And justice, Lianka? Don't you believe justice must be done?"

"Yes, I believe it must."

"So? Isn't the avenger a dispenser of justice?"

"Yes, but—"

"But what?"

"I don't know. I only know that I would never be able to kill a man in cold blood."

"Even a murderer?"

Shaken, Lianka pleaded, "I can't see myself as someone who puts people to death, kills unarmed men. Don't force me to say things I don't mean, Elhanan. Don't."

Touched, Elhanan broke off the conversation. They lay for an hour or two, or three, close together, giving each other courage. Outside it was springtime. In the distance there were trees; they could imagine the sun timidly exploring a cloud-streaked sky. Here in the ghetto there was a void, a strange void populated by ghosts.

Desiccation. Dust. Ashes. Here life was extinct: what remained of a community carried off by a tempest?

"I wonder," Elhanan said, "I wonder what's happening in my hometown."

"You'll know soon. Don't think about it. Think about now."

"You're tougher than I thought."

Lianka bowed her head. "There's a time for everything."

Two young people abandoned by a world thirsty for blood, fire and hatred. Two mouths seeking each other. Two hearts open to each other's pain. Two souls conversing, two memories calling, each to the other.

"When I was young," Elhanan said, "I was not afraid of dying but of waiting for death."

The hours passed, and the two partisans exchanged memories of childhood and times of trial, bound themselves together and shared secrets as if they were alone in the world, as in fact they were: the contours of the ghetto were the contours of their world, and that world had been drained of beauty and life. For how long? They did not know and had no way of guessing. They were the last Jews in Stanislav.

While they waited to go back to the main square, Feherfalu was ridding itself of its own Jews; but Elhanan and Lianka had no way of knowing that either. The ghetto in Feherfalu, invaded by Hungarian gendarmes and German officers, was evacuating its humble and unhappy inhabitants to an unknown destination, and Elhanan and Lianka could not know that.

Lianka was already an orphan. Elhanan had lost his father and was about to lose his mother, but the birds in the sky brought them no news of all that. Elhanan and Lianka had to cling to the present, to discover themselves in each other, to offer each other reasons for hope.

The afternoon seemed too long, yet suddenly too short. They were hungry and thirsty; exhausted. They would have liked to stay in that abandoned house with leprous walls until tomorrow, until the end of time. But they forced themselves onto their feet. A sense of duty? No, solidarity. Itzik and his men were already on the road. They would soon be in town and would look for their scouts.

"Ready?"

"Ready."

Everything went according to plan. No one suspected them. It was almost five in the afternoon. There was still a line outside the shop. Elhanan and Lianka joined it. Other customers came along, but the two partisans made room for them. From where they were they could observe the hotel and the restaurant. German officers crowded into both. Thank you, Lord. Let them eat, let them drink, let them shout their joy as masters of the humble and the pure in heart. Let them celebrate their power. Their lust for it will soon die.

Soon was now. Itzik arrived, sauntering casually. With his cap half covering his eyes, he looked like a workman hurrying nowhere. Lisa and Dora emerged from the alleyway on the left, hand in hand. In less than twenty minutes the whole team was in place. Four partisans kept watch in the next street: they would cover the retreat.

Itzik was standing behind Elhanan and Lianka. He greeted the girl just like a flirt. She smiled at him and blushed. They whispered a few words that Elhanan heard. It was all quite clear. Two grenades through the open door: Lisa and Dora to toss them. Four incendiary bottles through the window. And we run. When? At six-fifteen sharp, when it won't be hard to lose yourself in the crowd approaching the restaurant. The watch ticked, the shadows lengthened.

Now. Itzik casually slipped out of line and wandered toward the restaurant. He opened the door as if to take a peek inside. In the next instant a deafening roar shattered the main square. That's for Vitka, Itzik shouted in Yiddish. Lisa and Dora were already at his side. A window opened and everything blew up at once. It was like a bombardment, a barrage of shellfire. Furniture flew through the air, shards of glass carpeted the sidewalk. Elhanan thought, Ha! How easy it is to destroy! Shouts in German, in Polish. Men firing blindly. People running every which way. Police shouting. Germans issuing orders that no one understood. Time to regroup, and the partisans were already in a dark alley behind the square. They left town running, breathless. Suddenly Itzik cried, "Elhanan! Where the hell has he gone?"

Elhanan had been left behind. Dead? Wounded? Taken prisoner?

"I saw him two minutes ago," Lianka said.

"What held him up?"

Impatient voices rose. "He'll make out all right. He knows the area. There's not a minute to lose."

"I'll wait for him," Lianka said.

Itzik hesitated. Could he abandon his friend for the sake of his unit? Itzik was torn. Meanwhile the debate intensified. But Elhanan's return put an end to it. He was out of breath but satisfied.

"Let's pull out," Itzik ordered.

The sky was darkening now. Here and there a door opened a crack to see who was defying the police and the night. The townspeople had no idea that these were Jewish partisans; they thought it was the secret army, the Armia Krajova. "Good luck, men!" shouted a few old patriots. At last the partisans were sheltered by the forest. But Itzik allowed no respite. Hurry, he told them, panting. Hurry: only that would save them. After what seemed hours of running they reached camp, where David greeted them, almost mad with worry.

Itzik asked Elhanan, "Can I see you alone for a minute?"

"Of course."

"Tell me. Why did you stay behind?"

Elhanan's face clouded. "I'd rather you didn't ask me that."

"You endangered the whole group. I must know."

Elhanan rubbed his brow and thought. "Some other time, Itzik."

"Now." Itzik was angry. "Why did you endanger us all for no reason?"

"I didn't realize," Elhanan said, contrite. "It was a stupid impulse. . . . I wanted to—"

He broke off, but Itzik pressed him: "You wanted to what? You tell me, or next time I won't trust you."

Elhanan did not reply immediately. Why this sadness within? His friend's confidence and affection meant so much. "All right. I don't know how to tell you. I saw the grenades go off. I heard the wounded men shrieking. And I suddenly felt a crazy desire to go right up to the window and look inside, and see these killers laid out, flat on the floor, see them wounded, whimpering in pain, calling for help. Well, I saw them. Mutilated. Their faces twisted. I thought about the ghetto we visited once—do you remember?—and I was furious, and I pulled my pistol and fired into the whole bunch, roaring like a madman, 'That's for the ghetto! And that's for my uncle! And that's for all the Jews you persecuted, humiliated, starved, assassinated!' " A sigh prevented him from talking.

Itzik took him by the shoulders. "You stayed behind for that? For revenge?" Itzik was happy. He was proud of his friend. "Bravo, Elhanan! Bravo a thousand times! I underestimated you. Let's have a drink." And he dragged Elhanan into David's tent, where they were all celebrating their victory.

But Elhanan couldn't swallow anything.

Father and son often strolled the sidewalks of New York, exploring exotic neighborhoods and meeting colorful characters: a synagogue for black Jews in Harlem; a Chinese restaurant whose customers spoke Yiddish; Times Square and its passersby lost in the neon maze; the Village and its too rich or too poor street people in search of money, pleasure, danger; Brighton Beach with its Russian cabarets and cafés; a square for the lonely and uprooted, a forum for visionaries; a restaurant for jazz-lovers, a movie for jazz-haters. Malkiel knew the big city as well as his father had known his hometown.

"We too had our madmen," Elhanan said. In Brooklyn he was reminded of Feherfalu. In the American version of a shtetl, Jews lived in a sealed-off world. No business on the Sabbath, no school on Jewish holidays. They taught Talmud and mathematics in Yiddish. Life proceeded by the ancient Jewish calendar.

Once Malkiel took his father to the home of a great Hasidic master, who received visitors only after midnight. Impressive and even majestic, radiating strength and faith, arms stretched out before him on a bare table, the rabbi listened to Malkiel but gazed steadily at Elhanan.

"Rabbi," Malkiel cried, "I turn to you because ordinary medicine is powerless."

"Doctors are only God's messengers," the rabbi replied calmly. "I, too, am only His messenger. Men may be powerless; God is not."

Anxious, tormented, Malkiel crossed and recrossed his legs, trying to catch the master's gaze, which was fixed on Elhanan. "Isn't it a rabbi's duty to speak to God in our name?"

"God needs no intermediaries."

"But *we* need them!"

"Why do you speak for your father? If he has something to say, let him say it himself."

Elhanan heard and understood all of this. He opened his mouth, looked for the right words, found them. "Rabbi," he said, "I'm going under."

The rabbi's gaze remained steadfast. Abruptly he looked away.

"Is it hopeless?" asked Malkiel.

"God commands us to hope," said the rabbi, straightening his shoulders before hunching again in concentration. Outside, a drunk sang out his woes while policemen shouted, chasing a thug. Would the world's violence break and enter this room? The rabbi's voice deterred it: "Elhanan son of Malkiel, listen to me. In our prayers on the high holy days we beg the Lord to remember the near sacrifice of Isaac. What an idea! We beg God to remember? Can you imagine the God of Abraham as an amnesiac? The truth is, we make such requests in the name of memory to prove to Him that we ourselves remember. Next Rosh Hashanah you will go to synagogue; I command it. And you will remember. That too I command."

Outside, thirty disciples besieged them. "What were your impressions? What did he say to you? Which of his words struck you particularly?"

"It's confidential," Malkiel said.

Next day Malkiel told Tamar about the visit.

"You should have taken me along. I've never seen a Hasidic master."

"Next time you'll come."

Tamar pondered what Malkiel had told her. "I have every confidence."

"In him?"

"In your father. If he believes in the rabbi, that can only help."

On Rosh Hashanah father and son attended synagogue. Tamar was with her parents in Chicago. Elhanan followed the long service as always, with a prayer book in his hand. Then they invited him to the Torah. Malkiel panicked: how could his father recite the blessings without stumbling? Elhanan recited them from memory. Malkiel's happiness was unbounded. But it lasted only until the day after Yom Kippur.

"Let's see your rabbi again," Tamar suggested.

They were admitted at four in the morning. Malkiel stood near the table, Tamar in the background. The exchange between the reporter and the rabbi took on an unreal character. "My father's slipping again," said Malkiel. "We need more help."

"Help does not come from the mortal that I am. How many times must I tell you that?"

"Plead with God in our name."

"And why don't you plead with Him yourself, young man?"

"I'm sure my prayers don't reach heaven." Malkiel had to explain himself: he was too busy at the newspaper, too tormented by his father's illness, too harassed from too many sides.

The rabbi sighed. "Your father has priority. All the rest can wait. He cannot wait. Your father gave you everything; it is your turn to give it back to him."

"How should I go about it? The student can teach; the apprentice can become independent. But what can a son do for his sick father?"

"Speak in his place; pray in his name. Do what he is incapable of doing; let your life be an extension of his. Learn, since he no longer learns. Be happy, since he no longer laughs."

His throat dry, his head burning, Malkiel murmured his answer. "You're asking the impossible of me, Rabbi. How can I be happy, when my father . . ."

Laugh? Give himself over to life's pleasures? By what right could he be happy? He had never seen his father happy. An inconsolable widower, an uprooted man, Elhanan had never seemed carefree, capable of gaiety. Sometimes Malkiel was even angry with him for that; I'm here, he would think spitefully, I exist, I live, I love him and he knows it, isn't that enough for him? Doesn't he understand that when he wallows in melancholy and mourning he's putting space between us and condemning me?

"Rabbi," Malkiel said, "perhaps my father was happy once, in Palestine, before I was born—"

"All the more reason for you to be happier longer and more often! Will your father's sadness be less heavy, less burdensome, if it weighs the more on you? It is your duty to resist it. The person with you tonight will help you, I know. Who is she? Your fiancée? Marry her. Invite your father to the wedding. He will lead you to the *huppah,* I promise. He will recite the seven blessings; I promise that, too. It will be the happiest day of your life, and of mine. I shall remember it, and so will you."

The rabbi broke off; someone had knocked at the door, a discreet knock. An uneasy, fragile smile dawned in his bright, sharp eyes, but vanished immediately.

For Elhanan, Palestine was Talia. And Itzik. But while Talia was tenderness, Itzik meant violence. Talia or love. Itzik or friendship. During the last months of the war Itzik had but one purpose: revenge. For him it was as important as victory.

Born of sighs and sacrifices, the friendship between the two partisans was bound to last. And yet. As they said in Feherfalu, man acts and God laughs. No; in this case God would not laugh. God does not like to see friendship torn apart. God weeps for a parting as He weeps for a death. And in fact this friendship ended with a murder.

A few weeks after the attack on Stanislav came the liberation of Feherfalu. Summer sunshine warmed the red-brick roofs, the trees in bloom and the cottages with their closed shutters. The remaining villagers, sick with terror, awaited the invader. Some had fled to the mountains, others as far as Budapest. Still others went to hide in the cellars of abandoned Jewish homes. As always, great fear preceded the first offensive. Fear of falling into the hands of the last German unit, which, beaten, would kill before meeting death. Fear of bombs, artillery, stray bullets. Fear of Russian soldiers; propaganda said appalling but likely things about them.

Evacuated by the Germans and Hungarians, Feherfalu was a ghost town that day. Empty, the houses. Shut, the shops. Closed, the blinds. Deserted, the offices. The town was dead, breathing only in its grave. There was anguished silence, a wait heavy with foreboding.

Preceding the Red Army, David's partisans entered the town. The shooting lasted a solid hour. It was in fact pointless: the enemy was gone. Then again, you could never tell. They might flush out some stragglers. So the assault group moved in as if there were Germans in every building and Hungarians behind every window. Exploding grenades, the clatter of submachine guns—and then the terrified cries of women dragged by their hair and men shoved against a wall.

Elhanan said nothing and heard no one, but headed straight for his house. The gateway to the courtyard was open. The kitchen door, too. He rushed inside and ran from one room to another: no one. He cried out, he shouted, "Where are you?" No answer. Suddenly he noticed a muffled sound, a kind of scratching, from down below. They're in the cellar, he thought. "Come on out!" he shouted at the top of his lungs. "Come out! It's me, Elhanan!" The cellar door creaked open. An old woman's face appeared: it was the widow Starker. Elhanan knew her. She lived two streets over. What was she doing here? He told her to come up. "What are you doing in our house, Madame Starker? Where are my parents? Quick, don't stare at me like that, tell me, tell me, for the love of heaven! Where are my parents?"

She fell to whimpering and sniffling and hiccuping. "Then you don't know—"

"Know what? Come on, tell me! What don't I know?"

"Your parents, sir. They're not here anymore. They're—"

"Where are they?" Elhanan was out of patience and suddenly weak.

"They took them away. . . ."

"Where did they take them?"

"I don't know. They took all the Jews."

Elhanan wanted to scream, to strike out at someone, more than ever before in his life. He collapsed into a chair and stared into space. Madame Starker asked, "Would you like a glass of water?" He hardly heard her, he was not there, all this was happening to someone else. He, Elhanan Rosenbaum, was not armed; the woman before him was not a neighbor; the catastrophe had never occurred. Yet Madame Starker was talking. "I came to your house to hide . . . to hide in the cellar. . . . I said to myself that your shelter was safer than mine . . . especially since there are so many Jews in the Red Army." When Elhanan only sat there, she shouted down the cellar. Other heads appeared. Several women and some children. Frightened and obsequious, they kissed his jacket. "Thank you," they said, "thank you for letting us come to your house. Can we stay another day, another week? Until everything calms down . . . and the Russians get tired of looting and raping?" Elhanan stood up and walked out. In the house across the way—it belonged to the Cohen family—he ordered the living out. Terrified, they obeyed him, babbling explanations: "We had to hide. The Russian soldiers, they're capable of anything, everybody knows that." And why in Jewish homes? It seemed reasonable to them. Elhanan went to inspect the house next door: there the new inhabitants had been shrewder, affixing an old mezuzah to the door.

The synagogue: transformed into a stable by the Germans. The Hasidic house of study: a military brothel. The yeshiva: a museum of anti-Semitism.

Elhanan encountered acquaintances, who told him in breathless staccato about the ghetto and the cruelties inflicted on it by the Nyilas chief, a man called Zoltan. Here was Kovago, his old schoolmaster, saying to him, "Your parents left two candelabras and three ritual silver chests; they are yours." Vasaros, a former judge, told him, "Before the transports, I suggested to your father that they leave the ghetto." The transports. They described them to him, and he thought he must be living in a nightmare: the town betrayed all its Jews, and these men, these women, who looted their homes afterward, dared now to lament the Jews' fate in his presence. . . . He wanted to tell them of his revulsion but knew he could not. God, teach me wrath! Make me an avenger! But God did not will it so. Elhanan shrugged and went off to find other witnesses, other clues, other guilty parties. A voice called to him: Lianka, her cheeks aflame, was asking him if anyone in his family was alive. "Not one Jew survived," Elhanan said. "The town sold them all to their killers."

"Not all," Lianka said. "We turned up two. Come and see." He found them in the once stately home of Gershon Weiss, the manufacturer. The partisans surrounding them saw Elhanan and opened a path. "Do you know them?"

Yes, he knew them vaguely. They'd worked for the Weiss family.

"A Christian family hid them," David explained.

"Risking their lives," the survivors added.

"Are you the only ones left?" Elhanan asked.

"Yes," said one.

"There's a third," said a partisan. "The gravedigger."

Elhanan grew dizzy. The gravedigger? Why would God have spared the gravedigger? The two survivors turned to him: "If you have questions, go ahead. Ask them." Questions! No end to them, Elhanan thought. Why didn't the Jews flee to the mountains or the nearby villages? Why didn't their honest Christian neighbors take them in? The two survivors answered calmly point by point, adding details about this family or that, but each time ending with a sigh: "It happened so fast, so fast." As for Elhanan's parents, they had seen them in the ghetto. "Your mother told anyone who'd listen that she thanked God for saving her son. She consoled herself with thoughts of you, Elhanan; you were alive." Could she have guessed that he'd come back? "Ah," the survivors said, "if only she'd been able to see you like this, carrying a weapon, conqueror, avenger . . ." The word spoken aloud at last: avenger.

"Right," said a partisan. "We'll have to take revenge."

A brief discussion followed. Was that the way—the Jewish way—the way a Jew should go? To shed blood? Whose? Starting where?

Elhanan was lost in a vision of his parents and did not join the debate. Nor did Itzik. Itzik, who looked fierce. The others piled argument upon argument (most of them in favor of revenge) and interrogated the two survivors about collaborators and the Nyilas. One name popped up often: Zoltan, head of the Nyilas. Itzik made a note on a scrap of paper and stuffed it into his pocket. Then the partisans broke up. "Meet tomorrow morning at seven in the synagogue courtyard," David said. "Stay out of trouble. And don't forget, the war isn't over. We go where the Red Army goes. They're counting on us."

Torn between fury and despair, Elhanan paced the town's streets like a sleepwalker. At every corner he expected to stumble upon some childhood friend or cousin, or one of his parents. Constantly he saw his father or his mother beckoning him closer. . . . He wanted to speak to them, but no sound escaped him. He was alone. Yes, he had friends, comrades, and he would have more in the future, but it was not the same. Nothing can interrupt an orphan's solitude.

A Russian soldier called to him in Yiddish. "You want a watch? I have three. The watchmaker won't need them anymore. He was a fascist."

The soldier went off. Elhanan continued on his way but stopped abruptly. He thought he had heard a cry. A woman's cry. From where? He listened intently. He was wrong; his nerves were frayed. No, there it was again! A woman was shouting for help. Elhanan knew where the cry had come from. Suppose it was a Jewish woman being attacked? He burst into the house. The inner doors were wide open. A small room, all shadows, and two bodies intertwined on the floor. The woman was struggling, and the man was covering her mouth. Elhanan went to the window and threw back the curtains. "Are you crazy?" Itzik shouted. "Get out." Shocked and nauseated, Elhanan stared at his friend forcing the woman down with the weight of his outstretched body. Elhanan gazed upon the woman and was ashamed to do so. He knew that he ought to clear out, but his legs would not obey him. "Get out, Elhanan! Can't you see I'm not finished? Wait for me outside, unless . . . unless you want some too." Elhanan stared at the woman, stared into eyes that shone with indescribable shame, pain and protest, and he did not know what to do. Now Itzik's hands were rising on the woman as if to clutch her breasts, and she cried in horror as if she were possessed. Elhanan started toward his friend, went to touch his arm, changed his mind. "Itzik, my friend, come on. Please. Stop it. What you're doing is wrong." Itzik rebuked him: "You want to be a saint? Go to the synagogue—and leave us alone!" Itzik went at the woman fiercely; her mouth stopped again, she begged Elhanan with her anguished and anguishing eyes, as if he were her savior, as if he were almighty. But Elhanan was not. He stepped backward out of the room. In the street, he leaned against a wall and vomited.

Wait for Itzik? No. He decided to go. Go where? Home. Home? He had no more home. To the synagogue? To see it vandalized and profaned? Instead he wandered without purpose, from street to street. Here and there he ran across drunken Russian soldiers who invited him to join them. He heard women weeping. How long had he walked around the town? He was shocked to see that he had returned, unintentionally, to the house where Itzik . . . Not knowing why, he knocked at the door; no one answered. He knocked louder. He wanted to walk in. Perhaps he was hoping to find his comrade in arms Itzik, his friend Itzik the Long, who was no longer his friend. He needed to see him. To say what? Elhanan had no idea. Anyway, Itzik was not there. An old woman with a black scarf over her uncombed hair opened the door, sobbing, "Enough, enough! Go away, my daughter has suffered enough."

Elhanan gently pushed her aside and went to the young woman huddled in a corner. "I want to help you," he said gently. "Tell me what I can do." The young woman did not answer; she had not heard him. She was in another universe. Then Elhanan sat before her and took her hand; she was not even strong enough to pull it away. She seemed apathetic, listless; nothing more could terrify her, nothing more could interest her. "I won't hurt you," Elhanan said. "Look at me. Please look at me." He insisted: he had to help this woman. Time and will must be restored to her. Her features must relax. It was no use. Her vision seemed focused on some other reality, forever untouchable. Her stare was fixed in some other time. She was suffering a madness and a damnation that no one would ever fathom.

Elhanan turned to the old woman. "Who are you? Who is she?" The old woman wrung her hands and answered between sobs: "She's my daughter . . . no, my niece. We live at the other end of town, in a beautiful house. . . . We thought there'd be less danger here, less risk." Elhanan insisted: "Who is she? What's her name?" In the end, the old woman told him. She was the widow of a man who . . . who had collaborated. Elhanan whispered, "Her husband was a Nyilas? Is that it?" Yes, that was it. He was an anti-Semite and a fascist. His name was Zoltan. . . . Was he dead? Yes, assassinated. Yes, by Jewish partisans. The old woman was muttering and repeating herself. Zoltan, Elhanan thought. He went back to the young widow. "I'm sorry for what happened to you. I hope you'll believe me someday."

Later in the evening he heard Jewish songs in a big house. There he found a group of Jewish partisans with Russian-Jewish officers and soldiers; they were drinking and telling stories and laughing. Itzik saw him come in and walked toward him, hand outstretched. "Glad to see you, old friend."

Elhanan turned away.

"Let's go outside," Itzik said. "Let's talk." They went out into the street. "You're judging me," Itzik said.

"You shouldn't have done it," Elhanan answered, and again, "you shouldn't have done it."

Itzik squeezed his arm hard. "Do you know who she was?"

"I know who her husband was."

"And revenge? And justice? Are you forgetting what we swore?"

Elhanan's arm ached, but he ignored it. "Itzik," he said after a moment, "can you really believe that raping a helpless woman is an answer to what the enemy did to us? Can you really reduce our whole tragedy to one bestial act? And anyway, is it really a matter of justice? You wanted to take a woman and she was there, that's all. And even if it isn't all, what you did was . . . disgusting."

Itzik's suffering showed. "Who are you to tell me about morality?" he roared. "A bastard's wife, a killer's wife, doesn't deserve pity!"

Elhanan raised his voice. "And you claim you showed pity for her husband's victims when you raped her? You wiped out his crimes and righted injustices? The truth is, you raped her for your own pleasure, for your own animal satisfaction!"

Itzik took a step backward, as if to mark the distance that would thenceforth separate them. "You're not serious, Elhanan? Is that how you see me?" Elhanan had no need to answer; Itzik understood. "And anyway," he said, his voice breaking, "anyway, to lose a friend because of a lousy anti-Semite . . ." Exhausted, he trudged back into the house, where his comrades were still carousing. Elhanan stayed outside all night. Perhaps he was afraid to confront Itzik again. Perhaps he felt guilty for not acting quicker to keep his friend from going too far, not fighting for the raped young widow, a victim of uncontrollable Jewish rage and suffering.

He let the night take him. A pale moon reigned timidly over masses of stars. Here below, the alleys seemed darker and more menacing than during the day. And then the earth broke away and detached itself from the sky and the night. Dawn had won.

Malkiel felt a stab of panic, as if after a silent quarrel with a loved one: he realized that his quest was doomed to failure and had been all along.

Forgive me, Father. You'll have to forgive me, but I'm going to disappoint you. There is no such thing as a memory transfusion. Yours will never become mine.

I'm a stranger in this town that you knew so well. All the places you told me about are surely still here, but I don't recognize them.

You told me of a house set in a garden; I cannot find it. You told me that inside, past the courtyard, was the cheder *where your mother took you when you were small. All right, Father, I looked, I searched, and all these houses are much alike, and so are their courtyards.*

How can I use the images that appeared as you spoke? They're fleeting, they crumble like sand, they don't correspond to anything.

And yet I promised to remember, in your name and in your place. But I cannot. I cannot relive your life, see again the child and adolescent that you were, find traces of you in these walls that saw your birth and your childhood. I can live after you and even for you, but not as you. What you felt here when you explored the mystery of daybreak, I shall never feel. What you felt when you welcomed the Queen of Shabbat, I shall never feel.

Then why am I here? Why did you ask me to come? Why did you make me promise to remember all that you will have forgotten? Why did you show me things that only you can understand?

You told me of your own father's generous heart, of your mother's serenity and nobility; I remember your words, but that's all. I'll never be able to say them as you said them to me.

You described Stanislav to me, and I heard the pain that binds you to Stanislav. But that's all, Father. My pain is only an echo of yours.

You told me about your adventures among the partisans; I can see your comrades in arms, and I watch them as they rush into battle against the Germans, I hear the cries of the vanquished. I see pride on your friend Itzik's face as he fires; he shouts as he fires, he laughs as he fires; he's a happy man, Itzik—happy to be avenging Jewish honor, happy to be showing that the enemy of the Jews is not godlike but vulnerable, mortal. I see and understand all that you did and all that you saw; and yet I know that it will be impossible to keep my promise. Of course I'll bear witness for you, but my deposition will pale before yours. What shall I do, Father? Your life and memory are indivisible. They cannot survive you, not really.

I know that whoever listens to a witness becomes one in turn; you told me that more than once. But we are not witnessing the same events. All I can say is, I have heard the witness.

Yes indeed, Father, I have heard you. And in this foreign city, I still hear you.

In his hospital bed Elhanan was dreaming aloud. "The Book is open, and a hand is inscribing our deeds, good as well as evil. *The Ethics of Our Fathers* tells us so. Ah, if I could only read the page that tells of my glorious return to the town of my childhood on the day of its liberation . . ."

Despite Loretta's watchful eye, he had managed to slip out of the apartment three days before. He fell and broke several ribs. An ambulance took him to the emergency room.

Feverish, his gaze scanning something beyond space, was he aware now that his son was at his bedside?

"Be calm, Father," Malkiel said. "The doctor says no excitement."

"But the Book," Elhanan said. "And the hand. I see it writing. I'm afraid to read it. No medicine on earth can cure me of that fear."

He was not to move about, but he did so constantly. Ring for the nurse? Or the intern? Malkiel was about to step into the hallway, when his father's hand stayed him. "I told you about going back, didn't I?"

"Yes, you told me."

"And you're not angry?"

"No, I'm not angry."

Elhanan sighed before going on. "I'm mad at myself. I'm guilty, you know. And soon I'll be guilty without knowing why. I was there, you understand? I saw everything. I could have and should have stopped that rape. Itzik was stronger than I, but I should have kept at him until the woman could run off. Still, it broke my heart. I saw her eyes, this raped woman's eyes. If I'm sick now it's because of her eyes."

Malkiel had never seen his father in such a state. Under the influence of his illness, he took refuge in silence, but never had he let himself go like this. Even for the *Yizkor* service he hid his face. And here he was crying openly.

"We'll talk about it again sometime soon," Malkiel said. "Not now. Rest now. Doctor's orders. Otherwise he can't promise a thing."

"Who is he to promise me anything? God is the sole proprietor of the Book. It is the Book of His memory. And in that Book I'll be punished. I know it; I'm already being punished."

A nurse signaled Malkiel to follow her into the hallway. But Malkiel could not free his hand, which his father was clutching with astonishing strength.

"Your mother doesn't know. I'm ashamed of what she must think of me."

"We'll talk about it tomorrow, Father. The doctor wants to speak to me."

Elhanan did not hear him. "I loved your mother. I loved her the way your grandfather loved God. I loved her the way a traveler in the desert loves his jug of water, the way a dying man loves life. I promised her happiness, and we were happy. Someday I'll tell you about our nights in Jerusalem. Our long, rambling walks at night, before curfew. Every hour counted and every word was rich with meaning. Your mother was a good listener. She made me talk. She liked that. So I told her all about my childhood, my memories of school, my war. But not my break with Itzik, not that. I feared her judgment as I fear the judgment of heaven. Yet it was she who was punished, and not I. Do you know why your mother died? Because I was present at the rape of a human being, of her honor and integrity; I was present at a profanation of her sovereignty; I was present and did nothing. Here is the lesson I bequeath unto you, my son: Itzik blasphemed, I looked on, and it is your mother that death carried away."

He stirred and twitched again. Again the nurse signaled Malkiel to join her in the hallway. This time he broke away.

"Your father is weak. He has to rest."

"Forgive me, miss. He said he needed me."

"What he needs is sleep. Run along."

"You'll stay close by?"

"I promise."

Malkiel tiptoed back into the room. "Doctor's orders. I have to leave now. I'll be back. Tomorrow."

"But I need you. I have so much to tell you, so much I'll forget in the night. . . . Don't leave me alone."

"I'd like nothing better than to stay here all night. But—"

"One minute, then. Stay one more minute."

"Okay. One minute."

"Do you know what I'm thinking of, whom I'm thinking of, right now?"

"Tell me."

In spite of his pain, the sick man's face hardened, as if he were preparing to inflict pain on someone, perhaps himself. "The young widow." Overcome, Elhanan said nothing more. He did not fall asleep.

In his mind he was wandering great distances.

The camp began to hum with rumors, opinions, advice, promises, agreements: Were they going to leave, yes or no? Now or later? If you leave, will you write to me? Will you let me know when you get there?

Five hundred "displaced persons"—former partisans, deportees, stowaways—applied for the convoy. They were fed up with their marginal if not futile existence. Fed up with living off charity or the black market. Fed up with feeling like undesirables. Fed up with sleeping and waking on the ground that so many victims had damned and damned again before dying. When someone asked, "But hardship along the way? The obstacles? The dangers? Aren't you afraid?" they shrugged it off: "We've been through all that before, you know." And also: "At least we know where we're going now and why we're going there."

A week of preparation: learning a few key words of Hebrew, a few basic sentences of French. The truck convoy would stop at a transit camp in France before heading on to a port near Marseilles. They had to protect themselves against local informers and British spies roaming through Europe in search of Jewish "illegals." Practical considerations: how to dress, what to take along, or buy, or sell. The best advice? Take whatever the authorities advise and nothing more. They'll send the rest along afterward.

On the eve of departure Elhanan paid Talia a visit. She seemed happy; not he. "Hey now," she teased him, "you do look awful."

Shy as ever, Elhanan lowered his gaze. One question nagged at him: "And you . . . why are you so happy? Because I'm leaving?"

"Frankly, yes," she said.

"Thanks."

She pulled him close. "If you smile nicely I'll tell you a secret. A secret you'll like."

He tried, but he could only grimace.

Talia shook her head. "Try."

He tried. Same result.

"All right, I appreciate the effort. I have news for you. You're not leaving alone." Elhanan hardly had time to react. "I'm going with you."

At that Elhanan forgot to breathe. His head spun, and the earth went out from under him. What should he look at? How could he bear all this emotion?

"You see?" Talia asked. "I don't trust you. Once you're away from me, who knows whom you'll fall in love with." Her eyes sparkled. Her parted lips, full and sensual, demanded a response. More quietly she said, "You *are* stupid, really. My poor Elhanan."

"Why do you say that?"

"When we love somebody we ought to show it. But you hide it."

Did she really say "love"? Elhanan couldn't believe his ears. Elhanan was no longer Elhanan Rosenbaum. His life was no longer his own. He was dreaming an exalted dream. He saw Vitka again, and Lianka, and they said to him, "Now you will at last fall in love." He was dancing without moving, shouting his happiness without opening his mouth, less alone and more alone than ever, falling and rising at once all the way to seventh heaven, to the celestial throne where God, surrounded by Sages and Just Men, lavished upon him smiles and words at which his heart and his head swelled. Yet one fearful voice rose too: "So you love her? Be careful of the Tempter, Elhanan! He is always on the prowl, and spirits away the women we love." Another voice—or was it the same?—was mocking: "You happy, Elhanan? Why? Because you're off to the Holy Land or because a beautiful woman is going with you? Will the beauty of a woman mean more to you than the call of your ancestors?" In his confusion Elhanan turned to God, Who said silently, "All love implies love of me." Another voice—was it God's or Talia's?—added, "You must not be ashamed to love."

Talia kissed him. They stood embracing for a long time.

"I want to make love with you," Talia said, "but not in this place."

Elhanan saw again the mad eyes of the raped woman. He remembered his disgust. "You're right," he said. "Not in this place."

They broke apart. They had things to do, after all. Elhanan had books to return to the camp library. He had to say good-bye to his neighbors. Fill out forms. Everyone was tense, and the air was heavy with curiosity, with apprehension too. The convoy would run into detours and roadblocks. The forged documents would rouse the suspicions of a mean-spirited customs inspector bribed by British agents. The ship would sink. And if I die on the way? Hasidic texts taught that when a Jew, whoever he is, decides to go to the Holy Land, Satan will go out of his way to stop him. Satan and his tricks. Satan and his manipulations. How will he go about it now? At the end of time, when the Angel of Death slaughters the slaughterer, he, too, will be slaughtered by God. Why wait? Master of the Universe, why not step in a bit sooner? Take charge of Satan, who is the Angel of Death. For once come down on our side right away and keep this love story from fading into darkness. Be with us tomorrow.

Tomorrow arrived after a sleepless and tumultuous night. The convoy moved out at dawn. Elhanan and Talia traveled in the same truck. There were no speeches. There was no farewell ceremony. In shirtsleeves, the leader gave the signal, and the convoy rolled forward. The morning breeze was cool. Elhanan buttoned his jacket. A pious man said psalms. A boy and his fiancée held hands. Elhanan exchanged a wink with Talia. The words "not in this place" flashed into his mind. For two thousand years of exile, the Jews had said the opposite: "Also in this place."

The convoy rolled through sleepy villages, between tilled fields, into dense woods. Everywhere war had left its mark: demolished vehicles, burned-out tanks, the rubble of razed buildings. Fearful old men, women who walked submissively. Thus their punishment, Elhanan thought. They loosed evil upon the world, now let them live in remorse. They wanted to rule, now let them be ruled. An avenger's outlook? He was not comfortable in the role. He had broken with his best friend, who in taking revenge on a pitiless enemy had denied one poor woman her own right to pity. At the same time, he could not deny a rush of satisfaction at the sight of defeated Nazis.

What had become of the young widow? And where was Itzik now? He had joined the Czech army before the fighting ended. Elhanan himself celebrated the victory not far from Munich. Then, rather than be repatriated to Feherfalu, he had gone to the displaced persons camp. Was he right not to go home? There was no one waiting for him. And then he was afraid. Afraid to measure the emptiness left by so many dead. Afraid also to see the young widow again. End of chapter. End of European exile. End of wandering in the unknown.

The Briha, faithful to its reputation, had organized everything superbly. At the border, formalities took barely half an hour. That same evening the convoy reached the transit camp. A warm fraternal welcome. Cots, fresh linen, hot meals, religious services for those who wanted them, sports for the sports-minded.

During their lightning visit to France, Elhanan was separated from Talia. Busy with various preparations, she spent two days in the camp offices. When that world swallowed her up, Elhanan felt bereft. In a kind of delirium, he saw her climbing the clouds, at which he stared up for a long time before noticing her flying between heaven and earth, in search of refuge and certainty. Then he knew that he loved her truly, and that he would forever. You're never sure you love someone until you see her dangling from the clouds.

Talia reappeared only on the second evening, when the *maapilim* —as they called the illegals—were ready to start for the port. "From now on I stick with you," she said.

So, side by side in the truck, they yielded to the intoxicating hope that prevailed in the convoy. One man prayed. Another squeezed his wife's arm in silence. A boy said to his girlfriend, "Pinch me; I want to be sure this isn't a dream."

"There'll be eight hundred passengers," Talia said. "Three hundred and fifteen are already on board." And after a pause, "I hope the British don't know."

Everybody in the truck joined her in that hope. But if the British did know? Several theories were advanced. Of course they'll stop us for inspection. No, they'll escort us to Haifa. No, somewhere else . . . Talia took no part in these debates. What was she thinking about?

"Elhanan," she whispered, "have you ever seen the sea?"

"No. Never."

"Close your eyes, then. I'll tell you when to open them."

Elhanan felt like the unborn child who flies around the world with his guardian angel to choose a home.

"Now," Talia said.

Elhanan's heart leapt as it had when Talia first took his hand. He saw the sea, and it stopped his breath. He had not known that beauty could be so intense. He no longer doubted that the infinite existed, and not only in mystic philosophy. He found a sky so distant and blue that he understood why people looked at it with some anxiety. Where was the sea? Above? Below? Thousands and thousands of stars glittered in it. The sea: rocked gently and rhythmically by waves whose monotonous sound reverberated to the endless horizon. As he had when he studied the Zohar, he found in the sky joined to the sea a hallucinatory universe that he could not tear himself away from without a sense of loss and disorientation.

Talia said, "Sometimes the sea makes people want to die. I hope it makes you want to live."

The ship was an old Greek tub, the *Cretan*. Captain Nikos, a seafarer of the old kind, looked as if he were playing his own part in a movie: cap low on his forehead, a pipe in his mouth, a sardonic air that masked a romantic heart. His crew were sailors from all corners of the Mediterranean.

The real commander was Eytan, a strapping young man from the Palmach; they said he was a poet. Surrounded by a Palestinian crew, Talia one of them, he was in charge of the passage. If the British decided to intercept the *Cretan,* it was he who would organize resistance on board.

They weighed anchor after midnight. The passengers, jammed into stuffy cabins, were to come up on deck only in groups and according to a precise schedule. As interpreter, Elhanan enjoyed certain privileges. He could circulate freely. Soon, in fact, they considered him one of the Palestinian team.

The passage began badly. As if swirled by an immense hand, the sea screamed and danced: the planet was too small for her and aroused her fury. The sea summoned up all her grandeur and immensity; she provoked the depths to battle, howled at death like wolves at night, and refused to subside in daylight but gave herself up to the tempest. Beating against invisible shores, drowning in mist, she ate away cloud-shaped rocks, leapt toward the sky as if to defy it, and then fell back, like a squatting statue about to give birth.

When calm was restored, they had to worry about the British again. After thirty hours at sea, they faced the danger head-on: a warship approached at top speed.

Eytan gathered his crew. "They've spotted us. I radioed headquarters, and our orders are simple: change the ship's name to *Geula*"—the Hebrew word for "redemption"—"and resist, resist by any means possible. Public opinion, alerted by our friends, will then be heard."

His lieutenants brought the passengers to the upper decks. In groups, under the command of Palmach people, they were to delay the enemy boarding as long as they could. Elhanan stayed on the command bridge with Talia and Eytan.

"What will they do with us?" he asked.

"Internment camp," Eytan said.

"All of us?"

"Not the Palestinians. They'll let us go."

Another separation, Elhanan thought. Talia was thinking along the same lines; she turned to Eytan and said, "When will the boarding occur?"

"Tomorrow or the day after. As we approach the coast. That's what they usually do."

"Then we still have time."

"Time?" Eytan was startled. "For what?"

"To get married," she said calmly.

Eytan looked at her in disbelief. "Are you joking? You've picked quite a time for it."

Talia stood up to him. "If I marry Elhanan, that changes everything for him, doesn't it? As the husband of a Palestinian citizen he'll be entitled to go ashore with me. Am I right or wrong?"

Eytan admitted that her argument was sound. He asked Elhanan, "And you, poor boy, you have nothing to say about all this?"

"Yes, I have."

"Then say it."

"I say yes."

"You're sacrificing yourself for the cause, right?"

"Always ready, as they say."

Eytan looked him over, shook his head as if emerging from a poetic meditation, and burst into laughter. "This is the fourth ship I've commanded but the first time anything like this has happened to me."

He laughed and laughed, until Talia said, ironically but gently, "There's a nice wish in Yiddish: May nothing worse happen to you." And to Elhanan: "You see? In your honor I learned a few words of Yiddish."

Eytan said, "Talia, Talia. I'm supposed to be a poet, but you've outdone me."

The marriage was scheduled for the next day. Captain Nikos would conduct the civil ceremony, and an Orthodox Jew who spent all day studying the Bible would preside over the religious service.

The ceremony was a true event. A bridal gown was found for Talia and a white shirt and blue trousers for her groom. The officiating Jew recited the customary prayers and blessings. The bride circled the groom seven times under the tallith that served as a *huppah*. Elhanan said his vows—"by the law of Moses and Israel"

—and smashed the glass under his heel in memory of the Temple's destruction, and eight hundred men and women shouted *Mazel tov, mazel tov,* good luck to you, and may a lucky star light your way, and may your happiness last beyond this day and this week. There was even a sort of improvised reception. Everyone danced and urged the young couple to dance, and Eytan made a speech, and an amateur minstrel regaled them with funny verses. When night came, Elhanan and Talia took the captain's cabin. Pleasantly drunk, the captain announced over and over that it was the happiest day of his life, the happiest day of his life. . . .

Alone in the cabin, Talia took her husband's hand and placed it on her cheek. "When I was little my parents let their imaginations run wild about my marriage. They competed, inventing fantasies. But neither of them could have foreseen a wedding like this."

"You don't think they'll be disappointed?"

"They'll be happy. Like me. Because of me. And for me to be happy, you have to be happy too."

Elhanan recalled his own parents. They too must have imagined this day.

Talia said, "You won't mind if I weep for a moment?"

Nor could Elhanan hold back the tears.

"Good," Talia said. "We'll weep for our parents, who would weep if they were here."

Outside on deck, the guests were still celebrating.

And then on the horizon a second warship appeared, and then a third. Together they escorted the newlyweds to their destiny.

Three paratrooper units handled the operation. The illegals held out as best they could, but the outcome was never in doubt. In a few hours the boarding, inspection and takeover were completed. Thus ended the epic journey baptized "redemption." The passengers were transferred to a prison ship waiting off Haifa.

Was it a defeat for the Jewish underground? On the surface, yes; but only on the surface. Some fifty foreign correspondents, mobilized by the Jewish Agency, reported on the story, increasing the pressure on the British government. Newspapers and magazines in all languages, as well as newsreels everywhere, described the odyssey of these uprooted Jews. Driven by a millennial hope, they were determined to return to the land of their ancestors. Photos everywhere showed these refugees driven back by the haughty Royal Navy. And also a picture—so romantic that people laughed and wept—of the couple who had just been married at sea. Yes: Talia and Elhanan were celebrities, so much so that the authorities facilitated their disembarking. Never let it be said that the British lacked heart.

The couple were resting in Jerusalem, at the house of Talia's parents, when a letter came from America for Elhanan. A cousin wrote, "I had no idea that any of the family had survived the catastrophe." And Elhanan was unaware that he had family in the United States. Yet the cousin's letter proved that he was telling the truth. Names were accurate; dates and addresses corresponded perfectly. "Bring your young wife and come spend a few weeks with us," the cousin proposed. "We have a beautiful place in Westchester; your room looks out over the woods. You need time to recover, and you'll be able to do that here." A touching invitation, but Elhanan and Talia were in no mood for vacations.

In Palestine, Elhanan felt transported to a country at once familiar and mysterious. He seemed to recognize every stone, every tree, and every crossroad; but at the same time he felt a need to stop after every step he took, and cry out, "Is this only a dream?"

Hebrew inscriptions and street names—Yehuda Halevi and Don Itzhak Abrabanel—Jewish police speaking Hebrew, the Star of David gloriously displayed, the underground striking fear into the hearts of the British army: "Look, Talia! Read this! Listen to that!" Overcome by emotion, he passed from one wonder to another, in all the ecstasy of a teenager after his first date.

For the country, for the whole Jewish people, this was the finest hour. Each incident took on the dimension of an epic. After two thousand years of exile, a sovereign Jewish state was about to be reborn from the ashes. Everything would change: political structure and state of mind, foreign relations and self-esteem.

The first Sabbath with Talia's parents. Zalmen was a civil servant, Reuma an editor. After the kiddush, Zalmen and Reuma embraced the young couple. "Let's dance!" Zalmen shouted. Reuma needed no urging. Talia and Elhanan held back. "Come on, you too," Zalmen said. "Happiness is here to be shared!"

Elhanan and his in-laws got along beautifully. Mutual respect, affection, generosity, no misunderstandings and no afterthoughts. When people talked about "mixed marriages" between Sephardi and Ashkenazi Jews in the Mea Shearim neighborhood, they mentioned both couples.

Before looking for work, Elhanan and Talia went to the seashore for a few days. In a cabana on the beach they loved each other. Elhanan would always remember immense, violent waves.

Not far from them, two men walked slowly along the beach. Leaning on a cane and limping badly, an old man seemed to search for something in the sand. All these dramas that one observed. Some of the women were quietly beautiful but without sparkle; others seemed to light up the sea and the sun itself. The handsomest faces were those that did not reveal what they had lived through.

On their return, the days fell into a normal rhythm: attacks on the army and the police, curfew, repressions, demonstrations against regulations. Sensational news: the three resistance organizations concluded an agreement to cooperate. In one night ten bombs exploded at various nerve centers. The Lehi blew up military aircraft, the Irgun blew up a barracks, the Palmach and the Haganah brought in a few hundred refugees near Netanya. Unprecedented convulsions racked the country. Endless debates and discussions. When you're fighting for independence, where do your rights end? How do you respond to death sentences imposed by military courts? To a whipping by the police the Irgun replied by publicly whipping a British soldier. The British authorities threatened to execute "terrorists." These same terrorists took officers hostage: an eye for an eye, a life for a life.

Eretz Israel had not seethed like this since Bar Kochba's revolt.

(Any victory is temporary, a victory over time more so than others. Yet now Elhanan could not restrain himself. For him, every moment of clarity was a triumph that he earnestly tried to sustain. At those times he would speak until exhausted, not knowing if it would be granted him to finish the story he had begun.

So he often had the feeling that the memory he was summoning was the last. Like the scribe copying Holy Scripture, he wanted to bless God for each word that he succeeded in bringing to life.)

ELHANAN ROSENBAUM'S WORDS

Fool that I am, I never realized that Talia was leading a double life. I never guessed. She covered her tracks perfectly, she who never lied about anything. She claimed she was working for the secret service of an organization for underground immigration. In the evening she sometimes left me, saying in the most natural tone, "I'm on duty tonight. Don't wait up for me; I'll see you in the morning. If I sleep late, wake me. You know I love to have breakfast with you." Only later, lifetimes later, when I came back from Amman, did her parents tell me the whole story. They knew it all along.

At the time, I was working in the Czech consulate. I knew the vice consul. He'd studied at the yeshiva in Feherfalu, and my parents had suggested that he "eat a meal" every Wednesday. "I spoke to the consul about you," he told me one day. "We need someone like you, with Hebrew, Yiddish, German and the Slavic languages." They hired me as a translator. A decent salary and a reasonable work load. Talia couldn't get over it: "How did you manage to do so well so soon? Do you realize—you've barely arrived and you're already set!" What impressed her most was my consular ID. "If I understand this, you're almost a diplomat, aren't you? Do you have diplomatic immunity?" Talia laughed, and I too. I saw her happy, and I laughed.

I should have been more careful.

I remember one morning she was reading the paper and she turned pale. Overcome, she almost passed out. "What is it, Talia? Are you sick?" There was another question on the tip of my tongue, but I preferred not to ask it: Could you be pregnant? I brought her a glass of cold water. She took a sip, then another, as she stared at the front-page photo: five men, still young, chained together and surrounded by British police. "That's Saul," she said.

"Which one?"

She pointed: in his twenties, bushy-browed, an ironic smile. I asked, "Do you know him?"

She knew him. "A friend from school days." In fact, he was a comrade in arms. And the others? They, too, but she didn't know them: compartmentalizing was a rule of the underground. Arrested by British police during an attack on a military base, the five were to be tried by a military court. And then? The scaffold. "It has to stop," she said. I agreed. But I was against terrorism. Talia and I discussed this often. "And you don't oppose the British oppression that produces terrorism?" Yes, I did. "Then you're against everybody?" Yes. I was against everybody; they were all too violent for me.

Even so, she was noticeably preoccupied with armed resisters. Most of her reading was news reports and articles about them. Irgun, Lehi, Palmach, Haganah: she knew them all as if they were her domain. She knew their tactics and the names of their leaders. The Haganah? Moderate, prudent. The Palmach: an elite paramilitary unit. The Irgun: more extremist than the Palmach. The Lehi: more extremist than the Irgun.

In 1946 and '47, everybody talked about those four movements. Not a day went by without one of them sabotaging a bridge or a strategic building. Daring and ingenious, they penetrated the heart of civil and military administration. They extorted money from banks, cut telephone lines, stole vehicles and munitions, took hostages, and then issued communiqués: invisible, they were as ubiquitous as their too visible oppressors.

When I came home from the office one Sabbath morning I found Talia in tears. Rigid with pain, she was reading accounts of the trial of two underground fighters. Armed when captured, they refused to plead guilty. More, they denied the legitimacy of the proceedings. To every question from the judge they responded, "We're Jews, and this land is our land." The rest of the time, they sang. The prosecutor made speeches, the witnesses bore witness, the judge grew furious; but the accused sang. Finally the court tried them in absentia. To inform them of the death sentence, the judge and his entourage went to their cells. The two resisters received the verdict singing. One of them, Shimon, said, "You can keep us from living, but you cannot keep us from singing." Wrenched, Talia's father remarked, "Those words will live in the legend of Israel." Reuma wiped her tears and said, "May Israel's guardian keep them safe." Talia corrected her: "They're keeping Israel's guardian safe." I never intervened. Of course I admired the young Jewish heroes and grieved over their lot; but in my heart of hearts I thought, What a waste; haven't we lost enough blood? My in-laws, surprised at my silence, exchanged glances, as if wondering whether I understood. No, I did not understand.

I was a fool.

One Friday night we were waiting for Talia, who was late, something that had never happened before. We were always together for the first Sabbath meal. I liked to hear my father-in-law recite, in his heavy Russian accent, praise of his wife, that "woman of valor," and I liked my mother-in-law's Yemenite *zemirot,* and I liked the mood at table. Sometimes I could close my eyes and see myself once more in my father's house; I would tell him about Sabbath in Jerusalem.

Talia late? Where could she be? At the office? On a Sabbath eve? "Something must have come up," said my father-in-law. "Maybe a boat came in unexpectedly." He proposed that we sit down to dinner. My mother-in-law shook her head no. "Let's wait," she said.

"You're right. Sabbath isn't Sabbath without our daughter."

Talia came home after midnight. She was unrecognizable. Her hair was tangled, her eyes swollen, her skirt and blouse stained with oil and blood. "I need a hot bath," was all she said. She went upstairs, spent twenty minutes in the bathtub and came downstairs glowing, as if nothing had happened. Anguish fled from my mother-in-law's face; it was replaced by pride.

Next morning we heard on the radio that the Irgun had attacked a military convoy. Two soldiers dead, three wounded. The terrorists had sustained no casualties.

Everybody knows the rest. The world press told pretty much the whole story. The British command ordered a curfew. Gigantic raids, mass arrests.

"Was it worth it?" I asked Talia at dinner, later.

"Of course it was worth it."

"Look around: the whole country's suffering for one skirmish."

"Look around: that skirmish did permanent damage to the prestige of the British Empire."

"Are you sure? On one side, a pinprick. On the other, draconian punishments."

"A few more pinpricks like that, and the British army won't have enough medicine to treat themselves."

"Well, listen to you defending terrorists!"

"They're not terrorists. They're freedom fighters, they're the resistance!"

"If you admire them that much, what would you say if I decided to join them?"

Talia became serious. She seemed to be considering my question, which was only intended as a joke, and then she answered, "If you join an underground movement, I hope it's because you admire it and not just because I do."

The truth is, I wasn't ready. I recognized the resistance's courage and generosity, but from a distance. They chose danger, and that was their business. I'd been through enough danger in my youth. I broke with violence in 1945. Forever? Why not forever?

Was it perhaps because we felt that fate was about to separate us and that we had to live out our whole future in a few months, a few deeds? We loved each other with a perfect and all-consuming love that haloed our daily existence with a fragile mist of eternity.

Sometimes Talia said, half seriously, "All this has me worried. What's happening to us is too beautiful, too pure. The gods are jealous. Let's do something to appease their envy."

"What do you suggest?"

"A quarrel."

"About what?"

"Anything."

"All right," I said. "You first."

We argued for a moment and then burst out laughing.

I felt the threat everywhere. To wait for Talia when she worked late tested my nerves. One morning as I watched her drink her coffee, completely preoccupied, I felt my heart palpitating, as if it would burst. Usually the coffee mustache made me laugh. Not now. Now I suffered. Talia raised her head: "Are you in pain?" No, I was not in pain. It was something else, but what it was I could not say.

On November 29, 1947, an exuberant and profound joy surged through the country. Towns and villages, kibbutzim north and south, all applauded the United Nations vote in a delirious whirl. The world had finally acknowledged the validity of Jewish demands. Praised be Thou, Lord, Who granted us this victory. Everyone burst into song, into dance, into a celebration of history's meaning and a triumph over destiny. A groundswell stirred the

Jewish people's memory. Never again, the wandering; never again, the exile; never again, the fear. In a burst of happiness, Talia kissed her parents and took my arm. "Let's go make love," she whispered. "Now?" I was startled. "With the whole world looking at Lake Success, you want to go to bed?" "Yes. Later, when our children ask us what we were doing when the United Nations voted for Israel's independence, we can tell them, or at least think: we were making love." And truly the people of Israel everywhere made love, not physically but through the joining of all their memories of the past and their hopes for the future. Every one of them felt at home in history, at last; every one of them meditated upon fate and said Amen.

In Palestine as in ancient Judea, some attitudes quickly changed. After the United Nations vote I shared the general belief that war was inevitable and not to serve would be dishonorable.

Next day I told Talia I'd decided to join an underground group. "Which one?" she asked. I had no idea. For my purposes, one was as good as the next. I was not involved in politics; I trusted my instincts. Also luck, which decreed that on this day the Lehi's pamphlets would impress me by their lyrical tone and mystical content. A colleague at the consulate hinted that he had contacts with the movement. "Can you put in a good word with someone?" He could. A week later, December 10th or was it the 12th, I found myself in a cellar, before three men hidden by a curtain. They put me through a grueling interrogation. They insisted on hearing all about my past, my activities and opinions, my social relations. I wasn't offended. They were doing their job, after all; how could they be sure I wasn't an informer? "We'll be in touch," said a shadow. "When?" The same voice replied, "First lesson: don't ask questions."

Talk to Talia about it? Of course. I had to tell her. I shared everything with her. But this time she refused to listen. "Underground activities are serious matters. The less you talk, the better." I was offended: "Even to you?" She answered, "Exceptions to that rule can be dangerous." I was going to reply, "Tell me how you know so much about these rules," but the discussion was obviously over, and I didn't argue.

A few days later, I found a scrap of paper in my coat pocket: "Tomorrow afternoon at 5 outside the Eden Cinema." Probably my colleague had put it there. I took him aside. "Tomorrow's Friday, isn't it?" "Yes, Friday." "Don't you think the time and place are a bad choice?" "I don't know what you're talking about." "But—" "I'll say it again: I don't know what you're talking about." All right, I understood, security regulations made him play dumb. All the same, a good Jew like me doesn't go to the movies on a Friday night (the theater would be closed anyway); he stays home and prepares for the Sabbath. How was I going to explain my absence to Talia and her parents?

Next day I left the office at one in the afternoon. At four I announced that I had a toothache. "I'm going to the dentist." My mother-in-law made me promise to hurry back. Of course, of course. At five o'clock sharp I was in front of the Eden Cinema. Doors and ticket booth were shut. This is stupid, I thought, picking a place like this for a secret meeting. A voice jarred me from my thoughts. "Don't turn around or attract attention. Just walk. The next street on the right." A cold, neutral voice. Polish or Lithuanian accent. After a few steps I noted a dapper man beside me. Worked for a bank, maybe? He passed along some news: from now on I was part of Lehi. Caution and vigilance. For now, keep my eyes and ears open. Whatever I learned at the consulate or in consular circles, I would report back to him. He was my contact. I couldn't hide my disappointment: "Is that all? I was a partisan! I'd hoped for action!" "It's not up to you to determine where you can best serve," answered this bank clerk, who was called Yiftah.

I met him two or three times a week and passed along news and impressions. Anything of importance? No. But it was not my place to judge. In January, Yiftah told me I was to attend classes in ideology. All right, go for ideology; what won't a man do for his country? The courses were given at a dentist's: the history of Zionism, the origins of anti-Semitism, geopolitical theory. The difference between Herzl and Jabotinsky; the breach between David Raziel's Irgun and Avraham Stern's Lehi; their common adversary, the Haganah. . . . The courses came to an end, thank God, and I repeated my wish to take part in real operations. "If I wanted a political education I could have enrolled at the university." Yiftah didn't dignify that with an answer.

But he must have relayed my request to his superiors, because shortly afterward I was taking a crash course in sabotage, followed quickly by my first mission. "I'm going out tonight," I told Talia. "Things to do at the office." She smiled and kissed me. "Be careful."

The mission was a disaster. Our intelligence was poor, and our group walked into a trap. The arms depot we were to burgle was under surveillance. We were lucky: the British soldiers fired before we moved in. "Disperse!" shouted our commander. We made our way to the Kerem Hatemanim, the "Yemenite Vineyard," where underground patriots were always welcomed with enthusiasm and gratitude.

The second mission, in March, was more successful. We attacked another depot. A textbook operation. In no time we had the sentries bound and gagged. Wearing army uniforms, we walked around the camp unafraid and in no apparent hurry. The booty: two trucks piled high with machine guns, rifles and ammunition.

Back home again, I was itching to tell Talia. But she had more important news. She was pregnant. My head whirled. It was totally unexpected. "Are you disappointed?" Talia asked.

I took her face in my hands. "I'm happy, Talinka." Happy and worried. "When is our child due?"

"Why? Are you in a hurry?" No, I was in no hurry. "Late August, early September," Talia said.

"What shall we call it?"

"If it's a girl, we'll name her after your mother, all right? And if it's a boy . . ."

I said nothing. I couldn't speak. I had a vision of myself far off, with my parents.

On May 14, 1948, we were all gathered together at my in-laws', where our neighbors had joined us. Hardly breathing, we listened to David Ben-Gurion's speech declaring the independence of the Jewish state, which would bear the name of Israel. Should I be ashamed to confess that I sat there dizzied, with tears in my eyes? Talia, too. And the neighbors. And my in-laws. When old Rabbi Fischman recited the *shehekheyanu*—"Blessed be Thou, O Lord, king of the universe, that Thou hast let us live to see this day"—we all hugged and kissed for a long time. "Our child will be born in a free Jewish state," said Talia.

I went to the window. The past had seized me by the throat. I remembered my grandfather awaiting the Messiah, convinced that He was already on the way. I remembered my father asserting that the messianic promise dwells in each of us. I remembered my mother who—"Shabbat in a few minutes," said Talia's mother. "Let's light the candles." I thought of my mother most of all on the Sabbath. I'll never forget her because I'll never forget the Sabbath.

(Forgive me. I know that in dictating these pages I say things I no longer believe; how can I say I'll never forget when I'm plunging into forgetfulness? The day will come when I've forgotten everything. Even my mother? Even my mother. The Sabbath, too? Even the Sabbath. What can I do to preserve what keeps me alive? I don't want to forget, do you hear me, Mother? I don't want to. . . .)

"Don't think sad thoughts," Talia said, leaning against me. "Think of our child. It will be a boy. We'll name him for your father."

Across from our house a door opened. A Hasid appeared: he seemed to have stepped right out of my childhood. Suppose it was my grandfather? I called to him: "Where are you going?"

"What a question! Where do you suppose a Jew goes on Friday night? To services, of course!"

"Then you haven't heard the news?"

"What news?"

"We have a Jewish state."

"I heard it."

"And you're going off to pray?"

Grouchy, he pulled his beard and said, "If we have a Jewish state today, isn't it because the Jews never stopped praying? And now that we have it, you want us to stop praying?"

I turned to be closer to Talia's warmth. I saw other eyes looking at me through hers. And I wondered, Why us? What have we done to deserve this happiness from history, when for centuries history has given us everything but happiness? "Talia," I said, "promise me I'll always remember this hour, this minute."

"I promise," Talia said.

And yet a day would come . . .

(On this late afternoon Elhanan was happy. Malkiel, too. Elhanan was in a cheerful phase. His memories of Jerusalem had restored the vigor he seemed to have lost. He had been at it for two days. His voice was stronger. He rarely hesitated. His power and eloquence were renewed. The mist that had shrouded his past was dissipated; the altar of memory was brightly lit. Tamar teased her friend's father: "You're young again, Elhanan. If you go on like this, I'll marry you and not your son."

On the table, two recorders taped his account.

These restorations of memory were strange and unforeseeable. They came in the morning, or at night, and they lasted ten minutes or three hours. After which, weary, depleted, Elhanan relapsed into an apparent torpor, which, in fact, disguised increasing pain.

Everything went well today. Loretta hummed as she served dessert. Everything was happy today.)

Jerusalem, in those days: I remember it well. A blazing climate, stimulating and oppressive at the same time. The Old City was under siege by the Arab Legion. The Jewish quarter was still fighting but was succumbing to sheer exhaustion. They issued hourly calls for help to every staff headquarters in the Jewish city. They'd have to move fast if they wanted to preserve the honor of the city of David. Not easy. Officially Jerusalem was not part of Israel. This city's memories were the most Jewish in the whole world—but it had been internationalized. Did that hurt? All we could do was grit our teeth, wait, be patient.

In Jerusalem the four underground movements maintained their independent ways. Each kept its own infrastructure, its cadres, its bases. They collaborated, often successfully, on important objectives. All four were represented in the Jewish quarter of the Old City. All four knew they had to reinforce the last combatants there, men and women who could take it no longer. "Out of ammunition . . . three cartridges per man . . . a lot of wounded . . . a lot of dead . . . it's a matter of days—no, hours." What could be done? The Israeli army was fighting on all fronts—to the north, to the south—and the survival of the fledgling state hung on every shot fired. By what right did we sacrifice these rather than those? At all levels commanding officers were desperate: we have *got* to do something for the Old City, but what? Launch a counterattack? With what weapons? For the moment, the problem was to save the Jewish fighters in the Jewish quarter. Or at the very least to send in reinforcements.

On May 23 or so I attended an emergency war council in a Lehi camp. There were about fifty of us. Our commanding officer—was it Yiftah? I can't remember anymore—told us how grave the situation was. If no help broke through, the Jewish fighters would have to surrender. We'd need somebody who knew the Old City, the Jewish quarter. Maybe somebody who remembered a secret entrance. One voice rose above the rest: "I'm your man." I was startled, we were all startled: it was Absalom. I felt like laughing—this was a man? He was a boy. Not even bar mitzvah yet. "I used to live in the Jewish quarter," Absalom said. "I know every crevice. I even remember an underground tunnel; my grandfather showed it to me. He was a great cabbalist, my grandfather. He said the Messiah would use that tunnel. If you want, I can find it for you." Yiftah—was it Yiftah?—took a good look at the boy, called him closer, patted his head and thought it over in silence. Absalom stood easy, calm, sure of himself and his skills.

"All right," Yiftah said, "find the tunnel. But—"

He broke off; we held our breath; had he changed his mind? "You're not going in alone. I want somebody to go with you."

Arms shot up; everybody volunteered. Everybody but me. And yet Yiftah chose me. "You have a precious ID. You're practically part of the diplomatic corps. If anything happens to you, you'll have a better chance of talking your way out of it." Argue with him? It would have been unworthy. But . . . I thought of Talia, of her child, our child. Had I the right to run this risk? Had I the right to turn it down?

"Don't worry about a thing," Absalom told me. "We'll do just fine. I promise."

Yiftah added, "You'll leave tonight. Two in the morning, all right?" Absalom said it was all right, and I looked at my watch. Eight in the evening. I had time to go home, kiss Talia, hug her parents. "Is it all right?" Yiftah granted permission.

Talia suspected nothing and asked no questions. Nor did her parents. We made polite conversation: the situation on the various fronts, news from the United Nations, the glorious behavior of certain rabbis, openly violating the Sabbath to work on the city's fortifications. Talia was paler than usual and her father less talkative. I wanted to be alone with Talia and to tell her, "Talia, Talinka, if I die, don't wear mourning forever. Do it for our son. He'll want his mother to be happy." But I didn't say a word. Was it because I had premonitions that matters would turn out otherwise? I don't know. Our last evening together was punctuated by endless silences. Now and then I took her hand and squeezed it tightly. Or I looked into her eyes and smiled sadly. We said good-bye at midnight. I found myself back in the street, my heart heavy; I was thinking that I'd never see her again—meaning I was going to die. I never did see her again, and yet I am still alive.

Absalom took my hand as we moved toward the Old City. The ghetto in Stanislav came back to my mind. We slipped in and out of houses. I was totally confused by all the doors opening and closing. Were we in a cellar? An attic? We seemed to be walking across rooftops when we were actually crossing a narrow courtyard. Was fear doing this to me? I was sweating; it ran down my back. Absalom pulled me along, and I followed him meekly. Ask him to slow down? I'd have been ashamed. He might have told his grandfather, the cabbalist. "You won't believe this, Grandpa, but the guy they gave me for a partner said he was tired." No, Absalom, don't say that. I am no coward. . . .

How long had we been walking in the dark? I had no idea. Absalom stopped suddenly and whispered to me, "This is the Hurva, Rabbi Yehuda Hehassid's synagogue." Half demolished. He went as far as the ruins and came back: nobody there, he said. We continued on our way. Another stop. This was the prophet Elijah's synagogue. We listened. We heard noises inside. Absalom knocked very gently. A voice asked, "Who is it?" Absalom answered. The door opened.

We were greeted like saviors. They shook hands with us, clapped us on the shoulder, offered us brandy, promised us paradise. Suddenly I realized that we'd stumbled into the Jewish quarter's last line of defense. "Come over here," said a voice. It was an officer who wished to debrief us. I couldn't see his features in the darkness, but his voice seemed familiar. I couldn't quite place it. He asked specific and incisive questions: Where were the reinforcements? Why the delay? And the medical supplies? And the ammunition? I heard the voice, it penetrated, it nagged at my soul; that voice must own a face. But it was still dark. Dawn was on the way. It arrived. I saw the face: impossible! Itzik, my wartime comrade, my close friend, my sworn enemy. Itzik, faithful companion, ruthless rapist. A hallucination? I shook myself: no, I was awake, all right. Itzik got over his surprise in a hurry. He was an officer and would complete his mission whatever the cost. He'd hold this position to the last man, but he wanted to know, he *had* to know, what was happening across the lines, in the new city. "Do they realize how bad it is here? Do they know the civilians are exhausted and want us to surrender unconditionally?" I forced myself to answer: they realized everything, they knew everything, they were doing their best. . . . Absalom said shyly, "I'll go back the way I came and bring reinforcements in." Itzik was incredulous and asked, "Do you really know a secret passage?" I confirmed it; this little Yemenite Jew was something special. I loved him like a brother. I'd always loved Yemenites, with their hearts of gold.

"Good," Itzik said. "You rest, Absalom, and—"

Absalom refused. "Every minute counts," he said. "I'd rather leave right away." And he asked me, "Are you coming?" I wanted to say yes, but Itzik's presence changed everything; buried deep within me were words I had to say to him, words that had waited years.

"You won't leave before nightfall," Itzik ordered Absalom. "Get some rest. That's an order." The little Yemenite obeyed. He stretched out on a cot and fell asleep in seconds. "You too," Itzik told me. "Try to sleep. I have things to do." I pulled a blanket over me but didn't sleep a wink. Toward noon I sat in on a meeting of officers and leaders of what remained of the community. Some of them, courageous, preached resistance to the end. Others, no less courageous but more realistic, advocated a cease-fire. "We can evacuate the children and the sick," Itzik told them. "There's an underground passage. . . ." No one believed him. "Absalom here came in that way yesterday. Elhanan, too." He turned to me: "Tell them."

I told them. An old rabbi said, "It's possible. Miracles happen. When Moses fled the pharaoh's court, an angel struck the Egyptians deaf and dumb. The same angel can do the same thing here." The community leaders repaired to the cellar to talk things over, while the soldiers went to battle stations. The Jordanians kept up a continuous fire; our men answered, trying not to waste ammunition. From time to time we heard a shout: "Yaakov's wounded! Help, quick! Berakhya, watch out, get down!"

Late in the afternoon two rabbis were authorized to request an audience with the Jordanian commanding officer. They sought permission to bury our dead. By both Jewish and Koranic law, the dead must not spend a night within walls. Permission granted. I heard the rabbis chanting their lamentations. I thought, If I die now, they will also chant for me. Absalom was waking up; I looked at him in the half-light. Would my son be like him? I hoped so. Brave, reliable Absalom: I admired his courage as much as his wisdom, and I knew that in the Old City children were heroic. There was the story of a twelve-year-old boy who managed to set up and fire the only heavy machine gun the defenders had. Without these boys and girls, fearless messengers fleet as the wind, the Jewish quarter would long since have fallen into enemy hands. I'd heard that a boy of ten saved his commanding officer by dragging him through the rubble to a field hospital, after which he hurried back to the front.

Even in the time of the Talmud the sages boasted about the

intelligence, courage and passion of Jerusalem's children. Today, in this war without hope, no poet could devise a language rich enough to sing their praises.

Absalom, Absalom: only King David deserves to say how proud we were of you. Only he could give voice to the anguish that gripped me as I watched you prepare to move out.

"Can I leave now?"

"Not before midnight," Itzik said.

Absalom went back to sleep. And I felt a need to watch over him; and a need to pray to God to watch over all his friends, all those children who were defying death itself.

"I'm going with him," I told my onetime friend and enemy.

"All right."

We seemed to have said all there was to say. Nothing to do now but wait. Some of us were dozing. Others were daydreaming. Abruptly Itzik rose and came over to sit by me. At last, I thought. Time for a frank discussion. Why did he wait till now? Because death was lurking? Because this might be the last time we would speak? Itzik chatted idly. He didn't know how to broach the subject. Finally he plunged in. "Are you still angry?"

"Not angry. That's not the word."

"What is the word?"

"Disappointed. Disgusted."

"Then you can't forget."

"No, I can't forget."

I saw us back there, back then: him, sprawled on top of that poor woman; and me, standing by, a useless protester.

"Why did you do it, Itzik?"

"I told you. For revenge."

"But she hadn't done anything to you!"

"No, she hadn't. But her husband had, and his accomplices, and all her people."

"And you punished her because of them?"

"She was there, and the others weren't. They told me her husband was a sadistic son of a bitch, and to me she stood for him and all his filthy ways."

Go on in this vein? What good would it do? He knew my questions, and I knew his answers. Nothing would reconcile us. I thought so then, and I think so now. We do not make one human being suffer for the sins of another. Jewish morality forbids it. Vengeance is God's alone. King David reminds us of that in his psalms. Had Itzik repudiated King David? Had he hurled his Bible into the trash? The sons shall not be punished for the sins of their fathers, nor the wives for the sins of their husbands.

"How could you do it?" I asked him in a whisper. "How could you betray my admiration for you? My trust? How could you shame our cause by shaming a defenseless woman? How could you blaspheme, and betray the whole meaning of our struggle? On the eve of our victory over evil, how could you commit evil and call it glory?"

I saw him stiffen in the gloom. Itzik the Long seemed twice my size. He remained silent.

"And the divine image we all bear within us—what did you do to it? And the letter of the Torah that every one of us embodies—where did you leave it? And the Law that demands of us justice as much as mercy—how did you get around that?"

Itzik never moved a muscle.

"You, the fearless partisan, how could you stoop so low? You, a proud and inflexible Jew, how could you show such cowardice?"

The sorrow and anger of the past had come back to me. I wanted to hurt him badly, to shame him deeply. But I had to control myself: The enemy was not far. I had to speak softly. Even as I whispered I felt I was shouting, that heaven and earth heard my cries. The accused stood mute. Even after I'd finished blaming him, condemning him, he said nothing. He waited for me to continue, to go even further. And in the face of his silence I astonished myself by taking up his defense. In my mind, of course. Doesn't the Talmud teach us not to judge our friends until we have put ourselves in their place? Only then can we perhaps understand their true motivations. Only then can we put justice on a basis of truth. It is always the other within us that we reveal in displaying scorn or pity. He who judges himself may judge; he who judges judges himself. Me, a judge? Were we in the midst of a trial? A trial without magistrates or clerks, without bailiffs or spectators? A trial in which the accused declined to defend himself? Now he was murmuring. His murmur did not break the silence but on the contrary intensified it.

"I see, Elhanan. I see," he said. "So you'll never forget."

"I took a vow, Itzik. I vowed never to forget."

Who sighed? Did he? Did I?

It would soon be midnight. Absalom was saying his prayers. The prayer of *Ma'ariv*? Yes, and the one he prayed to his grandfather. "Guide us now as you guided us yesterday." We said good-bye to all, soldiers and civilians alike. Children were crying, and the wounded were moaning. We promised them all, "We'll be back before dawn." Itzik nodded in silence. Cautiously Absalom opened the door and slipped out. I followed him. No—I told myself I was going to follow him; I didn't follow him: a shot had just shattered the night. Someone cried, "No! Nooo!" Who was it? Absalom? Absalom never spoke again. We dragged him into the synagogue that bore the name of the prophet Elijah. I felt like screaming—Elijah, prophet of consolation, why don't you come now to console us? And who will console Absalom's parents? Because Absalom was dead. The bullet struck his heart, the heart that sang in silent longing for the Messiah. Tomorrow his dust would return to dust, and I would hear the rabbis' lamentations. And now? There was no more now. No more tomorrow either. The secret passage? There was no more passage. There was no one to bring reinforcements. No one to open the way for help. "Battle stations," said the commanding officer. "The Legionnaires may be mounting a night attack." I saw Itzik reaching for his weapon and heading for the doorway. Follow him? What good would that do?

The night passed without further incident. I watched over Absalom's body. I recited psalms. I knew many of them by heart. At dawn I fell asleep. In a dream I saw the Tempter applauding himself. I woke to the sound of heavy gunfire: bullets ricocheted off our walls. Before nightfall we buried little Absalom.

"Watch out!" Two powerful arms wrestled me to the floor. I looked up. It was not my father, and not Zalmen my father-in-law; it was Itzik. We stood up at the same moment. "You're too tired," he said. Side by side, we began firing again. A bullet grazed my hair. A Jordanian marksman almost did me in; Itzik did him in. "Thank you, thank you, Itzik," I told him. "Bravo." As in the old days, we were comrades in arms, covering each other. Was the past forgotten? Buried. Some other time. Later. But there wouldn't be any later. Next morning, what had to happen happened. The Old City's defenders could hold out no more. No more ammunition. No more rations. No more energy. No more hope. Between us and the rest of the world stood a wall more solid than time and as strong as death. We were alone. Sacrificed. I saw a few old men preparing a white flag. I heard a woman tell her children not to move. I heard a fool talking to the *shekhinah*—the divine radiance herself—asking if she would accompany us into exile.

A bullet in the shoulder knocked me to the floor; I didn't even see the arms that lifted me and dragged me backward. An image of my mother rose in my flickering memory. Why was I so cold, when my body was burning? Why was my mother so present when Talia, so near, was invisible? Had I gone mad? I heard a lullaby: "Sleep, little one, sleep; the enemy sleeps not, but neither does God; He watches over Israel, the God of Israel." Who was singing? Talia? A mother gone crazy? Not mine. Mine had wings, and I was being sheltered beneath them. I was rising and rising, ever higher; the earth could not hold me back; I was escaping its gravity. Sleep, little one, sleep; the earth is here and the sky is there; they will be there when you wake. But the wings would not be there for my old friend. You should have taken cover sooner, Itzik. In a burst of energy I raised my head; I saw my friend flat on the floor like myself. I clung to one thought: I am going to find my mother and my father, and be with them at last.

Someone distributed bread and water. I was not hungry. Or thirsty. I let my imagination lead me to Talia. I smiled upon her and said, Go see my parents, they're insane with worry. We dropped two levels, and I saw Zalmen and Reuma, I saw them chatting with my parents, I heard my father ask me, Did you say your prayers this morning? Let us recite psalms together. Reuma smiled at me; my grandfather told me that as long as a Jew is reciting psalms his enemy cannot defeat him. He's crazy, said Zalmen. Who's crazy? my mother asked. The man who thinks psalms do more good than weapons, Zalmen said. He's crazy, said a Jewish soldier. That's the way it is, said Talia. That's the way it is, said another soldier.

The Legionnaires attacked, and we drove them back. They renewed the attack, and we drove them back again. "Stand fast," the radio told us. "Trust us," said our superior officers from the other world. We trusted them, we stood fast. "Another few hours and you won't be alone," our leaders told us. We trusted them, we stood fast. An hour, a day. Then two hours more, one day more. And we were still alone. I less than my comrades. Thanks to Absalom and his cabbalist grandfather, I knew an underground passage; in my mind I went through it and joined Talia and her loved ones. I was sure my parents loved her too. And besides, they told me, we're proud of you. May you only be as proud of your own son. But be careful, said my father, raising his voice. "Hey, be careful," a soldier shouted. The Legionnaires pushed my parents away and took their place. They launched another attack, intensifying the violence. To my right a soldier collapsed. Behind me a young woman cried, "I can't see, I'm blind!" Standing at a window, behind tattered sandbags, I fired and fired. Suddenly, behind me, I heard the voices of rabbis praying for the dead.

"That May 28th, was it a Friday? I can't even remember. You'll have to check it, son. . . . Is it important? Very important. Everything is important. Why that particular detail? Because . . . I don't know anymore."

Elhanan vaguely remembered women wailing. They were out of candles. How would they greet the Sabbath? He remembered men arguing, as if in a mist. Should we go on fighting? Even on the Sabbath? A wounded man said, in a feeble but clear voice, Let's offer one more Sabbath to our eternal city. Other voices answered him, but Elhanan could not make them out. They mingled and fused. In the end they produced a bizarre medley of Hebrew, Yiddish, Arabic and other languages, which Elhanan could not identify. I'm delirious, he thought. He was not alone: Jewish history itself was delirious.

That afternoon the Old City's Jewish life, uninterrupted since its founding, was extinguished. Three hundred forty soldiers, from fifteen to sixty years old, departed for a prison camp near Amman. One thousand four hundred civilians marched toward the Jewish city. The two hundred dead would be transferred later.

The battle was over. The dream was over. Glory gave way to humiliation and defeat.

"Listen, Malkiel," his father said. "The Talmud tells the story of a wise man who dedicates his whole life to the study of the tractate Hagiga. After his death, they see a woman in mourning communing at his grave. She is the tractate. That's a love story, Malkiel. So is the story of the Old City. But a lost love. Within those walls, we could not understand why the whole people of Israel had not come to her rescue. They told us to hold on, and we held on. They promised us salvation, and we waited. Were we wrong to expect something from a young nation fighting on a dozen fronts at once? Were we asking too much? When I think back to my short time there, I feel an overwhelming, ancient melancholy. Luckily, I was wounded. Pain kept me from thinking clearly. It kept me from thinking of your mother and you. . . . But I can remember the Jordanian Legionnaires bent over me, talking to me, asking who I was and how I felt. I remember wanting to answer and not being able to. I was lying on a stretcher, and I knew they were carrying me off. I murmured, Put me down, I want to walk, I can walk. The stretcher bearers set me down. Two comrades helped me walk. Slowly, very slowly, we walked toward the trucks that would transport us to Jordan. In my mind I saw myself walking toward the train station with my mother and the last Jews of my village. For years I had hated myself for leaving my mother. Well, I found her again in Jerusalem."

(Elhanan was talking and Malkiel was listening. With a full heart he heard his sick father recall a time long gone, a world long gone. There was perfect harmony between father and son: the more the father let himself go, the more the son took in. In proportion as Elhanan felt his memory diminish, Malkiel felt his own expand.)

"I learned from the Red Cross that your mother was all right. In September they told me that I was the father of a son. Then I started to write letters to you in my head. I told you all about my life in the hospital and my life in the prisoner-of-war camp. I tried to make you laugh, because I was naive and believed my son was so intelligent, so precocious, that he'd understand my jokes. Oh yes, Malkiel, I was naive. I thought, Talia will read what I have not even written, and will laugh as only she can laugh when she's happy. She'll laugh so hard that our son, only a few weeks old, will laugh, too.

"It was in March of 1949, after I returned to Jerusalem, that Zalmen and Reuma, sicker at heart than the liberated prisoners, told me the truth. Your mother had died giving birth to you.

"The realization scorched my soul: I would never again be happy."

A LETTER FROM TALIA TO HER HUSBAND

You have been a prisoner for exactly one month. The Red Cross tells us not to worry. The newspapers here don't write about you anymore. My parents, adorable as always and even more so, do their best to keep up my spirits. My mother tells me funny stories; every day my father, good civil servant that he is, brings me more documentation on the laws protecting prisoners of war. "Believe me," he says, "the whole world is protecting Elhanan." My mother adds, "And God, too, no? Are you saying that God isn't protecting him?" You see how it is.

I'm angry with myself. I should never have let you leave for the Old City. I should have explained to your commanders that your health didn't permit it. And that we were expecting a child. I should have, I should have.

Will you be home in time for the birth of our son? I know it will be a son. Hurry home, Elhanan. The doctor says it won't be long.

In your absence, I talk to our son. I talk about you. And all we did together in Europe. Sometimes I burst out laughing. The look on your face, aboard the *Cretan,* when I announced our marriage!

I love you, and I want our son to know it. I love him, and I want you to know it. How happy we will be, we three together!

What is it that I love about you? Your excessive shyness? The attention you pay to other people's fears and desires? The way you turn aside when certain memories force their way into your mind? You know what? I'm going to surprise you. What I love about you is myself. Don't laugh; I love the image you receive of me. In you, thanks to you, I feel purer and more deserving. Because of you I feel closer to God. At breakfast this morning I even said so to my parents. Of course my mother wept. And naturally my father philosophized: "Normally it's the opposite. Because of God we feel closer to others. But you've always had the spirit of contradiction." After sighing, my mother said innocently, "What do you want from her? To me her vision and yours are the same." She is wonderful, my mother. Her shortcuts are as good as the ablest thinkers' eloquence.

I must tell you, for example, her comment about the *Altalena*. But I'm forgetting: do you know anything about that depressing and tragic story? *Altalena* is the name of a ship that the Irgun chartered in Europe to transport a thousand armed fighters and a lot of ammunition, which Israel needed, believe me. But our prime minister David Ben-Gurion claimed that the head of the Irgun, Menachem Begin, was in fact mounting a coup. How can we tell if he was right? At any rate, Palmach units shelled the *Altalena* and set it afire. The upshot was that twenty-odd Irgun fighters, survivors of the death camps, were killed by Jewish bullets. In a radio broadcast, a sobbing Begin ordered his troops not to retaliate: anything but a civil war, he said. For his part, Ben-Gurion told the Knesset that on the day the Third Temple is reconstructed, they would display the cannon that had shelled the *Altalena*. My mother's comment: "I weep for the Jews who fired as much as I do for those who fell." My father's? A brief and angry, "They're insane."

We do live in crazy times. Count Bernadotte, the big shot from the Red Cross and the United Nations, says he's strictly neutral, but everybody else says he's pro-Arab. Our administration is organized along British lines: civil servants take themselves very seriously. We have a finance minister without finances. In the meantime, refugees are streaming in from Germany, and deportees from Kenya and Cyprus. Jerusalem is still under siege: the road is open only for huge convoys. You can imagine how they're greeted—by general jubilation. Everything is rationed, meat, milk, bread. Our neighbor on this floor—you remember him? a skinny, distinguished-looking bachelor?—is leaving for Belgium, where he has family. By the way: to go abroad you need military authorization. You can't do anything anymore without permits. You see? We're finally a state like all the others.

Just the same, one thing surprises me: nobody talks about the Old City anymore. Abandoned? Poor thing. Since you left, I can imagine how demoralized it must have become. And yet, at the highest levels, they'd already decided on an operation to relieve it, involving combined forces of Palmach, Irgun and Lehi. With a reckless courage that everybody understood and was hoping for, the troops fought their way in. For ten hours the Old City was in our hands. And then, nobody knows how or why, they were forced to withdraw. An officer told one of our friends (Rafi, you know who I mean, a blond fellow, Yardena's buddy) that an elite unit had been ordered to evacuate a key point, thus letting the Jordanian Legionnaires retake it without a shot fired. Who's responsible for that mishap? In cases like that we always say, "History will judge." Always blame it on history.

And if you become a historian? I'd give a lot to hear you discuss these times with your son. Am I talking foolishness? You're right, Elhanan, my love. I'd give a lot to see you right now. And even more to see your face when you take your first look at our son, who will—yes indeed, my love—bear your father's name.

I hope he loves you, and I hope he is loved. I hope he learns all about our common past and is proud of it. You'll teach him his first lessons. Promise? It is your duty as a father. And I, poor woman, will hold my peace in the next room, or even in the kitchen, and listen to you; and if I weep, don't be angry.

In the first lesson I want you to say this to him (I had it from my own father): "To learn is to receive, and then it is to give, and then it is to receive again."

You gave me a son, my love.

You gave me life.

Bless me as I bless you.

"Why didn't you go back to Jerusalem to live?"

"I was afraid."

"Afraid to live there?"

"Afraid I wasn't worthy of living there. Do you understand? Without your mother, how could I wake beneath the same sky that we blessed together every morning? Jerusalem. I can see it now, and I can see us when we first arrived. I was full of faith in your mother and myself. I turned to her and said, 'I love you,' and through her I was declaring my love for Jerusalem."

"Tell me a memory of Jerusalem."

"A blue cloud shot with red, almost incandescent. A silence full of melodious prayers."

"Go on."

"A beggar."

"A beggar? Not my mother?"

"You're right—your mother is Jerusalem. But when I recall the road to Jerusalem, it's always a beggar that I see. He offers to share his meal with me."

"And you accept?"

"I accept everything from Jerusalem. Only in Jerusalem can a Jew learn the art of receiving."

The chambermaid knocked. "You're wanted on the telephone, sir."

"Me? On the phone?"

"Yes, sir."

"Who could be calling me here?" He went downstairs to the front desk. His heart racing, he picked up the receiver: let it not be about his father! "Yes?"

"Malkiel, is that you? How is everything?" It was the sage.

"Don't shout. If you do, we don't need the telephone."

"I may have a little assignment for you."

"I thought I was on leave."

"It won't take long."

"What's it about?"

"The head of state over there. There's a lot of talk here."

The fool! Didn't he know that this conversation was being taped by the secret police? "No need to shout. I hear you perfectly well. Too well, maybe."

"Will you do it, then? A thousand words on the man himself, his family, his public standing. There's nobody better qualified than you."

Malkiel was thinking, Come on, friend! You're not a beginner! Do you want the secret police all over me?

Later the sage would explain: It was a way to protect Malkiel. The Romanian authorities would know that the *Times* was behind him.

"I'll try. But I'm not sure—"

"Give it a shot. We'd really appreciate it. Incidentally, when are you planning to be back?"

"I don't know yet. A few days more, maybe. There're still a dozen inscriptions to work out."

When he met Lidia an hour later, she knew all about it. "I hope you won't write that article," she said.

"Why not?"

"Don't ask too many questions."

They walked toward the cemetery. Malkiel had the feeling they were being followed. "Is that possible?" he murmured.

"You could even say it was probable."

He turned: no one in sight.

"Listen to me," Lidia said. "In this country, caution is the first rule. The man is mad. And dangerous. If you said anything bad about him he could have you killed in an accident. If you said anything good you'd be lying, and anyway no flattery would satisfy him unless you treated him like God. You concentrate on your dead friends. You'll be better off, believe me."

"All right." The chief of state's crimes were not a priority just then. Maybe later, when he was back in the States. The man would still be news.

"Can I tell them that?" Lidia asked.

"Yes."

After a pause she went on: "I'm not sure I admire your good sense, but I approve of it."

Good sense? Me?

Lidia was making tea in her tiny kitchen. She moved gracefully. Even her silence was graceful, even her prolonged silence. She must have been unhappy. He could see it, he could feel it. She had a way of looking at him and smiling that revealed inner distress. Divorced? A spinster? A widow? How to tell? What good would it do him to know? He that increaseth knowledge increaseth sorrow, said the wisest king in the Bible. To hell with knowledge.

Malkiel and Lidia had dined at the hotel restaurant. There were few patrons. The service was slapdash. Conversation languished. Malkiel was not in a mood to chat, nor was Lidia. Malkiel wanted to go upstairs and sleep. Lidia suggested coffee or tea at her flat. "Don't be afraid."

"I can't help it," he said. "Beautiful women terrify me." She didn't crack a smile. Poor Malkiel. He wasn't too handy with compliments. Or with women, for that matter. He became awkward in their presence. Why so shy? He must see a psychiatrist. Someday. Later. After he completed the mission his father had entrusted him with. In the meantime he could pretend. He could pretend to be a shy fellow or a conqueror. None of that mattered. What mattered was that he was not good at pretending.

"So? Tea or not?"

"Tea," he said, wondering what he had let himself in for.

They had walked in silence to her flat. Why this sudden uneasiness between them? Malkiel could not explain it. Because she had finally lured him into a trap? Well, he thought briefly, here I am playing a spy taken *in flagrante*.

A modest apartment. Two dimly lit rooms. Living room, kitchen and shower. Malkiel sat on the couch and inspected the walls. A few pictures, naive landscapes. Where were the microphones? Under the lamp, perhaps. In the kitchen? No, inside the ashtray. Too bad he didn't smoke.

Lidia came back with tea. Sugar. She sat on the carpet. Their legs touched. Where were the cameras? "Why aren't you married, Lidia?"

She blushed. Her voice was husky. "It's a long story." She hadn't said "an old story."

"Where does it begin?"

"Are you really interested?"

"Everything interests me." Someone had to fill the silences; just as well to let her do it. As long as she was talking about her own life, Malkiel wouldn't think about his. His father: far, far away. The war: far away, farther still. Tamar: frustrated, drowning. Tamar, where was Tamar? "So, Lidia, your story?"

"We were young." She bowed her head. "Students. He was finishing medical school, and I was in modern languages. We knew each other by sight, ate at the same student restaurant, went to the same plays and the same demonstrations, where student attendance was obligatory. We danced, we flirted. Things looked good. He invited me home, and I met his parents. His father was an officer, no less. Colonel. A man of stature. Open features. Open eyes, open arms. His mother was an honest peasant, simple and affectionate. Always moving about, always serving: fruit, drinks, cookies. It was a close family, and hospitable. The picture of happiness. And then . . ."

Lidia had learned one day that the colonel headed up the secret police.

"He had my family checked out, because I was his son's friend and future fiancée. He had to be sure that there was nothing compromising in my background. I will never know why, but he had my father arrested. And my older sister. They were tortured. Each in the presence of the other. My fiancé—"

She interrupted herself. Malkiel wondered, Where are the microphones?

"My fiancé killed himself. I sank into one of those nightmares . . . black, black. I ran off . . . I quit school: to hell with school. . . . I moved here, far from home, as far as I could. So I'm alone now. That's the whole story. Are you satisfied?"

The tea had cooled. The apartment was cold. Malkiel was no longer thirsty and wanted to warm himself. He raised her chin. "Then tell me, why are you working for them?"

"You don't understand. That's perfectly normal. You can't understand. Be nice to me: don't judge me too harshly. Don't start mistrusting me."

Malkiel stared at his cold cup of tea. Should he believe her? Should he trust a woman working for the secret police?

"And you?" she went on, in the same confidential murmur. "Why aren't you married?"

"What do you know about that?"

"It's not magic. I went over your file."

"It's a long story," Malkiel said.

"I have plenty of time."

"I haven't."

"Too bad."

Yes, Malkiel thought. Too bad.

His thoughts took flight. His father. Tamar. Tamar and his father. "Go ahead and marry her," his father had said. "Marry her while I still have my faculties. Don't wait, son. In my condition I don't want to see anything put off." And again: "This *zivug*, this marriage, was made in heaven, I can tell. What have you got against this girl? She's radiant, beautiful, she's like your mother, if you only knew how much like your mother. . . ." Malkiel had seen his mother only in photographs or through his father's eyes, in his father's nostalgia. Yes, she was beautiful. Her Yemenite smile suggested unimaginable depths of fantasy, boldness, understanding, need. Whenever Malkiel thought about his mother he felt cheated of happiness that was his due.

Tamar, his mother, his mother's happiness, the curse on his father. Tamar, and the fear of losing her. "I'm not married," he said. "It's an old story."

Lidia was lost in reflections. "You're not drinking my tea," she said. "You reject my friendship. You refuse my body and all that goes with it. You lack courtesy, Mr. Rosenbaum."

"It has nothing to do with you, Lidia."

"Then with whom? With what?"

From the depths of his memory rose his father's tale and his mother's phrase "Not in this place." He had not undertaken this pilgrimage to sleep with a stranger. "It's a matter of place," he said.

"You don't like my flat?"

"It has nothing to do with your flat. It's this city. It's oppressive."

He stood up; so did she.

"Thank you for being honest," she said.

"Thank you for understanding," he replied.

She walked him to the door, stopped, and said, "To thank you in another way, I should repeat my advice: be careful."

"Why do you say that?"

"They're suspicious of you."

"What do they suspect? That I lack courtesy?"

But she was serious, even grave. "Be careful. I don't want anything to happen to you. They don't believe you. They think your passion for epitaphs is a ruse."

"Tell them they're wrong."

"All the more reason to tread lightly."

Malkiel was uneasy. Am I jeopardizing her security? Should I trust her? Tell her about the widow? And my father?

I'm a fool, he thought. A still young woman offers herself to me, and I look for excuses to sleep alone.

Malkiel recalled his father's encounter with the witch. It was all sharply etched in his mind. He saw the woman's face, noted her harsh expression, heard her deep strong voice as if he himself had been her victim.

A boy was walking down the street. It was early in the morning. He was shivering. The sidewalk was a sheet of ice. The boy had to be careful not to slip. He slipped. He fell. He hurt himself. Blood gushed from his nose and mouth. He was afraid. He would be late.

Fortune smiled upon him, in the guise of a woman who had just opened her window. She gestured: come closer. "Come here. Let me see your bruises." He made no answer. He did not know her. A boy did not speak to strange women. "You can't just walk on like that," she said. "Let me wash you off." She was already opening the door. He was already crossing the threshold. Now he was in a dimly lit living room. For some reason the shadows were reassuring. He had no idea why, but he let the woman take his overcoat, when it was only his face that needed attention. "You'll feel better," she said, as she took off his jacket and wiped his bloody eyes and lips with a damp handkerchief. "Your buttons," she said. "How can you breathe? You're suffocating, for heaven's sake!" Yes indeed, he was suffocating. Why had she sat him down on the sofa? Why was he just sitting there? He ought to stand up, dress himself, thank her and be on his way. He did none of that. She stopped him from doing it. "I'm not finished," she said every time he moved to free himself. "Sit still, boy. Be patient. I'm not finished."

He felt panic. He had just noticed that the woman was naked. She was wearing a dressing gown and nothing beneath it. He blushed. He recognized the Tempter. He must leave now, right now. He felt it, and his body told him the same. But he was glued to the sofa, his body damned. How could he save himself? His mind sought an answer, but it was too late. Holding a small handkerchief sprinkled with perfume that went straight to his head, she gazed upon him, transformed. Her cheeks flamed. Lips and eyes wide, she was panting. She dropped the handkerchief and made a gesture toward him, one that frightened him: he thought she would strike him, insult him, throw him out. "Take me," she whispered. "God Himself sent you this morning; let His will be done." In one quick motion she cast off her dressing gown. The boy closed his eyes to forestall sin. "Look at me," she ordered him. "Look at me and dare say that I am not beautiful." He refused to open his eyes. "Are you a virgin, or what?" she went on, her voice suddenly vulgar. He did not answer. "You are! Oh my God, how happy that makes me! I love virgins!"

She was trying to undress him, and he resisted. She forced him down, covered him with her body, ground her breasts into him, kissed him furiously as if to tear his flesh, chew him up, annihilate him. He was dizzy. His whole being was tense, overflowing with desire but obstinate in its refusal. "Take me, you idiot, what are you waiting for? Take me! Are you afraid? Have I frightened you? God will forgive you, I promise! Take me as hard as you can and you'll approach God—because you'll be in paradise." She whispered those words into his ear, onto his eyelids, and the lips he kept tight. "Be free, big boy. Be a man. Rape me and be king." But the boy was too young. Too timid, too much a believer. In a burst of energy he managed to break loose. Like Joseph in the Bible he ran for the door, leaving his coat behind. He was already outside, out of breath, when he heard the woman: "Hey, kid, you'll catch cold —here's your coat."

When he reached school, late of course, he did not dare go to class; he went to the washroom. Standing at the mirror, he studied his face for many moments, sure that he would find some outward sign of his sin. A master had once told him, "When one denies God, it is the first step that matters; one transgresses a law and realizes that nothing has changed. The heart beats as before, the blood circulates, people come and go, the universe remains the same. That is the beginning of separation." The boy wondered, Have I changed? Does my face still belong to me? Have I lost everything in losing my innocence, am I lost forever?

For a long time after that, he refused to look at a naked female body.

Grandfather Malkiel, I stand before you as before an invisible judge, a severe but charitable judge. Shall I confess to you what I've made of my life? After all, I bear your name; you have the right to know if I'm worthy of it.

First you should know that I have never betrayed that name. Even though in America immigrants and refugees rarely respect their original names. If you knew the transformations Ellis Island has perpetrated! Slomowicz became Salvatore if the immigration officer was Italian, Slocum if he was Anglo-Saxon or Irish. Isaac didn't sound right? Then they made it Irving. You cannot imagine how many people tried to mutilate or embellish or doctor "Malkiel." "What kind of name is that?" wondered Loretta, that splendid Southern woman. "Wouldn't you prefer Sam?" Everybody saw a linguistic barrier in "Malkiel," if not an obstacle. They suggested Melvin, Malcolm and even McDonald. Not a chance. I stuck to my real name. Only once did I hesitate, on the day when the Times *published my first piece. The editor looked at my byline and shook his head. "Malkiel?" he said, annoyed. "That just won't do. Is it a pen name or what?" I enlightened him. "I don't know anybody by that name. If you ask me, you'd do better to find another one, more familiar to our readers." For a few moments, I wondered if my stubbornness might cost me my career. Luckily the editor, busy with other aspects of the news, shrugged: "Do as you like. It's your name, not mine."*

As the years passed, the people I spent time with grew accustomed to my name. At least I think they did. Some accepted it.

Others gave me a nickname: Malki, or even Ki. At first I corrected them, with just a touch of irritation: "My name is Mal-ki-el." It was tiresome. And no less so when a new acquaintance asked me about it: "Malki-what? That's some crazy name. Who saddled you with that? What does it mean?" You're going to laugh, Grandfather: I won a beautiful woman's favors thanks to that name. She found it musical. To be perfectly honest, I ought to confess also that a fair number of no less lovely women rejected me because of that same name. Too bad. At home we say, "You win some, you lose some." That's life. You win and you lose. Tamar, for example—I think she loves me because she loves my name. She says it often, for no good reason, just to hear it. "Malkiel, you want to take a walk? Malkiel, are you hungry?" Or else, "Do you know Nepal, Malkiel? Ah, Malkiel, if we could make the trip together . . ."

Tamar often comes with me to visit my father; sometimes she goes alone. Then she says to him, "Talk to me about Malkiel." And my father replies, "My son?" If she'd asked, "Talk to me about your son," he'd have answered, "Malkiel?"

They understand each other. There's an intimate rapport between them that gratifies me. She owes him nothing, yet she denies him nothing.

One evening I found them shaken, sitting hand in hand, gazing into each other's eyes, as if sharing the same quest and hitting the same wall. "I'm afraid," my father said, his eyes half shut. "Everything in my head is muddled. Names, dates, words. I see a face in front of me and I recognize it, but I don't know if it belongs to the present or the past. Who are you, Tamar? Which period of my life do you belong to? Are you perhaps Talia? Am I reliving my past even as it deserts me?"

Tamar would do anything to help. And so would I. And you? Grandfather! Help him by helping me!

You who sacrificed your life for your people, for our people, guide me. Tell me what to do, how to defeat not death but the abyss that will swallow up the lives of the living and the memory of the dead. You whose memory shapes mine through my father's, tell me how I can keep silence from smothering the word, and also . . .

The handsome face, usually serious, now twisted and contorted. The pain was more than mental now; it was physical as well. "I want . . ." Out of breath, Elhanan stopped. His hand groped and waved in the air.

"What is it you want, Father?"

Elhanan opened his mouth, closed it, opened it again to gasp for breath. He wanted to speak, to ask for something.

"Yes, Father?" Malkiel stared intently at him. If only he could understand.

"I don't know. . . . I don't know. . . ." Huddled in his armchair near the window, he seemed harassed—but by whom? by what?

"What is it you don't know?" Malkiel was sinking into a depression as deep as his father's. Had the sickness crossed a new threshold? "You're upset, Father. Take it easy. You'll feel better soon."

Elhanan obeyed his son. Eyes shut, he folded his arms and seemed to drift slowly into a soothing lethargy. Relieved, Malkiel suddenly wanted to kiss his forehead as if he were a child, Malkiel's child, fallen asleep in the middle of a bedtime story. He noticed a single tear running down his father's cheek. Was he weeping in his sleep? But Elhanan was not asleep. "I want . . . I want an apple," he asked timidly.

Malkiel hurried to the kitchen. Seeing him, Loretta was worried; what had happened? "An apple. Quick. My father wants an apple."

Eyes still shut, Elhanan held out his hand. Malkiel put the apple in it. Elhanan caressed the fruit sensuously. "It's terrible," he said with a faint smile.

"What's terrible, Father?"

"I wanted an apple. But I couldn't think what to call it. Can you understand that? I envisioned the apple, I knew it was a fruit, I remembered its smell and its taste, I could have drawn a picture of it, but . . . its name escaped me."

Was that how the disease progressed? He would have to ask Dr. Pasternak. Tomorrow. He wouldn't be a bit surprised. He knew what was bound to happen, if not when: little by little the sick man would lose his vocabulary. Each day the sponge would grow thicker, greedier, more absorbent.

Malkiel was careful not to show his own distress. But Elhanan felt it and made few demands, so as not to increase it. Feigning sleepiness, he asked for nothing. If he was thirsty he would go to the kitchen himself. There, alone with Loretta, he would point to the teapot.

To ease the tension, Malkiel adopted an air of false gaiety. "I have a riddle for you, Father. Which is better, to hold a fruit in your hand or to be able to name it?"

A moment of truce, of reprieve. After the "crisis"—so each episode was called—Elhanan seemed to improve. In a lighter mood, he once again became the professor: "Adam's superiority lay in his ability to name the animals that God showed him. Not being able to name things was for the Romans the ultimate malediction: *Nomina perdimus rerum,* they complained. A deaf man does not hear the words, but he knows them. A mute does not say them, but he understands them. But what is an apple to a blind orchard keeper?"

"So here you are again on my turf! Who you talking to? The dead?" The gravedigger's guttural, hollow voice. Though Hershel laughed, his coarse features were frightening. "Leave the dead alone, Mr. Stranger. They have a right to peace and quiet, don't they? Come have a drink with me instead. They'll thank you for it, believe me."

"It's too early to go back to town," Malkiel said.

"Too early, too late. Meaningless words. If you have any sense you'll come along and trust me. I'll tell you more stories, about other meetings." His whole immense body jiggled when he laughed. His arms flapped and his chest swelled. He hopped and skipped like a carnival bear.

"All right," Malkiel said, "let's go."

In the street, people turned for a second look at this odd couple. The gravedigger was as slovenly as Malkiel was neat. Malkiel wondered if he was being followed. Hard to tell: there were too many people in the streets. After half an hour's walk they stopped before a seemingly empty lot surrounded by a crumbling wall. "It's the old cemetery," said the gravedigger. "They haven't used it for a hundred years or more." He pushed at a squeaky gate. A bare courtyard; way in the back, a little shack. "Here we are. This is where I live."

Inside, in the gloom, a man was sitting with his elbows on the table and his head in his hands. Surprised, Malkiel drew back.

"Fear nothing," Hershel said. "He's not dead. Sit down there." He pointed to a grimy chair. Malkiel overcame his reluctance and sat down. Across from him, the other man was breathing loudly. His hands clasped on the table now, he seemed to be staring off into space. Malkiel waited, calming himself.

"I lied," said the gravedigger, pouring himself a glass of brandy. "I'm not the only Jew in town. Ephraim here wants to talk to you. Just let him finish his prayer. Which prayer? Don't ask. You never heard of it. He invents his own prayers. Every night he has a new one. You want to listen? Be my guest."

"Adoshem sfatai tiftach," the man intoned. "Others have sealed my lips; it is for You to open them. For You to tell me if I should weep or sing; if I do one or the other of my own will, I'm damned; I know it. Can that be Your wish? I can't believe it; I'm too old to doubt You. I refuse to believe that man was created to choose between two maledictions. Show me the way. Tell me the answer. I'm afraid to decide all alone. I'm too old to allow myself the slightest mistake. That, too, I know.

"Upi yaghid tehilateha: I may never again sing Your praises. Silence would be easier. First of all, I'm in the habit. Since I lost my sight I have felt that my words too were blind. Can it be that You have forced me to take this road, to witness so much horror, for the sole purpose of blinding me? I am accustomed to the night, but not to the silence of the night. It is driving me mad. What is it that You wish? To deprive me of my sanity?

"I have traveled about the world, passed through towns and villages, met old men greedy for the future and children thirsting for dreams. . . . Will I ever see my loved ones again? Will they make me share their judgment of me? And of all of us? And of You?

"Decide for me, I beseech You. Let me see what my eyes can no longer see. Give me the power to speak without lying, or to be silent without turning my silence into a lie. Teach me how to interpret Your will, and how not to oppose it to the will of free men wrenched from life: that is the will I respect most deeply. Is it because Your will and theirs are not the same that You treat me as You treated the Seer of Lublin? At his wish, You deprived him of sight. But at whose wish did You deprive me of mine? Do You need it? So be it; take it. Bestow it on whomever You wish. But do not touch my memory. Does it hinder You? Does it weigh upon You? Too bad for me. But I cling to my memory as I cling to my life, I cling to it because it is my life. It is I, Ephraim son of Sarah, Your servant, who ask this of You. And he is weary and worn, Your servant: You know it, don't You?"

The seated man fell silent, but his words echoed throughout the room. "Who are you?" he asked suddenly.

"My name is Malkiel."

"Malkiel what?"

"Malkiel Rosenbaum."

"And what was your father called?"

"Elhanan Rosenbaum."

"Then you are Malkiel son of Elhanan?"

Malkiel cleared his throat; he felt as if he were appearing before a judge. In the end he only said, "Yes."

The seated man clapped twice. To summon someone? A ghost? "Malkiel son of Elhanan, you say? I knew him. He was a martyr. By what right do you usurp his name?"

"He was my grandfather."

Furious, the gravedigger knocked over his glass. "No fooling!" he shouted. "Ah, no! Not that!"

The unknown man stood up. "Come to the window," he ordered Malkiel. "I want to see you."

How can this blind man see me? Malkiel wondered, even as he obeyed. Ephraim walked with his hands straight out in front of him. Malkiel was feeling something new and was not sure what it was. He saw himself again as a child, on the eve of Yom Kippur. Hands outstretched, his father blessed him.

"Men are wrong to think that the blind cannot see. The truth is that they see, but differently. I would even say that they see something other." They were at the window. A dim light played on the old man's face. "Closer," he said. "Let my hands touch your head. Your eyes. I see with my hands. In your face I find your father again. And his father. One must know how to read a face. Only a blind man truly knows."

Malkiel felt his emotions swell. He had always been fond of old men and blind men. "Who are you, Ephraim?"

"You heard me. I am the caretaker."

"And what do you take care of?"

"What people throw away, what history rejects, what memory denies. The smile of a starving child, the tears of its dying mother, the silent prayers of the condemned man and the cries of his friend: I gather them up and preserve them. In this city, I am memory."

A madman, Malkiel thought. Another one. Unless it's me. Here, a gravedigger without a corpse; there, a blind caretaker. And where am I in all this?

With Hershel's help the blind man returned to the table. The gravedigger lit an oil lamp. Malkiel saw the caretaker more clearly: an angular, hollowed face, haloed by a sparse beard. Nervous hands. "How long have you lived here?"

"Since the war," Hershel answered, "which is like saying forever. I saved him. Not heaven, but the gravedigger, a man who lives by the earth. You want to know why I saved him? Because he was blind. You want to know how he went blind? He never stopped weeping from the time the war began, in 1939. You could say he was watering every desert in the world. I know all about people who weep. But I never saw anyone cry the way this one did. He was a foreigner—from Poland—so they put him in an asylum. That's where I saw him the first time. I invited him to come live in my hut. He sobbed his thanks. I did all I could to make him stop. His tears were stronger than my arguments. They flowed, and flowed. He got on my nerves sometimes, and I would ask him, 'Where do you find the strength to do all that crying?' He always answered the same way: 'Even when the celestial gates are locked, the gate of tears remains open.' His sight was dimming, of course, but that didn't bother him. It disappeared altogether the day the Germans arrived."

Ephraim raised his dead eyes to the visitor. "I wanted to remember, don't you understand? I knew I'd witness more bloody events. I knew my memory would not be able to hold them all. So to recall all that I saw and heard in Poland, I had to cease seeing."

The gravedigger interrupted. "I don't always know what he's talking about, it's too complicated for me, but I understand his tears. Every drop tells me a story. We've been living here together since the war. I pass along what happens in town and in the outside world, and he weeps about the old days, in his country, far away." The alcohol was inspiring him. He snickered. "You want to know why he agreed to stay here with me instead of leaving with the community?"

Malkiel waited without replying. He was a captive of these two men. He could hardly take his eyes off the blind caretaker's nervous hands; he wanted to cover them with his own, but dared not.

"You listen, young man called Malkiel son of Elhanan. Ephraim knew that every man, woman and child of our blessed community was going to be massacred and they'd have no decent burial, they wouldn't be buried in consecrated Jewish soil. He knew it better than they, better than I. So, Malkiel son of Elhanan, when I promised him I'd take personal care of him and pick out a grave among our most illustrious citizens, he finally agreed not to follow the others. The last time I ply my trade, it will be for him."

The blind man turned up his palms. Malkiel finally summoned the courage to place his own upon them. Two men, all that was left of a large community. How could they have . . .

"I know what you're thinking," the blind man said. "You're going to ask me a question, and I know what it is. You're going to ask me how I escaped the murderers, am I not right?"

Malkiel nodded, yes, the blind man was right. This blind man was a mind reader.

"I have powers, yes. I'm blind, but I see a long way. I'm old, but my brain is not worn out."

"But how did you—"

"You're in a hurry? I have all the time in the world. How did I escape the killers? I know the Cabala. An old master taught me the art of making myself invisible by pronouncing the names of certain angels. Am I not right, gravedigger? Didn't I make myself invisible?"

"That's right," said the gravedigger.

"It was so simple. I pronounced one word, one name, and the killers didn't see me."

Malkiel's hands still lay upon the blind man's. He did not want to withdraw them for fear of breaking the spell: for fear of interrupting the hallucination, for that is what Malkiel believed it was. He mistrusted all these stories of the occult. In India, too, the wise men claimed they could become invisible. In the end they died. Death alone is invisible. Man's end was the same everywhere.

"Since you could save yourself," Malkiel said, "why didn't you try to save some of the other Jews?"

"A good question, Malkiel son of Elhanan. And also pertinent. But we cannot teach such mysteries in one day. That takes time. Still, I tried. Didn't I try, gravedigger?"

"That's true. He tried."

"I did all I could to save . . ."

"To save whom?"

The blind man fell silent. Was he groping for a name? a face? a date? Finally he said, "He was called Malkiel . . . Malkiel son of Elhanan."

"What? My grandfather?"

"Yes, your grandfather. I tried to save him. To make him invisible in his turn. On the last night, before he was to join the SS officer, his executioner, I talked and talked to him. It was no use. 'Since all are to die, I will be the first,' he told me. I recall his last words; they were about your father. 'Tell him the date of my death so he can recite Kaddish.' " The blind man squeezed Malkiel's hand tightly. "Is that why you came? For the date?"

"I don't know," Malkiel said. "It may be, but I don't think so. My father knows the date. He commemorates it every year."

"Then tell me the truth: what brings you to this unfortunate little town?"

"My father."

"So I was right! Was I not right, gravedigger?"

"One hundred percent." The gravedigger laughed his abrasive laugh.

"Elhanan," the old man said. "Where is he?"

"He lives in New York."

"Is that far?" asked the gravedigger. "How big is it? Bigger than this town? What are the cemeteries like? Rich? Deluxe?"

The blind man and his visitor paid no attention to the drunkard's interruptions. The old man had flung his head back as if to read the low, dark ceiling. "Your father," he said pensively. "Your father is a wise man. I see him from here."

If he only knew, Malkiel thought, taking away his hands. If only he knew how sick my father is.

"Your father sent you here, and you don't know why. But I know. It was to see me. To receive my teaching. He too would like to become invisible."

This man's mind is wandering, Malkiel decided. Can he really see my father? Who knows? In this strange place all things are possible.

"And another thing," the blind man said. "He wants to become part of my memory."

He wants, he wants, Malkiel thought. Does my father still want anything?

Irritated that no one was talking to him, the gravedigger cried, "And me? I don't count? I have no memory? I can't see the invisible?" He put a bony arm on Malkiel's shoulders. "Remember what you seem to want to forget. I was the one who buried Malkiel son of Elhanan. And you, the other Malkiel son of Elhanan, you ought to respect me and honor me for it."

Had his father sent him to this town to listen to the two strange Jews? Could he have guessed that the gravedigger and the blind man were still here, as if forgotten by history?

"And if I were to tell you," the gravedigger went on, "that your father hopes you'll have yourself buried here? I'm the world's finest gravedigger, take my word for it."

"Let him be," said the blind man in a louder voice. "He is young and has much living to do. His father sent him here not to enter into death but to emerge from it. I can help him. You cannot."

"What do you know about it?"

"I know; let that be enough for you. Your job is to make people disappear; mine is to keep them among us."

Why did Malkiel now see himself with Tamar after one of their visits to Elhanan? They talked endlessly. Did hope help us to survive, or not? Too many families clung to it all through the war, thus falling into the enemy's trap. But would they have survived without hope? Hope is sometimes unworthy of us, Tamar said, but despair is even worse if it kills the will to act, to confront events, to protest evil, to shout, No! We are not blind, we will not submit! If the absurd exists, we'll respond. With reason or with more absurdity—but we'll respond.

The blind man leaned toward Malkiel as if to inspect him; their heads touched. The old man's breath entered Malkiel's nostrils. "You are young," the blind man said. "At your age a man is desperate and proud; at mine, pride vanishes. And yet it seems to me that I could teach you pride. And hope, too."

"You speak without knowledge."

"I know that. I am memory." He said "I am memory" as others might say "I am music" or "I am luck" or "I am death." "Listen, my young friend. Don't linger here. Get out. I implore you. What you seek, you can find in me. Look upon me and go. Feel the chill of my hand and go home. Your place is not with us. It is among the living."

"But my father—"

The blind man grew angry. "I have powers, I could force you, but I prefer not to. You've seen me, you've visited the grave of Malkiel son of Elhanan, and that's enough. I am your savior, your guide. The rest is none of your concern."

To avoid hurting the old man, Malkiel would have promised anything, but he could not lie to him. He would certainly leave. But not yet.

A memory was waiting for him. And calling to him.

"I'm afraid, son. If you knew how much."

"I'm trying to understand, Father."

"I'm afraid of failure. Of not passing along enough. At night I wake up sweating. There are so many things still inside me that I want to save. For you. For your children. Will I have time? At dawn

I can't calm my heart. This morning I wondered, Suppose God has forgotten His creation, and the Messiah His mission? Suppose the sun forgot to rise and the rooster to crow? Suppose my soul forgot it was a soul? Words are already playing tricks on me; they're all colorless, and bloodless; my mind is already ashamed of its limits, its opacity. What's to become of me, my son?"

"Such questions prove your faculties are still there."

"But someday I'll forget those questions, too."

"Someday . . . someday . . ."

"Tomorrow? Next week? I must hurry. The story I don't tell will be lost forever. The idea I don't pass along to you will never spring forth again. The event you don't hear about will be forever erased from history. Everything is already muddled in my head. Have I told you how I met your mother?"

"In a camp for displaced persons."

"Did I tell you that we became friends because—"

"Because you spoke Hebrew."

"I spoke it well. Better than now. My accent was perfect. I recited Bialik's poem called . . . I can't remember what it was called. It's about a student who neglects everything but his studies."

"Hamatmid."

"What did you say?"

"Hamatmid. *The assiduous student."*

"Ah yes, that's it. . . . I forgot. . . . I forget so many things. Soon I will forget where I come from and where I am going. Now and then my blood freezes at the thought that one day—who knows? —I will forget you, too."

Thus did Elhanan helplessly witness his own destruction. Forgetfulness was for him the death not only of knowledge but also of imagination, hence of expectation. Mentally torn, struggling vainly to control his actions, to transform time into consciousness, he submitted himself to constant examinations: What was the name of the man who . . . What happened on the day when . . . His reason, still clear, watched over a shrinking, progressively impoverished memory. In his brain a huge black sponge scrambled words and images. Time no longer flowed, but toppled over the edge of a yawning precipice. Overcome by a sense of inevitability, Elhanan decided that the end was approaching. He was losing sight of his landmarks. Forgetfulness was a worse scourge than madness: the sick man is not somewhere else; he is nowhere. He is not another, he is no one. Certainly Elhanan hung on; certainly he fought. With pills and potions he resisted, reading all he could on the subject. But, like Moses in the legend, he forgot at night what he had learned in the morning. "We can't do anything about it," the specialists repeated. "Forgive us; but medical science has its limits like everything else." Elhanan had to accept it: he was slipping down a slope, and at the bottom he would encounter nothingness.

Tamar came often to visit, between two assignments, alone or with Malkiel. Elhanan greeted her tenderly. Because she reminded him of Talia? Sometimes he talked to her as if she were his wife. She would not play the game: "I'm Tamar. But tell me about Talia." Other times: "Tell us about the war." Or: "And when you were a little boy. Tell us about when you were a little boy." Elhanan let himself go more easily when Tamar was there. When Malkiel decided that his father's accounts should be taped, Tamar approved. "It's good for him to talk. Words stimulate him. And it makes him feel useful." When the old man's brain dimmed, they worked together to brighten it. They gave Elhanan all their free time and lived according to his rhythms. But Elhanan was tiring more quickly. His memories were blurring faster. He repeated himself, or interrupted himself in midsentence, unable to finish. It was a kind of twilight, and Malkiel and Tamar felt it in their very being. It devastated them to see this man, once so proud of his lucidity and so attached to his past, lose both. Also, Elhanan was decaying physically. More and more he seemed extinguished. His voice no longer carried, his hands pointed aimlessly. But Malkiel and Tamar refused to resign themselves; they went on asking him questions. It was strange, but he seemed better on the Sabbath; he seemed more serene. He managed to express himself with his old eloquence.

"Remember what our sages teach us," he said to Malkiel after dinner one Friday evening. "It is given to man to know where he comes from, where he is going and before whom he will have to give an accounting. I still know where I am going, but I know less and less where I come from. My consolation? You, at least, you will know where I come from."

And later the same night: "You should go . . . go on a pilgrimage."

Malkiel was about to protest, when Tamar tugged at his sleeve. "Let him finish."

"Yes, my son. You must go to the town where I was born. You'd understand me better. You'd remember more. You may meet people who knew me. The woman . . ."

"What woman?"

"You know, the woman who . . ."

In the small hours Tamar turned to Malkiel. "Will you go, then?"

"I can't. He's so sick."

"I'll stay. I'll watch over him. Do what he asks."

"I'm afraid," Malkiel said.

"Of what?"

"I don't know, but I'm afraid."

"Sometimes I think your whole life is ruled by fear. Fear of loving, fear of not being worthy of love, fear of having children . . ."

He bowed his head. Tamar knew him well. "Still, I do love you," he said. "Fear doesn't keep me from loving you. And you?"

"I'm not afraid."

"What do you want?"

"From you? More sharing."

"Is that all?"

"That would be enough."

"Nothing else?"

"Nothing else."

Beloved Tamar. You, the beginning. You, the awakening. You, who will make sense of my father's disease. "Do you think a cure is possible in spite of everything?"

She did not answer immediately. She was lying down, and in the half-light of dawn she seemed asleep. In the end my father's agony will wear her out, Malkiel thought. A woman's role? To understand, to trust, to wait, to have faith and to share it. Then why have you fled into sleep, Tamar? Don't go away, don't leave me while I'm staring at you—as if you were a stranger—to give you shape and voice, so that your face, tense under my gaze, will become present again, human again, again filled with grace. "Tamar. Are you asleep?"

"No, I'm not sleeping." And after a moment, "Yes, I believe that even at the last agony, man is worthy of triumphing over death."

"We're not talking about death, but of oblivion."

"Oblivion is a way of dying."

"And you still believe?"

They clasped hands, as if to reaffirm their pact.

"I still believe. Do you want to know why?"

"Tell me."

"Because I love your father's stories. We won't forget them. Isn't that the beginning of a victory?"

Blessed Tamar.

Hershel the gravedigger came up to him at the gate of the cemetery. "You're leaving?"

"Maybe."

"When?"

"Soon."

"Too bad."

"Why too bad?"

"I wouldn't mind seeing you stay. I could dig a grave near your grandfather's. Can you picture it? Two graves, side by side, marked with the same name: Malkiel son of Elhanan."

Malkiel made no answer.

"You're not thirsty?" asked the gravedigger. "My throat is on fire." And when Malkiel made no answer, he went on slyly, "I'll sell you another story for a drink." Still Malkiel said nothing. The gravedigger insisted. "The story's a good one. You'll like it. I promise."

"A story about the dead? Another one?"

"If you like. Let's say a murder."

Malkiel stopped. Something in the gravedigger's voice had excited his attention. "What murder is that?"

"It takes brandy to revive my memory."

So there they were again at the table they occupied almost every afternoon. The gravedigger ordered a bottle and began his drinking. Malkiel did not touch the glass that the waiter set before him. He noticed suddenly that the gravedigger's eyes were bloodshot.

"Did I ever tell you I killed a man? No? I really didn't? Unforgivable. That's how it is; I'm getting old. I forget things. . . . I really never told you that during the war, after the ghetto was liquidated, I joined a partisan group? Our job was to punish the bastards who got rich denouncing Jews, stealing from them, selling them to the enemy. We executed a few. Matter of fact, we were the ones who took care of the head Nyilas here—well, not we but me."

Now Malkiel was all ears. The gravedigger was a missing piece of the puzzle. His story was part of the story.

"We sentenced him to death, you understand," said the gravedigger. "He was the worst kind of sadist, believe me. I know Death;

and I can tell you that Death itself detested that man. We knew he was in Stanislav the day the Germans massacred thousands of Jews. A survivor told us this bastard had tried to rape two girls before he killed them. They fought back, so he locked them in a barn and set fire to it. They burned to death.

"Well, I tracked him down, me, imagine that. One night we mounted an attack on a barracks. This fellow was humping a whore, and I knew the address. So with my famous rabbi's cane—I was never without it now—I broke down the door, and there I was staring at two naked bodies locked together. The woman screamed, and the man was scared stiff. I shut the whore in a closet and ordered the bastard to his feet. As he was, stark naked. I took a good close look at him. So this was Death's accomplice, I said to myself. All that ugliness, all that cowardice, all that flabby flesh: here's a man who must be an enemy to man. Why is he trembling?

"I glared at him like a lunatic; my gaze scorched him. Yes, sir: my gaze can burn. But the son of a bitch refused to give in. I felt rage mounting in me, and I wondered if I ought to keep cool. I was blinking too fast: I got my eyelids under control. Now his were blinking. Right: he realized he was finished. The bastard was all alone, and solitude can breed courage, but it can breed cowardice too. He began to snivel. 'I didn't do a thing, I swear it. I swear it on my unborn children's heads, on my sick mother's head I swear it. My hands are clean and my heart is clean—I did nothing, nothing bad.'

"He was a wreck. In a few seconds his outlines blurred; he began disintegrating before my eyes. Was this an officer? A fighting man? A lord decreeing the life or death of his subjects? What happened to his pride and his power? 'You're making a tremendous mistake,' he whimpered. His eyes and nose and mouth were dribbling, and his body was jerking and twitching. 'I'm not the criminal, not me, not me, not me.' And I thought, You little bastard, pretty soon you won't be able to say 'me' at all. You're about to die. I'm going to give you death, the death that suits you: I'm going to strangle you. You see these hands? They conceal death, your death.

"Why did I spend so long glaring at him? Sure, I could have gotten rid of him just like that, but understand, the relationship between death and its victims always intrigued me. Always. One defines the other. Neither can exist alone. 'What are you going to do?' this son of a bitch asks me. 'Are you really going to kill me?'

"No need to answer. Death is silent. Death imposes silence. And respect.

"Oh, I knew what was running through his head. When somebody thinks about his death, I can follow his thoughts. The son of a bitch was clinging to life. He wasn't offering it to his country or history or his family. He just wanted to hang on to it forever for its own sake. That was his nature and always had been. He wasn't looking for trouble, or complications. If living in peace and denying death meant living in a wasteland of sensual pleasure, or in the sensual pleasure of nothingness, that was good enough for him.

"Yes indeed, I knew what he was thinking. And he knew I knew. He was overcome; he jittered, he was full of anguish. Life fled his eyes, death entered his skin. I said to him, 'You're going to die; you're not dead yet but you're going to die, so look behind you. What do you see? Your victims are waiting for you. You won't get away. They'll be waiting for you when you die.'

"His face flushed and immediately paled. 'Don't kill me,' he begged. 'I'll say whatever you want. I'm a coward, I'm guilty, I'm whatever you like, only I want to live. I don't deserve to die.'

"He was standing right there in front of me, with his hand on his stomach as if he was sick. I suddenly wanted to laugh. He didn't deserve to die, he said. Nobody deserves it. But this pig killed people. Now he was really scared. My laughter terrified him. I was *laughing*. I asked him, 'Do you know who I am?' No, he didn't. 'A partisan?' he said. 'I'm your gravedigger.' I corrected myself: 'No, not yours. I'm your victims' gravedigger. To you I'm just death. And you make me laugh.'

"A grimace made him unrecognizable. His eyes gleamed oddly. I said again, 'I'm your death. No—I will be in a little while. First, I'm something else. For you, I'm God.' Did he take me for a madman? He agreed with me: 'Yes, you're God,' he said. 'For me, you're God.' 'You sincerely believe that?' He believed it. 'You're sure I'm not playing games?' He was sure. 'In that case, repent.' He had no idea how. I taught him. 'I want to hear your confession. Say it.' He beat his chest. 'Harder, harder.' He thumped it harder. 'Say that you were vicious.' He said it. 'That you were cruel.' He admitted it. 'That you rejoiced in humiliating your victims.' He admitted that too. 'Say that you deserve to die.' He deserved it. 'Implore God to pardon you.' He opened his mouth several times, but no sound emerged. Then he emitted a few groans that sounded like giggles. He beat his chest with both hands, as if to clear his conscience. 'Pray to God,' I told him. He prayed to me.

"But fortunately, God does not forgive."

"Hershel—will you let me ask one question?"

"Why not? Go ahead, Mr. Stranger, ask your question."

"The woman. His wife. What became of her?"

"I have no idea. I didn't even know he was married."

Malkiel's mouth was dry; he sipped at his *tzuika*. His head was burning, spinning. A false trail? Let's look somewhere else. The Nyilas was called Zoltan. Was it his last name or his first name? Hershel could not recall.

"Do you remember digging Malkiel Rosenbaum's grave?"

"You bet I remember it!"

Malkiel sipped again, nervously. "You told me you were laughing as you dug. Why were you laughing?"

The gravedigger leaned forward, and his massive head almost butted Malkiel's. "You'd rather I cried? It would have been easier, you know! You like things the easy way. Not me." His fist slammed down on the tabletop; he upset the bottle, which fell to the floor. He scooped it up. "Damn them," he said. "Damn them all. Him and his widow, too."

And he howled with laughter.

When Malkiel left the tavern, he walked downtown and mingled with the crowd.

Dusk had fallen, and night lurked in the mountains, waiting to be summoned by some poor desperate wanderer.

Tamar, where are you? What secret are you probing? What will you tell your readers tomorrow morning? What scandal will you expose? Death is a scandal. And life, too? Life, too.

Father, what are you seeing for the last time? What image are you trying to cling to? The whole world is an image. The past, too? The past, too.

Hey, passerby, I'm walking alongside you. You with your sack filled with misery, I'm talking to you. Don't look back.

You seem like a plainclothesman to me. Why are you following me? What do you expect to learn, tailing me through these city streets? Stop watching me.

A woman wrapped in a shawl slipped into the shadows: unknown. Another one, mute, fought the wind: unknown. And yet I am in such pain that I want to know; I want to know these women, to tear down their veils. I don't do it, and I feel guilty, and I don't know why. I give up. Resignation? No. Bad idea. My father needs me more than ever. And Tamar? She too, perhaps.

A project was taking shape in Malkiel's head: not to go straight back to New York from Feherfalu. He would spend a few days in Israel, and leave in time to spend the high holy days with his father. Why this detour? He had no idea. Perhaps he simply wanted to visit his mother's grave.

Malkiel knew Israel. His father had taken him there for his bar mitzvah. A sentimental gesture? Elhanan explained, "I celebrated my own bar mitzvah in exile; it would give me great pleasure to have yours in Jerusalem." At the Wall, dozens of boys from France, Australia and, most of all, the United States made the same gestures, wound the tefillin onto their left arms and then onto their foreheads, recited the same benedictions and roused the same mingled pride and joy in their parents.

But Malkiel's ceremony was less joyful. Only his father participated. Together they joined a Hasidic *minyan* and yet stayed somewhat apart as they prayed. "I have only you in the whole world," Elhanan mused. I have only you in the whole world, Malkiel thought. Elhanan offered an energetic Hasid a few shekels to call his son to the Torah. When he heard the ritual invitation—"Let Malkiel son of Elhanan rise and approach"—Elhanan choked on his own sobs. He covered his face with his prayer shawl.

It was true. They were alone in the world. The last of a long line that tied them to the famous author of *Tosafat Yom Tov*. And on the maternal side to a great medieval mystic, Rabbi Elhanan the Ascetic. In the shadow of the Wall, Malkiel meditated with deep feeling. His paternal grandparents had died *back there*. His maternal grandparents had died a year after their daughter. On the eve of the ceremony, Elhanan took his son to the Safed cemetery to commune at their graves. Talia had discovered this cemetery while strolling with her husband shortly after arriving in the Holy Land. She was astonished at the serenity of the place. "When I die, I want to be buried here," she told him. Elhanan teased her: "Not when you die, but if you die." She didn't smile. "Have I said something I shouldn't have?" Elhanan asked. She bowed her head as if searching for something on the ground. Then she raised it: "Look at me and tell me you love me." Why that pain in her eyes? Elhanan was surprised. "I do love you, Talia, you know that." After a moment she smiled. "One never knows it enough, my love."

In her agony, in the hospital, Talia murmured to her parents, "Elhanan promised me." "What did he promise?" "To take me to Safed."

In 1948 it was not easy to transport a dead body from Jerusalem to Galilee. Zalmen pleaded with an Irgun leader, who interceded with the army. An ambulance carried Zalmen, Reuma and the body of their daughter from Jerusalem to Safed. An eerie silence reigned in the cemetery; each tombstone was bathed in a blue-green light and caught the reflection of the copper-colored soil. During the burial, Zalmen repeated over and over, "Why, Talia, why?" And Reuma lamented, "And what will we do now, Talia?"

Elhanan told all this to his son, who, closer to him than ever, took his hand. "You must not weep, my son," said the weeping Elhanan.

After his release from the prisoner-of-war camp somewhere in the Jordanian desert, Elhanan became sick. Aftereffects of the war? A refusal to live? The doctors couldn't agree on a diagnosis. Some spoke of a general weakening; others, more romantic, shrugged: "He's still in love with his wife. He's heartbroken. It happens." The psychiatrists of course offered their catchall phrase, "Psychosomatic symptoms."

The indefatigable Reuma took care of the baby and the household. Zalmen took care of the rest. Elhanan was living on the fringes of his own existence. No one interested him, and nothing touched his emotions. Of battles, crises that flared, political tension, uncertainty, anguish, Elhanan knew nothing; he neither read the papers nor listened to the radio. The young people's bravura, idealism, spirit of sacrifice, were all at work somewhere else, in a world that rejected him. He sometimes looked upon his own son as a stranger. "It can't go on like this," Zalmen said, betraying his despair. "Do you hear me, Elhanan? You can't go on this way. If you don't make an effort you'll get *really* sick." And Reuma: "Look at me, son. You're destroying me if you destroy yourself, you're destroying all of us. Is that what you want? Think of your son: he needs a father, not a ghost. And who knows how many years are given us? Zalmen and I are not young, and when we're gone who'll look after Malkiel?" And both together: "Why not take a rest . . . take a rest abroad? Your son is still small, and he won't suffer much by your absence." Around that time, the mail brought Elhanan another letter from his American cousin inviting him to New York. Zalmen replied for him: "Your cousin is sick." The cousin: "Let him come here; our doctors are the best in the world." In the end Elhanan agreed, on condition that he could bring along his son. The cousin: "Of course! Our schools are the best in the world!" A heartbreaking scene at the port in Haifa. "You'll be back soon,"

Zalmen said, "quite soon." And Reuma: "Will you be careful? You promise?" They could not have guessed that they would never see one another again.

Elhanan had barely arrived in New York when he was rushed to a hospital: a serious relapse. The cousin and his wife smothered Malkiel with love. They kept murmuring, "So young and already an orphan," as if the two were mutually exclusive.

Back on his feet, Elhanan spent a couple of weeks with his cousin, who soon found him a modest apartment. "Leave the boy with us," they told him. "It will make life easier for you, and he can play with our Rita." Elhanan would not hear of it. The cousin's wife pleaded, "You're in no condition to take care of a child!" She was worked up: "What are you worried about? Someone stealing him from you?" Elhanan would not bend. "How are you going to make a living?" the cousin asked. Elhanan had no idea; he had not thought about it. He only knew that his son must not grow up among strangers. "But we're not strangers!" the wife protested. "Did you hear what he said?" she asked her husband. "He called us strangers!" The cousin calmed her down. "Let it go. He's not really back to himself yet. Don't upset him." A generous man, he pressed five hundred dollars upon Elhanan, who thanked him and promised to repay him. For the moment his problem was to find a woman who could take care of the child and the household while he, Elhanan, looked for work. "Try *The New York Times,*" his cousin said. "The classified ads." "Good luck," the wife murmured. "When you see how hard this is, you'll be banging on our door again."

For once luck was with him. Elhanan dialed a number and asked for someone called Loretta. She showed up that same day. She was in her forties, a widow, poor and kindly, hardworking and open-hearted; her melodious accent evoked the sunny hills of the South. "Oh yes, sir, I'm alone like you. Except that you aren't, really. You have that angel asleep over there. What a beautiful boy! It's a long time since I've seen a baby that beautiful." Her own two children were married and had stayed in Virginia. "I must be honest with you," Elhanan said. "I have five hundred dollars in the world, and that's all. I don't know how long it will take me to find work." Loretta protested with a wave of the hand. "Don't you worry about it, sir. You'll treat me right, and God will treat you right." "I admire your faith, Loretta." "You just keep your faith."

Loretta was wrong, and so was her God. Her employer got off to a rocky start. He pored over the classified ads and studied them as he had studied scripture in the old days. Which was better, to sell neckties or corkscrews? For a month he was a door-to-door salesman. People often slammed the door in his face. Sometimes charitable housewives bought one or two, even if they did not drink wine and didn't need the ties. "I feel sorry for you," they said. He muttered a thank you very much and went off in search of more dignified occupations: cantor in a small German synagogue (his German was not good enough), announcer on a Jewish radio station (his Yiddish was too Yiddish), presser in one of the last laundries left over from the Depression (his muscles were not developed enough), salesman of art books (his English was not refined enough). But he got along one way or another. He even enrolled for night courses at Brooklyn College. He studied everything, absorbed everything. He felt that there was not enough time; he wanted to make up for all the lost years and lost opportunities. He discovered Chaucer and Donne, Dickens and Thoreau, even as he deepened his knowledge of Maimonides and Crescas. He had never studied chemistry? He took chemistry. And physics. Nothing could keep him away from the theater of the Middle Ages. Mystical poetry, occult sciences, graphology, astrology. Ignoring advice from his physician, the young Dr. Pasternak, he worked hard, too hard: during the day giving private lessons in Hebrew literature to make a living, and at night preparing for his exams. His favorite courses: psychology and psychotherapy. Perhaps he hoped to cure himself by curing others.

He did not see his cousin too often. When Malkiel and Rita played together, Elhanan stayed home. His cousin was too rich. Too many secretaries, too many stocks and bonds, too many phone calls. In brief, too busy, too pretentious. Malkiel was more tolerant. Because of Rita? When he reached adolescence, he visited his relatives more often.

Malkiel turned out well, raised by Elhanan and Loretta. A gifted, alert child with no apparent problems. Coca-Cola and chewing gum, hot dogs (kosher) and baseball. He attended religious school, which took him in hand—a bit too rigorously—from kindergarten to high school. He was a good student and excelled at languages, mastering English, Hebrew and Yiddish. He made many friends and secretly loved to charm the girls in his classes.

Like his father, he was interested in everything; but he showed an obvious interest in literature.

His relationship with Elhanan was affectionate; he had not yet experienced the appeal of rebellion. That would come. For the moment they were close, friends and allies. At the end of the day they exchanged impressions and experiences. Malkiel described his friends and Elhanan his students, and later his patients.

At the dinner table they talked about current events. The situation in Israel. The Suez campaign. The Six-Day War. Politics and its scandals. There was one shadow, though: on Talia's birthday, Elhanan spoke only of her. They lit a candle and went to synagogue, where Malkiel recited the Kaddish. All that day Elhanan fasted: he neither ate nor drank. The rest of the year Talia was an absent woman shrouded in mystery. Elhanan thought much about her but rarely spoke his thoughts.

Malkiel would have liked to know more. Sometimes when his father was away he would contemplate the photograph of the beautiful Israeli woman that his father kept both on his desk and on his night table. Subconsciously Malkiel sought a reflection of his mother in all young women. They had to be dark, athletic, free and open, liberated and bold. Cheerful, active and outgoing. How many times did he fall in love? The woman in question, whether he met her in class or in the corridor, at a restaurant or a concert, filled his life for a week, a day, perhaps only an instant, until the surge of a new passion.

But the center of his existence was always his father, whom he respected and admired. Even when he resented him—for obscure childish reasons—he loved him. Sometimes he teased him. "Why don't you marry again?" Blushing in embarrassment, Elhanan would change the subject. And later, when Tamar appeared on the scene, Elhanan took pleasure in responding, "And you? Why don't you get married?"

One day when he came home from school—he must have been twelve—Malkiel had surprised his father, who was seated on the sofa beside a dark-haired woman. They both seemed cheery. Loretta, too; Loretta was glowing. One word and she would have burst into song. But Malkiel wondered, What's going on here? What's the big celebration? Somebody win a lottery?

"I know your name," said the young woman.

"I do, too," said Malkiel acidly.

"What a sense of humor!" she said.

Elhanan introduced her. "Shoshana is from Jerusalem."

"Mother was from Jerusalem, too."

"Exactly. Shoshana was a friend of your mother's."

Malkiel had the impulse to reply, "My mother is dead and you two sit here happy; you're glad my mother is dead." But he held his tongue. Elhanan invited him to sit down.

"Excuse me," he said. "I have homework." He went to the kitchen to look for a piece of cake.

Loretta scolded him. "That's no way to behave with your father. He finally asked a woman up. They're laughing and having a good time. Have you often seen him laugh that much?"

"Who is she?"

"Your father told you. An old friend of your mother's, may her soul rest in peace."

"Married?"

"I don't know anything about that. All I know is that your father's finally showing an interest in a woman. He's decided to live a normal life. Now, a normal man ought to live with a woman, preferably a normal woman. You won't say no to that? So are you going to sulk until he crawls back into his loneliness? Is that what you want? Is it?"

Malkiel put off his homework; he rejoined his father and the guest. When she laughed, her whole face lit up, her eyes, her lips, her nostrils. Every once in a while she touched Elhanan to stress a word or a memory.

"Shoshana was about to leave the DP camp when we did," Elhanan said.

"And if I hadn't been sick, you might have married me," Shoshana added.

And you'd be dead today, Malkiel thought.

"Your mother replaced her at the very last moment," Elhanan said. "What happened?"

"I've forgotten. The flu? A bad stomach virus, maybe. I hated Talia for being so healthy. I was in bed moping. But we were good friends, truly we were, Malkiel."

Why did Elhanan gaze so intently at her? Why did he insist she stay for dinner? How long would she be staying in the United States? Malkiel always remembered: he was jealous. For his mother? For himself, too.

Their guest returned the next day. And the next. Elhanan let her come along when he met Malkiel that day at the schoolyard gate. On the third night they went to the theater. Elhanan got home late. Malkiel was not asleep. As always, Elhanan came in to give him one last hug before turning in for the night.

"Did you have a good time, Father?"

"A very good time."

"That . . . that woman . . ."

"Yes?"

"Do you love her?"

Elhanan sat on the edge of the bed. A melancholy wrinkle deepened at the corners of his mouth. "I loved your mother only."

"But . . . this woman . . ."

"She was close to your mother. And for that reason she's close to me."

"Is she married?"

Elhanan hesitated, and then said, "No," before saying good night.

Shoshana never came back to the house.

Twice a week for four hours Elhanan contributed his psychotherapeutic services to survivors of the camps. These men and women felt a loyal affection for him that was not hard to explain: he listened without judging, and asked questions tactfully. He was always discreet, humble and honest. When he told a visitor, "I'm at your service," he meant exactly that.

Sometimes at the dinner table he would tell Malkiel about certain cases, naturally withholding the names. The lonely old man who had given up hope: he was the sole survivor in his family and knew that when he died his line would die. Despite his age he wanted to adopt a child. . . . The wife who had, for complicated reasons, lied about her past to her husband. Why was she so ashamed of her suffering? . . . The man who could not forgive himself for having refused a piece of bread to a friend, back there . . . The rich businessman who woke in the middle of the night, went into his study, locked it, and wept . . . The woman who, alone in her kitchen, stood in front of a mirror to watch herself swallow candy and cheesecake . . .

"One man said to me, 'In a camp in Poland I saw the extreme of human cruelty. I saw a German officer slaughter a father in front of his four children. That day I lost my faith.' "

"I can understand him," Malkiel said.

"Another man told me, 'In a camp in Poland I saw the extreme of human solidarity. I saw three strangers who sacrificed their sleep and their health to save a sick prisoner. That day my faith was restored.' "

"I can understand him, too," Malkiel said.

"And I might have seen it the other way: the first man might have been able to regain his faith, and the second to lose it."

"Do you help them by understanding them?"

"No. No one can really help these people. What they went through places them beyond reach. All you can do for them is listen."

"Do they feel better?"

"No."

"Then why listen?"

"No one has the right not to listen."

Malkiel thought, Someday I'll understand.

He and his father often talked about God. Like any adolescent raised in faith, Malkiel debated the notion of Providence. If God is everywhere, how do we explain evil? If God is good, how do we explain suffering? If God is God, how are we to conceive man's role in Creation? "God Himself likes an argument," Elhanan told his son. "But what is an argument? It is an admission of conflict and separation; these God creates and destroys, by His presence as much as by His absence. All is possible with Him; nothing is possible without Him. But the opposite is equally true. Never forget what the ancients taught us: God exists in contradictions, too. He is the limit of all things, and He is what extends the limit."

During another discussion, on a Friday night: "We must also consider the tragic situation of God Himself. He can only give His commandments to free men, to people with free will. But in considering the past and their future, men and women no longer demand that freedom which only God can grant. So they give it back to Him, and there is God dealing with people who are no longer free: is it to the greater glory of God if He rules, is obeyed by, a mankind diminished and enslaved? To take an extreme, we could suppose that it was God's will that mankind be superior to Him. Superior because it resents its limitations, because it aspires to the unattainable. Humanity is people who walk, who dance, who stubbornly pursue the perpetual conquest of their own freedom and their own innocence. . . ."

Malkiel thought again, Someday I'll understand.

Lidia stared at Malkiel as if he were out of his mind. "You're looking for *what*?"

"A woman."

"And if I understand you correctly, I won't fill the bill?"

"You always *mis*understand me."

"Your riddles are getting on my nerves, Mr. Rosenbaum!"

"Don't be angry, Lidia. Please."

He seemed so worried and miserable that the young interpreter softened. "I'm not angry. Only jealous."

"It's my loss, not yours. The woman I'm looking for is old. She must be about seventy."

They were sitting on their usual bench in the park. Late afternoon on a pleasant day. The park was swarming with people. The sun, white and cold in the transparent air, was setting lazily.

"And what's your dream girl's name?"

"That's just it. I don't know."

Lidia slapped her knees. "I have to hand it to you! Has it never occurred to you that there may be several old women in this city whose names you don't know?"

Of course she was right. He should have asked his father for more details. The Nyilas was called Zoltan. Was that his first name or his last name? Elhanan had never specified, and would he remember now?

"Let me explain, Lidia." He told her about the partisans and the Red Army. The liberation. Itzik the Long and his thirst for vengeance. The rape.

Her face betrayed horror and disgust. How could she have reproached him? "A question," she said, and cleared her throat.

"Yes?"

"What would you have done in your father's place?"

Malkiel had asked himself that question many times. He had tried to imagine himself in the room, standing over the two thrashing bodies. Would he have flung himself on his best friend to save him from himself? Would he have called for help? "I just don't know."

A couple sat down on a nearby bench. The man whispered in his companion's ear. Malkiel wondered, Do I exist for them?

The sun was truly setting now, and the sky over the mountains darkened and seemed menacing. The air was cooler. Cold.

"It's hopeless," Lidia said. She explained so calmly that Malkiel was annoyed. "There were plenty of raped women around here. Everybody knows about it, but nobody talks about it. Don't give me that look, Reporter. Don't tell me you didn't know. You didn't know that our liberators, the Russian soldiers, raped every woman they could get their hands on? Beautiful and homely, large and small, skinny and fat, innocent schoolgirls and shriveled-up grandmothers: they all went through it. That was life. The rules of the game. All's fair in love and war. The ransom, the warrior's reward, the conqueror's right to possess the conquered—call it whatever you like. Sometimes I suspect that my aunts, their friends, my own mother . . . They never talk about it. None of them will ever talk about the first days and nights of the liberation. It's an enormous act of collective repression. And you really believe you'll find the one your father saw on the floor, being tortured by his comrade in arms?"

Malkiel did not answer. She was right. It was hopeless. "I didn't think hard about it," he said in low tones, upset. "I know how stupid that is, but I can't help it. All I know is that it was only here, and I'm not even sure exactly when, that the real reason for my trip became clear to me."

Lidia teased him dryly: "A sudden revelation?"

"Sure, why not? I suddenly realized that I had to find that woman. See her, talk to her, hear her voice, see her eyes and her lips and her hands. I have to find her. I have to, Lidia."

Night had fallen. Malkiel could not see her features. A solitary stroller crossed the park and went to drown his sorrows God knows where.

"One question," Lidia said. "Suppose she's dead."

Again she was right.

"Would you regret your visit here?"

"No," Malkiel said. And after a moment, "I'm glad our paths crossed." Malkiel meant it. He liked her very much, this interpreter full of charm and information. If he had not met Tamar, who knows?

"All right," she said. "Let's go to work. The woman in question was a widow, and her husband was a Nyilas. He was called Zoltan. Unfortunately, there were plenty of Nyilas in our lovely garden spot under the Hungarian occupation."

"And Zoltan?"

"A common enough name."

"Famous for his cruelty. The terror of the ghetto. Excited by Jewish blood . . ."

Lidia listened carefully and asked some pointed questions. She had him repeat this incident and sharpen that detail. When he was finished she stood up. "All right, then. I'll see if I can be useful. After all, I know a lot of people. Maybe some of the oldest will remember. If so, we'll have a chance of finding her."

She said "we," Malkiel thought as he, too, stood up. A good sign. Another sleepless night. Should he spend it with the gravedigger and his blind companion? Maybe one of them could answer the questions: why had his father sent him to this city? To see the widow? For some other reason?

Malkiel almost lost his temper next morning when they shook hands in the hotel lobby. "Well?" he asked.

"Well, what?"

"Any luck?"

"Oh, luck; luck is a vague word."

"Have you learned anything?"

"Have I learned anything? Maybe."

"Are you making fun of me?"

"Calm down, my friend, calm down. You're in a country that requires iron self-control."

He took a deep breath to get hold of himself.

"Let's go have breakfast together," she said. "In peace and quiet, all right? That's a condition. Otherwise I'm through with you. I refuse to let you spoil my morning with your impatience."

Malkiel would have liked to tell her what he thought of her, but that would have been counterproductive. And what was the meaning of her game? Maybe police surveillance had tightened around them. "This hotel isn't famous for breakfast," he said, forcing himself to be amiable. "But I have some good American Nescafé. Will you do me the honor of sharing it with me?"

"But of course, kind sir."

By now used to Malkiel's generous tips, the waiter brought them fresh bread, butter, eggs and cheese. Lidia ate with good appetite. Had her woman's self-respect been wounded? Was she seeking revenge? She chatted about anything but the raped widow. The political economy under this regime, the Communist educational system, international current events as seen by Romanian commentators, literary analyses of the national folklore, funny stories about not so funny love affairs—for over an hour Malkiel played the game, never interrupting or betraying the slightest restlessness. And then with calculated nonchalance Lidia drew a folded sheet of paper from her handbag. "The whole works," she said. "Name, address, personal data."

Malkiel almost shouted, "Give it to me!" But he restrained himself. He stared at the folded sheet as if his life depended on it.

"Take it," Lidia said.

He grabbed it, and stroked it for a moment before unfolding it.

"Will you translate for me?"

"Elena. Calinescu. Linden Street, number fifty-two. Lives with her daughter and son-in-law. There's a granddaughter too."

Malkiel tried to keep calm, or at least not to show his anxiety. "She's alive," he said.

"And you are going to meet her," Lidia said.

"When?"

"Right away."

Without admitting it, Malkiel was somehow afraid to stand before this woman who had haunted his father for so long. What if she hurled reproaches at him? What if she screamed her hatred in his face?

Lidia asked, "Shall we go?"

Outside, it was drizzling. The city was sinister; its colors seemed less friendly, and the trees, in yellow leaf now, more depressing.

It was a silent, disturbing walk of ten minutes to a handsome little two-story house. Lidia rang for the second floor. The door opened a crack. Lidia spoke a few words in Romanian; someone answered. Lidia argued. The door closed. Lidia pursued the argument vigorously. The door opened again. Lidia and Malkiel entered. A disheveled girl led them to the living room. So, Malkiel thought, they have living rooms under the Communists. He wondered which Jewish family the house had once belonged to.

"Good morning, miss," a voice quavered. "Good morning, sir." It was a sickly voice, and barely audible. A distinguished-looking woman was standing before them, her head tilted toward her left shoulder. "What can I do for you?"

Malkiel inspected her: short, slight, dressed in black, her features delicate and sad. Was she in mourning? Hollow wrinkled cheeks. Heavy lips and eyelids. "Lidia," he said, "would you be good enough to explain . . . but carefully . . . kindly."

Lidia explained.

As the old woman listened, or seemed to listen, her head drooped more and more toward her shoulder.

The girl brought them glasses of mineral water. Lidia broke off to take a sip.

"What have you told her?"

"Nothing yet. A few words about you. That you're a reporter, that you live in the United States, that your father once lived here."

"Nothing else?"

"That's all so far."

The old woman was watching him, and waiting. Where should he begin? "Ask her to excuse us for imposing on her."

The old woman gave a barely perceptible nod. She picked up a glass of water and squeezed it with both hands.

"And forgive us for opening old wounds—I hope they're long since healed." The old woman's gaze was penetrating and added to Malkiel's anxiety. "Ask her if she understands what we're talking about."

Yes, she understood.

"Ask if she can recall the day of the liberation."

Lidia translated. The old woman stiffened. She raised her head. "No," she said. "I don't remember it." Was there defiance in this voice, weakened by the years?

"Ask her if she'd consider trying."

Lidia translated. The old woman, still stiff and proud, answered that she was old, she had lived too many years, too many seasons, too many tragedies. No, she did not recall that day. Besides, it was all so long ago.

"Insist, Lidia. It's important." Again Lidia translated.

"To whom?" asked the old woman.

"To me," Malkiel said.

"I don't know you. And anyway at my age the things that may be important to you aren't important to me."

Lidia translated, turning from one to the other.

"Tell her not to be afraid, Lidia."

"I'm not afraid," the old woman said.

"Then why refuse to help me?"

"I don't know you. So I fail to see how I can help you."

"By remembering the day of—"

"I've forgotten so many things, so many things," said the old woman. She dragged a chair closer and sat down. From then on Malkiel saw her only in profile. "So many things," she repeated wearily. "Luckily I've managed to forget them. God in His mercy has helped me erase them from my memory. You're still young, sir. You can't understand the virtues of forgetfulness. How could we go on if we remembered everything?"

Lidia translated in a neutral, professional voice.

"I'm not asking you to remember everything," Malkiel said. "Let's limit it to one day. The day of the liberation."

"It was wartime, sir. So many things happen in wartime."

"What sort of things?"

"Evil things, things that hurt us. Terrible things. Is there anything in war that isn't terrible?"

"Please tell me more precisely what you mean."

The old woman could not. She was very sorry. She was too tired and too old to pierce the mists that enveloped her memory. She was sorry, but he must understand that. . . .

"Forgive me, madam, but do you remember your husband?" Here we go, Malkiel thought, tense.

"What a question! Of course I remember my husband," the old woman said. "How could I forget him? He's right here in the next room. In bed with a bad cold."

Then she had remarried? Lidia had not mentioned that. Unless he had misunderstood her. He had fixed on the one fact that she was still alive. "Children?"

"Three. All married. Two live far away. We have seven grandchildren. Maria lives here with her husband and their daughter."

Three children, Malkiel thought. "How old is your eldest child?"

"It's a daughter, Silvia."

"How old is she?"

"Why do you want to know that? What do you care about my children's ages?"

"I promise to explain, madam."

"Well, let's see. I married my husband when I was . . . when I was twenty-five, maybe a little younger. Silvia? Thirty-eight, if I'm not mistaken."

Malkiel did some quick arithmetic and sighed with relief. No, Itzik the Long had no descendants in Romania. Yet how many times had it happened to how many others? "And your first husband, madam? Do you remember him?"

She stiffened again. Painful memories froze her bony face. Her silence became opaque. Her hands gripped the arms of her chair.

"He was an important man, wasn't he? A Nyilas officer. Zoltan—remember his name? Remember his uniform? His weapons? His whip? Have you really forgotten him? He detested Jews and hunted them down. Did you know that? He stalked them and beat them and tortured them. Isn't that true, madam—your husband killed Jews?"

In cutting, staccato tones Malkiel struck blow after blow. To hurt her? To rouse her from her torpor, to stir her up. But she, head high and gaze hard, sat mute.

Malkiel said, "Lidia, tell her I am not here to accuse her of anything, and even less to torture her, but . . ."

"But?" Lidia echoed.

"To understand. And that's the truth. I came to see her so I could understand my father better."

"What? In slashing at this poor woman you think you can help your father?"

"No, Lidia, it's not that. It's too late for my father."

"Is he dead?"

"No, he's still alive. Yes, my father is alive. But . . . never mind. I'll explain it some other time. Just believe me for now: Madame Calinescu's answers are extremely important to me."

The old woman seemed to have sensed the meaning of this exchange. She brought her hands forward and set them on her knees, and bit her lips before speaking again. "Tell him he's right. My first husband was a bad man. He liked to do evil, and he hurt me often."

"You? Why?"

"I used to beg him to break with his Nyilas friends. I wanted him to change. I wanted to live with a husband and not a hangman."

They had been married six or seven months before the liberation. He was the son of a friend of her father's. It was an arranged marriage, of course. She was young, very young, barely out of her adolescence. She dreamed of a Prince Charming. Her father said, "I've found your Prince Charming. He's a Nyilas, but that will pass." The man was called Zoltan. The girls liked him in his glittering uniform. "How could I doubt his character, his nobility of spirit? I was naive and stupid." He was a handsome fellow, sensual, vain, and he treated people with contempt. Yes, he beat his victims. Yes, he hated them, Jews most of all. Yes, he went to the ghetto to "clean it out," as he said. When he came back he radiated triumph. And she, his wife? While he was gone she stayed home with her many servants. Locked in her room, the shutters closed, she wept. "What are you crying about?" he asked. "You need everybody to be your victim," she answered. Then he whipped her. And she stopped weeping.

"Yes. How could I have forgotten my first husband?" the old woman said.

Actually, she could have escaped, gone home to her parents and told them, "Zoltan is a monster. I don't love him and he doesn't love me." Or, "We love each other at night, when we're alone in bed. But we're never really alone. His victims are always there; I can hear them groaning." Or again, "Yes, we still love each other sometimes, we love each other with a twisted love, a cursed love." Yes, she should have, she should have.

Malkiel could not help sympathizing. How can anyone go through life in a constant state of remorse? Why hadn't she left her jailer husband? Or fought back against the growing horror? She should have understood that such a refusal could have saved her—a refusal that ran with and not against life's grain, which transforms a handful of dust into a human being. Now it is too late.

Malkiel understood why she would want to forget. The days of the ghetto, and the humiliation of a people. Days of tenderness, too. Days when she loved her monster of a husband, when she sulked without him, when she embraced him and sought to mingle his breath with her own. She wanted to erase those images—what could be more natural? Had Malkiel any right to impose them upon her? An inner voice said, "Stop. Leave this poor woman alone. She's suffered enough, she has a right to rest, even if she can find it only in forgetting." But he knew he had to go on with his quest. Why? Pure instinct; he knew he had to.

"Your first husband, madam. Do you remember his death?"

Yes, she remembered. They came to inform her one afternoon in spring. She was in her garden. An officer stood before her, solemn and somber. Erect and respectful. "Be strong, madam," he said. "In the name of the minister of war and the commander in chief of the army, I must bring you sad news." She heard only the first words, "Be strong," and she guessed the rest. Wild thoughts tumbled in her mind. "He will never hurt anyone again." "I will never be humiliated again." "I am a widow. I am not yet twenty and already

I am a widow." And then? Then she must have fainted. Who killed her husband? She hardly knew now. Yes, she knew. Partisans. Jewish partisans. They lived in the forests and the mountains. Young people, who had escaped from the local ghetto, and other ghettos. "I saw his corpse. It was unrecognizable. I remember it. I said to myself, 'It is the dead who killed him. It is his own victims who punished him.' I remember because my parents were there. They told me that during the funeral services I kept saying one word over and over: 'Punishment, punishment.' The Russians moved in a few days or a few weeks later."

Lidia interrupted. "She's telling the truth. I got confirmation. She wasn't touched after the liberation. They said her conduct had been irreproachable."

Malkiel tried to imagine her young. She must have been beautiful. Fine features. Innocence itself. He tried to imagine her as victim. Victim of Itzik the Long. Screaming. Begging for pity.

It was still raining outside. A bird flew suddenly into his field of vision and seemed to be carrying shreds of cloud on its wings.

"As a young widow," Lidia went on, "she spent several weeks in a clinic not far from here. For mental disorders."

Of course, Malkiel thought.

"Of course," Lidia said. "Her husband's death. The shame of having been a Nyilas torturer's wife. The wild turmoil at the liberation."

Malkiel stepped closer to the old woman. He needed to look directly into her face. He gazed into her eyes. He saw nothing. There was no expression in her eyes. "Lidia, ask her if she sees me. If she doesn't see me, ask her what she does see."

The old woman did not answer the question. Lidia repeated it. Still she did not answer. She's tired, Malkiel decided.

"I'm tired," the old woman said. "These memories are a great weight."

Malkiel was not happy as an investigator. An inquisitor? All evidence points to this woman having also been a victim. Why add to her suffering by forcing her to relive the past? The same voice told him that this was enough. And again he did not heed it.

"Try to forgive me, madam," he said, leaning forward. "It will be painful, but I have no choice. My motives are honorable."

"Everybody says that," Lidia put in. "You can always find honorable reasons for inflicting pain."

Malkiel chose not to reply. "I am going to tell you about the worst day of your life. You are terrified. You have hidden in the cellar with an aunt. Do you remember?"

The old woman straightened her head. A deeper layer of shadow veiled her eyes. She placed her right hand on her breast and seemed to be measuring her own heartbeat, perhaps trying to quiet it.

"The Red Army is attacking, and the Germans and Hungarians have fallen back to new positions in a few buildings. Not for long. Resistance is useless and they know it. The battle lasts from dawn till midafternoon. From your shelter you can hear the sounds of war: tanks, shells, soldiers drunk on violence, bearers of death. . . . Suddenly you catch your breath. Somebody's broken down your door. An armed man is in the house. You can't see him, but you can hear him. He searches the house, opens the closets, inspects the rooms, knocks on the walls, opens the cellar door, stumbles on your aunt, who cries out in horror, flings her aside and runs down the cellar stairs pointing his rifle; and sees you. He's tall and slim and agile, and he's full of cold anger. He orders you up the stairs. You obey. He shoves you into a room and shuts the door. He turns to you and glares at you with hatred, and then he talks to you in a language you don't understand. Yiddish. Do you remember, madam?"

The old woman was panting, and stared at him now as if he were the man who had raped her. She pressed her hands to her temples. Was she trying to suppress some image rising irresistibly from the depths of memory? "No, sir, I do not remember."

Malkiel did not believe her, and harshly told her so.

"Stop it," Lidia said. "Can't you see she's suffering? Why do you make her suffer?"

"I did nothing to her," Malkiel said stubbornly. "Someone else made her suffer, not me. I'm part of her present, not her past."

"But you're making her suffer in the present," Lidia said.

"No. She's remembering pain from long ago. It's not the same."

"I don't remember," the old woman said tonelessly.

"The man barks an order: you don't understand. He explains in gestures. You still don't understand. Then with his rifle in his left hand he strips you with his right hand: tears off your blouse, your skirt; you're half naked. He drops his trousers." Malkiel was talking fast, without realizing it, much faster than usual.

Lidia cried, "That's enough! What kind of man are you?"

Malkiel could not stop. He would press this interrogation to the end and beyond. "You're lying on the floor in the dirt and the man is on top of you, crushing you, suffocating you, his breath makes you sick, he glares into your eyes, you fight him just as you fight the hysteria that might free you, and then you stop fighting, and suddenly . . ."

The old woman was absolutely motionless now. Reliving the shame, she seemed vanquished by shame.

"Suddenly a man appears. He's out of breath. He sees you before he recognizes your attacker. And you see him. You don't speak to him, but he understands you. You don't plead with him, but he comes to the rescue, or at least tries to. He calls out to your tormentor, in Yiddish also, and talks sense to him; but the other is deaf. He begs him not to be bestial; he raises his voice and cries out that what he is doing is cruel, immoral, inhuman; he shouts at the top of his lungs, but it does no good. And then he weeps, this new man. He sobs. Your eyes meet. You remember, madam?"

And in a hard, insistent tone: "That man, that unexpected knight who wanted to save you—do you remember him, Madame Calinescu?"

The old lady came out of her silence as an invalid comes out of illness: weakened but lucid. She seemed to have aged ten years in ten minutes. She opened her mouth, she started to speak, and suddenly it was Malkiel who panicked. He thought he knew, he did know what the old lady was going to tell him. She was going to reveal the hideous and abject face of her knight. "Ha! You see him as a noble creature, rushing to the rescue of a poor helpless woman. You are quite naive, sir. In war all men are beasts. All they want is to hurt people, to humble them, to possess them. Let me tell you what your knight did, that savior of yours whose heart was so pure: he waited for his friend to finish and then took his place. And you thought . . . You make me laugh, sir." That was what the old lady was going to tell him. To take revenge because he had troubled her peace? To see that truth prevailed? But then what sense was there in this quest? Where was hope? Was redemption still possible? A secret voice, the same inner voice, whispered to him, Go now, tear yourself away from this place, open the door and go and never come back! And as before, he paid no attention. Besides, his panic was baseless. The old lady would act out no such scenario. The knight's glory would remain bright and reassuring.

But the old lady's anger was nevertheless violent. "By what right do you reopen my wounds?" she asked slowly and distinctly. "Who authorized you to rifle my memory? Why do you force me to see myself again soiled, bruised, dishonored in my flesh as in my soul?

What have I ever done to you? Haven't I suffered enough? I prayed God to let me forget, and God heard me; I finally buried my memories. And wiped out the traces of that day that was blacker than night. I finally forgot the ugly leers, the hands, the sounds that tied me to that man. Why must you undo what God has done? By what right do you come to transform His divine compassion into human malediction?"

She did not raise her voice; she contained her anger, but her fury brought back her somber gaze. Stricken by remorse, Malkiel said nothing. She's right, he thought. How can I tell her she's wrong?

"I forgive you," the old lady went on. "A man's character always shows in his face, and I know that you are not cruel. You wanted to show regret, and pity? That is no concern of mine. Since you were in my house, I listened to you. Since you looked at me, I spoke to you. And now please leave me. I need rest."

Malkiel bowed in thanks. He signaled to Lidia that it was time to leave. And yet he knew that he must ask one last question: "The man who tried to help you—do you think of him from time to time?"

"Thanks to him I believe from time to time that not all men are evil. I believe that he was honest and a man of charity. But in my need to forget it all, I finally forgot him, too."

She rose to show her visitors out. As she shook hands with Malkiel she said, "That man of courage and humanity, I see him at times, as if behind a smoke screen. An illuminated shadow, so to speak. But I saw many shadows that day, and in the days that followed."

Malkiel held her hand in his own. "I hope you won't be too angry with me, Madame Calinescu. Thanks to you I've learned something useful and perhaps essential: forgetting is also part of the mystery. You need to forget, and I understand. I must resist forgetting, so try to understand me, too."

For the first time she attempted a smile. Malkiel was affected by that more than by her words: "I could lie, but I don't want to. The truth is that I don't understand you. Aren't you too young to learn someone else's past in addition to your own? A little while ago I wondered if the man was perhaps you. But of course that's impossible. You were not even born then."

"It was my father," Malkiel said gently.

The old woman swayed, shuddered. Fearing she would collapse, Malkiel put his arms around her and went on just as gently: "My father was the man who tried to save you, not the other one."

Relief softened Elena Calinescu's face. Little by little she grew calm. She gazed at him for some time before murmuring, "Then will you allow an old woman to thank you? And to kiss you?" She kissed his forehead. "Thank you for coming." She kissed him again. "And thank your father."

Malkiel embraced her and then, on the verge of tears, left without a word. Lidia followed him. They went downstairs without speaking. In the street Lidia turned to him. "Will you allow an interpreter, not so young anymore, to kiss you, too?" She kissed him on the mouth. And Malkiel saw his father again, who had never known love here in the city of his birth; no woman here had ever sealed his lips with hers.

It was time to go back.

Tamar. He would see Tamar again. He would love her; love her with his whole heart. Weeping, laughing like a child, she would take him back, he was sure. Or at least he hoped so. Was she angry? That was all in the past. Their quarrel? Ancient history. The incident? She held it against him, but given his past and even more his father's past, could he have done otherwise? Tamar was unjust. With her chin in the air, she'd glared at him. "You're lying. You're lying, and you want me to lie, too!" Good thing it happened at his place and not at the newspaper. The foreign editor and the sage himself would have settled the matter for them: all real news must be published.

Israel was at the heart of it. And an article that might do Israel harm, might tarnish its image and harm its interests. Malkiel said, I love Israel. Tamar said, I love truth. They spent a sleepless night debating, shouting familiar arguments and old recriminations back and forth. Malkiel tried to bring her to the "right way of thinking," as they say; it was no use. Proud, arrogant, sure of her knowledge and her right to pronounce judgment, she proved stubborn, determined, unyielding: she punctuated everything she said with, "Freedom of information comes first." Malkiel replied, "And if your sacred freedom of information causes real harm? Harm to our people? Will you swear by it just the same?" Tangled in their maze of pride and loyalty, they forgot how to listen. So the couple broke up. Hurt, each saw in the other an obstacle.

Tamar had interviewed a young Palestinian from Bethlehem who was on a lecture tour in the United States. He was a professor of political science at Bir Zeit, and he accused Israel's government, police and army of suppressing and torturing the Arabs of the West Bank. Even before she turned it in to the foreign desk she showed her piece to Malkiel, who blushed as he read it. "Come have a cup of coffee," he said.

"Right now? It's five o'clock—we'll miss the first edition."

He insisted. "Please, Tamar. Come on."

"Is it that urgent?"

"Yes."

They went up to the cafeteria and took a small table in the corner. "What's so urgent? Something about your father?"

"No."

Tamar was short with him. "Come on. There's not much time. If you have something to say, say it."

"That article. Have you shown it to anyone?"

"No. I was going to give it to the sage once you'd gone over it."

"You'd better not," Malkiel said.

"What? But it's explosive! It'll be quoted all over television tomorrow."

"That's just it," Malkiel said. "That's why you'd better not." Malkiel too had to go back to work. "Let me make a suggestion," he said. "Wait one day. Nobody's going to beat you to it. This guy is too eager to see the story in our paper. We'll talk about it tonight. If I don't persuade you, run it tomorrow."

She looked at him for a long moment, then rose suddenly and walked toward the door. "See you later," she said hastily.

At seven o'clock, as usual, Malkiel went to visit his father. In his heart he had hoped to find Tamar there; she often arrived first; but she was surely in no mood to please him that evening. Loretta was all smiles.

"Everything all right today?" he asked.

"Just fine," she said, "except he wouldn't take his nap."

Malkiel told his father, "You should rest in the afternoon. It's good for you."

"I can't sleep. I don't want to," Elhanan said. "I'm afraid of not waking up. Or of not knowing I've awakened."

To make him talk, Malkiel asked all kinds of questions, to which Elhanan replied distractedly. "Your mind's somewhere else," Malkiel said.

His father paused before answering. "Our sages teach us that two angels attach themselves to a man at birth and never leave him. One walks before and helps him climb mountains, the other follows in the shadows and pushes him toward his fall. I have a feeling that the second one is now stronger. I feel sorry for the first."

"Don't underestimate him," Malkiel said. "He's there to protect you; and God protects him."

Elhanan thought that over, and his voice was full of anguish. "And who protects God?"

Malkiel was in a hurry to go home. Tamar was already there. Curled up on a sofa with a stubborn look on her face, she was sipping a whiskey-soda. "All right, let's get right to it, Mr. Censor." It was beginning badly. When Tamar wanted to be bitchy, she was unbeatable.

"You'll allow me to sit down?"

"Yes."

"On the sofa?"

"No. Take a chair. That one, so you face me. Okay. I'm listening. Start explaining. What right do you have to censor me, violating all my principles?" When Tamar uttered the word "principles," nobody could stand up to her. They were sacred, those principles. Inviolable.

Malkiel tried his luck anyway. "You met with this Palestinian, right?"

"Of course I did. His facts were solid and specific."

"Were they also true?"

"What do you mean by that?"

"Did you verify them?"

"You read the piece—didn't I report official Israeli reactions?"

"When you publish both versions—and don't give much space to the Israelis—you leave room for doubt."

"What's wrong with shaking up the simpleminded reader?"

The argument degenerated. They both fell back on clichés and emotions.

"It's a question of truth," Tamar said. "Do you want me to suppress it?"

"You dare contradict the truth of Israel by any other truth?"

"If what this Palestinian says is true, then Israel is contradicting its own truth—its ethical calling, its prophetic mission!"

"Who are you and who am I to set ourselves up as judges of an ancient people, and furthermore our own?"

"Who are you and who am I not to help an ancient people, and furthermore our own, refrain from serious error? Their salvation may depend on it, and ours certainly does!"

"You call yourself Israel's savior?"

"Your irony is misplaced. I'm neither a prophet nor a moralist. I'm a journalist. I intend to do my job as honestly as I can. And you're only a sad little preacher trying to stop me with childish and sentimental arguments."

"And you don't give a damn for Israel's welfare—admit it! You don't give a damn about their security—go on, admit it! All that matters to you is your scoop, and the boss's congratulations, and if that piece brought you a Pulitzer Prize you'd jump for joy, and if Israel had to suffer for it, what the hell! Do I overstate the case?"

"Yes, you overstate the case, damn right you overstate it! I love my work. I love it passionately, and not because of the rewards but because it's my weapon! I like to think that because of me men and women will be a little happier and their lives a little easier."

"You worry about everybody in the world except your own brothers and sisters in Israel!"

"That's a lie!"

"Then prove it!"

"How do you want me to prove it? By concealing what happens there? By accepting injustice there and passing over it in silence?"

"And the injustices perpetrated against Israel? You don't care about them? The terrorist raids? The assassination of children? The murder of innocent civilians?"

"The paper we work for talks about them all the time, and often on the front page. Don't you think the Palestinians' fate deserves a little attention too?"

"Ah, there it is—finally admitting it's the Palestinians you care about."

"No. It's the truth I care about. And I love Israel as much as you do."

"But you're prepared to do them harm and put them at risk."

"No! I'm prepared to keep them from doing harm to themselves!"

"Oh, magnificent, Tamar! You're going to help Israel in spite of itself! Bravo!"

The battle raged all night. Malkiel demanded a "special" attitude toward the Jewish state because of its past sufferings. Tamar, too —but with this difference: Malkiel said they had to "understand" Israel's shortcomings, that the world had to be more tolerant of a country traumatized by five or six wars, while Tamar held that precisely because of Israel's past sufferings the world had to be more demanding; it was a community that should be helping its victims instead of oppressing them.

After that sleepless night Tamar filed her piece. The next day it got the front page and provoked an uproar. Jewish organizations issued protest after protest; the State Department refused to confirm charges that, in any case, Jerusalem hurriedly denied; and at the United Nations, five Arab delegates quoted the article in question to prove that Israel was violating the rights of Palestinians on the West Bank.

That night Malkiel found his father in tears. "I saw the article," he said. "I read it three times, seven times. . . . I don't understand. . . ."

"I don't either, Father. I don't understand either."

Between Tamar and Malkiel, there were now the tears of Elhanan.

It's unfair, Malkiel thought. It's unfair for Israel to separate us while it should bring us closer. Help us, Father, as you have helped so many others.

I'll go home soon, Malkiel thought. I'll see Tamar again. I'll tell her I love her with a love that we can make fruitful. Then I'll see my father and tell him I love him with an unhappy love: I'll confess my failure. I found nothing, Father. Nothing that could help you or us. Here you are on the brink of despair, you who've helped so many of the sick invent hope for themselves. Here you are on your knees, you who taught pride. You used to say, "The most miserable creature on the face of the earth can still make someone else happy." You hadn't thought about what might happen to you, what's happening to you right now. There is an evil that contradicts all theories. When your mind was clear you admitted that yourself: you can't help anyone, and no one can help you. Or is it *because* you can't help anyone that no one can help you? What difference does it make? I am finishing my journey empty-handed.

But isn't it your fault, too? Why did you wait so long to speak to me, to share your past with me? Why didn't you tell me the true purpose of my trip? What did you want to see me accomplish in your town? To walk on its soil and curse it, to open the cemetery gate and bless it? Or simply to sleep in your house, to pray in your synagogue? The latter no longer stands, and the former is occupied by strangers.

You wanted me here? I am here. To see the widow? I have seen her. And now? How has my presence here been useful to you? I breathe the air you breathed, I see the sights that made you drunk, I take in fragments of memory that have been chipped away from yours: is that enough? I bring you a smile, the widow's. Is that enough?

I'm afraid, Father. If you suddenly burst into speech as you used to, to ask me questions as you used to, what would I answer? If you suddenly decided to reclaim what you've given me, how would I fill the void you'd leave in me? If you accused me of wanting to enrich my memory at the expense of yours, how would I justify myself?

Stop worrying, Malkiel, thought Malkiel. Father will say no such thing. Father will say nothing ever again. As ill as he is, he'll let his thoughts disperse in a fog. His eyes open, his mouth half open, he will neither accuse nor complain. To the last moment, a father like yours will try to spare you, to protect you.

But now it's up to me to protect him. If I only knew how. Does Tamar know? Truth is, I ought to consult a new specialist. My father was a specialist, in his own field. They came to consult him, and went away comforted. He knew how to listen. He knew how to console, too. Who in turn will console him? God?

And what if I began praying?

Malkiel surprised himself by meditating upon Job. Poor Job. God spoke to him, and Job was silent. God asked him questions, and Job did not answer. God spoke to him of the very origins of the universe, and Job said nothing. Had he, too, lost all links to the past? Did God make him lose it? Was there a more terrifying, more unjust suffering for him?

Rage, Job. Shout your anger, Father. That may be a cure. Cry out. Pound your fist, shatter the walls. He who suffers misfortune and submits to its laws has a slave's heart, a slave's soul and mind. Never submit, Job. Never resign yourself, Father. Show us all that your heart is bursting. Curse, break your silence, transform it to a conscious outcry. Rebel against unwilled oblivion, the most inhuman of evils. Banish the black-winged ravens with your anger.

Can you still help me to help you, Father?

Grandfather Malkiel, I've come to say good-bye. I'm on my way. I'm going home. Tamar is waiting for me: I need her love. Is my father waiting? Does he still need mine?

I'm leaving you, and I wonder: in coming here, did I find the answers to my questions?

Tomorrow I board a plane for Bucharest. There I board a plane for Israel. I want to visit my mother's grave and to say a prayer. To restore my soul at the Wall in Jerusalem. To meditate beneath its sky, so laden with meaning.

I leave you the old woman and her wounded memory. Watch

over her. Let her old age be more serene than her youth. May she live in the promise of renewal and not in the remorse of actions frozen in time.

Watch over Lidia, too, Grandfather. She's a good honest woman, and alone, so alone. I trusted her and never regretted it. Let her be there for someone who will stand beside her; let no one do her harm.

And from afar, from up there in heaven, lend me your protection, too. I need it. Whatever happens, I will have to justify my father's faith in me. He made me his messenger; I will have to prove myself worthy of his message.

My father, my poor father! It's hard to talk that way about someone who was once the powerful embodiment of intelligence and eloquence. Disarmed and defenseless, he is presiding over his own disintegration: he pronounces words that crumble in midair, dead words; the sentences he speaks are dead sentences. He himself is dying. For him, the passing moment is gone forever. He is unquestionably still alive, but in him time is dead. My father is living a dead life: his time is dead time.

Can you see all this from where you are, Grandfather Malkiel? Your son has suffered greatly. At first, when he was still lucid, he realized that he was slipping down a fatal slope and that there was nothing he could do to stop himself. A maniacal hand was tearing away the pages of his life one by one. Every morning he knew a little less, and every evening he felt diminished. Sometimes, watching him, I wept without tears: I could hardly bear his agony. He would search for a name, a word, and I saw his brain working, digging, digging; sweat beaded on his forehead; terror filled his eyes, empty of memory; I saw his lips move, his tongue groping, I saw his heart breaking, and because I could not help him without humiliating him I turned away, I went out, leaving Tamar to fight the battle alone.

And now?

Nothing can be done, the doctors say, nothing can be done. . . . It's a disease, an incurable disease. Once the destructive process has begun, nothing can stop it.

Your poor son, Grandfather Malkiel, has become the poorest of human beings. He has nothing, and he is no one.

And now?

Is there still a now for him?

Will he recognize me? When I left, I was the only one he could identify. Tamar? He confused her with my mother. Loretta? He thought he'd met her somewhere in the Ukraine. Everybody else was a stranger to him. My father proceeds through a universe populated by strangers. Do they smile at him? Do they frighten him? Can he distinguish friend from foe?

"There's nothing that can be done," the great specialists declared. Too late for unknown cures. The brain is being dismantled. And miracles, Dr. Pasternak, what about miracles? There comes a moment when God Himself refuses to intervene.

I know: even the most eminent doctors are sometimes wrong. I sometimes wonder if the diagnosis is correct. I wonder if my father is suffering from amnesia or some other disease. He may know everything that's happening to him, everything said in his presence, everything going on around him and within him, and he may want to react, to respond, but he may be incapable of it. Or he may not want to. He may be disappointed in mankind. And in its language. He may reject our worn and devalued words. He may need others altogether. And as there are no others, he may be choosing to feign forgetfulness so that he can remain speechless.

An improbable theory? So much the worse. What matters, Grandfather, is that your son is no longer in touch with the world of the living. Did he know what would strike him down? That might explain why he agreed to open up, why he undertook a kind of memory transfusion as one has a blood transfusion. Was it his wish that my memory substitute for his own? That I do the remembering for him? Is that even possible?

Grandfather Malkiel: I, Malkiel, your grandson, will fulfill his wishes, I promise you. What he has buried within himself, what he has entrusted to his extinguished memory, I will disclose. I will bear witness in his place; I will speak for him. It is the son's duty not to let his father die.

At his grandfather's grave, Malkiel imagined Tamar. Doubtless at Elhanan's bedside. She would not punish the father for the sins of the son. We are going to be married, Tamar. I want my father to see us together again.

Don't fight it, Tamar. Don't say no just for revenge; no more revenge. No more games. Let's take whatever comes along—the good and the less good alike—simply and in harmony. Despite pain and sorrow, we'll put our trust in what exalts us—my father's relentless sufferings—and in what thwarts us, too—the ambiguities of life, most of all Jewish life in the diaspora. We'll forge new links from which new sparks will rise. Spoken words will become signs, words unspoken will serve as warnings. And we'll invent the rest.

And my father's memory will sing and weep in mine.

And yours will blossom in our children's.

You win: we'll have many children, Tamar.

And one day, Grandfather, they'll tell the story of your son, in their turn.

Elhanan son of Malkiel.

Malkiel son of Elhanan.

FAREWELL

It comes back to me now . . . the well. . . . I'm afraid of the well; it's always night in the well. Afraid I'll answer its mysterious call . . . Before I was born, a peasant woman threw herself into that hole. . . . They said she was in love . . . pregnant . . . couldn't resist the Tempter's laughter. . . . Yes, it comes back to me: the Tempter sent for me at midnight. . . . Ah, but the rabbi had taken me under his wing. . . . I remember the rabbi. . . . I remember my bar mitzvah. . . . The synagogue crowded . . . people I knew, that I've forgotten now . . . My father, proud . . . My father, uneasy . . . The rabbi smiled upon him. . . . I love the rabbi, I love him greatly, but the image is hazy. . . . Vague features, a bushy white beard; I remember his bushy white beard. . . . He's speaking; the rabbi's talking about . . . I don't know what he was talking about. Maybe the danger of the Tempter: he steals what is most precious to us. From some he steals the heart. From others, vision. He stole my tongue. For a joke . . . How to protect myself from him? The rabbi didn't tell me. Perhaps he did, but I've forgotten. . . . He's speaking. . . . Soon it's my turn. . . . I'm afraid I'll forget my speech, and yet I know it by heart. I've delivered it many times to a friend at the yeshiva. . . . I'm perspiring, I'm short of breath. . . . If I forget one sentence, one quotation, it will all be lost. . . . One word, if I forget one word . . . I look at my father, I think of my mother. . . . The rabbi has finished. . . . I step up on the bimah, I kiss the velvet cloth that covers the holy ark. . . . I begin . . . my voice is feeble, too quiet. . . . Someone coughs, the rabbi gives me an encouraging glance, the Tempter's laughing raucously, and I'm doing all I can to drown him out. . . . I raise my voice, or at least try to. . . . The words fight me, they won't come, the Tempter's holding them prisoner. . . . But the rabbi is stronger; he closes his eyes and murmurs an incantation, and the Tempter flees, releasing my words. . . . Now I can't get them out fast enough. . . . I have no idea now what I said. . . . I recall one quotation, only one . . . from the Gaon, yes, the Gaon Reb Eliahu of Vilna: "The goal of redemption is the redemption of truth." How did I use it? I can't remember. Why does it linger like a lost soul in the ruins of my memory? Perhaps because my father had said it over and over from my earliest childhood: Truth, my son, truth, truth must not die. . . . All else matters less. Take care to be truthful always. . . . Truthful with your friends, truthful with God, truthful with yourself. . . . Most of all, he said, most of all, at the hour of your death you must know that you have not helped to kill the truth. . . . Truth dies every time a man turns away from it. . . . I'm thinking about it now, Malkiel my son. Oh, I know, I'm nowhere near death; but my reason is. At night, in the dark, I wonder: where is truth, in the light or in the shadow? In presence or in absence? And I wonder: was the life I lived the life I was destined to live? Did I never mistake the path? Have I been a good son, a good husband, a good father, a good Jew? I should have thought of that long ago . . . when I had all my faculties . . . when I still knew how to fit the pieces together. . . . No more, not now . . . Sometimes I tell myself, God is cruel, as cruel as the Tempter. . . . Since He has not permitted me to know the answer, why did He reveal the question to me? Why does He insist that this old man die in remorse and doubt? What has He to gain by my loss? What is His goal? The goal of redemption . . . of which redemption? Why must it have a goal? Do I myself still have a goal? Is there anything tangible, durable, real left of me at all? . . . I have nothing, I am nothing . . . more than a shadow and less than a man . . . But what is man deprived of memory? Not even a shadow . . .

The light is dimming within me, and I don't know if it's night or weariness or the rain. It's exasperating, but my eyes are heavy as their gaze wanders around me, far from me, drawing nameless images. Who has stepped between me and the world, between things and their shape?

Malkiel my son, you are in me but you are somewhere else; you are my life but you are on the other side of my life; I no longer know what you're looking for. I wonder if I'll still be here when you come back: I mean, I wonder if I'll know it's you.

All I know at this moment is that God has punished me. Our sages are right: the Tempter is not sin but punishment. . . . Ah, my son, I will not rise up against God's will. I have no doubt deserved

His punishment. But why this one and not another? I'd have preferred anything, even death. I'd have preferred death to this agony of memories wrestling and drowning.

What have I done to be reduced to this? If you hear me, God, answer me. No, I take it back, forgive me: answer me so that I can hear You.

But even if You answer, my question remains: What can I have done, as a Jew or as a man, to bring down upon me not damnation but obscurity, not death but dissolution?

Taking your advice, Malkiel, and Tamar's, too—love her, my son, love her as I love you, as I loved your mother; I mean, love her with utter and ever greater love—I began to trust in the word, that is, in the human voice. I told you, I told both of you, so many things. . . . I forget what they were.

But I think I know this: I did not tell you the essential. Yes, Malkiel, I am still lucid enough to admit it: there is something important, vital, that I especially wanted to pass on to you, perhaps a kind of testament. And each time, I said to myself, That can wait. I said to myself, This is so essential that I won't forget it, even if I forget all the rest. And now I've forgotten that, too.

But I am trying to remember. I must. More than my honor is at stake; my right to survive is at stake. I must not take this essential thing to my grave with me. It must stay on here, in this world, as an offering or a sign, all that remains of a vanished life.

I try, believe me. I turn pages, I dig up graves, I search every corner of my being. Who or what was it about? A person? Friend or enemy? An event? A glorious moment, or an infamous plot? I don't know, my son; I no longer know. There are words I will never be able to speak again.

I don't even know why I sent you to that remote village where I knew happiness as a child and a youth, Sabbath eve with your grandparents, and the anguish afterward, at midnight, when I heard the Tempter's icy laugh.

What message were you to bring back to me?

What answer to what riddle?

I will forget everything; I know that. Talia's name, too? No. Not hers. Nor yours. Names are important to a Jew. You will have a son one day; what will you call him?

Nothing is more important to a father than to earn his son's admiration. Have I earned yours? You won't hold it against me too much if I desert you along the way? Will you forgive me, will you?

Is it not a father's duty to help his son remember, to magnify his past, to enrich his memory? I cannot shake the depressing thought that I have failed you in this respect. In leaving you, I bequeath to you a black curtain.

Is that enough for you to think of me without bitterness?

How I wish I could have seen you in the role of father! Will you tell your son how I yearned for it? Will you tell him I did my best to reach you, in the name of my parents and ancestors? To remain a Jew? Never to abandon the memory of his forefathers? To remain faithful to the image a Jew ought to have of himself? Never to deny the Jew in him but to urge him to solidarity with his people—our people—and through them with all of humanity? Will you tell him about his grandfather's love for the strange and magnificent community of Israel, which extends from you to Moses? And from you, Tamar, to Sarah? Thanks to them, I shall live on; thanks to you, Abraham lives. What will I become without you two? Don't tell your son, and don't tell your father, that we must belong to the world at large, that we must transcend ourselves by supporting all causes and fighting for the victims of every injustice. If I am a Jew, I am a man. If I am not, I am nothing. A man like you, Malkiel, can love his people without hating others. I'll even say that it is because I love the Jewish people that I can summon the strength and the faith to love those who follow other traditions and invoke other beliefs. A Jew who denies his Jewishness brings shame upon all who preceded him. Tell your son not to bring shame upon me. A Jew who denies his Jewishness only chooses to lie. If he lies to himself, how can he be honest with others?

All that, Malkiel my son, all that, Tamar my daughter, is part of the essential thing but is not all of it. And even this I can tell you only thanks to the rare flashes of light that God in His mercy still grants me.

They say that before dying a man sees his whole past. Not I. All I see is bursts and fragments. But perhaps that is because I am not yet going to die, not physically, at any rate. Is that why I still cannot recall the essential thing that I want so much to pass on to you, Malkiel?

That doesn't matter, my son.

Even as I speak to you I tell myself that you will discover in your own way what my lips cannot say.

God cannot be so cruel as to erase everything forever. If He were, He would not be our father, and nothing would make sense.

And I who speak to you cannot say more, for

Note: unfinished ending of book is Correct.

Per M.D.

ABOUT THE AUTHOR

ELIE WIESEL received the Nobel Peace Prize in Oslo, Norway, on December 10, 1986. His Nobel citation reads: "Wiesel is a messenger to mankind. His message is one of peace and atonement and human dignity. The message is in the form of a testimony, repeated and deepened through the works of a great author." He is Andrew Mellon Professor in the Humanities at Boston University and the author of more than thirty books. Mr. Wiesel lives in New York City with his family.